Mike sta
mesmeriz   *curves*
and pouty lips. "Gina—"

Suddenly a key sounded in the front door.

"Madre Dio! It is my uncle!" Gina panicked. "You should not be here!" To her left was a closed door. She grabbed Mike's sleeve and pulled him into the dark room with her. Only, it was a closet.

Mike started to protest but stopped abruptly at the sound of her uncle—*his boss*—calling for Gina. The closet was small and crowded and he was pressed against Gina and her tight, skimpy dress. She moved her arm and her breasts rubbed against him. At his sharp intake of breath she froze.

Mike tightened his arms around the bare skin of her back. She stood on tiptoe to whisper in his ear. Soft silky hair brushed his jaw, robbing him of rational thought. "What are we going to do?"

Mike wished he knew. If he weren't so aroused maybe he could figure it out. How could he explain *this* to his boss? He tried to shift, but only managed to stroke her hip with his erection and press closer to her breasts.

There was nothing he could do but enjoy the delicious agony....

Blaze™

Dear Reader,

This book is a favorite of mine. Writing about Gina and Mike was like telling the story of two old friends. After it ended, I genuinely missed them for days. I think part of the reason I bonded so quickly with the characters is that I really identified with Gina.

Like her, I went to an all-girls Catholic high school, though in a small town in Hawaii. A grand total of one hundred and sixteen girls made up the tenth, eleventh and twelfth grades. Obviously there is some of me in Gina, although which aspects, I'm not saying. After all, my mother will be reading this book.

You all take care. And don't forget to check out tryblaze.com!

Debbi Rawlins

Books by Debbi Rawlins

HARLEQUIN BLAZE
13—IN HIS WILDEST DREAMS

HARLEQUIN DUETS
46—THE SWINGING R RANCH
46—WHOSE LINE IS IT ANYWAY?

HARLEQUIN AMERICAN ROMANCE
780—STUD FOR HIRE?
790—OVERNIGHT FATHER
808—HIS, HERS AND THEIRS
860—LOVING A LONESOME COWBOY

EDUCATING GINA

Debbi Rawlins

HARLEQUIN®

TORONTO • NEW YORK • LONDON
AMSTERDAM • PARIS • SYDNEY • HAMBURG
STOCKHOLM • ATHENS • TOKYO • MILAN • MADRID
PRAGUE • WARSAW • BUDAPEST • AUCKLAND

This is for Sue H., the real Gina.
Thanks for all your wonderful stories.
You're a fun and gutsy lady. Have a great eightieth!

ISBN 0-373-79040-6

EDUCATING GINA

Copyright © 2002 by Debbi Quattrone.

This edition published by arrangement with Harlequin Books S.A.

® and TM are trademarks of the publisher. Trademarks indicated with ® are registered in the United States Patent and Trademark Office, the Canadian Trade Marks Office and in other countries.

Visit us at www.eHarlequin.com

Printed in U.S.A.

1

"NICE LEGS. Is she new?"

Mike Mason shook his head in disgust. "Have you heard anything I've said?"

His friend and co-worker, Robert Scarpetti, kept his attention on the tall blonde at the water cooler outside Mike's office. "Maybe she's a sales rep for one of our distributors. I haven't seen her before, have you?"

"*Rob.*"

Robert looked at Mike. "I heard every word you said. You think California wine sales are up on the West Coast because gas prices are up and it costs too much to ship our wine across the country." His gaze went back to the young woman who'd briefly stopped at their secretary's desk. "Good. Cori should know who she is."

"Dammit, Rob, if you weren't the boss's son, your ass would be fired by now."

Robert slid off the edge of Mike's desk and flashed him a big grin. "Not when I have you to make me look good."

Mike grunted. He was tired and hungry after missing another lunch hour. Normally Robert didn't annoy him. After fifteen years of friendship, he'd learned to take the overgrown kid with a grain of salt.

They'd met during their sophomore year in high school soon after Mike's mother had started working for the Scarpetti family. The company distributed wine in the States from their vineyard in Italy and she had been their bookkeeper. The job had been a godsend. A recent layoff had left her unemployed and penniless. Mike's father hadn't been in the picture for ten years, ever since the bastard had walked out on them.

"Don't worry, bro." Robert clapped him on the back. "I'll talk to Pop about looking into Daly City as a possible site for a distribution center. It's near enough to San Francisco but not so high rent that it'll inflate Pop's blood pressure."

"You checked it out already?"

Robert snorted. "Hey, I'm not a total waste. Want to go have a beer?"

"It's only four-fifteen."

"Your point being?"

Mike rubbed his eyes and loosened his tie. "I still have another couple of hours of work to finish."

"Damn, Mike, I wish you'd relax. This company's been around for over a hundred years. It ain't going anywhere."

"Right." Easy for Robert to say. He was a Scarpetti. Automatically entitled to a secure position in the family business.

As great as they'd all been to Mike, giving him a job, even contributing to his college education after his mother's death, he was still not one of them. It didn't matter how hard he worked or how many holidays he spent at their table, he would never be a part of the inner circle.

Robert and Antonio would both deny it if questioned. Not that Mike would ever broach such a subject. He was grateful to be the only non-family member in management, and he knew he had a good chance to head the West Coast operation someday. They already trusted him to handle a major part of the business.

At twenty-eight, he had no student loans to pay off, and he made a damn good salary. More than most guys his age. No question he owed them big time. But he could never shake the need to belong, to have their unconditional acceptance.

"If you change your mind about that beer, Joe and I will be down at Angelo's." Robert stopped at the door, checking his reflection in the glass inset, and then pulled out his comb. "But I'll only be there until five-thirty. I've got a date with Melanie tonight."

A date. Mike couldn't remember the last time he'd had one. He'd caught a couple of movies and late dinners with Daphne from the real-estate office upstairs last year. But she thought he was too work-obsessed, and when he'd called a couple of months ago, she told him she'd be washing her hair for the next year or so.

"Count me out today." Mike opened his middle drawer looking for chips or anything to quiet his noisy stomach. "I still have the quarterly budget to work on."

"Screw that. Work on it tomorrow."

Mike found an open package of cheese crackers and sniffed it. Smelled okay to him. "I want you to review the figures before you go on vacation."

An incoherent bellow interrupted them.

Mike looked up.

"Dammit, I gotta go." Robert threw a disgusted glance down the hall. "The old man is hollering for me. How many times have I told him to use the intercom?"

"But you're not in your office."

"That's not the point." Robert stalked off, muttering under his breath.

Mike smiled as he tore into the cheese crackers. The Scarpettis sure were a boisterous bunch, especially Antonio. He'd left Italy thirty years ago but still clung to some of the old ways, personally and in business. Good thing the company was so well established and making a lot of money. But then again, there was a downside to their fairly easy success. No one seemed particularly interested in expanding or modernizing.

Except Mike. Once he got the West Coast operation into action, he knew he could double the company's profits. Wouldn't that make him nice and cozy with the family?

The blonde walked past his office again, this time slowing to smile at him. He nearly choked on the stale cracker. He had to admit, she did have great legs.

Hell with it being a long time since his last date. It had been a century since he'd gotten laid.

"JEEZ, POP, that damn cigar is stinking up your whole office. Put it out." Robert waved a hand through the smoky air. "Disgusting."

"This is my office. I do what I like in here. Sit down."

Robert opened his father's window, ignoring the humid August air that rushed in. Traffic noise from the street below the three-story Brooklyn office rose to compete with their conversation.

"All right, all right," he grumbled over the din. "I'll put out the cigar. Now close the damn window."

Robert gladly shut out the warm air and noise. But that was the least of the problem. His father smoked too much, ate and drank to excess and stayed out late every night, a pattern that began after Robert's mother died last year. It worried the hell out of him.

"What did you want, Pop?" He took a chair across the old scarred desk that belonged in a junkyard.

"Your cousin Gina is coming from Italy in three days."

"Gina?" Robert frowned. He hadn't seen her in eight years. Not since his last trip to Tuscany. She'd happened to be home from Catholic boarding school in Milan, shy, quiet, the perfect convent-school student. "Why?" Robert couldn't imagine his timid cousin flying across the Atlantic alone. "Not that it won't be nice to see her, but…how old is she now?"

"Twenty-three. She's just finished all her schooling

and your aunt says she's been a little rebellious lately.'' Antonio shrugged expansively and muttered something in Italian. Robert knew only a few choice words. "You know your aunt Sophia, the drama queen.''

"Is she coming alone?''

Antonio sighed and mopped his forehead. There seemed to be more and more of it each day, and Robert shuddered at the thought his hairline would one day recede like Pop's.

"Unfortunately, yes, and she'll be here for a month.''

Robert started to get a bad feeling. "I still don't understand why Gina would come here.''

"To cut loose.'' Antonio waved a hand. "That's how you say it, right? You know, get the wildness out of her system.''

"Oh, brother.''

"What's this?'' Antonio scowled. "You suddenly don't have time for family?''

"Me?''

"Who else should I ask to escort her around the city?''

"Oh, no.'' Robert abruptly stood. "I'm on vacation starting this weekend, remember? I already paid for the cruise. Two weeks. Me, Melanie, lots of sun and piña coladas. I'm not baby-sitting anyone.''

"I will reimburse you for the cruise.''

"No way.'' Robert backed toward the door. "Melanie pulled a lot of strings at work to get two weeks off.''

"Roberto." Antonio slammed his palm on the desk. "This is family. This is important."

"I understand." But Melanie sure wouldn't. "I'll only be gone two weeks. Let Mike show her around in the meantime."

"Mike?"

Robert mirrored his father's expansive shrug. "He's practically family, right?"

Antonio frowned. "Practically isn't good enough. He's a male, and she's a female. You do the arithmetic."

"Yeah, but we're talking about Mike."

"I'm talking about hormones or testosterone, or whatever those things are." He shook his head in that stubborn way Robert hated. It meant the subject was closed. "You will pick Gina up at the airport and stick to her like glue. End of discussion."

"Pop, don't make me say something I'm gonna regret."

Antonio narrowed his dark eyes. "What?"

Panic assailed Robert. He couldn't cancel this trip. He and Melanie had been planning it for six months. What a damn mess! "It's about Mike."

"Yeah?"

"It's confidential."

"Roberto, I remind you." He picked up the cigar he'd put out. "You brought up the subject."

"You can't tell anybody, Pop, including Mike. This is a very sensitive issue."

"All right, already."

Robert took a deep breath. He really hated involving Mike, but what else could he do? "It's no problem if he accompanies Gina around the city." He cleared his throat. For this lie, he would surely go straight to hell. Not to mention Mike was going to kill him. "Mike bats for the other team."

Antonio's bushy brows drew together. "What are you talking about?"

"You never heard that term before, Pop?"

"I know what it means." He looked uncertain. "It means he could be an interior decorator or something. Am I right?"

Robert choked back a laugh. "I guess you could say that."

"But Mike? I've known him half his life. He's not that way."

"When was the last time you saw him with a girl?"

Antonio toyed with the cigar as he thought for a moment. "Last year, Thanksgiving, he brought that short redhead to dinner."

"That was three years ago, she was his neighbor's daughter and she was fifteen."

Antonio frowned. "How come he doesn't look like one of those kind?"

"Pop, don't be so old-fashioned. He doesn't have to look any particular way. The important thing is, he can show Gina around the city without you worrying."

Antonio chomped on the cigar, his bushy brows drawn together as he thought. "Okay, tell him to get in here."

"OH, MAN." Mike winced at the brass clock on his desk. She'd be here in less than an hour and he still had two reports to fill out for customs and a stack of invoices to approve. Of all the jobs the Scarpettis had asked of him, baby-sitting had to be the lowest. He'd almost told them to kiss off on this one, but then he had a staggering realization. The trust Antonio had placed in him was pretty damn remarkable.

Most of the older Scarpetti men were still old-fashioned, especially about their women, and that included Antonio. They liked their women pretty, obedient and chaste. Trusting Mike with the care of his niece was the closest Mike had ever gotten to the inner circle. In a way he felt as if he'd finally been given the keys to the house.

Too bad all his work wouldn't resolve itself while he was playing nursemaid. He pushed the stack of invoices to the side to make room for his day planner. The way he figured it, he could still come to work early in the morning and late in the evening. Even though Antonio had instructed him that Gina was to have close supervision, Robert had given Mike a heads up on what to expect.

From what Rob remembered, Gina was a bookworm who was just as happy to spend her day in a library or sitting in front of a computer as she'd be sightseeing. She'd flip over the New York Library. Mike figured that alone would keep her busy for half her stay.

He studied his day planner, arranging and rearranging his priorities for the next week and listing them in the order they required his attention. The intercom rang, surprising him. The company's two secretaries were at lunch, Robert was picking Gina up at the airport, and none of the other three Scarpettis working in the office bothered to use the device. When they wanted someone, they just opened their mouths and let it rip.

"Mike, Robert's back with—" Clicks and static interrupted Antonio's voice, and then the connection was back and he muttered, "How the hell do you work this thing?"

"Keep this button depressed." Robert's voice came through. "Go ahead, talk."

"Mike?"

"I'm here."

"Would you come to my office, please?" His abrupt change in tone, obviously for the benefit of his niece, had Mike grinning all the way down the hall.

It never failed to amaze him that the company ran profitably. Antonio was a shrewd enough businessman who kept close watch on the operation and the finances, but his refusal to modernize came at a cost. Robert understood that, but he wasn't ambitious enough. If Mike could only get a foothold, he knew he could make some innovative changes that would make them all take notice.

Rob passed Mike as he left his father's office and gave him an apologetic smile. Antonio's door was already open, but Mike gave a brief courtesy knock before entering.

"Ah, here he is." Antonio gestured him inside.

Antonio's desk was the neatest Mike had ever seen it. Even the papers in the In box in the corner were in a tidy stack. The nude painting that usually hung on the wall behind the boss had been removed.

Mike cleared his throat to disguise a laugh. It was a perfectly tasteful and expensive painting. This Gina had to be some prim and proper—

Then he saw her. Sitting at Antonio's conference table, bundled up in a big, bulky tan coat, her hair stuffed into an ugly knit cap. She must be roasting in this August heat, Mike thought.

"This is my niece, Gina Ferraro." Antonio made a sweeping motion with his hand, urging Mike inside. "Mike is our distribution manager."

"Hello," she said in a throaty voice, her sultry accent wrapping around Mike like a cashmere blanket. She sent her uncle a quizzical look out of almond-shaped brown eyes. "I thought that was Roberto's job."

Antonio looked as surprised as Mike that she'd asked the question. But he only shrugged. "They share the title. But Mike does most of the work."

Gina switched her attention back to him, but Mike was still reeling from Antonio's surprising but astute remark. He hadn't realized Antonio was aware of the situation.

"And now you have to baby-sit me," she said, her lips pursing slightly in a pout as she extended her hand. "I have explained to everyone that I do not need an escort."

"This is a big city, *cara*." Antonio gave his niece

a patient smile. The kind he reserved for nice Italian women from whom he expected obedience.

"Yes, Zio," she said meekly, looking directly into Mike's eyes as he accepted her hand. Small. Incredibly soft.

"It's really no trouble. We have a terrific library in—"

Annoyance flickered in her eyes, and she withdrew her hand. "I have made a list of places I would like to visit."

"Oh, okay. Sure."

"Have you had lunch?" Antonio rubbed his meaty palms together. "Either of you?" He didn't wait for an answer. "Let's all go to Angelo's. You two can get better acquainted over a nice bowl of linguini and clams."

Gina made a slight face, but then said, "Yes, Uncle."

Mike stepped aside and waited until she stood. She was petite, about five-three in sensible black-laced shoes, the kind Mike's grandmother used to wear.

Antonio gestured for them to precede him out the door. "After we eat, Mike will take you to my apartment so you can unpack and rest awhile. Later, if you aren't too tired we'll have dinner together. Okay?"

"Whatever you say, Uncle Antonio."

"And take off that coat before you die of heatstroke and your mother makes meatballs out of me."

She touched the top button with reluctant fingers and then slipped it free. By the time she got to the third one, the sudden tension that had coiled in Mike's gut about knocked him over.

What the hell was wrong with him? He didn't have time to analyze this odd reaction. She was on the last button.

She pulled the lapels apart and shrugged the bulky fabric off her shoulders, revealing an unattractive, shapeless black dress over hose that were too thick.

Mike let out a disappointed breath and took the coat from her. But the smile she gave him made his insides tighten again. It was the almond-shaped eyes and full lips. He was a sucker for both. Good thing she wasn't his type. As if he had one after such a long dry spell.

They all got to the hall and Antonio bellowed for Robert to join them. So much for the intercom.

The restaurant was crowded for midafternoon, but Antonio's regular table was reserved and they were waited on quickly. Everyone ordered pasta but Gina. She wanted a cheeseburger and fries.

As soon as she excused herself to go to the ladies' room, Antonio chuckled. "A cheeseburger." He muttered something in Italian. "This is the rebellion my sister is so worried about."

Robert shook his head. "I kind of feel sorry for her." His gaze followed Gina. "She's twenty-three and she looks like forty dressed like that. Maybe Mike should take her shopping."

Mike snorted. "Yeah, right."

Antonio tore off a piece of bread from the loaf in the center of the table and then peered at him with open curiosity. "You guys know how to do that kind of stuff, right?"

"Pop."

Mike caught Robert giving his father the eye. "What do you mean?"

Antonio shrugged and busied himself with slathering enough butter on his bread to clog an artery. "I don't want her to get crazy, but maybe a nice pink dress would be good. Black is so old-fashioned."

Mike and Robert exchanged amused looks.

"It's Sophia. My sister still thinks she lives in the nineteenth century. Black is for mourning." He looked up and nudged his chin at Mike. "Help her find a nice pink dress. Just not too short, okay?"

Mike grabbed a hunk of bread before he said something he'd regret. Robert damn well better be right. Gina had better prefer spending time at the library or computer, and not Bloomingdale's and Bergdorf's. If she wanted to shop, she could find just about anything online.

Robert signaled the waitress for another beer. "Gina went to Catholic boarding school all her life. I'm sure the nuns had a lot of influence on her choice of clothing."

"Here she comes. Stop talking about her." Antonio reached for a second piece of bread, and Robert deftly grabbed the butter.

"Come on, Pop. Too much of this stuff isn't good for you."

"You, who ordered a second beer in fifteen minutes, is telling me this?"

Mike let the familiar argument fade into the background as he watched Gina approach the table. As conservatively as she was dressed, she didn't have a timid way of walking or carrying herself. As unbecoming as her hairstyle was, the severity of it accentuated her exotic eyes and full lips, and a couple of heads turned when she passed a table of four men.

Antonio stood when she got to the table, and he gave Robert and Mike the evil eye until they gave in and followed his lead. Gina reclaimed her seat, pressing her lips together as if trying to hide a smile.

She caught Mike watching her and quickly looked away. When Antonio tried to take the butter, the other two started in again. The genuine affection between father and son always impressed Mike, and he barely paid attention to the petty squabbling.

Apparently Gina didn't, either. She glanced around the restaurant, her hands folded primly on the table, yet barely able to contain the excitement in her eyes.

Poor kid. Had she really been hidden away at a convent school all her life? Mike didn't doubt it. The Scarpettis clung to some odd traditional values. Even Antonio had his quirks in that department, although he'd never admit it.

Mike continued to watch how her eyes widened with interest as she took in the rowdy but good-natured interplay at the bar. The TV positioned high on the corner wall was showing a baseball game, and some fevered cheering escalated the noise level.

When Cindy, a cocktail waitress in a black miniskirt and a tight blouse endorsing the Mets walked by with a tray of mugs, Gina's eyes widened even more. She watched the woman deliver the beer to a table and blinked in astonishment when the redhead leaned over to unload the tray. The way the skirt rode up, not much was left to the imagination.

"So, Gina, what kind of things do you like to do?" Mike asked to distract her. And himself.

Her gaze settled on him. "Me? Well, I read a lot." Her shrug was apologetic. "I sew and I spend time on the computer. I am afraid I do not have a very exciting life."

"Nothing wrong with that. Mine isn't all that exciting, either." Unfortunately that was the truth. All he did was work.

"But this is a city full of fun and excitement and..." Her voice rose with excitement, drawing her uncle and cousin's attention. She gave them a serene smile.

Antonio gave her a patronizing one back.

Mike sighed. Poor kid. It wouldn't kill him to show her the sights a little. He'd have to check the entertainment listings. Maybe *The Lion King* was still on Broadway.

2

GINA WAVED GOODBYE to her uncle and cousin and blew them a kiss as the elevator doors closed. She could not wait to get out of their office and go to the apartment. She loved her family, but she hated the black dress more. Mama had insisted she wear it on the plane, and Gina had figured it was a small price to pay for a month's freedom in New York City.

"Where is your car?" she asked when they got outside.

Mike gave her a funny look as he stepped off the sidewalk onto the street. "I don't have one. We'll take a cab."

"You do not have one? I thought everybody in America had two cars and two televisions."

Laughing, Mike raised his arm to hail a cab. "Not in New York they don't. It would cost too much for me to keep a car here. Anyway, I don't need one."

She liked the way his light-brown hair curled at the ends and touched the back of his white collar. He was tall, almost a foot taller than her, and she liked that, too. "Uncle Antonio...he does not pay you enough money?"

His sea-green eyes unexpectedly met hers, and she

felt a tingle at the back of her neck. "I make a very good salary. Keeping a car simply isn't sensible."

Gina sighed. Sensible. She did not want to hear that word ever again. Regina Marie, please be sensible, Mama had said a hundred times since Gina had returned from school. You cannot have an apartment in the city, she had said. Living alone would not be sensible for a single girl about to be married.

Marriage. Gina cringed at the thought. She had nothing against the institution, but the family expected her to marry Mario, who owned the neighboring vineyard. But he was old, almost forty, and as exciting as shriveling grapes.

Sometimes when she was home from school she would stroll through the vineyards in the evening and she could see the lights in his house go out at ten o'clock. Her friends did not even leave their houses for the clubs until nine.

"Gina?"

She blinked and saw that a cab had pulled over and Mike was holding the door open for her. Arranging the bulky coat she had put back on over the dress, she slid across the back seat, where she stayed close to the middle of the seat.

Mike put her luggage in the trunk, got in, gave the driver an address and settled back and loosened his tie. His suit was made of a dark-blue lightweight material that clung to his thighs. He was thin, but not too thin, just right, really, with no spare flesh around his middle. Without the jacket his shoulders were broad and straight.

He was definitely the kind of guy the girls at school talked about when they had been lucky enough to sneak away to the city for a night. Gina had been brave enough only once, and she had almost gotten caught by Sister Maria Therese. Even though she had made it over the fence unseen, she had worried the entire night that her empty bed would be discovered and so had no fun at all.

Mike continued to look out the window and she edged an inch closer until their thighs nearly touched. He rubbed his shadowed chin, pushed a hand through his hair, but did not even give her a second glance.

Gina sighed. She hated being ignored almost as much as she hated the black dress. But that was all right. She would soon get a reaction from Mike Mason.

ANTONIO HAD CALLED ahead to alert the doorman at his building to let them in. Mike left one of Gina's suitcases with the guy while he escorted her to Antonio's apartment. Leaving the bag was a safety net. In case he had to make a quick getaway.

Something about Gina was giving him hot flashes. Maybe it was her subtle vanilla scent or her soft unconscious sighs. Or maybe it was the innocent way her thigh kept brushing against his as they'd sat in the cab.

Gina walked ahead of him, her swaying hips revealing a few curves. She had them in the right places, that was for sure, not to mention full high breasts not even the ugly black dress could hide.

Shit! What a jerk. He was supposed to be watching Gina. Not *watching* her.

Ever since he and Robert had noticed that blonde outside his office a few days ago, Mike had been acutely aware of how long it'd been since he'd been horizontal with some sweet young thing. Maybe he ought to lower his standards for a night. Be like Robert and pick someone up at a bar who had the same idea in mind.

But that wasn't his thing. He'd have to be really horny, and the situation wasn't that bad yet. But he had gone so far as to find out that the blonde's name was Heidi and that she was a sales rep for one of their outside distributors. He'd also found out that she'd asked about him.

That gave him the green light. Now he needed time away from his baby-sitting duty.

"Do you know which bedroom will be mine?" Gina asked once they'd gotten inside the apartment.

"Why?" he asked quickly, his mind racing.

She blinked. "So we know where to put the suitcases."

"Oh, right." He flexed his shoulder, trying to loosen the mounting tension traveling to the back of his neck. "Maybe we should just leave them in the living room for now."

"But I want to unpack." She stepped closer, peering into his face. "Are you not well?"

"I'm fine." He headed down the hall, not sure which bedroom to go to. He'd been to Antonio's at least a dozen times, but had never made it past the living room and kitchen.

It ended up a simple choice. Besides the master bedroom, there was only one guest room. The third bedroom contained only a desk, computer and love seat.

He set down the suitcase between the white-oak armoire and four-poster queen-size bed. When he turned to leave, he ran into Gina. She stumbled backward and he caught her upper arms.

Her eyes widened. *"Scusi."*

He stood, paralyzed by the sultry beauty of her eyes, how thick inky-black lashes highlighted the golden flecks. The firm muscle he found under his touch surprised him. He didn't know what he expected, maybe more fleshy softness. But to be this toned and sculpted, she clearly worked out.

Man, she was in better shape than he was.

At the depressing thought he dropped his hands. He didn't move back, though, and neither did she. They just stood looking at each other for a long heart-stopping moment.

"Uh, I'd better go get your other bag from the doorman," he said finally, stepping back and then taking a wide swing around her.

"You will be right back?"

"Of course." He made it to the door. "But if you want to start unpacking or take a nap or whatever, go ahead. I'll leave the bag outside the door."

"You will not leave me here alone?" Her eyes had gotten wide again and a little frightened.

Mike sobered. He was supposed to be taking care of her, not running away because he couldn't keep his libido under wraps. "I'll be either in the living room or in your uncle's office making some phone calls and checking my e-mail."

"Good." She smiled. "I would like to unpack, but do not need a nap. Perhaps we could go to Central Park?"

Mike checked his watch. No way was he getting in rush hour traffic all the way to Manhattan. "We'll save that for another day when we can get an earlier start."

"I understand," she said, but her lips pursed in a pout. And then he realized she wasn't pouting at all. The look was natural because of the fullness of her lips. A sexy look that women paid thousands to surgically duplicate.

He rubbed his clammy palms together. "Okay, I'm going to go now. Take your time."

Mike got the hell out of the apartment before he said or did something really stupid. The elevator was slow to get to the tenth floor and that suited him just fine. Only a fool would be anxious to get back too quickly.

Gina was going to be more trouble than he anticipated. But not if he got a grip of himself. Oh, shit, he wanted to be gripped, all right. That was the problem. But she was a kid, and he should be ashamed.

Okay, so she was only five years younger than he was. But if age were measured in experience, she'd be a baby. Robert's description of her wasn't the only clue. Gina looked sexy—that was a quirk of nature—but she was still inexperienced and naive. A guy could tell that sort of thing.

Experienced or not, she was off-limits.

He gave the elevator down button another impatient jab and then wished he could recall the asinine gesture. No sense in hurrying back to temptation. Not that he'd act on any of his impulses. Unless he wanted to get his ass fired.

The elevator doors opened and as soon as he got in, the car shot down to the first floor as if it were a friggin' express. The doorman was talking to someone, so Mike perused the building's notice board. There was an ad for a dog-walking service and beside it, was a flyer for massage therapy. In the top corner was a picture of the busty blond masseuse. And she made house calls.

Mike groaned. He wasn't that desperate. Was he?

GINA BEGAN UNPACKING the clothes her mother had insisted she bring. Those things she shoved in the closet, unconcerned about the wrinkles. She would only need them when she dined with Uncle Antonio or visited with him in the apartment. The rest of the time she would wear the clothes she had made herself or had bought with the allowance her mother had sent her while she was at school.

Carefully she unrolled the cropped T-shirts, Capri leggings and miniskirts she'd hidden beneath her assorted underwear. One dress in particular she shook out and then laid across the bed. It had wrinkled during the trip, but the material was stretchy, and once it was on her body, it would be so tight she would not have to worry about ironing it.

She kicked off her shoes and knelt on the floor to root through her second suitcase. Two pairs of strappy sandals had been hidden among her toiletries. She fished them out, along with the red nail polish for her toes.

Not even a sliver of guilt dampened her excitement. She was tired of wearing ugly dresses and having to act like an old woman. None of the other girls at boarding school or the all-girl university she had attended had parents as strict as hers.

And for what? She had been a good girl, studying hard, getting good grades, staying away from the boys who hung around outside the school's stone wall. She had not gotten into trouble like some of the other girls, or at least nothing that her parents knew about. The two times Gina had made the sisters angry by staying out past curfew, she had been able to talk them into not writing her parents a report.

She pulled off the dreadful black dress, wadded it into a ball and threw it on the closet floor. She would not need it until her flight home. Just the thought of having to return to Tuscany to plan her wedding depressed her. She quickly chose an outfit that would lift her mood, and then sat on the floor and shook the bottle of red polish.

The scandalous color made her heart race so fast that her hands shook. She had to keep stopping to wipe the excess polish off the brush so that she did not make a mess of her toes. While letting the first coat dry, she leaned back, her arms outstretched for support, her legs straight out in front of her so she could admire her work. She wiggled her toes and was pleased when the light reflected off the shiny gloss.

She hoped Mike was not growing impatient. The thought of him made her smile. He was tall and handsome and she liked the way he smelled, too. Fresh and clean, like pine trees washed by the rain.

She wished the girls back at school could see him. They would all be jealous. Especially Maria Scalia, the nasty witch, who had nicknamed Gina Virgin Mary, as if Maria knew all about sex. How Gina would love to see her mouth drop at the sight of Mike and his beautiful green eyes.

She slumped back against the bed and pictured herself casually mentioning to her graduating class how Mike would be her personal escort for an entire month. Of course she would refer to him as Michael. That name suited him better.

The fantasy made her smile as she applied the second coat of polish. She wondered what Mike would say when she told him she wanted to lose her virginity.

With him.

THREE-THIRTY AND STILL no sign of her. Mike began to wonder if she'd fallen asleep. Not that he'd knock on her door to find out. The longer she stayed in her room, the better for him. He lifted the phone to return another call he'd picked up from his voice mail.

In the short time since he'd gone to lunch and arrived at Antonio's apartment, four messages had been left for him. What the hell would happen when he was out of the office for most of the month? This was going to be a disaster.

Robert wouldn't be leaving for vacation for three more days. He'd have to step in and entertain his cousin. Melanie or Melody or whoever his newest love interest was would just have to wait until the cruise for his undivided attention.

His last call returned, Mike hung up the phone and heard a door click. He glanced over his shoulder down the hall but saw no sign of Gina. Relief and disappointment washed over him in alternate waves. Part of him wished she'd stay out of his face for a while and give him a chance to regroup. The other part of him wanted to get lost in her seductive eyes.

It was the accent, he told himself. That's what turned him on. His first major crush had been on his French teacher. He'd been thirteen and she had probably been in her early thirties. She was pretty enough, but it was her accent that had him reaching under the covers at night.

He sat at Antonio's desk and flipped on the computer. He was surprised his boss even knew how to use a computer, much less have one at home. At Mike's touch, dust flew off the keyboard, and he shook his head. He should've figured Antonio didn't actually use it. Knowing him, he probably thought it made him look in touch with the business.

He had only two new e-mails to answer and had

just finished signing off when he heard Gina clear her throat. Taking a deep breath and wondering what the hell he should do with her now, he pushed back from the desk.

He turned toward the doorway and his jaw went slack. His mouth opened. Nothing came out.

"You like?" she asked, skimming her hands down the sides of a red dress that fit like a second skin. Her long thick hair was down. Dark and glossy with chestnut-colored streaks, it reached just past her shoulders.

She had put on makeup, not a lot, but enough to accentuate her eyes and cheekbones. Before she was pretty; now she was a stunner.

"Mike?" Worry lines formed between her brows.

"Um…" He had to say something eventually—when his mouth worked. Instead, he made the mistake of checking out her dress again. Made of some type of stretchy material, it left no doubt where every curve started and ended. The neckline wasn't too low, but Gina's breasts were so full that…

"You're not going out like that."

She frowned, her red-tinted lips forming that sexy pout again. "Why not?"

"Why not?" His gaze automatically ran down her body. If her dress was two inches shorter… "Because women don't dress like that here." Most of them couldn't get away with it—and look that good.

"Yes, they do."

"Not in the daytime."

Gina folded her arms across her chest, pushing everything into the right place, and Mike had to look away quickly. "I have seen them."

"You've been to New York before?"

She shook her head. "I have seen *Sex and the City.* Twice. At my friend Lucia's house."

"Sex and the City?"

"On the television. It is—"

He sighed. "I know what it is, Gina. But women don't really— What?"

"That is the first time you said my name." Her lips curved in a smile that made his chest tighten. "I like very much the way you say it. Please, say it again."

"Don't try to distract me."

She blinked, confusion clouding her eyes. "I do not understand."

How was he going to explain? Admit that just looking at her gave him a hard-on? Thank God he was already sitting down. He grabbed the edge of the desktop and pulled the chair and himself closer to the desk.

He forced his thoughts back to last Sunday at the grocery store when he'd splattered a ripe juicy plum at the feet of a pretty blond shopper. Recalling the embarrassment of her shocked scream and accusing eyes barely did the trick. He was still pretty damn hard. At least he had the desk for protection.

"Ah, I understand," Gina said after a discomfiting silence. "Distract. It means I take you off the subject." She looked pleased. "I do that?"

He groaned. "You have to change your clothes."

Her eyes got dark and wounded. "Because I look fat."

That startled a laugh out of him. "No, trust me, you do not look fat."

She shrunk back, her shoulders hunching forward, and then hugged herself.

"Come on, Gina, you look terrific." He started to get up and thought better of it. "You look absolutely beautiful."

Guarded pleasure lightened her eyes. "You say that not to hurt my feelings."

"Wrong, and you know it."

She blinked a couple of times, fret drawing her brows together and doubt so plain in her face, that he got it. She really didn't know that she was a stone fox, built like a brick house, the object of men's fantasies.

Unbelievable! She had no friggin' idea. Not a clue. She really *had* been sheltered. Probably had worn a conservative schoolgirl uniform most of her life. This was all experimentation to her.

But heart failure for him. "The reason I want you to change has nothing to do with how you look. I'm worried about what your uncle will say."

Defiance flashed in her face. "I am doing nothing wrong."

"No, you aren't. But would he approve?"

She sighed heavily and paced to the window.

Mike clenched his jaw. He hadn't seen the back of her until now. Or had gotten down far enough to notice how the black spike heels made her legs look longer and shapely. That wasn't even the best part. She had the most perfect rear end known to man. He tried to look away. He couldn't.

She stared out the window long enough for him to give himself a thorough mental shake, and then she undid his hard work by turning around and meeting his eyes. "I do not want to displease my uncle, or my mother. That is not my intention." She shoved her fingers through her hair, letting the thick strands fall in a curtain of silk. "I am just trying to have fun, to be like other girls, to enjoy life before…"

She pressed her lips together and turned back toward the window. "You are very kind to worry, Mike, but how I dress is not your problem."

The hell it wasn't. He was going to get fired over this. All the accurate forecasts and tight budgets he'd produced weren't going to mean squat to Antonio if he thought Mike wasn't doing right by his niece.

In the back of his mind, Mike recalled how Antonio liked to play up his Italian heritage, make references that he was related to a godfather in Sicily. Some of the guys at the warehouse chuckled about it behind his back. But maybe it wasn't a joke. Maybe he'd have someone whack Mike and make it look like an accident.

"Look, Gina, since I'm your guardian…"

Her eyes blazed.

"I mean, escort, while you're in New York, I kind of am responsible."

She smoothed her palm over her hip and down her thigh. His gaze helplessly followed. "I am not a child."

"No, you definitely aren't." He swallowed, cleared his throat. "Will you excuse me a moment?"

He had to talk to Robert. This arrangement was not

going to work. No way. Not without Mike ending up with his butt in a sling.

Gina stood there looking uncertain, and Mike realized she was waiting for him to get up and leave. That could be a problem, yet he couldn't very well make the call in front of her. He shifted in hopes of loosening his pants.

"Is something wrong?" she asked, moving toward him.

"No." He shot off the chair. "Nothing. I need to go make a phone call."

She followed him out to the hall.

"In private."

Her eyes narrowed and she drew her lower lip into her mouth. "Is it about me?"

Mike hesitated, fascinated with the new contortion of her lips. "Sort of."

She stepped closer. "What have I done?"

All she had to do was glance down at his fly and she'd know exactly what she'd done. He backed up toward the living room. "Nothing. I have to go."

She followed. "But, Mike..."

Thinking he heard something, he held up a hand for silence.

"But I—"

"Wait! Did you hear that?"

She stopped short and listened.

A click broke the silence.

"The door." Mike cursed under his breath. "It's your uncle."

3

"MADRE DIO." Gina's gaze flew toward the living room. For all her brave words, she did not want her uncle to see her like this.

"Go to your room. I'll tell him you're napping."

Not anxious to be sent back on the next plane, she started to obey when the door opened.

She would never make it to her room before Antonio saw her. To her left was a closed door. She grabbed Mike's sleeve and pulled him into the dark room with her. Only, it was a closet.

"What the hell did you do—?" Mike cut himself off at the sound of her uncle calling for her. He muttered a word she did not understand, his warm breath gliding across her cheek.

The closet was small and crowded and they were pressed so close together, Gina could hardly breathe. She moved her right arm and her breast rubbed against him. At his sharp intake of breath she froze.

Only one other time had she been this close to a boy. Diego was a classmate's brother and he had been all hands. It had been fun and exciting at first, but then he scared her by reaching between her legs.

When he would not stop as she had asked, she had bitten his arm.

But Mike's hands were nowhere near her. She wondered what he would do if she placed her palms on his chest. She smiled when she realized there was nothing he could do. Not without alerting her uncle. And Mike would not do that.

"Mike?" she whispered.

"Shh." He put a finger to her lips, missing at first in the darkness, but then finding her and making her heart race like a runaway horse.

She parted her lips ever so slightly, and he let his finger trail away, dragging across her lower lip as he withdrew. A warmth spread over her body, and she closed her eyes and snuggled closer, pressing her breasts lightly to his chest.

His heart beat wildly against her. She swallowed hard. She wanted to kiss him. She wanted him to put his arms around her. She wanted—

Her uncle coughed, and she jumped. It sounded as if he was just on the other side of the door.

Mike's arms instantly came up to hold her still. She laid her cheek and one palm against his chest. He didn't move at first, and then he tightened his hold. Not much, but enough to make her knees weak.

Tentatively she splayed her hand on his chest. He jerked slightly and then stilled, and she did not think she imagined that his hand moved down her back. Just a little, and not in an obvious way, but it was enough of a caress to cause goose bumps to march down her arms.

She stood on tiptoe so she could get close to his ear and whispered, "What are we going to do?"

Mike wished like hell he knew. If he wasn't so damned aroused, he'd be angry as all get-out. Gina hiding in the closet was one thing. The two of them—together—could he explain *that* to Antonio?

He lowered his head to her ear. Soft silky strands of hair brushed his jaw. Her exotic scent briefly robbed him of all thought. She was so close she had to feel the erection that wouldn't quit. And there wasn't a damn thing he could do about it.

"We'll have to sit tight," he finally managed to whisper, and when she abruptly tilted her head back, he realized she probably didn't understand the phrase.

He didn't bother trying to explain. She'd keep quiet. That was what counted. He had to think. Which wasn't easy with her breasts rubbing against his chest. He shifted, hoping for more distance, and her hip stroked his arousal. Sucking in a breath didn't help. It only pushed him in harder against her breasts.

Like a flash of lightning, it occurred to him that he still had his arms around her. He loosened them and his hands fell to the curve of her backside. Fighting the temptation to cup her to him required every ounce of his willpower.

Gina was like the girls in high school he'd watched from afar but never had the nerve to ask out. They were the cheerleaders and song leaders, and God forbid they'd go out with anyone who didn't throw a football.

"Mike?" She touched his chest to get his attention.

Yeah, that did it, all right. "I think my uncle has gone into the bathroom," she whispered, her warm, intoxicating breath another nail in his coffin.

Dammit. He should have been listening for Antonio.

"Mike?"

"Wait." With his thumb, he touched her lips. They were moist, and he had the insane urge to lower his head and kiss them.

Her hand moved restlessly against his chest. She had to be able to feel his heart pounding—pounding so hard he thought it might explode. That wasn't the only thing about to explode, and he knew she could feel that, too.

He straightened, listened and thought he heard a water faucet. That was enough for him. He disengaged himself from her tempting hands, carefully turned the knob. A quick glance down the hall assured him the coast was clear.

"Go to your room. Now," he said, and took off out the apartment door as though the devil himself was on his heels.

MIKE WAS THE FIRST one in the office the next morning. He got there early, about six-thirty, after a nightmare woke him before the alarm went off. In the dream, Antonio and his brother-in-law, Augie, had chased Mike with butcher knives. They had nearly caught up to him when he'd bolted upright in bed in a cold sweat.

The memory made him look over his shoulder as

he turned on the office lights. After he got the coffee started, he emptied his In box and started to sift through the reports and invoices that required his attention.

His mind kept wandering to Gina. She wasn't easy to figure out. Did she have her family fooled? Or had she really been that sheltered? He couldn't deny the unguarded innocence in her eyes or the uncertainty in her voice when she tried to assert herself. *Don't judge a book by its cover* was one of his mother's favorite sayings. Gina made a good case for that old adage.

"Hey, Mike."

At the sound of Antonio's voice, Mike jumped and dropped his pen. It rolled toward his desk clock. Seven-fifteen. "What are you doing here so early?"

Antonio grunted and reached into his pocket for a cigar. "It's Gina."

Shit! He was going to get fired. Or worse.

"I couldn't go out last night," Antonio said. "I had to stay home with her and got too damn much sleep. Where were you?"

"Me? Home. I, uh, figured she was too tired to go anywhere."

"Tired? She drove me crazy. She has a list this long of places to go." He held his hands an exaggerated distance apart. "I told her she has to wait for you to take her. I don't know these young people's hangouts."

"I thought she liked hanging around libraries and computers."

Antonio snorted. "Her *mother* likes her hanging

around libraries and computers. Sophia is too old-fashioned. Gina should go to a dance or a movie sometimes. She should do what other young girls do.''

Mike didn't think so, but he kept his mouth shut.

Antonio eyed the stack of paper in front of Mike. ''You are not planning to work today.''

''I have a few calls to make and—''

''No. Gina is at home eating breakfast. She will be ready in an hour. Today I want you to take her to Central Park.''

''Maybe Robert can—''

Antonio gave his head an emphatic shake. ''Robert is going to New Jersey to check a location for a new distribution center.''

''In Jersey?'' That didn't make sense. Not if they were looking into a West Coast site. They couldn't afford two new locations at once.

Antonio shrugged. ''It's close and cheaper than any of the boroughs.''

''Why didn't I know about this?''

''No decision has been made.'' Antonio waved an impatient hand. ''Worry about Gina. Your work can wait.''

Mike bit back a curse. What the hell was going on? Was the West Coast proposal just a carrot to keep him placated for a while? He had to talk to Robert. ''I'll take care of your niece.''

''Good.'' Antonio reached into his pocket and pulled out a wad of cash stuck in a gold money clip. He threw a couple of large bills on Mike's desk. ''Tell her to buy something nice, huh?''

Mike watched him leave. He'd always liked Antonio. The man had been good to Mike's mother, paying her a more-than-reasonable salary and being generous with bonuses for Christmas and her birthday. He'd been generous with Mike, as well. But he didn't like the way Antonio ignored Gina. For all his talk about family being everything, he sure didn't have much time for his niece.

Of course the Scarpetti men's attitudes toward women were not always admirable. Not that they overtly disrespected them, but they coddled them too much, failed to give them enough credit for having any sense outside the home.

It surprised Mike that Gina had attended college. Made him wonder what she planned to do with her education. Probably enter the family business on the Italian end, where they made the wine. It was logical she'd stay there where her father and Antonio's older brother Guisseppi ran the vineyard and harvested the grapes.

Other options could keep her in Europe, as well. Antonio's other brother, Dominic, headed the wine distribution in Paris, and the younger one, Pietro, handled the marketing and warehousing in Rome. Gina would do well on the sales side of things. What red-blooded man wouldn't want to place an enormous order with her? Sexist, he knew, but it was the reality of the male-dominated business.

So why did the idea annoy the hell out of him? Why his sudden interest in Gina's future? He had enough to worry about keeping her out of trouble for the next month. And not getting himself fired.

He plowed through the paperwork that couldn't wait, left a voice mail for Robert to contact him as soon as he got back and then grabbed a cab and headed home. If he was going to spend the day in Central Park, it wouldn't be in a suit.

GINA SAT ON THE WINDOWSILL, staring down at the crowded sidewalk, watching the streams of people hurry to work. Many of the women wore suits and tennis shoes. An odd but practical combination, she figured, envious of their freedom of choice.

She wished she owned a suit. Mama thought they looked too manly. As if the ugly black dresses she liked Gina to wear were not too grandmotherly.

Sighing, she checked her watch. Would Mike ever show up? She hoped he was not angry about yesterday. All her courage had faded when she heard Zio Antonio outside the door, and she panicked. No harm had been done, though. Her uncle thought she had been in her room alone.

She slid off the sill and adjusted her skirt. Wearing skirts so short was not easy. She was constantly tugging and pulling and trying not to feel self-conscious. Some of her school friends had encouraged her. They wore skirts equally short, some of them even in front of their parents.

The knock at the door had her tripping over the unfamiliar high heels, and she hopped to the door on one leg, trying to adjust the fit. Before she opened it, she slipped the other shoe back on.

Mike did not look happy, and her mood fell. "Gina, why didn't you ask who it was before you opened the door?"

She shrugged, more interested in the snug fit of his jeans and black T-shirt. "I knew it was you. Zio Antonio said you were coming."

His gaze ran down the front of her, something in his eyes making her get hot and prickly. "Since I didn't call from downstairs for you to buzz me in, you should have been more cautious. Next time find out who it is before you unlock the door. New York is not the safest place."

"Why are you trying to frighten me?"

"I'm just trying to make you more aware." He walked in and locked the door behind him. "Your uncle told me you wanted to go to Central Park."

"Oh, yes. The sky is so blue and pretty. It would be a perfect day, yes?"

His eyebrows dipped in a frown. "Then why are you dressed like that?"

She looked down at the pink blouse tied at her waist and denim miniskirt. "You do not like this outfit, either?"

"I like it fine, but not for a day in the park. What if you want to sit in the grass?"

"I do not have any pants," she murmured, and looked away.

"Pardon me?"

"Mama does not think women should wear pants."

Mike laughed. "And she would want you to wear this?"

His amusement fueled her embarrassment. Sometimes her parents' old-fashioned attitude made her ashamed. "No, but I sewed this myself in secret. Pants are harder and take longer to make."

Surprise, then understanding flickered in his eyes, and he smiled. "How would you like a pair of jeans?"

"Oh, yes. The kind with a ripped knee or—"

He chuckled. "Let's get a whole pair for now, okay?"

WHY DID HE SET himself up for this kind of torture? Mike had never had masochistic tendencies before now. Why had he foolishly thought shopping would be easy with a woman who looked like Gina?

"What about these?" She pranced out of the dressing room and twirled around so that he wouldn't miss the back view. "Do you like them?"

The faded denim was skintight and accentuated her narrow waist and full hips. Her belly was remarkably flat, considering how he'd seen her wolf down the entire cheeseburger and fries yesterday. Her rear end was round and perfect and begged for a man's hands—*his* hands—to mold themselves over the taut curves.

"Mike, are you all right?" she asked, a worried frown wrinkling her brow.

As soon as his heart started again, he'd be fine. "I like the other pair better."

"But they were too baggy."

Exactly. ''Can you even sit down in those?''

She grinned and walked toward him. ''Do you want to see?''

Mike held up a hand. ''Never mind.''

No telling what she'd do. He was sitting in the only seat outside the women's dressing room, which made his lap the likely target for her demonstration. Oh, yeah, that would be great. It wasn't as if they hadn't attracted enough attention from the other Blooming-dale shoppers.

Both men and women eyed Gina as she modeled the different styles of jeans. She seemed oblivious to the mixture of envy and admiration in their stares. She was too excited about the whole prospect of shopping.

''I have one more pair to try on.'' She spun toward the dressing-room door, then stopped and asked, ''May I have two pairs? *Per piacere...*please?''

If he said no, two guys, who hadn't once taken their eyes off her, would probably gladly buy her anything she wanted. A woman about his age who'd overheard Gina gave Mike a hostile look as if he was a vile controlling husband.

''Fine. Just hurry up.'' He stood and got out his wallet. Antonio had given him a nice piece of change. Enough for the jeans and a dress—an appropriate dress, like maybe a muumuu. Hell, Mike would gladly pay for it himself.

She came out to show him the third pair, which looked so much like the last pair that he didn't know she'd changed. At Gina's request, the saleswoman cut off the tags so she could wear them out of the store.

After their purchases were wrapped and paid for, they headed for the escalator. They got as far as the lingerie department. Gina stopped and stared at the red and black silk G-strings on display.

Fear gripped the back of Mike's neck. "Come on. We're going to be late."

Her eyes widened. "Central Park closes?"

"That's not what I meant."

Gina sidled up and took him by the arm. "Can we not stay for ten more minutes?"

He darted a look at the mannequin wearing the G-string and tried not to think about the way Gina rubbed the inside of his arm.

"Per piacere." She made her lips look pouty. "I mean, please."

"Just ten minutes."

"I promise." She smiled and then kissed his cheek.

An innocent touch that threatened a major hard-on. Oh, man, he was in bad shape. No way was he going to stand around and watch her select underwear. "I'll wait for you on the first floor."

Her expression fell. "Why?"

"Because I have something to do down there." He reached into his pocket and withdrew some money. "Here."

"Grazie, but I have my own money." She lifted her chin and headed in the direction of the G-strings.

What had he done wrong? "Ten minutes," he called. "At the bottom of the escalator."

She waved without turning around, which was good enough for him. Let her get her G-string or whatever.

He didn't have to know what she wore under her clothes. And he didn't have to subject himself to watching her select it.

He used the time to go to the washroom and splash his face with cold water. On the way back to the escalator, he stopped at the men's cosmetic counter and squirted himself with one of the testers. The stuff smelled nasty, and he let out a rude grunt that netted him several stares. No wonder he never wore any of that junk.

With a minute to spare he arrived at the escalator. No sign of Gina yet. Not that he expected her to be early. She'd been like a kid in a candy store all morning, excited by simply trying on sunglasses. She'd explained that her mother didn't allow unchaperoned shopping, which basically meant it wasn't worth going.

Such strict rules and morals were hard to understand. Particularly since Gina seemed to be a good girl, genuinely concerned about what her parents and uncle thought. Even the way she'd wanted to dress had more to do with normal and healthy rebellion than attracting male attention.

That was the thing that floored Mike the most. She didn't even get how hot she was, or that men tripped over themselves watching her walk across the street. She was more interested in gawking at shop windows and staring at young women with blue hair and navel rings.

He checked his watch. Eighteen minutes. No sign

of her coming down the escalator. He'd give her another two and then drag her out of the store.

After another five minutes, he took the escalator steps two at a time up to the lingerie department. He didn't see her, and flagged a saleswoman.

"I'm looking for my friend," he said. "Petite, dark hair, pretty—"

She smiled. "Italian accent?"

"That's her." The relief he felt was ridiculous. She was probably still in a fitting room.

"Yes, she went that way." The woman pointed in the opposite direction of the escalator. "With two other gentlemen."

4

"WE WERE SUPPOSED to meet at the bottom of the escalator a half hour ago." Mike blew into his clammy palms. "Are the elevators and escalators the only ways to get to the first floor?"

The security guard nodded. "For shoppers."

"What do you mean? Are there stairs we haven't checked?"

"Don't worry, Mr. Mason." The older man glanced at the notes he'd taken so far. "We have a good description of her. We'll find your daughter. How old did you say she is?"

"Twenty-three," Mike muttered.

"What?"

"I never said she was my daughter."

The man closed his notebook and glared. "Is this some kind of joke? We're talking about a grown woman, not a *kid?*"

Mike shook his head. "No, definitely not. She's new to the city—"

"So are a third of the people in this store." The security guard crossed his arms over his big round belly. "I ought to have you arrested."

"That's absurd. On what charge?"

"Anything happens in this store, like a theft or something, while you have us distracted, and I gotta believe you were in on it."

Mike groaned. The guy had one hell of an imagination. "Look, I'm telling you the truth. She's Italian and she doesn't speak much English."

"Guess what, pal? Half the people who live in the city don't speak English."

"Yeah, but—"

"Mike!"

At the sound of her voice, he spun around.

She ran to him and threw her arms around his waist, burying her face in his chest.

"Gina, are you okay?" He held her tightly and stroked her back when she refused to release him.

She mumbled something in Italian but wouldn't look up.

Another security guard, tall and lanky, walked over and stood beside them. "She's fine," he said, exchanging a look with his paunchy co-worker then glancing around at the gathering crowd. "She just had a little fright, is all."

"Those two guys have anything to do with it?" Mike asked, a fury rising in him he didn't know he possessed.

She looked up. "They said you sent them to find me. That you had an accident."

Mike stared down at her pale face. "Did they hurt you?"

She shook her head. "I punched the short skinny one."

He swallowed a startled laugh and then glanced at the taller security guard. "Did you catch them?"

The man's grim face was answer enough. "If you want to file a report, let's go to the office."

"No." Gina straightened and stepped away from Mike. "We are going to Central Park."

"But, Gina—"

"They ran. You will not catch them. And if Zio Antonio finds out what happened, I will be on a plane back to Italy."

She had a point. Mike looked at the security guard again. The man shrugged. The other one was trying to break up the interested group of onlookers.

"I want to go now, please." Her accent was heavier, probably because she was upset. In her eyes was an odd mixture of pleading and determination. Her mind was clearly made up.

"Okay, but you stick close to me. Got it?"

She nodded enthusiastically and slipped her arm through his.

He pulled her closer still, unsure of what he was more afraid of—her or the unknown.

"I WANT ANOTHER hot dog." Gina dug into the pocket of her jeans for money. "And a Coca-Cola with lots of ice."

"You're going to be sick."

She wrinkled her nose. "Why?"

"Because you've already had two Cokes, a hot dog *and* popcorn."

"Yes, and?" She passed the vendor her money and then doused her hot dog with mustard and relish.

She had the most incredible appetite for a woman, especially one her size. Of course she did a good job of burning off calories. He got winded just watching her play Frisbee with the two twelve-year-old boys they'd met earlier. She ran and dove for her catches as if the free world depended on her.

No wonder she was in such excellent shape. The woman could move. Hell, she'd even gotten him off his ass to catch a few throws.

She took a big bite of the hot dog and ended up with mustard on the tip of her nose. He got it off with his thumb. She smiled and took a gulp of Coke. Not Diet Coke, but the real stuff.

That was another thing he liked about her. How she did everything with such gusto, totally unselfconscious. There was no worrying about how she looked or acted. When she got excited about something, the whole world knew it, and she didn't seem to care.

And God knows, she got excited a lot. Her accent would get thick and she'd throw in a few Italian words. Mike understood some of them from listening to Antonio and his two brothers-in-law, Augie and Lorenzo, talking at the office.

"Let's go find some shade." He carried the bag with her skirt and the other pair of jeans they'd bought.

The sack with her lingerie purchase got lost in the scuffle she'd had with the two men, and Mike had to ruthlessly push the reminder aside. There was nothing he could do except get angrier than he could remember ever getting in his life.

It wasn't only about being responsible for her welfare on Antonio's behalf. But the idea that her trust and innocence could be stolen by two low-life jerks made his blood boil. That it could happen practically under his nose made him feel guilty as hell.

But to her credit, she was resilient. She hadn't let the incident affect her mood. When Mike had mentioned how admirably she was handling things, she'd looked at him with round trusting eyes and said she'd never be frightened with him near to keep her safe.

Fool that he was, his ego had inflated like a balloon. And then headed straight back to guilt. What if something had happened to her? What if—

"We will sit here?" She stopped at an oak tree, its roots bulging from the ground. But that didn't stop her from finding a narrow spot in the grass.

She plunked down and then patted the area beside her. He didn't have much choice. He settled in close. Too close.

"I like Central Park very much." She smiled at him. "We can come again, yes?"

"I don't know. You wear me out."

She frowned.

"I'm kidding."

"Oh." She took the last bite of her hot dog and wiped her mouth.

His gaze lingered on her lips. Moist and peach-colored, they alone got his adrenaline pumping. Her tongue darted out to swipe a tiny crumb from the corner of her mouth, and he had to look away.

"What kind of exercise do you do?"

He brought his gaze back to meet her curious eyes. "Exercise?"

She nodded. "Everyone needs to exercise."

"I get enough running around the office."

She made a face. "That is not the same thing."

"I work a lot of hours. I don't have time."

"Does my uncle work you that hard?"

Mike snorted. "*I* work me that hard."

"That is not good," she said, shaking her head with concern. "Do you swim?"

He shrugged. "I haven't for a while."

She extended her hands behind her and leaned back. The reclining position showed off her flat belly and made her breasts jut out. "Tomorrow, we will swim."

Amused at her confidence, he asked, "Where?"

"You do not know of a place?" She frowned, and then her eyes brightened. "Coney Island. I read about it on the airplane."

He hadn't been there in years. "Maybe."

"Why maybe?"

"Because I have a lot of work to catch up on. I thought you could go to the library for the morning and—"

She groaned. "I can go to the library at home. I want to see New York."

Great. "We can't go out every minute."

"Why not?"

He laughed. "Look, how about if you go to the

office with me and use my computer while I get some paperwork out of the way, and then we'll spend the afternoon out."

"At Coney Island?"

"I was thinking a museum. The Guggenheim?"

"Oh, yes, that is on my list."

"Oh, great, you have a list." He sighed. "You have any rest time on that list?"

She laughed. "Come," she said, sitting up straight and then scooting backward until her back rested against the tree trunk.

"Where?"

"Here." She tugged at his sleeve until he leaned toward her. "Closer."

What the hell was she doing? Knowing it was trouble, he shifted his butt a foot closer.

She put an arm around his shoulder and urged him to put his head on her lap. He resisted, but she gave him a smile that sent his resolve floating off in the warm breeze.

"What? You think I'm too old to keep up? I need a nap?"

"Yes."

"Hey." He started to lift his head.

Laughing, she splayed her fingers through his hair and gave it a small tug, forcing him to rest his head on her thighs. He complied, but she left her fingers in his hair and gently massaged his scalp.

He briefly closed his eyes at the soothing sensation.

"This is not a good idea," he finally said, yet made no move to get up.

"Why not?"

He opened his eyes. She looked down at him in innocent confusion, her fingers continuing to work their magic. "You don't know?"

She blinked. "Papa used to like when I rubbed his scalp. He said it relaxed him."

Mike snorted. Obviously her mind wasn't in the gutter with his. God, he was a dope.

Her fingers stilled. "But I never got a funny feeling in my stomach with Papa."

Mike sat up.

"Did I hurt you?" she asked, her eyes filled with genuine concern.

He shook his head as he got to his feet. Was she really this naive? "We'd better start back. In another hour it's going to be tough to get a cab."

She held out her hand and he pulled her to her feet. Without warning, she kissed him on the cheek. "Thank you for the nice day."

"Don't mention it." He quickly backed away.

"*Scusi.*" She made a sound of impatience. "Excuse me, I do not understand. I did something wrong?"

He smiled. "It's a term that means what I did was nothing. Don't give it another thought."

"Oh, but that is not true." She slid her arms around his waist and looked up into his eyes. "You have given me the perfect day."

"Yeah, well, I'm glad you liked it." He tried to disengage her arms. "I don't think you should be doing that."

She held on tightly. "Why? Because you make my stomach, um, what is the word? Jump? Flutter?"

"Gina." He drawled her name into a warning she ignored.

"Mike?"

"Yes?" He took a step back. She moved along with him.

"Can I ask for one more thing?"

"What?" he asked slowly, his gaze hopelessly tangled with hers.

"Will you kiss me?"

His gaze stayed locked with hers another moment, until he realized he was actually thinking about giving in. "Holy shit! Gina, don't even think about stuff like that."

She blinked. "Why?"

"Because."

"You have a girlfriend?" She slackened her hold.

"No."

"Good." She tilted her head back farther and closed her eyes. "You can kiss me now."

The sun shining on her lips made them glisten. He swallowed. "No kissing."

She opened her eyes again, hurt gathering like storm clouds. "You do not like me. You think I am too much trouble."

"Of course not."

She dropped her arms and moved back. "That is all right. I understand."

"No, you don't." He hated the hurt look on her face. What had she been told by her parents? Or maybe it was the nuns who'd undermined her confidence. "It's just that it's too public here."

She stared at him, her eyes growing wide, and then her lips curved in an expectant smile. "You must be planning some kiss."

Mike groaned. She'd probably been asking for a peck. Now she'd expect much more. Gee, no pressure here.

"ROBERT, WAIT UP." Mike shot up from his desk to catch him before he disappeared for the day.

"Coffee. I need coffee right away." Robert turned and headed for the office's small kitchen.

Mike followed, but stopped at Augie's office when he noticed the door was open. "I didn't know you were in already. We could have had a coffee together."

Augie shrugged and stared down at the newspaper spread across his desk. "I had a lot of stuff to catch up on."

Mike frowned. Yeah, Augie looked as if he were really busy. What the hell was going on? Augie always had time for coffee with him, even if only to find out what was happening with sales so he could try to stay on top of things.

"No problem," Mike said. "Maybe tomorrow."

"Sure," Augie looked up briefly and went back to his paper. Mike continued to the kitchen, his concern growing, but waited until his friend poured a cup of the strong black brew. It was pretty early. For Robert, anyway. "Your office or mine?" Robert asked after he'd taken a sip.

"Mine. My coffee is sitting on my desk." Mike led the way back down the hall. At least Robert didn't seem to be avoiding him. Although he still hadn't volunteered anything about his trip to Jersey either.

"What's up?" Robert sprawled in the chair opposite Mike, cradling his mug in his hands.

"I was hoping you'd tell me."

Robert's eyebrows shot up. "Come again?"

"What's with this trip to Jersey?"

Robert made a dismissive sound. "Nothing. You know Pop. The warehouse lease is up for renewal and he thinks the rent is going up and he's panicking."

Mike frowned. Not good. A move would mean a delay in opening the West Coast distribution center. "It probably will be raised."

"I don't think so. Pop's been doing business with the Einsteins for over twenty years. He pays promptly." Robert took a slow sip and then studied Mike over the rim of his mug. "You didn't think I was doing anything behind your back, did you?"

"No, but I don't understand why you didn't mention going to Jersey."

"Pop asked me to go at the last minute." He shrugged. "Probably trying to keep me busy so I don't seem totally useless."

"Knock it off, Robert. Nobody thinks that."

"Right. I need more coffee."

"You got another minute first?"

"Don't worry, Mike." He rose to his feet. "The

West Coast distributorship will be yours. Unless Pop doesn't think I can handle things at this end.''

Guilt nudged Mike. The thought had crossed his mind. Not because Robert wasn't capable. He simply didn't seem interested. ''Since when do you give a rat's ass what your dad thinks?''

''I don't,'' Robert said without conviction, ''but I overheard him talking to my cousin.''

''Which one?'' Three of them worked at the warehouse.

''Gina.''

''About you?'' he asked when Robert didn't expand.

''Forget it. What did you want to talk about?''

Mike didn't want to forget it. He knew Robert, and something was really eating at him. Maybe he regarded Gina as a threat. Maybe she wanted... No! Did she want to work at the New York office? Even if she did, she'd hardly be qualified to do anything more than entry level work while she learned the ropes.

Oh, man, he couldn't talk to Robert about Gina now. If things got political or messy, Mike didn't want to end up in the middle.

''I bet it's about Gina,'' Robert finally said after a lull.

''What about her?''

''That's what you wanted to talk to me about, right?'' Robert grinned. ''What? She's boring you to death already?''

''Not exactly,'' Mike murmured. It felt wrong discussing her with anyone. And not just because of the possible business aspect. It was more about her, about not betraying their relationship. Crazy thinking since they'd only known each other for two days, but there it was.

Robert frowned and studied him closely. "What's up?"

"Nothing. I was just thinking about how much work I have to do."

"Ah." Robert nodded thoughtfully. "And Gina's taking up all your time."

Mike shrugged, suddenly worried that Robert might want to step in and take Gina off his hands. He blinked. But that's what he wanted, right? "She's good about giving me time to get caught up. We're working it out."

Robert rubbed the back of his neck, his brow furrowed. "Look, I know you guys are supposed to go to Coney Island today. I could take her."

It was obvious that was the last thing Robert wanted to do, so Mike knew he wouldn't get an argument when he declined the offer. "You leave for vacation tomorrow. Go home and pack and get your last-minute stuff done."

"Okay, but don't say I didn't ask."

Mike snorted.

Robert gave him a sheepish grin. "When I get back I promise I'll take over."

"Don't worry about it." Mike got up for more coffee. He had at least another hour to sort his mail, dictate a couple of letters, and then brace himself for another day of hurricane Gina before he had to go get her. "I have everything under control."

"I hope so." Robert nudged his chin in the direction of the office lobby. "Look who Pop brought with him."

5

GINA SAT AT MIKE'S computer in the corner of his office while he studied a piece of paper at his desk. She tried to stay focused on the computer screen, but her gaze kept wandering over to him. He looked particularly handsome this morning with his light-brown hair a little messy and his chin stubbly.

She wondered if today they would kiss, how his beard-roughened jaw would feel on her skin.

She realized she had sighed out loud when he looked up and met her eyes. Quickly she forced her attention back to the computer.

"I won't be much longer," he said. "About another fifteen minutes."

"Do not hurry. I am fine." She was in a great mood. Nothing could ruin her day. Zio Antonio had not said anything about her new jeans.

She found the *Sex and the City* Web site she was searching for and helped herself to a tablet of paper and pen lying nearby. She had misplaced the list of nightclubs she had printed off her computer at home. The clubs the four women on the show went to. Mike would probably not want to go to most of them. He would worry about upsetting Zio Antonio, but she would persuade him.

It took more than ten minutes to copy everything she wanted. Although she had learned to speak English at a very young age, she had never read or written the language much, except during high-school English classes. She reviewed the list and realized she had written it half in Italian.

"Just a few more minutes—"

The phone rang and Mike groaned. He snatched it up and gave his last name, instead of a greeting.

She thought about leaving the room, but it was obviously a business call and not a personal one. Besides, she loved listening to him talk about work. He sounded very confident and smart. She liked the way he looked, too, his face so serious and focused as he described the latest merlot they had bottled.

He hung up and gave her an apologetic smile. "Are you ready for the beach?"

She nodded. "But if you still have work to do, I do not mind waiting."

"I could work until midnight and never get caught up. Let's go."

"Maybe I could help you."

He laughed. "That's okay. It'll all still be here when I get back."

His attitude wounded her. "I know many things about the business."

He gave her an odd look. "Probably more than me. What made you say that?"

"You are overworked, yet you do not want my help."

"It's not that. You're on vacation. This is probably your last fling before you start work."

"Me start work?"

"When you get back to Italy."

She frowned. It was an odd thing for him to say.

"I assume you'll be working at the home office in Tuscany." He shrugged, but his eyes were watchful. "Maybe you plan on working at the Paris or Rome office."

She stared back at him, wondering if he was trying to make a joke. If so, she did not understand. Women in her family did not work in the business. They married and made babies. Just as they all expected her to do.

The phone rang again, and Mike muttered a word she had not heard before. He started to reach for the receiver and then stopped. "I'll let it go to voice mail."

"But it may be business." Guilt cut into her. He was neglecting his work for her. "It might be important."

He laughed. "Are you sure you're related to Robert?"

"Scusi?"

"Never mind. It was a bad joke." He grabbed the phone but was only on for seconds.

"Is something wrong?" Gina asked when he hung up and grunted with impatience.

"One of our distributors is here to see me." He threw up his hands. "Just a few more minutes, okay?"

"No sweat." She had heard him use the phrase a couple of times.

The corners of his mouth twitched. "Be careful what you repeat. Do you want to wait in your uncle's office or maybe in the kitchen area?"

"Oh." She wanted to listen to him talk some more, but she stood, realizing it would not be proper for her to be present during a business meeting. "I have not spent time with Zio Augie yet. I will find him."

"I'm sorry about this, Gina."

"This is business, Mike." She stopped at his door and gave him a reassuring smile. "I understand."

"I'd make the guy wait since he doesn't have an appointment, but he's thinking about giving up the truck space of our wine for more Mondavi stock."

She gasped, appalled at the idea. "Our grapes are far superior. Why would—"

Mike cleared his throat and focused on the doorway behind her. "George, good to see you."

Gina turned around to find a man approaching. Shorter than Mike and maybe a little older, he had a dark bushy mustache and small black eyes.

"Glad I caught you, Mason." He eyed Gina with curiosity as he shook Mike's hand. "You going on vacation?"

Mike glanced down at his jeans and red polo shirt. "Nah, I'm headed out for the day. I have an out-of-town guest." He gestured to Gina. "This is Gina Ferraro, Antonio's niece. This is George Zacharias."

The man took Gina's hand, and the firm shake she gave put surprise in his eyes. "I am pleased to meet you, Mr. Zacharias."

"It's George, please. So, you're from Italy?"

"*Si*. Tuscany, where we have the finest grapes in the country."

George gave her an amused, rather patronizing look that made her want to scratch something. "Yes, you make some fine wine."

"Our merlots cannot be surpassed." She waved a dismissive hand. "Even for a grape that has been overplanted and overproduced. We are very careful about our selections. Our merlots are very reliable grapes."

Mike watched, fascinated, as Gina described their cabernet sauvignon, and how they had become so well respected that more of their wine was being sold *en primeur,* or as futures, when collectors or merchants agree on a price before it is bottled.

She was a natural at selling. Not just because she looked like a million bucks in her new jeans and clingy T-shirt, but because her passion for wine was genuine. But that Gina looked like sin in jeans did nothing for George, who never hid the fact that he was gay. Still, Mike could tell he was impressed. Oh, man, did she know her stuff.

After holding George's rapt attention for several minutes, a faint pink tinged her cheeks. "Forgive me. You came to see Mike. I did not mean to intrude."

"No problem. What you said is very interesting." George took a seat at Mike's urging. "Actually I'd like to hear more sometime.'' He glanced at Mike. ''Assuming we're still doing business after this meeting.''

''What's going on, George?'' With grim acceptance, Mike sat in his own chair. ''What's making you unhappy?''

Gina started to leave, but Mike waved her back inside. ''Stay if you want,'' he said. ''This is your business, too.''

Surprise flickered in her eyes, and then a pleased smile lifted her lips and she reclaimed the chair in front of the computer.

George snorted. ''Need reinforcements to help me change my mind?''

Mike hated being baited. ''Tell me what the problem is and I'll see if I can fix it.''

''Simple.'' George shrugged and pursed his mouth in an annoying show of indifference. ''Mondavi is willing to give me a larger percentage.''

''That's hard to believe. You know damn well we pay top commission.''

''I'm telling you straight.'' George smiled. ''Maybe Mondavi wants my business more than you do.''

Mike drummed his fingers on the desk. The guy had to be bluffing. ''Well, like I said, we're already paying top dollar. I don't know that there's anything more I can do.''

''Okay, but you understand...'' George shrugged again and started to get to his feet. ''I like you, Mike. I've enjoyed doing business with you. But that's the point—this is business. I have to go for the highest profit.''

"*Scusi*, um, excuse me."

Gina had been so quiet Mike had almost forgotten she was sitting in the corner. Both men looked at her.

Her lips were pursed, her brows drawn together. Confusion never looked so pretty. "May I ask a question?"

Mike figured no harm could be done at this point. It looked as if he was losing an account. "Go ahead."

George sank back into his seat with a condescending nod toward Gina.

"You are an independent distributor, *si?* You work for yourself?"

George nodded patiently, but Mike narrowed his gaze. She was up to something. Her accent was more pronounced and she looked entirely too innocent—in spite of the shrewd gleam in her eyes Mike had not seen before.

"You sell and distribute the Scarpetti wine to retail stores, *si?*"

George glanced at Mike, the corners of his mouth lifting in amusement, and then nodded at Gina.

"And you do not feel it is profitable enough to continue to sell our wine."

"I wouldn't go that far," George said. "It's just more profitable dealing with Mondavi."

A pleased smile lit her face. "I understand."

"If you say so." George chuckled.

"We'll talk about it later, Gina," Mike said.

"Oh, yes." She sighed. "I was so worried the distributors would be upset with the new catalog. But now I see there is no problem as it has nothing to do with your decision. Everybody will be happy.''

"What catalog?" George looked from Gina to Mike, his eyes growing angry. "I didn't hear about any catalog."

Shit. Mike hadn't, either. Had he been left out of the loop again? What the hell was going on?

Gina's eyes widened. "Perhaps I should not have said anything. My proposal has not been approved yet." She shrugged. "But it makes sense to me to ship direct to retailers. We have been established for a long time. Our wine sells itself."

"What are you guys trying to pull?" George's eyes blazed at Mike. "You can't cut out the distributors. We have a contract."

A contract the idiot was trying to weasel out of, but Mike didn't point that out. He leaned back in his chair. "I frankly don't know enough about the plan at this time to discuss it. But considering your reason for being here, it's a moot point, isn't it?"

"I said I was *thinking* about going with Mondavi." George abruptly stood. "I haven't made up my mind yet. Until I do, I expect you to have my normal shipment ready each week."

He stormed out of the office before Mike could say another word.

"Mondavi. Ha!" Gina grunted, and then rattled something off in Italian.

He turned to stare at her. She looked awfully pleased with herself. Calling George's bluff didn't give Mike the same satisfaction. A catalog business could screw up his West Coast plans. The real bite is that it made sense. "You want to tell me about this catalog proposition?"

Her triumphant look promptly faded. "There is nothing to tell."

"Right."

She folded her arms across her chest and he tried not to get distracted by the way her shirt pulled across her breasts. "When I was in school I did a paper on such a plan, and I got a very high grade."

"But you haven't presented it to your father or Antonio yet?" he pressed anxiously.

Her eyes got wide. "No. I have not."

Mike sighed at his own paranoia. Still, when Gina did implement her plan, he would undoubtedly be affected. The crazy thoughts started to spar in his head when he abruptly realized what had happened with George.

"Gina, you could have really pissed the guy off. We can't afford to chase away business."

She frowned. "I am sorry, but he made me angry. He comes in here speaking of Mondavi as if—"

"Gina." Mike waited for her to chill out. She lifted her chin but gave him her attention. "When you do get involved with the business, you're going to have to hold on to your temper, be a little more tactful. Even if a distributor or a supplier does make you mad, and believe me, there'll be plenty of times when some of those idiots will drive you up a wall."

She gave him a funny look. "What do you mean, get involved with the business?"

"When you go back home and take your place at Scarpetti Wines."

She blinked, looking utterly stunned. "I have no place in the business. No Scarpetti woman does."

"Of course you do. You studied business in college, right?"

She nodded, her expression grim. "It does not matter."

Mike shook his head. He knew the family was old-fashioned, but Gina was from a new generation. Surely they wouldn't hold her back. "What a horrible waste of talent."

Her eyes lit up. "Me?"

"You obviously know more than enough about wine making and sales. Maybe you'll be surprised." He locked his desk, mostly out of habit, and then stood, suddenly anxious to get the hell out of the office. "Maybe you'll get back to Tuscany and your father will have a job waiting for you."

The sadness returned to her eyes. "The only thing waiting for me will be a wedding."

SHE TALKED HIM into taking the subway. But Mike was so damn dazed she could have talked him into just about anything. A wedding? Gina married? To some stranger?

No, of course the guy wasn't a stranger. But he was to Mike. Which made no difference in the entire scheme of things. Except he had this damn proprietary feeling going on. He didn't understand it, but there it was.

"Are we almost there?" Gina turned her big, almond-shaped eyes to him. She looked all of fifteen.

But he knew that once she got up, with the tight jeans and snug shirt hiding nothing, the illusion would be gone. "About ten minutes," he said, and quickly looked the other way, out the opposite window.

Still, she was too young to be married. Dammit. She was inexperienced. She had to ask to be kissed. Most women nowadays took what they wanted. He wondered if she ever *had* been kissed. A real tongue-sweeping, down-your-throat kind of kiss. The kind that made a guy so hard he thought he might explode.

Hell, he wanted to be the first one to show her what it felt like to press bare skin to bare skin, to make her wet and needy. To make her mindlessly grope for him, to make her part her thighs and welcome him inside.

She was getting married. Shit. She was forbidden fruit. Damn, but he suddenly wanted a taste.

He had to get his mind off this dangerous track. Bad enough they sat so close he could feel her body heat. With each bump of the train, they seemed to get closer. "Gina, I know you don't want to talk about it, but tell me about this guy you're going to marry. You said he's your neighbor?"

Her face immediately darkened, which cheered him considerably. "He is old and boring."

"So why marry him?"

"I do not know that I will."

That information shouldn't have made his heart

soar. It was immaterial to him what Gina did. "Earlier you sounded as though the plans were all set."

She sighed. "My family thinks so."

"But if—"

She laid a hand on his arm. "Please. It is not a subject I like to discuss."

"No problem." He covered her hand with his, intending to reassure her, but the casual contact was like a jolt of awareness that jump-started parts of his body better left dormant.

He quickly retreated, lifting his hand to plow his fingers through his hair, and then inched away until his thigh no longer touched hers. She dropped her hand from his arm and slanted him a wary look. Was she reacting to his abruptness, or had she felt something too?

For the next five minutes it took to get to Coney Island, they didn't speak. Mike kept telling himself he shouldn't be so damn glad she didn't want to marry this guy. What she did was none of his business. After a month, he'd probably never see her again.

He almost missed their stop. He jumped up and pulled Gina to her feet just as the doors started to close. They made it outside without a second to spare.

Gina sagged against him. "You frightened me."

"Sorry." Her body molding to his was not a good idea. He took the tote bag she carried and used it as a shield. "I'll carry this."

She didn't let go but smiled, looking slyly at him. "Today when we are not in public, we will kiss, yes?"

"The beach is public."

"Ah, but we can go in the water."

Man, she was going to be the death of him. "Are you going to let go of this?"

She made a face and released the tote. "If you do not want to kiss me, Michael, you can say so."

"You haven't called me that before." He liked it.

"I am upset with you." She lifted her chin and started to walk away.

"Uh, Gina, wrong direction," he said, reluctant to give up the great view of her backfield in motion. He'd been too young to understand the song the first time he heard it. He sure got it now.

She turned around and headed in the opposite direction. He caught up to her and, grabbing her shoulders, steered her to the left. He didn't ask why she was upset with him. He didn't want her to bring up kissing again.

The beach was crowded for a weekday, beach towels and mats occupying much of the sand. Lines had formed for both the roller coaster and Ferris wheel already. The crowd and water quality were two of the reasons Mike never came here anymore, but in spite of that, an unexpected excitement churned in his gut.

He'd had some memorable times here as a kid. Behind the carousel he'd gotten his first kiss from Dee Adams. His gaze immediately went to Gina. Man, why did he have to think of that now?

"Let's go find a place to sit."

Gina blinked at him and then went back to gawking at the throng of people in a multitude of shapes and stages of undress.

Clearly she'd forgotten her annoyance with him.

He took her hand and led the way toward the water, torn between snagging a safe public spot in the middle of everyone or finding a more private area off the beaten path. Weak bastard that he was, he headed for the most isolated patch of sand way off to the side.

It wasn't as if anything could happen with all these people around. A kiss, maybe, or—

No. No kiss. No nothing.

Gina was so busy looking over her shoulder at something she nearly tripped over an unattended beach chair. Mike pulled her out of harm's way, and she gave him a smile that made him swallow hard.

"May we ride the roller coaster and carousel?" she asked, tossing another glance behind her.

Man, he hated roller coasters. "Later, maybe."

"And have a hot dog?"

He laughed. "*After* your ride."

She gave him another one of those sexy smiles. Amazing how she could look young and innocent one minute and cut him off at the knees the next.

Using his foot, he smoothed the surface of the sand and then spread out two beach towels about two feet apart. He kicked off his shoes, along with a spray of sand he'd collected under his soles.

He pulled off his shirt and heard Gina's clothes rustling behind him. His chest tightened in anticipation. What sort of swimsuit would she be wearing? Probably nothing too racy, but on her anything looked hot.

He took a deep breath and turned around at the same time she dropped her shirt onto the towel.

Her breasts were totally bare.

6

MIKE STARED for a moment, unable to look away. She was perfect. Round and firm. Large pink areolas and nipples that stuck out like—

"Gina!"

He dove for her shirt, but grabbed his, instead, and then dropped it when he tried to cover her up. Their nearest neighbor, an older couple about four yards behind Gina, were shading their eyes and squinting.

Mike threw his arms around her and pulled her against his chest. Her skin was silky and warm, her hair fragrant with a flowery scent. Her firm nipples beaded against his chest.

"Michael?" She tilted her head back, her startled eyes searching his face.

He glanced past her at the couple. The woman scowled in their direction. "Gina, this is not a topless beach."

"I do not understand."

"Work with me here." Just what he needed—Gina to get arrested. Antonio would do more than kick his ass. He'd be calling his friends, the kind who wore shoulder holsters. "We're going to slide down to the towel together, okay?"

She frowned, and then understanding flickered in her eyes. She slid her arms around his neck. "We're going to kiss now, yes?"

"Yes. I mean, no. Put your arms down."

Hurt darkened her face as she slowly let them fall to her side. No time to explain that he simply wanted her covered as much as possible. He cocked his head to the side and saw the woman who'd been watching them march toward the lifeguard stand.

"Shit." Mike let go of Gina long enough to grab their towels. He threw one around her shoulders and snatched their discarded clothes and bag, and then drew her along with him down the opposite side of the beach where the shoreline wasn't so nice and the crowd considerably thinner.

"Mike, I do not—" She stumbled.

He put an arm around her. "I'll explain in a minute."

He didn't look back until they'd passed the last group of sunbathers and made it to an old abandoned concession stand. No one had followed.

They stopped on the far side of the building where no one could see them. One side of Gina's towel had slid down her shoulder, revealing the top swell of her left breast.

Mike swallowed and sank back against the wall. His gaze lifted to her confused face. He should adjust the towel and cover her up. What he wanted was to take the damn towel and bare her.

Gina shifted, gripping the towel more tightly. "Mike, you are frightening me."

"I'm sorry." He straightened, but there was nothing he could do about his racing heart. God, what kind of suggestive looks had he given her?

She moved closer and splayed a hand on his chest. "Why were we running?"

He relaxed. It wasn't him she was afraid of. Maybe she should be. "You have to wear a swimsuit."

She blinked. "I am."

"Not just the bottoms."

"But in Europe—"

"This isn't Europe."

She pursed her lips in a pout. "Americans. They worry too much about their bodies."

Mike laughed. "Most of them should."

She studied his face long enough for him to get edgy. "I embarrassed you?"

"No," he replied honestly. "You're beautiful, Gina."

The way she blushed amazed him. Women who looked like her knew it. He brushed his thumb down her cheek. "I just didn't want you to get in trouble."

"With Zio Antonio?"

"Him, too, but you could have been arrested."

She frowned.

"By the police."

Her eyes got wide. "But in Europe—"

His thumb rested on her lips, silencing her. "I know about the different view most Europeans have of nudity. But in America it's different. And would your mother or father approve?"

The look in her eyes told him she wasn't thinking

about her parents right now. Neither was he, for that matter. He quickly pulled back his hand.

"I have only been to the beach three times. And never with them. I do not know what they think."

"Gina."

At the doubt in his voice, she lifted her chin. "This is the truth. The beach is for swimming and making a tan. It is not the same thing as being naked with a man."

"Right." Mike sighed and looked around. They were alone, and if he shielded her with his body, she could get her top back on without incident. The sooner the better. He was lucky to have one shred of common sense left.

"Michael?"

He looked down at her and she lifted herself on tiptoe and brushed his lips with hers. She started to lower herself, but then came back up for another soft kiss.

Mike didn't move. He let her experiment and control the pace. But at her soft whimper of frustration, something inside him snapped and he grabbed both her arms and kissed her hard, slanting his head and trailing his tongue over her lips.

She tensed at first, and then slowly opened her mouth.

He'd wanted the kiss to be gentle, but it was too late for that. His tongue swept inside her mouth as he tasted her with a greediness that shocked him. Her tentative response was the only thing that slowed him down.

With too much reluctance, he finally drew back.

Gina stared up at him, her eyes as round as pizzas. He'd really scared the hell out of her now. "Can we kiss some more?" she asked.

His breathing ragged, he hesitated. "I shouldn't have done that."

"Yes." She pressed against him, the towel slipping entirely off her shoulder and bringing her bare breast into contact with his skin. "I want you to do it again."

He briefly closed his eyes at the incredible feel of her nakedness, at the way her nipple blossomed against his bare chest. He wanted to take it into his mouth and suck it hard, make her moan, make her ask for more.

"Michael, please?"

He snapped out of his trance and stared down at her. What the hell was he thinking? This was Gina, his boss's niece. He straightened away from her, his gaze helplessly targeting her breast. He barely forced himself to look away from her. "Gina, we can't do this."

"Why?" The hurt and confusion in her voice was like a slap across his face—a well-deserved one.

"*I* can't do this. It isn't right."

"You like me, yes?"

He looked her straight in the eye and held her gaze. "Have you ever been with a man?"

She blinked and color lightly tinted her cheeks. "Of course."

He sighed. "It was a rhetorical question."

She squinted, clearly unable to translate what he'd said.

"I don't think you've been with a man, Gina." She started to protest, and he added, "Not the way I mean."

"How do you mean?"

"I think you know."

She didn't respond. She didn't have to. The apprehension in her face gave him his answer. It turned to shame and she pulled the towel around herself, covering her breast.

"Gina?" He lifted her chin. "You are beautiful and very tempting. Please don't make things harder for me."

Hope lit her eyes. "Maybe we could just kiss."

He drew back his hand. "That's the thing. It won't stop there."

"It can," she said, reaching for his hand and pressing her palm to his.

"You give me way too much credit."

She got that puzzled look on her face again, as if she wasn't quite sure what he meant. "You will not hurt me, Michael. I know that."

"Certainly not intentionally." They had to get out of here. She might trust him, but he wasn't sure he trusted himself. Especially with her looking at him the way she was. "Come on, put your shirt on and let's go ride the Ferris wheel."

He started to turn around to give her privacy, but she tugged at his hand.

"Michael, I lied."

He got a bad feeling. "About what?"

"I want to do more than kiss." She pursed her lips in that irresistible pout.

He swallowed, but his mouth got so dry it was almost painful. "Definitely not a good idea."

"You were right. I have not been with a man." Embarrassment bloomed in her cheeks and her gaze skittered away.

He brought it back to his, and he smiled. "That is nothing to be ashamed of."

The way his heart raced and blood rushed to his groin was a damn good reason for *him* to be ashamed, however the knowledge that she was a virgin and wanted him to be the one made his ego swell as much as his cock.

"I know," she said, shrugging, her hand still tight around his. "And I am not asking to, you know, do everything. But I am asking you to do one thing for me...."

So enthralled with the color of her eyes in the sunlight, he hadn't noticed her guiding his hand until his palm met with a mound of soft yet firm flesh. He stared down at his hand sandwiched between her smaller one and her abundant breast.

She moaned softly, and he looked at her face. Her eyes were closed, her lips lifting in a slight sensuous curve. Tentatively flexing his fingers, he explored the swells and dip, until he couldn't stand it, and then gently pinched her nipple between his thumb and finger.

Whimpering, she thrust herself against his hand. "It

feels good," she whispered, and then murmured something in Italian. Her lids drifted open and she looked at him with dazed eyes. "Touch me some more."

He moved his hand to her other breast, just for a moment. Just to appease her curiosity. God, he wanted to put his mouth on her. He wanted her to find his thickening arousal. But neither could happen.

He squeezed gently, liking the way she filled his palm. He found her nipple, already big and ripe, and he fought the urge to lower his mouth. Instead, he touched his lips to hers, lightly, knowing this was it. He had to stop. Now.

"You throw any more sand at me and I'm telling Mom."

The kids' voices came from just around the corner. Mike and Gina sprang apart.

"You're such a baby. Go ahead and tell her." The second voice seemed to be drifting farther away.

Gina gathered the towel around her, clutching it at her breasts, a blush climbing her neck.

"No one saw anything," he whispered. "Here." He held up her shirt. "I'll block you."

She quickly took the shirt and turned around. But not before he saw the humiliation in her eyes. They were in a public place. What did she expect?

That wasn't fair. He couldn't blame her for his guilt.

He held up the towel when she let it go and waited for her to pull on her shirt. Had he been too busy beating up on himself to notice if she'd put on her bra?

She turned around and took the towel from his hands.

Oh, boy. She definitely was not wearing a bra.

"We'll find a rest room," he said, and dragged his gaze away.

"What for?"

"So you can finish dressing." Dammit, he'd told himself not to look there again. He wondered if it was possible to die of a prolonged hard-on.

She glanced down at her chest. Her nipples poked at the light cotton T-shirt. "Oh." She hugged the folded beach towel to her chest.

He took a deep breath. His body hadn't quite settled down yet. He might need the other towel. "Do you even have a swimsuit top?"

She shook her head.

"I guess we head for the Ferris wheel, then."

Her troubled frown began to clear. "And the roller coaster?"

He groaned. "And the roller coaster."

"Mike?" She fell into step beside him. "At the top of the Ferris wheel it will be private. Maybe we can kiss again."

Mike's steps faltered. The roller coaster sounded better already.

GINA TOOK EXTRA TIME to shower. She knew her uncle had late dinner plans, and she hoped he would leave the apartment before Mike picked her up. Zio

Antonio would definitely not approve of the dress she planned to wear tonight.

Mike would, though.

She smiled at her reflection in the mirror as she pulled a comb through her wet hair.

He would say she should not wear something so short or tight or low-cut. But then he would look at her the way he had today when she had bared her breasts to him. She got hot and tingly thinking about the way his nostrils had flared and how he had sucked on her mouth so hard it was as if he wanted to swallow her whole.

The way he had cupped her breasts and pinched her nipples had been both scary and exciting, and if she did not stop replaying the afternoon in her head, she was afraid she would have to take a shower again.

She blow-dried her hair and then took extra care with her makeup. Tonight they were going dancing, and she wanted to look perfect. If she did, maybe he would kiss her again. Maybe he would even kiss her breasts.

The thought sent a shiver down her spine. Would he suck her nipples hard or lick them gently?

To her amazement she had unconsciously slipped her hand inside her robe and touched her breast. Her nipple stuck way out and she lightly pinched it the way he had. She closed her eyes, imagining it was his hand on her, making her grow warm and shivery.

Excitement erupted in her belly and she withdrew her hand, frightened, embarrassed by her thoughts and the reaction of her body. The nuns would go crazy if they saw the desire growing in her heart. If they knew how much she craved Mike's mouth.

It was a strange feeling, nothing at all like having a fantasy about Brad Pitt or Ben Affleck while she lay in bed at night. Mike was real flesh and blood, yet he had touched her in a place no man ever had before.

And she had let him. She had wanted him to. And she wanted him to do it again.

She would surely go to hell for all this wantonness. So why did it not seem wrong? Not with Michael, anyway. He did not push or coax, and if at any time she told him to stop, she had no doubt he would. He tried very hard to be a gentleman. But then he would get that helpless look on his face and give in to her.

She wrapped her robe more tightly and hugged herself. But what she liked the most about him was that he thought she was smart, that she would be good for the company, that she was capable of being more than a hostess and making babies.

The idea made her smile and she twirled around, imagining herself in a business suit, just like the women she watched from Zio Antonio's window in the morning.

A knock at the bathroom door sobered her.

"Gina?"

"*Si*, Zio Antonio."

"I'm leaving now. What time did you say Mike is picking you up?"

She looked at her watch. "In half an hour."

"Okay, then. You have fun. Be home by midnight and I'll see you in the morning."

Midnight. Gina scowled. The night would be just beginning. Even Antonio did not get home until midnight, his breath heavy with too much wine. *"Si, Zio Antonio."*

She listened for his footfalls to fade and then the click of the front door. Hurriedly she finished the last of her makeup and then shimmied into the black dress she had been saving for a special occasion. It was snug and not easy to zip, even when she sucked her tummy in as hard as she could. No dinner for her tonight, that was for sure.

After checking her nail polish for chips and giving her hair a good brushing, she sat on the edge of her bed and studied her only two pairs of suitable shoes. Wearing the right one was most important, according to the women on *Sex and the City.*

She selected the pair of black stilettos, even though she had already worn them. Obviously she would have to talk to Mike about taking her shopping again.

There were certain disadvantages to dressing in this new manner. Men looked at her as they never had before. She supposed that was what she had wanted at first. But mostly she had wanted to be like her friends, or the other young women who frequented the nightclubs in Milan. And not like Grandmother Scarpetti.

She did like the way Mike looked at her, though. The way his eyes got a little glassy made her body temperature go up. He never made her uncomfortable like other men had at times. Of course, he had instructions from her *zio* to take care of her.

A heaviness settled in her chest. Was that why Mike paid attention to her? Because it was his duty? No, she was being silly. He liked her. How could he kiss her as he had if he did not like her?

She sighed as she slipped her feet into the heels. She wished she had more experience with men. All she had for information was her friends' gossip. Not that she knew whom to believe. Maria thought she knew everything about men, but Gina suspected some of Maria's claims were fantasy.

As Gina stood, her dress rode up her thighs and she had to tug and rearrange the clingy fabric until seams matched and nothing showed. She looked in the mirror and had second thoughts about wearing such a revealing dress. Then she imagined how Mike's eyes would get glassy and his gaze would run down her body, and she started feeling warm and giddy.

The doorbell rang and she quickly checked her teeth for lipstick before going to answer it. Even though she knew it was Mike, she peeked through the peephole as he had counseled her, but saw no one.

She grinned and then called out, "Who is it?"

"It's Mike."

"How do I know it is you?"

Silence, and then he said, "Come on, Gina."

"Step back so I can see you."

"Very funny." He did as she asked. "Okay?"

"Another step back."

"Gina, do you want to go out tonight or not?"

She smiled when he moved back and she got a good view of him. He wore a silky, burgundy printed shirt and black jeans that were snug enough to start that funny flutter again. She flattened her palms against the door, pretending it was his chest, and watched the way he rubbed his jaw and then pushed his hand through his hair.

Maybe they should stay in the apartment tonight. She could make him some pasta and then they could get comfortable and then maybe—

"Gina?"

"Yes, Michael?"

"Are you going to let me in?"

She unlocked the dead bolt, opened the door and kept a straight face. "Turn around so I know it is really you."

His gaze met hers and a thrilling intensity in his eyes made it impossible for her to look away. He moved forward and she automatically took a step back. One side of his mouth started to lift.

Ah, so he was playing a game. When he moved toward her again, she grabbed the front of his shirt and pulled him close. "There is one way to tell if you are really Michael Mason."

His left eyebrow shot up, but he did not try to move away or pry her hands from his shirt. He stared down at her, expectant, watchful, while he reached behind and closed the door.

She swallowed and resisted the impulse to release him and back away. "A kiss would reveal who you really are."

"Is that right?" His gaze lowered to her mouth.

Her breath caught and she could only nod.

"Like this?" He lightly brushed his lips across hers.

It was maddeningly brief and chaste. "You are not Michael Mason."

He smiled, his mouth curving in that sexy way that made her want to squeeze her legs together, and she braced herself for a real kiss.

He glanced at his watch. "Are you ready?"

Disappointment dampened her mood. "I have to get my purse. Michael?" She had started to turn, and when she suddenly looked back, she saw him eyeing her dress. "We could stay in the apartment tonight if you want."

His gaze narrowed. "Why?"

"My *zio* will not be home until late." She shrugged. "I thought if you were tired from today, I could make you some pasta." She shrugged again, a touch of uncertainty creeping into her thoughts. "Rub your shoulders."

Mike drew his head back and made a funny noise. "I think we'd better stick to the plan. We'll just make it an early night."

"Early night?" The phrase was unfamiliar to her.

"We won't stay out late."

"But nothing happens until late."

He smiled. "Right. What time's your curfew?"

She smiled back. "Two-thirty."

7

STAYING HOME might not have been such a bad idea. They stood in the doorway of the posh uptown club, and Mike gritted his teeth at the way two men openly ogled Gina. She didn't seem to notice. She was too busy staring wide-eyed at the nude posters hanging on the walls. Admittedly they were tasteful works of art, but that didn't make him any more comfortable. Antonio would not be happy with this place. Not one bit.

How the hell had she come up with it? A bad feeling gnawed at him. She had a sizable list of nightspots she wanted to visit, half of which he'd never heard of. He was going to have to do some quick research.

"Gina, what do you say we skip this place?" He watched a couple dancing in the corner of a small dance floor. They seemed to have their tongues down each other's throats. If the woman had one less inch of fabric on, she'd be arrested.

"Why?" Her fascinated gaze was still on one of the posters—the back of a nude man who was crouched in a position that left no doubt as to his sizable assets.

He laughed. "You don't think this place is a little odd?"

"Is it?" She turned her eyes on him. "I have never been to anything like this before."

"No kidding." A waitress smiled at him as she passed. She wore a thong and a shiny gold bikini top that barely covered her breasts.

"Good evening." A man in a tuxedo approached them. He was big, both tall and so broad his shoulders required a Wide Load sign. Probably a well-dressed bouncer. "Will you be staying downstairs for a while?"

Mike frowned. "As opposed to…?"

The man's brows drew together as he looked from Mike to Gina. "Have you been here before?"

They both shook their heads.

He smiled. "Ah, we have the best club in Manhattan. I'm Darin, your host for the evening. There are two more floors." He gestured toward a curved staircase. "Of course here we have the dance floor and in the corner is a light buffet, mostly cheese and crackers and fruit, that sort of thing, while you mingle."

Mike's gaze went back to the couple who were pseudo-dancing. He didn't think he and Gina would be doing too much mingling. Only two other couples sat in the corner talking and drinking.

"It's early. The usual crowd normally gets here around eleven," Darin said as he followed Mike's gaze. "And of course there are about a dozen people in the community room on the second floor right now. The third floor has only private rooms."

"For dinner?" Mike asked.

Darin smiled. "If that's what you wish."

Gina had wandered a few feet away and stared at the top of the staircase. "Can we go upstairs and look?"

"Of course." Darin's overly interested gaze rested on Gina's rear end.

Mike stepped between them and put a possessive hand at her lower back. A private room for dinner sounded pretty good. Leaving sounded even better. Something about the place made him uneasy. He whispered in her ear, "I know a great restaurant around the corner."

"Oh, I am not hungry. Are you?"

"I thought we were supposed to have dinner."

"Shall I leave you two to wander around on your own?" Darin asked, and took a diplomatic step back.

"Yeah, thanks." Mike waited until the guy left. "I don't like this place. Let's get out of here, huh?"

"But I have not seen upstairs."

"Look, the guy said it doesn't get jumping until later. Maybe we'll come back." *Right.*

"But we are already here." Gina took his arm and gave him one of those smiles that scrambled his common sense. "Come on, Michael, are you not curious?"

"Not really."

"I am." She tugged at him. "Come. Maybe the music is better upstairs and we can dance."

His gaze went back to the couple on the dance floor. Granted, it had been a while since he'd tried any fancy footwork, but he didn't call that dancing. The man's hands molded themselves to his partner's nude back, slowly following the curve of her nearly exposed buttocks. He cupped her against him while he did a slow grind with his hips.

To his humiliation, Mike's body reacted to the display and he quickly looked away. "Okay, we go upstairs for a look, but then we leave."

Gina gave him a tolerant smile and led the way. He followed closely, that bad feeling niggling at him again. No way would he let her talk him into staying. The city had a slew of clubs they could go to, ones he knew, ones that didn't make him feel so damn uneasy.

The top of the stairs gave way to a well-appointed landing with another nude on the wall, this one an oil painting, and two love seats upholstered in plush burgundy velour facing each other. Between them, on a dark wood coffee table, sat a large glass bowl of green and red grapes.

A short hall led to two closed doors. Soft music came from behind one of them. Gina looked questioningly at him, and he shrugged. The door was slightly ajar, so he gave it a light push.

Inside, the lighting was soft and reddish, and it took a moment for his eyes to adjust. Gina hung on his arm and craned her neck to see into the unexpectedly cavernous room. It appeared to be sectioned off by two panels of red velvet drapery, which blocked their view.

A woman's laughter, mingled with the sounds of the Moody Blues song "Your Wildest Dreams," came from behind one of the drapes. Gina took a few tentative steps inside. Mike followed, curious himself about what was going on. Darin had said there were a dozen people up here, but it was awfully quiet—

A low, primal moan pierced the strains of the song, and in that instant Mike realized where they were. How could he have been so friggin' naive?

Before he could stop her, Gina stepped up to the part in the drapes and froze. Mike reached out to pull her back and caught a glimpse of a naked woman lying on some floor cushions. He got a hold of Gina but stopped cold.

One guy was sucking the woman's nipples as another guy lay between her thighs licking while she bucked. A third guy with long, wild, blond hair knelt beside her, his eyes closed, the veins at his neck bulging as she stroked his erection.

Gina mumbled something in Italian, her voice barely a whisper. Loud enough to bring Mike back to his senses. He grabbed her arm and she stumbled backward, her gaze glued to the scene.

"Don't go." One of the men had come up for air, his mouth and chest slick with moisture. "Join the party."

The guy getting the hand job opened his eyes and stared at Gina.

Mike gave her a firmer tug and she moved back. "Let's go."

She looked at him, her face a mass of confusion. She started to revert to Italian again, but stopped and asked, "What are they doing?"

Was she kidding? "We'll discuss it outside."

She nodded but looked back, eyes wide with disbelief, as he dragged her out of the room.

Man, he felt like a jerk. Talk about stupid. Even though he'd never been in a place like this before, he certainly knew they existed. Couples who swung used them, or singles who went for orgies. He should have figured it out immediately. The nude posters and paintings, the dirty dancing... Shit! Private rooms?

His only defense was that New York was a city where just about anything went, including racy art in public places. Darin and his fancy threads had thrown him, too.

They got to the stairs and Gina said, "But we have not been to the third floor."

Mike gave a startled laugh. "That wasn't enough for you?"

Her eyes met and held his. "On the next floor, the rooms are private, yes?"

"Yes. I mean, no." That he had even a moment's crazy hesitation scared the hell out of him. "No."

"But, Mike..." She wrapped her fingers around his forearm and stroked up to his elbow. The motion inspired a totally inappropriate image.

"Gina, we need to leave." Dammit, he sounded as convincing as a kid turning down candy. "Now."

"But, Mike, I have to go to the rest room."

"Oh." His gaze went to the other door. It was unmarked just like the first one. "Can you wait a few minutes? I think there's a McDonald's nearby."

She shrugged and bit her lower lip.

He sighed. Upstairs was private. Private was better. Right? ''Come on.''

He took her hand and led her to the next floor. Unlike the large furnished landing on the second floor, the top of the stairs immediately gave way to a long hall. On either side was a series of doors, all closed, two of them with Do Not Disturb signs hanging from the knobs.

Other than that, the doors all looked alike, with no indication that one was a washroom. He stopped and listened. It was eerily quiet in the hall. No sounds came from behind any door. Thank God.

And then he heard a lock disengage and turned, surprised to find Gina opening one of the doors.

''Wait!''

Too late. She stepped inside.

Mike followed, holding his breath, prepared for the worst.

The room was empty. Furnished but no people. Set up like a hotel room, an attached bathroom in the corner, for which Gina immediately headed.

A soon as she shut herself behind the door, he glanced around at the furnishings. Nothing sleazy or cheap about them. The queen-size bed was covered with a rich, royal-blue duvet, and a half-dozen matching pillows were spread against an artsy chrome headboard, the kind you saw in Park Avenue store windows.

The floor was polished hardwood and the Oriental rug expensive. How the hell did they pay for all this? No one had hit them with a cover charge when they came in. Drinks were probably twenty bucks each. But not even the waitress had pushed them to buy.

He heard the bathroom door open and he turned around. Gina had her arms crossed over her chest as if she was cold. Her breasts were round and high, creating a valley headed toward more hidden treasure, and to his disgust, arousal stirred in his belly.

The tableau downstairs was not his kind of thing, but the image of the foursome lingered in his mind and did nothing to help the semi-hard state the experience had left him in. Hell, he was only human. And male.

Gina seemed a little wooden as she came toward him.

"Are you okay?" he asked, wondering suddenly what kind of sick gadgets they had in the bathroom.

"Fine."

"You don't look fine." The room was dimly lit and he moved around the bed to get a closer look at her face.

"What are those?" She stared past him toward the nightstand.

He turned and groaned. Sitting there was a collection of condoms and some kind of feather contraption. He could guess what you did with something like that, but he wasn't about to explain it to Gina. "Let's get out of here."

"I want to see." She walked past him, her fascinated gaze glued to the nightstand.

"I don't think so. Uh, Gina I wouldn't touch that…."

She picked up one of the foil packets and squinted at it. "A condom, yes?"

"Yup."

"I have never seen one before. What a pretty color."

She looked at him, excitement dancing in her eyes. "May I open it?"

"I'm guessing tonight you've seen a lot of things you haven't seen before." The blush that climbed her face made him regret the remark. "I'm sorry, I didn't realize what kind of place this was."

"I asked to come. It is not your fault." She returned her attention to the foil packet.

"Did you know…?" The sudden suspicion was ludicrous. "Well, I'm sorry you had to see all that."

Her head came up and uncertainty clouded her eyes. "I am not sorry."

Mike swallowed. "You'd better put that back on the nightstand."

She seemed nervous, but she wouldn't look away as she approached him. "Watching those people gave me a funny feeling here." She pressed a palm to her belly and then slowly let it slide lower. She stopped before getting to her crotch.

His mouth got so dry he wasn't sure he could speak. His first attempt failed. He cleared his throat. "What you saw is not normal lovemaking."

"I know," she said quickly. "And I would not want to—" she gave a helpless shrug "—do anything like that. But it makes me want to kiss you." She moistened her lips. "It makes me want your—" She covered her face.

"Ah, Gina..." He didn't know what to say. "Don't be embarrassed."

She still wouldn't look at him.

"Hey." He took her hands away from her flaming face. The temptation to ask what she'd been about to say was nearly too much. But it wouldn't do either of them any good. "You got excited. It's a perfectly normal reaction."

She gazed at him with trusting eyes. "Did you get excited?"

He wanted to lie. He wanted to press her hand to his swelling penis. "Yes, I did."

Desire flared in her eyes. An experienced woman could have hidden the response. Or used it to her advantage. Damn, he wished she weren't so young and naive. Maybe then they could have had a thing for the month. Two mutually consenting adults enjoying each other's company—

"Michael?"

He realized he had hold of her hands. One of them grasping the foil packet. He promptly released her. Hurt darkened her eyes.

"Gina, look..." He exhaled slowly, at a loss for words. "You know I think you're beautiful and smart and sexy but—"

He didn't know what hit him. Her untutored lips pressed hard against his. She briefly put her hands on his chest, her fingers curling into him. And then she backed away.

"We can go now," she said, her voice unsteady, her gaze wavering.

He pulled her to him. Her brief resistance came from surprise, and then she relaxed. He tilted up her chin and lightly kissed her lips. When he tried to withdraw, she moved with him. He kissed her again, this time using the tip of his tongue to part her lips.

Shyly she touched her tongue to his. Heat shot to his groin. What the hell was he doing? He couldn't...not with Gina...and not in a place like this...

She found his tongue again, something so sweet about her tentative exploration that his resolve weakened. One more kiss wouldn't hurt a damn thing.

He cupped her face with his hands and kissed her so thoroughly he left no doubt as to how much he wanted her. It was agonizing to finally pull back. The effort was almost too much. "Now," he said, trying to regain his breathing, "we can go."

She slowly opened her eyes, and then blinked. "But Michael—"

He put a finger to her lips, took the foil packet out of her hand and tossed it back on the nightstand. He wasn't even sure he hit his target. He didn't look back. He got them outside to the hall and down the stairs before he did something really stupid.

They'd barely made it to the first floor when Darin appeared. He held out two champagne flutes to them. "I hope everything is satisfactory."

"No, thanks." Mike declined the champagne and was surprised to see Gina accept hers.

She sniffed it but didn't take a sip.

"May I get you anything else?" He signaled the waitress. "We have a very fine twelve-year-old scotch if you prefer, or perhaps a cognac."

Mike took the flute from Gina's hand and looked around for someplace to set it. The waitress came and he placed the glass on her tray. "Actually, we were on our way out, but thanks, anyway."

Darin drew his head back in surprise. "Leaving so soon? The action won't start for another hour."

"What action?" Gina asked, her eyes wide and curious.

Mike took her arm. "I think we've seen enough action for one day."

"Pity you're in such a hurry." Darin smiled and clasped his hands in front of him. "But there is one small matter we have to address."

"Which is?"

"Your bill."

The champagne Gina took, of course. Well, here went the twenty-dollar drink. No problem. Mike would pay fifty for it just to get out of here. He withdrew his wallet and pulled out a couple of bills. "How much?"

"Let's see. Since you were here for less than an hour—" Darin thought for a moment "—I'll give you a break. Three hundred should cover it."

Mike's jaw slackened. "Dollars?"

Darin nodded, his smile still intact.

"For one drink?"

The man frowned. "That was complimentary."

Shit! He didn't have that kind of money on him. A hundred and twenty or forty maybe, but that was it. "What the hell is the three hundred dollars for?"

Darin gestured toward a small plaque at the entrance with a patience that annoyed the hell out of Mike. "Like the sign says, anything upstairs goes for two hundred on up. Go look at the price list if you like. You'll see that I'm really giving you quite a deal."

"But we didn't do anything. We only looked."

Darin shrugged, his pleasant smile beginning to fade. "I only enforce the club policy."

It wasn't worth arguing. Mike pulled out his American Express card. "Here."

"Sorry, we don't take credit cards." Darin pointed to the obscure sign again.

Mike muttered a curse. "I don't have enough cash on me."

"Then we have a problem."

"I have some money." Gina dug into her tiny black bag and produced three twenty-dollar bills.

Darin looked at Mike. "I guess we still have a problem."

"You've got to be kidding. You won't accept almost two hundred dollars for basically nothing?"

The man's shrug was far from apologetic. "I don't make club policy."

Mike's temper started to flare. "Looks like you'll have to make an executive decision, pal. Because that's all the money we've got."

Darin looked from Mike to Gina, his brow furrowed in thought. "You have no other solution, huh?"

"Nope."

The big man turned toward the bartender. "Larry, call the police."

8

GINA LET OUT a string of angry-sounding Italian. Then, in English, "You are going to call the police for a matter this silly? Do they not have enough to do in a city this big?"

Darin seemed as surprised as Mike at her outburst. The guy hesitated and then said, "If you consider a hundred dollars so silly, then cough it up."

She frowned, obviously unfamiliar with the term.

"How about I bring the rest of the money back within an hour?" Damn, now he wished he had an ATM card. He'd always shunned the idea, figuring he'd never keep his checkbook straight.

"And I'm supposed to believe you'll do that?"

Gina gasped. "You think we would lie?"

Darin laughed. "Imagine."

The bartender called out to him. "What do you want me to do, boss?"

"It's up to these good people." Darin's smile was really pissing Mike off.

"We don't have a lot of options," Mike began. "Either you let us bring back the money or you call the police."

"No." Gina took the cash from Mike's hand and

shoved it into Darin's, along with two of her twenties. She held back the third. "This we need for cab fare. You will take this money and this ring." She pulled off a small diamond ring from her pinkie finger.

"Gina, no."

She put it in Darin's meaty hand. "When we bring back the money, you return my ring. It is done."

Mike touched her arm and looked at her meaningfully. "I'm not going to let you do this."

"Michael, I said, it is done." The anger and determination in her face gave him pause.

Darin studied the ring, looking for the gold stamp inside the band. He held it up to the light. "Okay, you have a deal. But you only get one hour."

"I would like a receipt, please."

He glanced at Gina with amusement. "You'll get your ring back, lady. All I want is the 120 bucks."

"And I am supposed to believe you?"

In spite of everything, Mike chuckled at the look on Darin's face. "She's got you there, pal."

"Don't push it," Darin warned, and motioned to the bartender.

The young man gave him a piece of paper, and Mike watched Gina watch Darin write out the receipt. She constantly surprised him. The ease with which she had just taken charge blew his mind. No way she'd be happy being a housewife. As worthwhile a position as it was, Gina wasn't cut out for the job. Nor would she be content being some man's trophy. She was an innocent when it came to sex, but not about life in general.

It occurred to him this was the second time she'd jumped in and helped out. Man, his ego was taking a beating.

"Here." Darin passed her the piece of paper. "One hour."

She took her time studying his messy scrawl. Finally she nodded and grasped Mike's arm. They walked out and he immediately hailed a cab. They didn't have time to waste. If traffic was bad, an hour might cut it close.

Gina slid in, stopping halfway across the seat. When Mike got in, she didn't budge even though their thighs pressed against each other. She didn't seem to notice. Her distracted gaze wandered out the window, but he noticed her hand shook slightly.

"Hey." He sandwiched it between his palms. "We'll get your ring back. I promise."

"I know. But he made me so mad." She let out a sound of exasperation and then lapsed into Italian, not even stopping to take a breath.

The cabdriver's head came up and he stared at her in the rearview mirror. Great. All they needed was for the guy to think she was a nutcase and kick them out of his cab.

"Calm down." He squeezed her hand, but she kept rattling off. "Come on, Gina."

The driver pulled over to the curb.

Mike cursed under his breath. They were going to get thrown out. "What are you doing? We're in a hurry."

The man ignored him. He turned around in the seat

and directed his dark gaze at Gina. And then he said something in Italian.

She answered, her voice rising, her hands waving excitedly.

Mike squinted at the man's license posted near the meter. Luigi Caliguri. Great. Just great. "Gina, we're in a hurry, remember?"

Luigi gave him a curious glance, then went back to talking with Gina. In Italian. And so fast Mike couldn't understand a word of it. All he knew was that Luigi looked pretty steamed. At whom, Mike had no idea.

When the guy jammed the cab into drive and made a perilous U-turn and headed back toward the club, Mike had a clue.

LUIGI HADN'T LOOKED so big sitting in the cab. But nose to nose with Darin, his size was damn impressive. He had two scars on his chin and jaw, battle scars, no doubt, and his untamed black hair made him look like someone Mike would avoid in a dark alley. Hell, any alley. He'd never been in a fight. Had no desire to be in one.

"Gentlemen," he began, "I'm sure there is no need for any bodily contact."

They both ignored him.

So did most of the customers who'd wandered into the club. Two couples barely spared them a glance as they headed directly upstairs. A group milled around the buffet table. The bearded guy sitting alone at the bar seemed to be the only interested spectator.

"Gentlemen, please…" Mike started again.

Gina tried to pull him out of harm's way. "I did not mean for this to happen. I was only talking. I did not know Luigi would do this. I am so sorry, Michael."

"You taka this poor girl's ring," Luigi growled. "What kinda pussy boy are you?"

Darin clenched his fist. "The kind that's going to smash your face into the wall."

"Come on." Luigi started to dance around like a boxer while he made hand signs for Darin to come get him. "It will please me to breaka your nose."

Gina grabbed the cabbie's sleeve and said something in Italian. Distracted for the moment, he didn't see Darin's fist before it crashed into his face. He stumbled backward. Darin was about to take another jab at him, but Mike stepped in to break it up.

The blow landed on the side of his jaw. His head whipped to the side. The punch hurt like a son of a bitch. He saw Darin draw back for another swing at him, but Gina swung her purse into Darin's face. The bag was too small to do any damage, but it momentarily stunned him. Long enough for Mike to grab his arm and yank it up behind his back.

Luigi lunged forward to take advantage of Darin's immobility. Mike pulled him back in time but lost hold of his arm. Dammit. Mike had not wanted to do this…

Darin aimed for his face and Mike had no choice. He flipped him over so that he lay prone, and then put his knee on the bigger man's back.

"What the hell did you just do?"

A uniformed policeman frowned at the dazed and incapacitated Darin, who had at least fifty pounds on Mike. Two more officers carrying nightsticks came in behind the first cop and eyed Mike with malice.

"Was that karate?" the shorter one asked as he got out handcuffs.

"Whoa!" Mike got off Darin. "This isn't how it looks."

All three officers chuckled. "Gee, I never heard that one before. What about you fellows?" the first one said.

"Let me explain." Gina stepped in between Mike and the cop with cuffs. "Please."

"I want these deadbeats arrested." Darin got up off the floor and tugged down his tuxedo jacket sleeves. "I'm the manager here and they tried to skip out on their tab."

"Bull!" Mike started to get in his face, but then thought better of it. "You gouged us and you know it."

"Everybody shut up." The officer with the potbelly turned to Gina. "Except you, little lady. What do you have to say?"

"This is a terrible, terrible mistake. We were on our way to get the money to get my ring back when Luigi turned the car around and—"

"Are you Luigi?" the officer asked Mike.

"No, Luigi's the cabdriver," Mike said, and turned to Luigi—except the man wasn't there. He'd disappeared. Mike swore.

The cop narrowed his gaze. "Watch your mouth, young man."

Gina gasped. "Luigi left?" She spun around looking for him. Flustered, she alternated between English and Italian until the officer finally told her he'd heard enough.

"Tell you what," he said, flipping open the cuffs. "I'm gonna let you explain it all to the judge."

"DOES IT HURT?" Gina touched Mike's jaw and he flinched.

Then he jerked away from her. "What do you think?"

She pressed her lips together. He had been in a bad mood ever since they'd left the police station. How many times did she have to say she was sorry? She had already explained she had not asked Luigi to go back to the club. He had surprised her, too.

"I'd better go before your uncle gets home." He started to get up from the couch, but she clutched his arm.

"I know you are angry with me, but please do not leave yet."

He sighed and settled back down. "I'm not angry. I just don't want your uncle to see me with a bruised and swollen jaw. Nor do I want to explain why I've been sitting in jail for the past two hours."

"We will not tell him." She lightly trailed a finger across the bluish skin that stretched across his jawbone. And then she leaned over and kissed it.

"Hey."

"What?" She pursed her lips in a fake pout. "I am trying to make you all better."

"Yeah, well, I think you caused enough trouble for one night." He tried to get up again, but she stopped him.

"I thought you did not blame me."

"I don't." He shoved a hand through his hair. It was still messy from the fight. She liked the way it looked. "But from now on, we don't go anywhere unless I've checked the place out first."

She nodded and snuggled up to him. "I have never seen anything like that before. My friends will not believe it."

"Oh, man. Don't tell anybody about the place, or about us being there."

She swallowed and looked down at her hands. "You are right. I am ashamed."

"That's not what I meant." He forced her chin up. "The reason no charges were pressed against us was because the desk sergeant remembered that Darin had pulled the same thing on two tourists last year. Who knows how many other people he's conned out of money? If we'd had the cash on us, we'd have paid him just to get out of there pronto."

"Then he should be in jail."

"You get no argument from me."

"How did you know how to flip him in the air like that?"

Mike made a face as if he was not happy about what he had done. "I took karate and judo when I was a kid."

"For a long time?"

He shrugged. "My mother worked two jobs and she didn't want me hanging around the apartment after school by myself. It was karate or piano lessons." He rolled his eyes. "I ended up getting a black belt."

"That is good?"

He smiled. "Depends on who you ask."

She liked him in this mood. "Tell me about when you were a child."

"Nothing to tell. I went to school and then to karate. When I got older, I got a job after school. That's it."

"Did you have a girlfriend?"

"Only two, one in tenth grade, and then Stacy and I went together for half our senior year."

"What happened?"

"I had to work to pay for college. That didn't leave much time for a social life. Look, enough about the past. Your uncle is going to be home at any minute."

She shook her head. "He comes home very late every night and I smell too much wine on his breath. I am worried he does not take care of himself." Before she left, she would have a talk with him.

"I'm sure he's okay." Mike's worried frown said something different. "He never gets to work late."

"Perhaps I am like my mama." The sudden thought terrified her. "I worry too much."

"This is a vacation." His lips stretched into a beautiful smile. "The only thing you need to worry about is staying out of trouble."

She sighed. Michael did not understand. She did not

look for trouble. Tonight had been a mistake. But now, she kept thinking about the blond man's aroused body. She wondered what Michael's nude body looked like. It frightened her to have so many obsessive thoughts about sex. The nuns had warned all the girls that such ideas would lead to trouble.

Gina touched his arm and used the tip of her finger to draw a swirly pattern in the light-brown hair. How much of him was covered with this fine hair? He had a little on his chest, she knew, and around the waistband of his shorts. Did the trail stop or go all the way down...

"I'm heading home now, and you go to bed. Tomorrow we'll visit a nice safe museum."

"You forgot something."

He had a cute frown. "What?"

She cupped his face as he had done with her and kissed him on the mouth. He sank back against the couch cushions and she took advantage of his mouth opening in surprise. She forced herself to make the kiss more leisurely, using her tongue to explore inside his mouth.

She had made the mistake of being too feverish the other times she had kissed him. Slow was better. The way he kissed her. Slow. Deep. Thorough.

"Gina..." he moved his head back so that their lips barely touched "—your uncle..."

She liked the way his lids lowered to hood his eyes. "We will hear him unlock the door."

He tried to straighten, but she sat on his lap and put her arms around his neck. His gaze touched her cleavage, but he quickly raised his eyes to meet hers. "You're determined to get me fired, aren't you?"

"Now look who worries for nothing." Again she kissed the spot where his jaw was bruised. His skin was a little rough from his beard and she wanted to feel it on her breasts.

She wriggled into a more comfortable position, and he groaned. She watched his eyes drift closed, and excitement bubbled in her stomach. Her already short dress had raised an indecent amount, and she silently willed him to put his hand on her bare thigh.

He did something better. He put his arms around her and she felt her zipper give. It glided down her back, the fabric parting in its wake. His fingertips touched her bare skin and he hesitated. She did not want him to stop. Please, no.

He leaned back his head and looked at her with bewilderment in his eyes. "You're not wearing a bra."

She shook her head, feeling shy again. Had she done something wrong? She had taped her nipples so they would not show— Oh, no! The tape. It would be horrible for him to find the two strips. Models used them all the time, but still...

"You're so..." He reverently cupped each breast with his hands. "I couldn't tell."

She swallowed hard. Pride and shame went down slowly. "Would you kiss me there?"

He blinked, some unidentifiable emotion flaring in his eyes. She thought he might try to leave again and she slipped her dress off one shoulder. He hesitated and then lowered the other side.

She reached inside her neckline to grab the tape and heard his sharp intake of breath. At first she did not understand, and then she remembered how the woman on the pillows had fondled one of her own breasts.

The idea both scared and excited Gina. Could she do that in front of Michael? His glazed eyes watched her every move. The hunger she saw in his face chased away her shyness, and she pulled the neckline down to expose both breasts. Carefully she removed the narrow strip of tape from each nipple.

His obvious fascination encouraged her, and once the tape was gone, she touched one beaded nipple with the tip of her finger. His lips parted and she felt his chest expand. Sitting on his lap as she was, his mouth so close, she need only move a little for him to reach her breasts with his tongue. Could she be so bold?

Gina took a deep breath and moved at the same time she guided his head toward her. His breath was hot and ragged against her tender skin, and when his cool wet tongue touched her, she sighed with pleasure. He made a funny sound that sent little jolts of excitement down her spine as she watched her nipple disappear between his lips.

Strange sensations swept her and the more he suckled, the greedier she became. The feel of his mouth there in that private place was the most incredible sensation of all. When his gentle exploration turned to eagerness, she thought she would surely die from pleasure.

Michael brought his head up suddenly and laid it back against the couch as he caught his breath. "Ah, Gina, this was not supposed to happen."

Startled, she nearly pulled her dress back up. But his heated gaze went to her glistening nipple and she knew it was not over. She cupped a hand beneath her neglected breast and offered it to him.

His throat worked as he swallowed, but his gaze stayed fixed on the ripe pink nipple. "I should go."

"No, Michael, please."

"God, Gina." He groaned and took her in his mouth with far less gentleness this time. His hand slid up her leg and rested on her exposed thigh. Another three inches and he would find her panties, wet from the moisture pooling there.

His head came up again and just when she thought he would push her away, he found her mouth. His tongue dove between her lips and his hand inched a little higher on her thigh.

She no longer felt awkward. Michael did not care about her inexperience. He kissed her hard and made her want to do things that would have frightened her a month ago. There was so much more to sex than she had imagined. And she wanted it all. With Michael.

His kiss slowed and he nibbled at the corner of her mouth, then along her jaw. When he got to her ear, she almost jumped off his lap. Amazing how she could be so sensitive there.

When he withdrew she was going to protest, until he cupped a breast and sucked the nipple into his mouth. She closed her eyes and tried to concentrate. So many odd sensations were happening to her body and she wanted to feel them all. She wanted to feel Michael beneath her palms.

Slowly she rocked her bottom over his hardness and his breath caught. He stopped suckling and looked questioningly at her. She wished she knew what he wanted. She wished she dared ask.

His lips quirked slightly, making him look a little sad, and he dragged the back of his knuckle down her cheek. "What are you doing to me?" he asked in a low gravelly voice she almost did not recognize. "I swore I wouldn't let this happen."

Shame filled her. She was pushing him to do something he did not want to do. She tugged at her neckline to cover herself. He put his hands on hers, his fingers trailing over her nipples. His gaze lingered on her breasts, longing in his eyes, replaced with regret as he helped her pull up the neckline.

Without the tape, her nipples were well defined by the clingy dress. He touched them through the fabric, watching how they responded. Beneath her bottom she felt him stir.

He lowered his hands to her waist and guided her off his lap and onto the couch.

He confused her. Aroused her. Even with her limited social life she had met boys from time to time, at neighboring school dances or her friends' brothers, and she knew when a man was interested. Michael was definitely interested. So why did he push her away?

Is that what made her want him so much? He was nothing like the other men she knew. None of them made her feel sexy and needy the way Michael did.

"I have to go," he said. "Are you all right?"

She nodded. "Put ice on your jaw when you get home."

He smiled and gave her a quick kiss.

And then he was gone.

9

"Is EVERYONE at the office going crazy, or is it just me?" Mike asked Robert as he drove him to the airport the next day.

"It's you. Oh, shit. I forgot my snorkel and fins."

"I put them in the trunk." Mike let the conversation lag as he pulled Antonio's car onto the freeway and merged with the traffic.

Mike seldom drove. Normally he would've told Robert to take a cab, but he seriously considered confiding in his friend about his problem with Gina. A bit difficult, perhaps, because Rob and Gina were related, but they weren't close cousins, and Robert definitely did not share his father's attitudes about family, anyway.

Still, Mike hesitated. Something odd was going on at the office. The guys gave him funny looks. Antonio's brother-in-law, Augie, had always stopped in Mike's office on the way back from getting his first cup of coffee in the morning. Not anymore. He hurried past as if he was late for an appointment. Except the guy hadn't had an appointment in three years. He knew the business, but he was lazy. Mike liked him, anyway.

"You haven't noticed anything odd in the office?" he asked Robert again when the Mercedes behind him had finally gotten off his tail.

"Like what?"

"I don't know." He felt foolish all of a sudden. "Like some of the guys seem to be avoiding me."

Alarm flickered in Robert's eyes and then he looked away. "It's your imagination."

"Bullshit!" Mike knew that reticent tone of voice. Robert was hiding something. "What's going on? Is it about the West Coast distributorship?"

"No." Robert's quick denial was almost believable, but convinced Mike he did know something. "I swear, nothing is going on about that."

"What, then?"

Robert turned to face him. "I don't know what to tell you, buddy. Everything is kosher as far as I know."

Mike concentrated on his driving. He couldn't think about Gina right now, or what he should or shouldn't tell Robert. With all his guilt chewing at him, it was highly possible nothing was going on in the office. It really was just him.

"How's it going with my cousin?"

"Don't ask."

Rob chuckled. "Where is she now?"

"At your pop's apartment."

"What's she doing—refiguring the Dewey decimal system?"

"She's got a lot more energy and curiosity than you give her credit for."

"Yeah? So what have you guys been doing?"

Mike coughed. That part he wasn't prepared to discuss. "Nothing much. Central Park, Coney Island, the usual tourist stuff. The thing is—"

"Ah, crap. Where's your cell phone?"

Mike took it out of his pocket and handed it to him.

"I was supposed to call Melanie. She wanted to get to the airport on her own, but she has a habit of oversleeping."

Mike returned his attention to driving while Robert punched in his girlfriend's number. His friend's self-absorption sometimes annoyed Mike, but at the moment he was grateful. The interruption gave him time to come to his senses. It wasn't right to discuss Gina with Robert, or anyone. She wasn't just another woman.

The notion struck a chord of fear in him. That wasn't to say she was anyone special to him. Sure, he liked the way she was unafraid to jump into tough situations. Or used her brains and not her femininity to make a point. And man, did he like the way she looked.

Even more, he liked the way she looked at him. He got hard in two seconds just thinking about that sexy pout of hers, the way her gaze melted into his, begging for his touch. And the sounds she made when he tasted her breasts. It was the most awesome—

"Yo, Mike!"

He blinked and glanced at Robert.

"You're gonna miss the exit."

"Dammit." He changed lanes just in time and managed not to hit anybody.

"You just took three years off my life." Robert twisted around to look out the back window.

Mike checked the rearview mirror. A guy he had cut off was giving them the finger. "Next time wave the other four at us," he muttered.

Robert chuckled. "This isn't like you. What's got you so distracted?"

Nothing was like him anymore. Ever since Gina had arrived, he hadn't had a moment's peace. But he was having fun, too. It'd been a long time since he'd been interested in anything but work. Why the hell did she have to be the boss's niece?

He darted a glance at Robert, who'd already moved on to checking his plane ticket. "Question."

"Shoot."

"Will Gina be offered a position in the company?"

Robert grunted. "You know Pop. He's kind of old-fashioned about that stuff. My aunt Sophia is worse. She wouldn't let Gina work."

"Does anybody in your family realize this is the twenty-first century?"

"Nope." Robert grinned. "Only me. I don't like my women barefoot and pregnant."

"I'm serious, Rob. Gina is smart, and she knows the business. She'd be an asset."

"I wouldn't let Pop hear that kind of talk. The last thing he'd want is for you to encourage Gina." Robert sent him a speculative frown. "Something else is bothering you."

"Me? Like what?"

"I don't know. Maybe it's just your paranoia about the office gossip."

"What gossip?" Mike's heart sank. Was it about Gina? His job? "I haven't heard anything."

"There's nothing to hear. I only meant that you keep worrying that something is going on." Robert shook his head. "You're the one who needs a vacation, buddy. When I get back, you'd better think seriously about getting away for a while."

"Right." Signs to the various La Guardia terminals popped up all of a sudden. "Pay attention to the signs. I don't want to get stuck in the arrival lane and have to circle the airport."

Conversation ceased while they navigated their way to the right terminal. Cabs hogged the curb and space was at a premium. Mike pulled over as close to the skycap station as he could and then popped the trunk.

Robert jumped out and hurriedly yanked out his bags. "Thanks for the lift," he said into Mike's open window. "I'm serious about you taking a vacation when I get back. I figure I can manage to hold down the fort for a week or two without everything falling apart."

"Yeah, I'll think about it. Have a good trip." Mike started to raise the window as Robert headed for the curb. "Hey, Robert—" his friend looked back "—how about taking Gina off my hands for about a week when you get back?"

"No problem." He gave him a salute and then turned to the skycap.

Oh, yeah, there was a problem. Gina was going to be pissed off and, even worse, hurt and confused. But this had to stop before things went too far.

Mike suddenly felt guilty as hell.

A WEEK HAD PASSED since that night at the weird club, and Gina and Mike had spent every day together, going to museums and the Statue of Liberty and the Empire State Building. In the evenings they sometimes went to dinner or a play. But he had not kissed her again, and Gina was growing impatient.

She had done nothing wrong. And she now knew him well enough to know he thought about kissing her. Often. Every day. But he stopped himself and was careful to keep her at a distance so she could not act. Which frustrated her. And what Michael did not know was that when she grew frustrated or impatient, she became determined.

Mama called her stubborn. Gina preferred determined.

She watched him read the entertainment section of the newspaper. Tiny lines formed between his brows when he concentrated, and his mouth looked very stern. She liked it better when it was soft and sucking her breasts.

"How about we go see a movie for a change?" He looked up when she did not answer right away. "Anything you want to see?"

She sighed. She wanted to go dancing, but for the past two nights all he said was maybe later. Later she would be back in Tuscany under her mother and grandmother's eagle eyes. The thought depressed her.

"Gina?"

"What?"

"I asked what movie you'd like to see."

"I do not want to see a movie." She plopped down beside him on her uncle's couch and sat cross-legged. The freedom of wearing jeans would be something else she would miss. "I want to go dancing."

He tensed at her nearness. Did he think she would bite? "What's wrong with seeing a movie?"

"I can go to a movie back home."

"You can go dancing, too."

She shook her head. "I am not allowed."

"To dance?"

"If I took a chaperon, I would be permitted. My aunt Gabriella went with me once. She has a big heart but a mean bulldog face, and the boys would not ask me to dance."

He laughed.

Gina stared down at her red fingernails. He did not understand how strict her parents were.

"I'm sorry I laughed." He touched her knee where she had made a tear in her jeans. "I thought you were kidding."

She looked up to find pity in his eyes. It made her angry and she looked away again.

"So what *do* you do all day back home?" he asked, and it was hard to stay mad while he still touched her. He had not removed his hand, and she prayed this meant he would no longer treat her so distantly.

Get Your
Coventry Romances
Home Subscription NOW

And Get These
4 Best-Selling Novels
FREE:

LACEY
by Claudette Williams

THE ROMANTIC WIDOW
by Mollie Chappell

HELENE
by Leonora Blythe

THE HEARTBREAK TRIANGLE
by Nora Hampton

A Home Subscription! It's the easiest and most convenient way to get every one of the exciting Coventry Romance Novels! ...And you get 4 of them FREE!

You pay nothing extra for this convenience: there are no additional charges...you don't even pay for postage! Fill out and send us the handy coupon now. and we'll send you 4 exciting Coventry Romance novels absolutely FREE!

SEND NO MONEY, GET THESE
FOUR BOOKS FREE!

CO881

MAIL THIS COUPON TODAY TO:
**COVENTRY HOME
SUBSCRIPTION SERVICE
6 COMMERCIAL STREET
HICKSVILLE, NEW YORK 11801**

YES, please start a Coventry Romance Home Subscription in my name. and send me FREE and without obligation to buy. my 4 Coventry Romances. If you do not hear from me after I have examined my 4 FREE books. please send me the 6 new Coventry Romances each month as soon as they come off the presses. I understand that I will be billed only $9.00 for all 6 books. There are no shipping and handling nor any other hidden charges. There is no minimum number of monthly purchases that I have to make. In fact. I can cancel my subscription at any time. The first 4 FREE books are mine to keep as a gift. even if I do not buy any additional books.

For added convenience. your monthly subscription may be charged automatically to your credit card.

☐ Master Charge 42101   ☐ Visa 42101

Credit Card # _____

Expiration Date _____

Name _____
(Please Print)

Address _____

City _____ State _____ Zip _____

Signature _____

☐ Bill Me Direct Each Month **40105**

Prices subject to change without notice.
Publisher reserves the right to substitute alternate FREE books. Sales tax collected where required by law. Offer valid for new members only.

RENEGADE GIRL

by

Mary Ann Gibbs

FAWCETT COVENTRY • NEW YORK

RENEGADE GIRL

Published by Fawcett Coventry Books, a unit of CBS Publications, the Consumer Publishing Division of CBS Inc.

Copyright © 1981 by Mary Ann Gibbs

All Rights Reserved

ISBN: 0-449-50198-1

Printed in the United States of America

First Fawcett Coventry printing: August 1981

10 9 8 7 6 5 4 3 2 1

Chapter One

To Vicky Lingford and her brother James, Costerley had always been their home. They were born there, James five years after his sister, and until their father became involved with the awful Mr. Grammidge and his railway company, with the result that Costerley was lost to them, they could not imagine living anywhere else.

It was a pleasant large country house, much too large for Paul Lingford's means, and the six hundred acres that went with it brought in very small rents. But it had a small park and lawns studded with old trees, and if the kitchen gardens were overrun with weeds only the children, besides an old gardener and a young undergardener, knew about it.

Costerley was a haphazard household, in keeping with its owner. Paul Lingford was happy-go-lucky, handsome, and with little idea of responsibility or the management of money. By nature he was essentially light-hearted, absurdly trusting, and with a deep affection for his wife—who had defied her family's disapproval to marry him—and his two children.

After his wife's death when Vicky was twelve years old he decided that he had had enough of governesses, and that his daughter should go to school. This was largely decided for him by the action of his father-in-law, Sir Hector Macalister, who had never spoken to his daughter since her marriage. He attended her funeral, however, and before returning to Edinburgh informed Paul's lawyer, Mr. Larkin, that he was prepared to educate James on condition that his father saw that his sister was brought up as the daughter of a gentleman should be.

Mr. Larkin, a member of the London firm of Philimore, Larkin and Philimore in Lincoln's Inn Fields, suggested that the boy should start as a boarder in the junior school of St. Chad's, an excellent London school with a first-class reputation, and Paul, not to be outdone, selected for Vicky an even more expensive and select girls' school in Chiswick.

Most of the girls attended daily, accompanied by their maids or brought in their fathers' carriages, but unfortunately for Vicky most of her companions had the advantage of having had good governesses before they became pupils at Chiswick Academy. She suffered considerably from the fact that no governess had ever stayed at Costerley very long.

The reason for this was a simple one. Her father engaged them at excellent salaries, to be paid six-monthly, and when the end of the first six months came he was either away or abroad and payment had to be postponed until the end of the year. As many of them were clergymen's daughters anxious to send the money they earned home to help support brothers and sisters, they left, and new ones would take their places. Nobody made inquiries as to the capabilities of these ladies. Some were good teachers, some were bad, some were indolent, others with little education, so that the children gained very little from them.

James was naturally clever, and once being given the chance to catch up at St. Chad's, did so with speed, but Vicky became resigned to sitting at the bottom of her class throughout her schooldays. She had a friendly disposition, however, and one of the girls with whom she became most close was Emily Sellinge.

This young lady, whose looks, accomplishments and general knowledge far surpassed Vicky's, sometimes asked her out to tea on a Sunday.

The Sellinges lived in Brook Street and consisted of Emily, her widowed mother, her brother Sebastian, a young man considerably older than his sister, and, from time to time, Mrs. Sellinge's brother, Judge Calvert.

Vicky heard a great deal about "my uncle the Judge," just as she heard about "my brother Sebastian," but she never met the Judge and only once saw the brother, who struck her as being a serious-minded young man with a mind set entirely on his work. At that time he had left Oxford with a degree and intended to become a barrister, following in his uncle's footsteps. During the time that the girls were at school he was at first for a year in a solicitor's office, learning the practical side of legal procedure, and after the year ended he became a pupil in a barrister's chambers in the Temple. By the time Emily left school he had eaten his dinners and been

6

called to the Bar, and with his uncle's influence behind him became a junior on the Northern Circuit, so that his family saw less of him than ever.

In the meantime the young Lingfords spent their school holidays at Costerley, where an elderly and distant cousin by the name of Miss Crampton had been persuaded by Paul to act as their chaperon and companion. It was a duty that she accepted with strong misgivings, as she had never had much to do with young people. Her life had been dominated by church work, by organizing bazaars in aid of foreign missions, by Sunday schools and working girls' clubs, and by visiting the outlying parts of the town where she lived, to see if the poorest people needed free coal tickets and extra blankets in the winter. She very much disliked having this charitable routine interrupted by being asked to take charge at Costerley, although Mrs. Berney, wife of the Squire of Davington a few miles away, and her children, who had known Vicky and James all their lives, did their best to entertain her.

She did not rebel openly until the Christmas of 1878, when Vicky was eighteen and the Grammidges and their still more awful friends were invited to stay at Costerley. She then sought out Paul and said that she refused to stay any longer.

"With so many in the house you will not need me," she told him clearly and distinctly when he tried to persuade her to change her mind. "I am sorry, Paul, but it is not my fault if you choose to fill your house with such people. When they are gone, if you still wish for my services, you have only to write."

"My dear Edith, you are being very stupid," said Paul, smiling with his usual charm. "Mr. Grammidge is one of the wealthiest men in London."

"Wealth does not make a gentleman," she replied severely. "And nobody appears to know how he came by his money."

"He made it all abroad," said Paul airily. "It does not concern us."

"It should concern you," she said. "With two young people of your own here to be considered."

When the Grammidges arrived, she gave one look at the lady, extended two fingers to her husband, bowed to the rest of the guests and went upstairs to finish her packing. She left after a luncheon at which Mr. Grammidge and his wife were

7

the chief guests, and Vicky saw her elderly cousin go with dismay.

The thought of being left to the company of Mrs. Grammidge appalled her. The lady's vulgarity in dress, speech and manners had never been witnessed at Costerley before, and she could scarcely believe it when after Miss Crampton left, she heard her father inviting Mrs. Grammidge to take her place as his hostess there.

The Berneys did their best, asking Vicky and her brother out to their young people's parties, and ready with excuses when invitations were extended to them to take dinner at Costerley.

When the Grammidges left it seemed that Paul Lingford was a great deal better off. More servants were engaged, while their master took rooms for himself in Sackville Street and spent a great deal of time there, saying that he had to be "on the spot." It seemed that Mr. Grammidge had made him the secretary of a large railway company that was being built in South America.

After James had gone back to school in the new year, Vicky was taken to the Sackville Street lodgings so that she could have dancing and music lessons. These she enjoyed, but she did not enjoy the parties in the house that Mr. Grammidge had hired in Bruton Street for the season. No doubt Mrs. Grammidge, fat, vulgar, overdressed and loud-voiced, meant to be kind to the motherless girl, but the young men she introduced to her were never like any the Sellinges would have entertained. It was when the lady suggested that "dear little Vicky" should have a coming-out dance at Costerley, and that she herself would select the dress she would wear, that she protested to her father in much the same way as Miss Crampton had protested at Christmas.

"I am sorry, Papa," she said, in the privacy of their sitting room in Sackville Street. "But I will not wear any dress chosen by Mrs. Grammidge. I know exactly what it will be like—all flounces and lace and knots of ribbon and bunches of artificial flowers. If it is important to you that I should have this ball at Costerley"—and here her eyes met his and she saw them drop away from hers quickly—"then I will ask Mrs. Sellinge to choose my dress. She will know what I should have—a white silk dress like the one that Emily wore at her coming-out ball."

8

"To which they did not invite you," said her father unkindly.

"It was held last Christmas, when Costerley was full of the Grammidges," she reminded him.

His eyes rested on her moodily. "Perhaps you are right," he conceded. "You're not a little beauty like Emily Sellinge, and I should have thought that a dress with a bit of color in it would have softened your lack of looks. You will have to wear some jewelry, though. Larkin refuses to part with the jewelry your godmother left you until you are twenty-one, as it was left like that in her will, so I suppose I shall have to hire some."

"I wish we had not got to have those dreadful Grammidges to my ball," sighed Vicky.

Paul frowned. "I'd like you to be careful how you speak about my friends."

"Your *friends?* People like the Grammidges? Oh, Papa, how can you call them your friends?"

"Because they *are* my friends," said her father. "And what is more, my dear, Grammidge is footing the bill for the ball in any case."

"Mr. Grammidge, paying for my coming-out ball!" For a moment she was too horrified to speak. Then, "I cannot believe it," she said.

"You do not suppose that I have the money to pay for London caterers and the best champagne and Hungarian orchestras and all the rest of it? Pull yourself together, Vicky, and do not be so stupid. The ball is a business affair. Grammidge wants to make the acquaintance of some of our neighbors, and this is a good way to set about it."

It dawned on Vicky then, young as she was, that her father and his friends intended to use her as a decoy for the furtherance of the railway company, and suddenly the late April sunshine outside the windows lost its soft beauty and became bright and harsh. "And you really think that our friends will accept invitations sent out by Mrs. Grammidge?"

"The invitations will be sent out by me, my dear. Mr. Paul Lingford will request the pleasure of his friends' company at the coming-out ball of his daughter at Costerley Park on June twelfth at ten. And when they arrive and find the Grammidges there I trust that they will behave with their usual civility and courtesy."

The weeks went by, the invitations for the ball were out,

9

and one morning Vicky received a letter from Mrs. Grammidge asking her to accompany her to William Whiteley's the following day to select her ball dress. In despair Vicky called a cab and went to appeal for help to Mrs. Sellinge, and when she poured out the whole story of the coming-out ball she saw her face grow grave.

"You do not know Mrs. Grammidge?" said Vicky as she finished.

"Oh no, my dear. But I have heard her spoken of as a most vulgar woman, and she cannot be allowed to select a dress for you."

"Dear Mrs. Sellinge, what am I to do? I cannot refuse the dress when her husband is paying the expenses of the ball."

"No, you cannot refuse." Mrs. Sellinge remembered her uncle's opinion of Mr. Grammidge, and had no wish to become involved with Mrs. Grammidge herself. Then a way out suggested itself.

Nearly opposite them in Brook Street was the house of the Dowager Lady Taversham, who had at one time been very much attached to Vicky's mother, having been a lifelong friend of Lady Macalister's.

She lived alone with a companion by the name of Miss Sedge, a thin lady with a lively and alert air, reminding Vicky when she had first met her as a schoolgirl at the Sellinges' of a fox terrier. She had a habit of sitting on the edge of her chair, waiting as a terrier might wait for a ball to be thrown. In Miss Sedge's case, however, she was simply waiting for a request from her employer to run upstairs or down on errands such as the fetching of books, spectacles, or embroidery materials.

"I know what we will do," said Mrs. Sellinge brightly. "I will put on my bonnet and we will go across to see old Lady Taversham. I am sure she will be able to suggest a solution."

The bonnet was put on, and Vicky was conducted across the street to the Dowager's house, a tall building whose modest and grimy appearance belied the spaciousness of its interior.

The square hall with its marble floor had a central staircase leading up to the main drawing room, large enough to be used as a ballroom should the need arise, with a smaller drawing room leading off from it.

The doors that opened off the hall led to a dining room where thirty or forty guests could dine at ease, a breakfast room, a library, and a small morning room where her ladyship usually received morning callers.

It was to this apartment that a footman conducted them that morning, and when she heard their names the Dowager handed the piece of embroidery she was working on to Miss Sedge and got up from her chair to receive them with a grave pleasure.

She held Vicky at arm's length to consider her, with her head on one side. "You have grown up since I last saw you at one of Emily's schoolgirl parties," she said then. "You have your father's fair hair—the color of ripe oats, your mother called it—but you have her dark eyes and determined chin."

"We have come to you, dear Lady Taversham, for your help and advice," said Mrs. Sellinge, and related the story of the disastrous coming-out ball and Mrs. Grammidge's offer to buy Vicky's dress.

"She cannot be allowed to do that, of course," Lady Taversham agreed. "But as she has been kind enough to offer she must not be snubbed." She considered the problem for a moment. "Have the Grammidges a house in London?"

Vicky told her that Mr. Grammidge had taken number 74 in Bruton Street for the season.

"Then what could be simpler? I will call upon Mrs. Grammidge this afternoon and suggest that she might like to lunch with me and my young friend Miss Lingford here on Thursday next. I shall say that I understand she wishes to give Miss Lingford a dress as a birthday present for her coming-out ball, and suggest that after lunch we might go in my carriage to Regent Street at the fashionable shopping hour in the afternoon, and visit one of the shops there that has my custom. We can decide on a suitable dress there and the dressmaker will make it up for Miss Lingford."

The strain left Vicky's face, and she laughed. She had an infectious laugh. "That is an excellent idea," she cried.

"I have heard," said Lady Taversham, smiling rather wickedly, "that Mrs. Grammidge loves titles. She will enjoy a ride in my carriage in Regent Street, I think, at that time of day."

The call was made and Mrs. Grammidge was all delight, and on the following Thursday she arrived at Lady Taversham's to find Vicky waiting for her. They lunched together and her ladyship talked and listened and behaved as if Mrs. Grammidge was the sort of lady she was accustomed to entertain. The visit was made to Regent Street, and the dressmaker, after a glance at Vicky that took in her slender height, fair hair and dark eyes, ordered one of the beautiful young ladies who were walking about the department as if they had nothing to do to put on one of the dresses that were on display.

It was a white dress in silk, with the plain apron front so fashionable just then, the apron edged with deep flounces and bunched up at the back in a large gathered bow. The white straps decorated with forget-me-nots on the shoulders were altered under Madame's orders. "This young lady is too tall and dignified for forget-me-nots and rosebuds," she pronounced. She ordered some white camellias to be fetched instead.

They were brought and declared perfect, and when Mrs. Grammidge, slightly awed by Madame's authority, suggested brighter colors in the dress, she was told firmly that a young lady's coming-out dress was always white.

"A white dress for the belle of the evening will be looked for by her friends," she reminded the perspiring Mrs. Grammidge in a superior tone, and when the lady suggested a diamond necklace as a nice touch she was again crushed with a decided, "Oh no, Madam. A young lady always wears pearls at her coming-out ball. I have no doubt that Miss has a necklace to wear."

"If she has not," said Lady Taversham firmly, "I will lend her one of mine."

So Vicky's measurements were taken and the dress promised by the first of June, and Lady Taversham took Mrs. Grammidge and Vicky back to her carriage well satisfied with the afternoon.

"Do not forget to tell your father to invite me," she told Vicky. "I shall be mortally offended if I do not receive an invitation."

And as a beaming Mrs. Grammidge was sent back to Bruton Street in a carriage with a coronet on its doors, she sat down and wrote a note to Mrs. Sellinge telling her of the happy outcome of the afternoon, and expressing a wish that she hoped to see her and her son and daughter at the ball.

"I have a feeling," she wrote, "that little Vicky will be in need of all her friends. Mrs. Berney has kindly offered to have me to stay and hopes that you and your family will be able to take advantage of her hospitality too."

Mrs. Sellinge was made unhappy by this suggestion. "I

had not intended to accept the invitation, as you know, my dear," she told Emily as they sat in the drawing room after dinner that evening. "Your uncle was quite firm about it. He said that on no account must we allow ourselves to be on friendly terms with the Grammidges. Indeed he went so far as to call Mr. Grammidge a scoundrel."

"As little is known about Mr. Grammidge except that he made a great deal of money in ventures abroad, and is now engaged in promoting a large railway company in South America," observed Sebastian from the armchair usually occupied by his uncle, "I do not quite see how we can regard him as a scoundrel. But if he intends to be at Costerley with his wife and his associates I cannot help feeling that Lady Taversham is right, and that Miss Lingford will want all her friends about her at her coming-out ball." He glanced at his sister. "Isn't she one of your old schoolfriends, Emily?"

"Yes, and quite the plainest of them all," said Emily spitefully.

"As far as I remember most of them were plain, and the few that were pretty could only giggle in corners," said her brother.

Emily pouted and said she was sure her brother did not intend to go to Costerley and added, "You know that you hate balls."

"Nevertheless I shall go," said Sebastian. "At the risk of offending my uncle the Judge." The truth was that he was becoming increasingly tired of his Uncle Horace. Not only did he appear to regard his sister's house as his own, but he behaved as if he were its master and paid the bills, which most assuredly he did not. "Come, Mama," he went on pleasantly, "you know that Mrs. Berney will be delighted to have you and Emily to stay. I shall put up at the Star and Garter in the village; it will do very well for me and Herbert." Herbert, who was well on in his fifties, had been his father's valet before he became his.

"You will take Herbert?" His mother was horrified. "But—what will your uncle do? He always expects Herbert to wait on him."

"Then he will have to make do with a footman, will he not? Jakes will take Herbert's place quite well, I am sure. I think my uncle should remember that Herbert is my servant and that I pay him."

He left the room, saying that he had some letters to write,

and his mother found some consolation in the thought that Adela Berney was to be at the ball. Sebastian had always had plenty to say to Adela, and his uncle the Judge had given his opinion that she would make him a good wife. Moreover he had expressed the opinion that it was high time that his nephew got married. So her acceptance of the Costerley invitation might not incur the wrath she had anticipated.

The drawing room at Costerley was the only room large enough for a ball, and when it was cleared of its furniture and its carpets, and flowers banked in the empty fireplaces, it made quite a reasonable ballroom.

In spite of the Grammidges, directly Sebastian entered the room he knew he had been right to persuade his mother and sister to come.

Vicky's white dress with its camellias and its short train was exactly right, and the string of pearls lent by Lady Taversham was a perfect complement. Her mother's painted fan with its ivory sticks inset with mother-of-pearl was the only colored thing she carried, and the little bouquet made up for her by the head gardener at Costerley was of white hothouse roses and stephanotis.

As she stood there beside her handsome father she no longer looked plain: the excitement had given her cheeks color, and her dark eyes were sparkling. As they received their guests, Vicky's gloved hand in her father's arm, with James, who had been allowed leave for the occasion, on her other side, it seemed as if they alone were the center of the ball.

As he glanced about him Sebastian could see that there were more than a sprinkling of the Lingfords' old friends there too, gathered as perhaps James was to surround and protect Vicky from the bad manners of her father's new friends. But in the meantime there was too Adela Berney, looking extremely handsome and happy to be his partner for the first dance.

"It is a pity," she said as they moved off on to the floor, "that Vicky Lingford is so plain."

"Do you think her plain?" he asked.

"Do not you?" She laughed up at him, but he was looking at Vicky, who was dancing with one of the Berney boys.

"No," he said.

"But you cannot call her pretty?"

"Oh no. Nobody could call her that." But there was an air

of dignity and distinction about Miss Lingford that he could not fail to notice.

Miss Berney began to talk about the Grammidges. "My father says he cannot imagine what induced Mr. Lingford to take them up."

"It might be a matter of business."

"Then why not keep them to the City?"

He smiled down at her. "My dear Adela, do not ask me to explain other people's behavior."

It was some time before he could get near Vicky to ask her for a dance, and then her program was full, except for the last two dances. "I have promised James the gallop," she said, smiling. "But the one before is the final waltz."

"Then allow me to have that." He wrote his initials on her little card, but it was already early the next morning before his dance with her came, and the summer dawn was sending a pale line of light across the sky.

The ballroom was hot, and the Grammidges' friends had taken rather too kindly to the champagne, and Vicky said her head ached.

"Come out on the terrace," Sebastian said, sorry for her and wondering what the future would bring this slender, dignified girl with such a feckless, handsome father. "It is cool out here and getting light."

The Chinese lanterns in the trees had burned themselves out, and she put her hand in his arm and walked out onto the terrace beside him, and in the soft warm air of another summer day she suddenly said, "It was very kind of you to bring your mama and Emily here tonight. I am sure your uncle the Judge did not approve of it."

In spite of the smile around her mouth in the half-light she looked tired and depressed. He said, "I hope you have enjoyed your ball?"

"But it was not mine," she said quietly. "The Grammidges paid for it all."

"That was kind of them." His voice was dry, and she raised anxious eyes to his.

"I wonder if it was?" she said. "Mr. Sellinge, you are a lawyer, and you know about these things. I have been torturing myself into thinking that Mr. Grammidge gave this ball because he wanted to get some of our friends interested in his railway company. People like Lord Emersham, and Sir

Hartley Random, and Lord Bury. Names that would entice other people to invest money in the railway too."

He thought it quite likely, and he wondered that she had been astute enough to see it. But he also remembered that it was her coming-out ball, and he wanted to reassure her.

"These rich men and their wives have a great ambition to get accepted by society," he said smilingly. "It is amusing to watch them make their efforts at entering a circle that is closed to them, but it has its pathetic side as well."

"And you think that is all it is?" Her face brightened, and she laughed in her attractive way. "They want to be recognized by London society, and this ball for me was their way of doing it, because my father has many titled friends."

"I would say that is all it is," he agreed. The dawn was spreading across the sky, touching the summer landscape with rose and gold. For a moment her hand tightened on his arm.

"You have lifted a weight from my mind," she said, and then James came to remind her that the gallop was about to start and she had promised it to him.

Sebastian refused the offer of a carriage and walked the three miles back to the Star and Garter at Davington, enjoying the freshness of the country air. His mind, far from dwelling on the awful Grammidges, on the lavishness of the entertainment, or even on the vivacious Miss Adela Berney, was unexpectedly held by the girl for whom the ball had ostensibly been given. He had expected her to be just another of Emily's rather dull friends, but he had found a young woman who had attracted him oddly.

All through the evening he had noticed that she had met the invidious position in which her father had placed her with a quiet dignity usually to be found in a woman twice her age. It was only at the last, when weariness of the Grammidges overtook her, that she had appealed to him as she might have appealed to an older brother, or even to Mr. Larkin, her father's lawyer, for advice.

Emily and her friends called her plain, but the dark eyes that had met his were large and beautiful, their black lashes long and silky, their eyebrows finely marked. Her hair, simply dressed in a knot at the nape of her neck, with a fringe that curled naturally, was so pale that it was almost silver under the gas chandeliers. And she showed personality and character rare in the girls he met at balls and dinner parties in London.

He remembered her sudden laugh, charming and sweet, and hoped that he would see more of her in London now that she was out. But as it happened it was to be some time before he was to meet her again and a great deal longer before he was to hear her laugh.

Chapter Two

Vicky was up early that morning, and although she had had only a few hours' sleep, she was down in time to have a hasty breakfast with James before the carriage took him to the station on the way to St. Chad's, knowing that it would be only a few weeks before he was home again for the start of the long summer holidays.

When he had gone she asked for her horse to be saddled, as she wanted to be out and away from the house, where the Grammidges and their friends were still sleeping off the effects of the champagne. It was refreshing to be in the leafy lanes leading to Davington, and in a small bag attached to her saddle she carried Lady Taversham's pearl necklace. As she rode she dismissed from her mind the dreadful young men that Mrs. Grammidge had kept bringing up to dance with her, and instead she found herself thinking about Emily's brother. Being older than herself by nearly nine years, to nineteen-year-old Vicky he appeared almost middle-aged, and she had turned to him instinctively, drawn by his look of understanding. He was a little taller than she was, dark-haired and clean-shaven, as most barristers appeared to be, with a steadiness in his gray eyes that reassured her as much as the advice he had given her.

Perhaps he was right, and her father's new friends were only social climbers, Mr. Grammidge seeing himself with a title one day and Mrs. Grammidge looking forward to the time when she would be "my lady." The thought made her smile, and the day seemed brighter for the kindness Mr. Sellinge had shown to his sister's old schoolfriend.

She arrived at Davington Hall at eleven and was told that Lady Taversham had been up for some hours and would be pleased to see her. She was shown up into the comfortable sitting room that had been set aside for her ladyship and found her looking remarkably sprightly. Indeed, gray-haired though she might be, her eyes were as shrewd as ever and one would never have guessed that she had been up nearly all night.

She thanked Vicky for bringing back the necklace so promptly, rang for her maid to put it away in her jewel case, and then offered her young friend a glass of sherry.

"You will observe that the housekeeper has allowed me several glasses as well as the decanter," she said, smiling. "She must have known that I would have callers. I am afraid Emily and her mama are not yet down."

Vicky was not surprised: Emily had never been fond of early rising. She accepted the sherry, however, and as she drank Lady Taversham regarded her critically and asked when the Grammidges were leaving.

"At the end of the week," Vicky said, relief in her voice. "And then my father's cousin, Edith Crampton, is coming back to chaperon us for James's holidays. I expect she will stay until the shooting season starts, when I understand Mrs. Grammidge is to come back to Costerley to act as hostess." Her slender brows knitted in a frown. "I cannot tell you, Lady Taversham, how much I hate to see her taking my mother's place."

"I can understand that." Lady Taversham thought of the contrast between fat, vulgar Mrs. Grammidge and the acid sanctity of Miss Crampton and wondered which was worse. "I have a suggestion to make," she said then, "to which I hope your father will agree. After James has gone back to school in the autumn I hope Mr. Lingford will spare you to stay with me in Brook Street until Christmas. Would you care to come?"

"Care to come? Oh, Lady Taversham, it would be lovely." Vicky's dark eyes lit up with delight and her cheeks flushed, and her ladyship thought that the girl was not as plain as people liked to make out. Certainly her face had character, and her eyes were beautiful.

"Then that is settled," said Lady Taversham, smiling. "You must write to me directly James has gone back to school, giving me the date of Mrs. Grammidge's arrival at Costerley, and come to me the day after. It will give you time to be civil to her and explain that your mother's old friend wishes to have you to stay. I do not think she will object."

Paul was asked for his permission as soon as Vicky got home and gave it with reluctance.

"If Lady Taversham wants you, then I suppose you had

better go," he said. "But I don't think Mrs. Grammidge will like it, and it will be infernally rude for you to walk off the instant her foot is in the door."

Vicky compromised by promising to stay at Costerley for the first week of the Grammidges' visit, feeling that she could endure seven days of the lady's company if at the end of it she was free to go to Lady Taversham.

Miss Crampton arrived in June after the ball, when the Grammidges and their friends had departed, and with her at Costerley Vicky was invited out to all the summer festivities arranged by their friends. Archery parties and picnics and small dances and croquet and tennis parties filled the afternoons and evenings, Miss Crampton only objecting to tennis for her niece as it meant wearing a skirt above her ankles, which she did not consider proper.

Paul returned to his rooms in Sackville Street, saying that he had business affairs to attend to, not explaining what they were. Vicky thought they might be connected with Mr. Grammidge's new railway company.

The ball had not been as advantageous as Mr. Grammidge had hoped, and when his wife suggested having Vicky to stay with them in Bruton Street he refused to allow it. "No good throwing good money after bad," he told her grumpily. "If the girl had looks and a bit of life in her, instead of standing about the room like a statue, I would have her here for a time. But she will not draw the young sparks in. At least not the sort I'm after. No well-to-do young aristocrat is going to come courting Paul Lingford's plain daughter."

Mrs. Sellinge's letter of thanks for Paul's "delightful ball" made no mention of Vicky, neither did it express the hope that she would see her in London in the near future. Miss Crampton, when Vicky remarked on the coolness of the letter, tossed her head and said it was no more than she expected.

"Your papa is far too friendly with those dreadful Grammidges," she said. "If he continues with that friendship you and James will suffer. You mark my words. People like the Sellinges are not the only ones to drop you like hot cakes."

Vicky did not believe it. "At school Emily was my greatest friend," she protested."

"School friendships do not last, my dear," said Miss Crampton shortly. "No doubt Emily is enjoying the London Season far too much to remember you."

She did not think that Sebastian would be likely to remember her, but the thought that his mother and sister would drop her hurt Vicky more than she admitted. But if it were so, she thought, putting up her determined chin, they were welcome to go their own way. She and James had no need of fair-weather friends.

James had invited a schoolfriend of his by the name of Tom Timberloft for the long summer holidays, and the days slipped by, too energetic and too happy to allow many thoughts of the Sellinges to intrude. Timbers, as James called him, was also a boarder at St. Chad's, but as his father was an Army colonel in India he had to spend his holidays with a sour old aunt in Putney, or at St. Chad's, which the headmaster's wife, Mrs. Dacres, did not like at all. She said that boys were under her feet all the term and she did not see why she should suffer them during the holidays.

Vicky welcomed Timbers, however. He was a nice, red-haired boy with a face covered in freckles, utterly good-humored and not likely to lead James into any scrapes. But after they had gone back to school and she was left to welcome Mrs. Grammidge in their place and Miss Crampton had returned to the West Country, she wished she had not stayed on for a week out of politeness instead of flying off to London the next day.

Looking back afterward she wondered if she had been responsible for the disaster that followed, but at the time all that had been in her mind was that she must save Mr. Bassett from losing money to the insufferable Grammidges.

It was the day before she was to leave for London when two gentlemen who had been at Costerley for the partridge shooting left. It was in the morning and she was sitting in the small library writing to James while her father saw them off when she heard Mr. Grammidge's loud voice in the large library that communicated with the smaller one by a door, now half open.

"Well, my dear," said Mr. Grammidge to his wife, "those pigeons were easy for the plucking."

"I hope you plucked 'em clean?" said Mrs. Grammidge with her loud laugh.

"Not a feather left on 'em," said her husband. "I hope the next will be as easy."

"When does he arrive?" asked Mrs. Grammidge.

"Tomorrow evening. Name of Bassett. He's an astute kind of bird, so we shall have to be careful. But Paul says he is a good shot and enjoys going out with the guns, which the others did not. All they thought about was the fortune they were going to make out of my railway." Mr. Grammidge chuckled. "They are far the easiest to pluck."

Vicky took up her letter and fled through the far door and up to her room. There she sat for a time unable to continue with her letter, her thoughts on what she had heard. If only she could have told somebody about it, but there was nobody to tell. Miss Crampton had been gone a week, and tomorrow she was herself leaving in the afternoon for London. As Mr. Bassett was not expected until the evening she would not even meet the poor man. He would just walk into a house where two men, and one of them her own father, waited to pluck him like a pigeon.

She did not sleep well that night and was thankful when after luncheon her father said goodbye to her and took Mr. Grammidge off to the billiard room, while Mrs. Grammidge retired to the small drawing room to indulge in a slumber after her heavy meal.

The carriage was just coming around, loaded with her luggage, to take her to the railway station, when a cab drew up in front of the house and a gentleman, accompanied by a servant and cases of guns, stepped out of it. He paid the cabbie and was ushered into the hall by the new butler, an obsequious man that Vicky did not like very much.

He was afraid Mr. Bassett had not been expected until the evening, he said, but Mr. Lingford was only in the billiard room. It would not take a moment to fetch him.

"I would not disturb his game on any account. Your housekeeper can show me to my room and then I will have a stroll around the park out there to get some air into my lungs after the smoke of the train."

Mr. Bassett came into the hall, and Vicky suddenly made up her mind. This pigeon should not be plucked without a warning. She came out of the morning room where she had been waiting for her carriage and said she was pleased to welcome Mr. Bassett before she left on a visit to an old friend of her mother's.

"I am Mr. Lingford's daughter," she explained. "While your luggage is being taken upstairs perhaps you would like to come into the morning room for a moment. My train will not leave for a little while yet—our coachman always allows too long a wait at the station. So I shall have time to make acquaintance with you before I go."

Mystified by her abrupt manner, he followed her into the morning room, and directly they were out of earshot of the servants she said quickly: "I have something to say to you before I go. You may or may not believe me, but it is true." She told him quickly and in as few words as possible what she had overheard the day before, and saw his pleasant open face grow suddenly grave. "You may wish to accompany me to the station and take the next train back to London," she finished, looking at him anxiously.

"I think that might be unwise. One does not wish to cause trouble between you and your father's guests, and he would be very annoyed if he thought you had been eavesdropping." He saw her head go up and smiled. "Do not think I meant that unkindly. You have done me a great service. But I am very fond of shooting, Miss Lingford, and as I have been invited to Costerley for a week with my guns, at Costerley I will remain. As to the plucking of this nice fat pigeon, Miss Lingford, I can promise you that not a feather will fall." He held out his hand. "I hope you enjoy your visit to London. I am sure I shall enjoy my visit here."

And then he turned about, holding the door open for her to go out to the carriage and her London train.

She would have been consoled had she been present at the final evening of Mr. Bassett's stay in Costerley. All the week he had enjoyed the shooting, being an excellent shot—in fact, the head gamekeeper said it was a treat to have a gentleman who was not a danger to himself or to the beaters. At the end of it, however, when Mr. Grammidge and Paul pressed on him the prospectus of the new American railway company, with its list of officers headed by Mr. Grammidge as chairman and Mr. Lingford as secretary, he examined it with interest and asked if he might take it away with him to show it to his lawyer.

"Being a man with a number of interests in business matters," he told Mr. Grammidge, "I never allow my name to be used in connection with any new investment before I see my lawyer, who will send an auditor to see the company's books. That, you will agree, being a businessman yourself, is only common sense. I expect the books of your railway company are at your London office and can be seen in a matter of days?"

23

"Oh, certainly." Mr. Grammidge helped himself to a strong brandy. "Unfortunately they are in York at the moment—a small matter of the investment of twenty thousand pounds—but I will send for them at once and let you know the moment they are back in my hands."

"Excellent," said Mr. Bassett cheerfully. "Let me see, your offices are in"—he took up the brochure and examined it again—"in Bruton Street. I thought that was your home address, Mr. Grammidge? I could not have been paying attention."

Paul Lingford, catching a warning glance from Mr. Grammidge, swiftly changed the subject to the day's sport, and Mrs. Grammidge rose from the table, saying that if they were going to talk of dead birds and suchlike she would go to the drawing room. "I wish little Vicky—Mr. Lingford's daughter—were here to entertain you, Mr. Bassett," she added. "She has a nice little voice and sings very pretty, though she hasn't 'ad many lessons."

Mr. Bassett replied politely that he would look forward to meeting Miss Lingford the next time he came, and after an evening at billiards he said goodnight and the next morning left for London.

"I'm glad to see the back of 'im," said Mr. Grammidge as he smoked a cigar in the smoking room with Mr. Lingford after he had gone. "That feller smelled a rat, Lingford, old boy."

"Smelled a rat? What do you mean?" Paul's blue eyes regarded his partner with some amazement. "I suppose there is no harm in his lawyer or his auditor or whoever it is seeing the books?"

"No 'arm at all, if there was any books," agreed Mr. Grammidge. "The trouble is, Lingford old feller, there ain't."

"But you said they were in York."

"To give us a chance to breathe and make plans," said Mr. Grammidge comfortably. "Though mine have been made for some time, let me tell you."

"Are you saying that this—American railway company—is like your books?" asked Paul, going rather white. "That it does not exist either?"

"'Course it don't. But we've made a lot of money out of it between us. One 'undred thousand pounds, my dear Paul, which I am willing to split with you, as a lot of people wouldn't have taken no shares if your name hadn't been on the pro-

24

spectus as the company's secretary, all nice and proper. I'll take sixty thousand, as it was my idea in the first place, and you can 'ave the forty thousand what's left. How does that strike you?"

It struck Paul very forcibly then that he had been the dupe of a man who had built up a large fortune by many devious methods. He would have liked to refuse to touch the money and declare that he would have nothing to do with swindlers, and threaten to have him arrested for fraud. But it was too late for that, and Grammidge would only laugh at him. Was his name not on the prospectus as the company's secretary? Who would believe him?

"I shall be leaving London tomorrow afternoon," went on Mr. Grammidge, as easily as if he were talking of setting off on a pleasure trip. "If you call at my 'ouse in Bruton Street I will give you your share of the money in bank notes, but you must not call later than ten o'clock. The missus 'as been packed up for some weeks now. She knows my little ways and is allus ready to go off on journeys at short notice. We will leave Costerley this afternoon, and England tomorrow night. I advise you to leave for France too not later than the day after. Don't leave it any longer or you may have the perlice around to see you in Sackville Street, and once you're across the Channel they can't touch you."

After a little thought Mr. Lingford decided to take that advice. Indeed, there was little else he could do.

The church that the Dowager attended on Sunday mornings was St. George's, Hanover Square, and as the Sellinges attended it also, the two families would meet after church and stroll back through Hanover Square to Brook Street, the younger ones usually going on for a walk in Hyde Park before luncheon.

When Vicky came to stay with Lady Taversham she would walk back with Emily and her brother, who remained rather silent on that first Sunday morning as if he had a difficult case on his mind.

Emily, however, chattered on as usual about the balls she had been to and the young men she had met and the new dresses her mother was buying for her.

On the second Sunday of Vicky's stay the Sellinges' behavior was quite extraordinary. Not only did they not wait for the Dowager but after acknowledging her with somewhat

25

distant bows and not a glance at Vicky, the Judge and his sister walked on, while Emily went with them.

It was Sebastian who made up for their rudeness by waiting behind to greet her ladyship with smiling gravity and to ask if he might accompany them back to Brook Street.

Her ladyship said with equal gravity but with no smile at all that she would be glad of his company, and they set off, allowing the rest of Sebastian's family to proceed some way ahead of them.

"Mr. Sellinge," said Vicky, as they left the churchyard, "have I done anything to offend Emily? She would not look at me this morning and neither would your mama. I cannot think how I could have upset them."

Sebastian regarded her smilingly. With her smart little brown hat tilted over her dark eyes, her dress of amber silk under a cape of the same color, she was certainly worth looking at that morning. But as her eyes went to the retreating backs of his family with a puzzled frown, his own met the Dowager's with a question in them, and he saw her slightly shake her head.

"There is no accounting for Emily," he said lightly. "I have long ago given up trying to follow the twists and turns of her mind." He asked if they were returning home, and when Lady Taversham said that they were he suggested taking a turn in the square, as the October morning was almost as warm as summer.

"I shall give up the pursuit of my family," he said, "and lunch with them later."

As they walked along together he told them that he had moved to rooms in Gray's Inn.

"I heard that you had your own chambers there now, but did not know you had left Brook Street," said Lady Taversham, acknowledging a cool bow from an acquaintance who overtook them with equal coolness and a slightly heightened color.

"Mama was not pleased with me for moving, I am afraid," said Sebastian in his easy way. "I have taken my valet, Herbert, with me, and for some time my uncle had regarded him as his own."

"You cannot be popular with the Judge either then," agreed her ladyship, who had always found Judge Calvert more than autocratic. She asked what his rooms were like, and he described them amusingly as being comfortable, and said that Herbert had found him an excellent cook, and that altogether the change had pleased them both considerably.

So, keeping to light topics, he strolled on with them around the square and eventually into Brook Street, where they parted, and as they went up the steps to her own house the Dowager remarked rather puzzlingly that she thought he was a very chivalrous young man.

Vicky understood the reasoning that lay behind this remark only when she had gone to her room to remove her hat and cape and get ready for luncheon and her ladyship followed her there, a folded newspaper in her hand.

"You may have noticed, Vicky my dear," she said in some agitation, "that I did not ask you to read the *Times* newspaper to me yesterday. There was a paragraph in it that I did not wish you to see until I had made up my mind what to do. The behavior of some of my friends and acquaintances this morning, however, has decided me, and I think you should read it for yourself. Sit here quietly, child, and read what it says, while I tell the servants to delay luncheon by half an hour."

With astonishment and increasing dismay Vicky read the marked paragraph on the page where the paper had been folded back.

"It is understood," it stated, "that an enormous fraud has recently been perpetrated on an unsuspecting public. For the last year a company purporting to be that of a railway in South America has been launched by Mr. Alfred Grammidge, an individual whose enormous wealth has for some time been regarded with suspicion in some quarters. In this latest venture Mr. Grammidge was joined by Mr. Paul Lingford of Costerley Park in Berkshire, a gentleman of supposed honor and integrity. As secretary of the company one would suppose that not only was he fully aware of what was going on but that he aided and abetted it. Between them the two gentlemen have gathered in upward of one hundred thousand pounds, leaving the shareholders worthless certificates for a railway that it is now certain never existed except in the fertile brains of Mr. Alfred Grammidge and his friend, Mr. Paul Lingford. The two gentlemen left England in a hurry a short while ago, leaving no address. It is feared that those they defrauded will never see their money again."

Vicky read the paragraph twice, unable to believe it, and then, remembering the Grammidges and her coming-out ball, and the "pigeons" who were invited to Costerley to be "plucked clean," she knew that it was true. The behavior of Emily and her mother that morning had confirmed it.

Not only was Paul Lingford branded as a swindler and common thief, but his son and daughter would also be branded because they were his children. Sebastian Sellinge's "chivalry" on which Lady Taversham had remarked a few minutes ago filled her with resentment. He had known, as his family had known, and everyone who had welcomed her as a friend of Lady Taversham's would know about this detestable paragraph.

Somehow she must leave London, and at once, but where could she go? If she went to Costerley, friends like the Berneys would have seen it, and their welcome too must be cool and distant. Invitations would neither be issued nor accepted. Their father's iniquity must follow his children even to Costerley.

And then another question came to tease her. The boys at St. Chad's would soon know about this news in the *Times*, if they did not know already, and when they did, what would be their behavior to poor James?

Chapter Three

Usually Lady Taversham's son and daughter-in-law lunched with her on Sunday, but today her ladyship had sent a note early asking them to come that evening instead. She and Vicky lunched alone with Miss Sedge, waited on by servants whose glances at her ladyship's guest were not without curiosity.

The topic uppermost in their minds was not discussed until the meal was over and her ladyship took her young guest into her boudoir to ask if she had formed any ideas on the subject.

"I think I should like to walk to the Sackville Street lodgings this afternoon," Vicky said quietly. "I must see Mrs. Norris."

"Your father's landlady. Is she likely to be troublesome?"

"Not at all." A faint smile touched Vicky's white face. "She is the kindest of women, and most obliging."

As it happened, Mrs. Norris was a great deal more obliging than Vicky realized, as Paul's account for the last three months had not been paid, and beyond slipping it in front of him on the first of every month, Mrs. Norris had refrained from anything of a stronger nature. Her account was at once consigned to the fire or the wastepaper basket, and although she was perfectly aware of it, Mrs. Norris assumed, totally without reason, that as her lodger was a gentleman the account would be settled in due course.

"There may be a letter for me there," explained Vicky, her voice more than a little strained. "And I am sure there will be Mr. Larkin's address. I think if no directions have been left for me in Sackville Street I should go and see him tomorrow."

Lady Taversham approved of this, pleased that the girl exhibited so much composure. That the news had been a tremendous shock she had no doubt, but she was certainly keeping her feelings under control with remarkable fortitude.

"I will send my maid with you," she said. "And no doubt Mrs. Norris will be able to summon a cab to bring you back later."

So Vicky set out on foot for Sackville Street—Lady Taversham did not approve of having her horses out on a Sunday—accompanied by Crofton, a rather severe-looking woman of forty or so. No conversation was attempted between them, except an exchange of directions as to the best way to approach Sackville Street, and when they arrived at Mrs. Norris's house Vicky parted from her companion with relief.

She received a warm welcome from Mrs. Norris, a motherly creature with a disposition that was always being imposed upon by her lodgers. Yes, she said, there had been a letter left for Miss Lingford, but she did not send it to her because Mr. Lingford had told her his daughter would come and fetch it. She was very glad that Miss Lingford had come, however, because Mr. Lingford had left a great many things in his rooms and she would like to relet them if he was not coming back.

"Of course." Vicky accompanied her up the stairs to the first floor, where her father's sitting room, a large and well-furnished apartment, had decanters of wines and spirits and a box of cigars unfinished on the sideboard.

"He always liked to entertain his friends here after you had gone, Miss," explained Mrs. Norris.

The letter that Paul Lingford had left for his daughter was on a table in the middle of the room, and as Vicky picked it up Mrs. Norris left her to read it alone, saying that she would fetch her some tea.

The letter was short and to the point. Paul stated briefly that he found himself obliged to leave the country for a time and advised her to go to her uncle, Harold Lingford, in Westborough. He was a very rich man and would give her a home until her father could send for her. Mr. Larkin, of Philimore, Larkin and Philimore in Lincoln's Inn Fields, would give her his address. It was signed, "Your affectionate father, P. Lingford."

No money was enclosed with it, and neither was there mention of any. How then, Vicky wondered, did he expect her to get to Westborough, a railway journey of over sixty miles? Was she perhaps to walk?

She went on into his bedroom and found chaos there, as if he had packed in a hurry, thrusting things as he thought of them into a portmanteau. His ivory-backed brushes were gone, as were his Russian-leather slippers and his silver shaving mug, and a heavy overcoat. He had left simply the things he was unable to take in one portmanteau, and the wardrobe was half full of them.

A portrait of her mother lay with its frame broken on the floor. She picked it up and set it on one side, and then piled everything from the wardrobe and drawers onto the bed, anger with her father mounting as she did so.

If there had been any honesty in him, her heart told her, he would have stayed to face his creditors, promising to pay them as and how he could, even if he had to sell Costerley to do it. He would at least then have shown courage and innocence of complicity in the affair, and his friends might have forgiven him. But to slip away with his horrible friend Grammidge was to brand himself as guilty as his partner.

She went back into the sitting room and collected a silver inkstand and some gold seals from the desk, together with an ivory paper knife, and when Mrs. Harris came back with a tray nicely set out with a pot of tea and some fruitcake Vicky told her that she had her permission to sell everything that her father had left behind. When Mrs. Norris hesitated, she said that she would tell Mr. Larkin to write her a letter to this effect when she saw him the next day.

"And there is another thing to be discussed," she added. "Did my father pay your account before he left?"

The landlady admitted reluctantly that Mr. Lingford had left four months owing. "Not but what I don't trust him to pay, Miss," she added hastily. "I'm sure he'll be back soon and everything will be settled. He was such a nice gentleman."

It was evident that she had not seen the paragraph in yesterday's *Times*.

Vicky choked down the fruitcake and drank the tea and then went through her father's desk in the vain hope that she might find some explanation for his conduct, but she only came upon one old letter among a pile of unpaid bills. It had an Edinburgh address on it, and it had been written soon after her mother's death, informing Mr. Paul Lingford that his wife's father, Sir Hector Macalister, would take upon himself the education of his grandson, James Lingford, on condition that he, Mr. Paul Lingford, brought up the boy's sister, Victoria Mary Lingford, as a lady should be brought up and educated.

Vicky sat on the floor and studied the letter gravely: there was an implacable tone about it that frightened her a little. If her Uncle Harold Lingford refused to take her into his house it did not seem as if she could appeal to her grandfather for help. If he knew that his son-in-law had deserted her he would in all probability wash his hands of both of them, and poor James would be the loser.

She took the letter with her father's when she went back to Brook Street that evening, and hearing voices in the drawing room that indicated that Lady Taversham was entertaining her son and his wife, she told the butler to make her apologies to her ladyship and that she was retiring to her room with a bad headache. She asked him to send a few sandwiches to her there later on.

Left to herself, the more she thought about her father's actions the more sick at heart she became. Not only had he robbed countless people of what had possibly been their savings, or indeed their only source of income, but he had lent his name to encourage them to invest in Mr. Grammidge's fraudulent schemes.

She was up early on the following morning, and leaving a note for Lady Taversham telling her what she was about to do, she took a cab to Lincoln's Inn Fields, taking the two letters with her.

Mr. Larkin received her with courtesy and kindness. He was in fact a kindly man, and had been distressed at the possible plight of Paul Lingford's children.

"I have come to you, Mr. Larkin, for your help and advice," she said, coming to the point at once with a directness that he had to admire. "You know, of course, that my father has left the country?"

"I am afraid there are not many people who do not know about it, Miss Lingford," he said. "Has he left any directions as to where and when you are to join him?"

"On the contrary, he has told me to go to Mr. Harold Lingford," she said, putting the letter in front of him. He took it up and read it in silence, and she saw his face go grave.

"Certainly Mr. Harold Lingford might give you a home with him in Westborough until this unhappy scandal has blown over," he said. "Have you ever met him?"

"Never. I believe my father borrowed money from him at sometime and it was not repaid. I know there was trouble between them. If he will not take us into his house I do not know to whom I can turn for assistance. As I found this letter in my father's desk it does not seem to me that my grandfather would be willing to help. In fact, if I applied to him it might seriously imperil James's future."

She put the letter in front of him, and he glanced at it and nodded. "I have a similar letter in my possession," he told her. "But I do not think you need have any apprehension that he will withdraw the money he placed with my firm for your brother's education. Even if he should hear that Mr. Paul Lingford has left the country under—ahem—unfortunate circumstances, I believe he will conclude that you are with him."

Vicky could see the sense of this, although the thought of having left the country with her father was not a pleasant one.

"If my uncle in Westborough does come to our rescue," she said, her face brightening a little, "is there a good school in the city where James could continue his education?"

"Yes. The Westborough Grammar School has one of the oldest foundations in the country, and an excellent reputation," said the lawyer. "It would be a very good thing if he could be moved there, because only this morning I had a letter from Dr. Dacres, the headmaster of St. Chad's, asking me to remove your brother from his school."

"Remove James from St. Chad's? But why? What has he done?" Then as her eyes met the lawyer's, understanding came. "He will not have Paul Lingford's son in his school," she said.

"Dr. Dacres says that as far as he is concerned he could not have a better scholar. But the good doctor is afraid that if Mr. Lingford's son remains at St. Chad's the parents of some of the other boys may feel obliged to take their sons away. He writes regretfully, saying that he will be extremely sorry to part with your brother."

It seemed so grossly unfair that Vicky could have wept with anger. The sins of the father were being visited on his children indeed. She controlled herself with some difficulty and said coldly that of course James must leave, that very day if it could be arranged.

"I do not know where to take him," she added. "Costerley—"

"I am afraid we must not consider that for either of you until I have heard from Pargeter's Bank," said Mr. Larkin. "Your father took out a large mortgage on the house and estate to purchase a directorship in Mr. Grammidge's railway company, and now he has left the country the bank may be forced to foreclose."

So Costerley was gone. "I know Mrs. Norris would find rooms for my brother and myself for the next week while I go down to Westborough to see my uncle," Vicky said slowly. "But I scarcely like to impose on her good nature. You see, my father owes her a great deal of money."

Mr. Larkin undertook to settle Mrs. Norris's account, and to write three letters immediately: the first to Dr. Dacres asking him to see that James Lingford was packed and ready to be fetched that evening from the school, the second to Mr. Harold Lingford telling him that his niece and nephew would be calling on him at Westborough Hall on the following morning, and the third to Dr. Eccrington, the headmaster of Westborough Grammar School, asking if he had room for another boarder in his establishment.

"I shall mention no names," he added. "Because I think it might be wiser for you both to choose another name than that of Lingford for a time. I shall simply say that through no fault of his own the young gentleman has been forced to leave his school in London and that his friends would like accommodation found for him at the grammar school if it is possible. Shall I suggest that you might call upon him with your brother tomorrow afternoon? You will by that time have seen your uncle and will be more assured of what your future there might be."

Vicky agreed, and added, "You said you thought it would be wise for us to change our name. How can we do that?"

"By deed poll, or simply by taking another name."

She thanked him for his kindness and advice, said she would think it over, and went back to Sackville Street. There she engaged rooms for herself and James for a week, Mr. Larkin having promised to settle up everything for them when they left.

Mrs. Norris was delighted to have them and bustled off to prepare suitable rooms while Vicky went on to Brook Street to pack her clothes and to say goodbye to Lady Taversham.

"I shall leave my coming-out dress behind," she said. "One of the maids can have it. I could not possibly wear it again,

34

however pretty it is, knowing that it was paid for by Mrs. Grammidge."

"Then you can make your mind easy on that score," said her old friend, smiling. "She did not pay for it."

"Not pay for it?" Vicky stared. "Then who—"

"I wrote to her thanking her for her kind offer," said Lady Taversham, "adding that I was sure she would understand if I had the coming-out dress of the daughter of my old friend put down to my account. So you may pack it with a clear conscience, my dear, with my love and hope that the day will not be long before you will be wearing it again."

Vicky could only thank her with a kiss. She was too choked with emotion to speak, and Lady Taversham went on:

"You know how gladly I would give you a permanent home here. You would not cause me the slightest embarrassment: I am old enough to be able to meet sneers and innuendoes with impunity. But you are young and vulnerable, and unkind people can make their arrows sharp and penetrating. It is wiser to find a home with your uncle for the time being, and you will be safe with him. His friends in Westborough will be kind to you, I am sure, and your brother will settle down in time at the new school."

Before Vicky left, Lady Taversham went to her little escritoire and took from it a small purse. "I want you to take this, my dear," she said, "in case you find yourself stranded without money. There are ten sovereigns in that little purse, and you are not to hesitate to call upon me for more if you find yourself in need. You have the Macalister pride, I know, but pride will not pay your bills."

They parted with words of affection from her ladyship and promises from Vicky that she would let her know directly she was settled with her uncle in Westborough. But all the same, Lady Taversham could not help feeling some measure of relief when one of the Taversham carriages took Vicky and her luggage back to Sackville Street.

From across Brook Street, Emily saw her go and ran to tell her mother.

"Mama," she cried, "I do believe Lady Taversham has asked Vicky to leave. She has just been driven away with all her luggage."

Mrs. Sellinge said she would call on her ladyship in a day or two and find out. But Lady Taversham was not one to forget a snub and did not easily forgive the coolness of the bow she had received from Mrs. Sellinge on Sunday.

When she arrived at the Dowager's, to her mortification and astonishment she was told that her ladyship was not at home. It took some weeks before she realized that Lady Taversham had temporarily crossed her off her visiting list.

In the meantime Vicky found that Mrs. Norris had rooms all ready for herself and James, and very soon after she arrived in Sackville Street James himself drove up in a cab, with his luggage and tuck box and a selection of schoolbooks.

"Well, James?" Vicky said, after she had paid off the cabbie and they were left alone in what had been their father's sitting room.

"Well, Vicky?" he said, returning her kiss. "It seems the guv'nor has left us to our fate."

"Have you had a very dreadful time at St. Chad's since it all came out?" she asked.

"On Saturday and yesterday I was sent to Coventry—except, of course, by Timbers, who has promised to write to me. He is going to write to his father to ask him if he cannot leave St. Chad's and go to another school. He hopes the Colonel will send him to one of these new schools, Haileybury or Wellington, that cater to the sons of Army officers."

"And Dr. Dacres? What had he to say to you?"

"Nothing. Mrs. Dacres would not take the least notice of me—not that I cared. She is a hateful woman. But this evening when I was ready to go and waiting for the cab, Dr. Dacres came out of his study and into the hall to shake my hand and to wish me luck at my new school. He was not such a bad old soul, after all."

"Poor James. I am glad you have left St. Chad's all the same." Vicky told him that Mr. Larkin thought they should first visit their Uncle Harold at Westborough in the morning.

"It only takes an hour and a quarter by rail from Paddington Station to Westborough, and if Uncle Harold consents to have us we will go on and see the headmaster of the Westborough Grammar School before returning here to Sackville Street. We shall have to pay a short visit to Costerley sometime this week to pack up what we want to keep." She told him about the mortgage on the place and how Mr. Larkin was pretty certain the bank would foreclose, and saw his face fall. But he soon had questions to ask about the Westborough Grammar School. "Is that where I am going?" he asked.

"Will you mind, Jamie? Mr. Larkin says it is a very good old school, and as it will not be so expensive as St. Chad's I hope there will be enough of Grandfather Macalister's money left to send you on to Oxford."

"But what will you do?"

"I hope that our uncle will be able to find me a situation of some sort in the town, so that I can be near you."

James approved of this, and that evening after a splendid meal supplied by Mrs. Norris he slept soundly, while even Vicky had more sleep than she had had the night before.

After breakfast the following day they made their way to Paddington and caught a morning train to Westborough. It was a beautiful morning, and the colors of late autumn were beginning to thrust their way into copses and over country lanes. As they left the smoke of London behind the sunshine became stronger every moment, and it was exactly half past eleven when they saw Westborough, with its clusters of red-tiled roofs surrounding the gray stone of the great cathedral in its midst.

High above the town stood the ruins of the castle that had once protected town and cathedral, and now only provided interesting and picturesque ruins for visitors to see, to sketch and to ramble over as they admired the view.

In the stationyard there was a cab rank with rather jaded-looking horses in the shafts, their drivers talking together in the cab shelter as if the acquiring of a fare was the last thing in their thoughts.

After some minutes Vicky succeeded in attracting the attention of one of them, a large gentleman with a spotted neckcloth under his driving coat, who was suitably impressed when she gave him their destination.

He helped them into his cab with some deference, and in a few minutes they were off leaving the city by West Gate. Almost immediately they began to ascend a gentle incline on a country road with a stream running gaily beside it. Beyond they saw a covey of partridges, moving across the field like animated wine bottles. The covey reminded them of Coster-ley, and they looked at each other and smiled, and their spirits rose as the horse began a slow climb to the top of the hill.

A new life was beginning, a life quite unknown to them, a life that mercifully would have no Grammidges to spoil it. A life where at all events they were now on their own and together.

Chapter Four

They saw the Hall when they reached the top of the hill. It was an imposing building, standing in a large park with a roadway leading from the lodges at the gates to the house itself.

The park was planted with fine trees, and cattle were grazing there, and as they drew near they could see what a very large mansion their uncle's house was, with its red-brick battlements and Gothic windows and the great carriage sweep in front of it.

They descended from the cab in front of massive steps flanked by ornamental vases in terra-cotta, and as she paid off the cabbie and turned to look up at the house before ascending the flight of steps to the front door, Vicky was reminded of Emily Sellinge's scornful description of the magnates of Surbiton, where the wholesalers looked down on the retailers and the retailers looked down on the wholesalers.

James pulled the iron bell handle, and a butler answered it, correct in black and white and looking rather like one of the penguins in the Zoological Gardens in Regent's Park. Vicky told him that Mr. Lingford was expecting them, without giving her name, and he stepped back and led them across a very large hall to an even larger library, the shelves filled with expensively bound volumes that looked as if they were never taken down or even intended to be read.

A large important-looking gentleman was seated in a swivel chair in front of a writing table in the window with his back to them. He turned as they came in, and Vicky saw with some interest that he was as dark as her father was fair. But where his brother's expression had usually been one of lazy good humor, Harold Lingford's was nothing but one of hard arrogance and conceit.

He stared at them now with an expression of disgust, if not with positive hostility. He had Mr. Larkin's letter in his hand, and it was obvious that it had made him very angry indeed.

"So you are my brother's children?" he said, frowning at them from under beetling brows.

"Yes, sir." Vicky's chin went up, as it had a habit of doing if she was challenged.

"Have you any idea what is in the letter that I received this morning from a Mr. Larkin, who says that he is your lawyer?"

"No, sir, I am afraid I do not. I leave it to Mr. Larkin to write his own letters," said Vicky. She guessed that her impertinence would shock him, as indeed it did.

"Then I will tell you what is in it," he said icily. "Your lawyer informs me first of what is common knowledge by this time, namely my brother's disgraceful behavior and his flight from England to escape a probable prison sentence because of the frauds he has perpetrated. And secondly he has the impudence to suggest that I should give you and your brother—the children of a common criminal—a home in my house. What do you think of that?"

"Only that Mr. Larkin, knowing you to be our next of kin, possibly thought you should be given the chance to provide for us before he could decide what else could be done."

"That's as it may be." Finding himself worsted by this slender, dignified girl, Mr. Lingford began to bluster. "It did not occur to him that I have my own family, and my position in Westborough to consider, and that both would be harmed, if not actually degraded in the eyes of my friends and acquaintances, if I brought the children of a man like my brother to share our lives?"

"I do not suppose any such idea occurred to Mr. Larkin," agreed Vicky pleasantly. "He is a very nice man. But now that we are here, are you able to advise me what I should do?"

"Return to London by the next train and find yourself some sort of gainful employment. I understand your maternal grandfather is providing for your brother, so you have only yourself to consider."

"That is very true, and I am sure your advice is very sound, sir. It is advice that I shall have no hesitation in taking." Vicky slipped her hand over her brother's, which was slowly doubling itself into a fist. "Come, James, let us be on our way. But before we go, Mr. Lingford, I would like to reassure you on one point. It was suggested by Mr. Larkin that we should change our surname. My brother and I talked it over on the way here, and we did not like the suggestion, because we had no idea that any members of the Lingford family would find it degrading to extend a hand of friendship to us, as we are not responsible for what our father has done. But I can see that we were mistaken, and Mr. Larkin was right. My brother and I will at once change our name from Lingford to Macalister, so that you and your family need have no fear of disgrace from an association which is as unpleasant to us as it is to you. Neither James nor I will recognize any kinship with your family in the future. Come, James."

She took his arm, and, turning their backs on their unhelpful relative, they left the room.

"He might have given us luncheon," James said as they started off on foot across the park.

"It isn't very far to walk back to the town, and it is a lovely morning," said his sister happily, thinking of Lady Taversham's sovereigns in her new purse. "I saw a large hotel—I think it was called the Mitre—in the High Street as we turned out of the street to the railway. We will have a lovely big meal there and then we will go and see Dr. Eccrington, because he too will have received a letter from Mr. Larkin this morning."

"I only hope he does not treat us as our uncle did," said James, and then his eyes met his sister's and he laughed. "Wasn't he a brute?" he said. "You have got to get yourself 'gainful employment,' Sis. Have you any idea how to set about it?"

"I daresay Mr. Larkin will find something for me," said Vicky calmly, refusing to look on the dark side of things. Since she had read the newspaper paragraph on Sunday she seemed to have suddenly grown up. The rather shy, awkward girl had gone, and her place had been taken by a self-possessed young woman.

The Mitre was the best hotel in the town. It was an imposing building, and in the old days before railways had come in it had been a large posting inn. Even now, their waiter told them, there were stables for at least fifty horses at the back.

"I know that no lady should enter a hotel dining room without a gentleman escort," said Vicky. "But I have one today in you, Jamie, so I am quite safe."

The waiter had found them a table in a small alcove that overlooked the High Street, so that it was almost as if they had a private room to themselves. And there they dined on excellent roast beef, followed by James's favorite treacle pudding, fresh baked bread and cheese, washed down by some extremely good cider.

Vicky allowed James to pay the bill, passing him one of her gold sovereigns under the tablecloth, and with a shilling tip to the waiter it came to four shillings and sixpence. They set off for the grammar school afterward feeling much more cheerful and refreshed.

The grammar school was situated at the bottom of College Street, which was a cul-de-sac. It was not a wide street, and most of the houses that fronted on it were as old as the school itself, although some of the timbered fronts had been replaced by Georgian facades, with long sash windows looking onto the street.

The grammar school faced up the road, a forecourt with gateposts decorated with pineapples in front. Over the arched door there was carved the date 1527 in the stone, and above it the school crest, which might have been an eagle or equally well a hawk, and the motto *Labor Omnia Vincit* beneath it, both almost obliterated with the centuries.

Behind the school were large gardens, playgrounds and playing fields, spreading out under the shelter of Castle Hill, and as they were ushered into the paneled hall they felt an air of antiquity, as if here at least time stood still.

When Vicky told the manservant that she would like to see Dr. Eccrington on a matter of some importance, she and James were shown at once into the doctor's study.

Dr. Eccrington got up from his desk and came to greet them. He was a dark-haired, fine-featured man in his middle forties, with a pair of shrewd blue eyes, and the warmth in his face was so different from her uncle's cold indifference that Vicky's heart lifted as he took her hand.

"You must be the young lady Mr. Larkin wrote to me about," said the doctor genially. "I had his letter this morning. It is here on my desk." His eyes rested penetratingly on James. "This, I presume, is your brother, for whom Mr. Larkin requested a place in my school, if we can accommodate him. He did not, however, give me your name."

Vicky said that their name was Macalister and that they

were the grandchildren of Sir Hector Macalister, who had made himself responsible for her brother's education.

"And why," asked the doctor, "do you wish your brother to come to us? Have you relatives in Westborough?"

For a moment Vicky hesitated, and then she said quietly: "We thought we had one relative in Westborough who, if he felt he could not welcome us, would at least have given us a home until we could discover what was best to be done. But he made it plain this morning that he would have nothing to do with us."

"I see." And yet it was plain that the doctor was still puzzled. She thought his wits were probably as sharp as his eyes and he missed little of what went on around him. He asked them to sit down, and as they settled themselves in chairs before his desk he said questioningly, "And yet, Miss Macalister, you still wish your brother to come to our grammar school?"

"If you please." Vicky's eyes met his. "It seemed to me as we walked back from—our relative's house that it is just the kind of city where we should both be happy. I have never lived in a cathedral city before, and there is a charm about it that won me over." It was also a city where it would be possible to hide from one's friends until the shame of her father's behavior had been forgotten.

Dr. Eccrington referred again to Mr. Larkin's letter. "Your lawyer says that your brother was at St. Chad's," he said thoughtfully. "And that for private reasons, he was asked to leave. May one ask what those private reasons were—or is it too delicate a question?"

"No, it is not. And far from being private, I am afraid those reasons are very public ones by this time." Vicky spoke bitterly and suddenly made up her mind to tell this man the truth, even if it meant that he too refused to have Paul Lingford's son in his school. She felt that if James did not start with a clean slate he might be smeared by some imagined scandal, and the scandal that faced them was surely worse than anything that could be imagined, even by their most unkind friends.

She told them their real names, and how James had been sent to Coventry at St. Chad's because of what his father had done. She hid nothing from him, stressing the kindness of Lady Taversham to herself, and the fear of Dr. Dacres that the fathers of other pupils might remove their sons from St. Chad's if James were to remain.

"Lingford," said Dr. Eccrington musingly as she finished. "Yes, I quite understand that Mr. Harold Lingford would not welcome you. He is not renowned for his charitable attitude even toward his own friends. I believe he has totally disowned his brother, putting a notice to that effect in the local paper last Saturday, so that it should coincide with the *Times* paragraph. He could scarcely receive his brother's children after that, however innocent they may be."

"I suppose one cannot blame him," agreed Vicky. "I daresay he has an important position in the town." Her eyes went to the playing fields outside the windows, where a game of soccer was going on with enthusiastic support from the boys watching it. "I suppose," she said sadly, "that even with a changed name it is going to be difficult to hide ourselves from what our father has done."

"Difficult, but by no means impossible," said Dr. Eccrington cheerfully. "If James comes to us I do not think anyone will be likely to question a suggestion that he has been ordered to a country school by his medical man because the London fogs were harming his health." His eyes dwelt on James's excellent physique, and he gave a small smile. "What do you think of that, Miss Macalister?"

"You do not think that some of the boys might find out the truth and give him a bad time?" asked Vicky.

"Your brother looks to me as if he is quite capable of taking care of himself," said Dr. Eccrington. "But if anything of the sort reaches my ears, the offenders will be summoned to this study and I will teach them a lesson in human kindness and charity to others that they will not forget in a hurry." And here he glanced at the cane that lay across the top of his desk. "But I do not think you need fear for James, Miss Macalister. Most of the boys are day boys. We have twenty boarders, and they come from families of farmers and of small country squires, who find it too difficult in the winter to bring them daily along our muddy country lanes. The day boys come from the town, sons of clergy, lawyers, doctors—even the proctor has two sons with us—besides the sons of the richer tradesmen. There are a hundred of them all told, and I do not think your brother will be unhappy here. Our boys are good-natured country boys—high-spirited, of course, and some too free with their fists, but I feel that James will be able to take things as they come. What do you think about it, boy?" And now the blue eyes were turned probingly on James.

James met them fearlessly. "I agree with my sister in liking the town, sir," he said. "And I would like to come to the grammar school. But now that my uncle has refused to have anything to do with us I am wondering what my sister will do. You see, sir, my father left her with nothing but unpaid bills."

"Which Mr. Larkin will settle for us, Jamie, and claim from the sale of the estate," Vicky reminded him. She smiled at the doctor. "We are seeing Mr. Larkin tomorrow, and I have no doubt he will help me to find a situation of some sort where I shall not be too far from Westborough. Indeed, I shall tell him that he must." And she set her chin in a way that Dr. Eccrington admired, and made him think that under the circumstances Mr. Larkin certainly would find Miss Macalister a situation near Westborough.

"I suggest then that James come to us here as a boarder next Saturday," he said. "That will give you time to see Mr. Larkin and to pack his clothes and so on." He noticed the cut of Vicky's gray silk dress, that her cloth cape was lined with fur, and that her hat had the stamp of a good milliner. He guessed that her clothes had been purchased from leading London shops and wondered if the accounts would ever be paid. Her face was an honest one, however, and her eyes were as brave as the set of her chin. He added gently, "If Mr. Larkin cannot find a situation for you, my wife is always meeting the parents of our boys, and many of them ask her if she knows any young ladies who would take the place of governesses in their households. Something of that sort might suit you."

Before leaving they met Mrs. Eccrington, a nice motherly woman, who looked after the health and welfare of the boys assisted by a housekeeper, Mrs. Broom, and as they walked back to the station their hearts felt considerably lighter, while Vicky did her best to dispel the uneasiness James felt for his sister's future.

"What *will* you do, Sis?" he asked. "If you have no money and nowhere to go?"

"The sovereigns dear Lady Taversham gave me will last quite a little while," she said, smiling. "And then there is my godmother's jewelry that was left to me. I know I am not allowed to touch it until I am twenty-one, but Mr. Larkin might advance me something on it. I believe there is a diamond necklace that is quite valuable. As my twenty-first birthday is two years away, the jewelry is not going to be much use if I die of starvation in the meantime."

They arrived back to find that Mrs. Norris had a good meal for them, and the following day they traveled down to Costerley and spent a little while there, selecting what they wanted to keep of their possessions and arranging for them to be packed up and sent to their lodgings in Sackville Street. Mrs. Norris had large dry cellars under her house and had promised to store such cases for them until they had a place of their own.

They said goodbye to the few servants that remained, and as they traveled back to London, to lessen the grief of leaving Costerley for the last time, they talked of the house they would have in the future. It was to be quite small, a cottage, no more, where James was to come to spend his holidays and his furlough when he was a man employed on some important engineering work abroad. It began to take shape in their minds, and they grew more cheerful as they neared London. The next day Vicky went through her brother's clothes, sorting those he would need for school. James spent the time in Mrs. Norris's cellar, busy painting J. MACALISTER on the lid of his trunk to obliterate the J. LINGFORD that had been there before.

In the afternoon they called on Mr. Larkin and told him what they had arranged with Dr. Eccrington. They also told him of their reception by Mr. Harold Lingford, which did not seem to surprise him, and he promised to make inquiries about a post as companion or governess for Vicky in the vicinity of Westborough.

He also approved of the change of name, and if Macalister was not quite the one he would have chosen he did not show it.

By Saturday all was completed, and Vicky traveled to Westborough that afternoon to see James as far as the school. Mrs. Eccrington showed them around, and especially the light airy dormitory where James was to sleep. She then invited them to tea, and as they sat in the headmaster's dining room eating bread and butter and honey and excellent plum cake with the Eccrington children, Vicky was even more reassured as to her brother's happiness there.

45

After tea he was allowed to walk to the station with her, and it was then that her destiny took another turn.

It was getting dusk and the shops were all lighted up, and they had come up College Street and across the bridge over the river that ran through the town, into Market Lane. From there they made their way past the Mitre and into the High Street, and it was just before they reached Railway Street that Vicky caught sight of a milliner's shop on the other side of the road.

"We are early for the train," she said, "and before we go on I must have a look at those bonnets. They look remarkably fashionable for a country shop in a country town."

The hats and bonnets in the shop window were lighted from above by a single gaslight outside. It was encased in a metal shield directing the light down upon the goods in the window, and as Vicky paused with James beside her the shop door burst open and a small servant girl came running out, almost knocking them down in her fright.

"Oh, ma'am," she cried, catching at Vicky's arm, "will you please come? I think the missus is dead. Dropped down like a stone she did, and all the work girls is gone, seeing as it's Saturday when they go at five instead of seven, and Miss Fosbery isn't in today, and Miss Silcocks is gone to a lady in the country what wants her bonnet urgent, and Mrs. Bellon isn't here, and I dursn't touch her—"

"Of course I'll come." Vicky tried to soothe the frightened girl. "My brother will run for a doctor if you will tell him where he can be found."

"The missus allus has Dr. Warren, ma'am. In Bridge Street."

"Where is your mistress?"

"Down there by them shelves, ma'am. She was trying to lift one of them 'eavy rolls of silk when she suddenly let it drop and fell, and she looks like as if she is dead."

The girl ran back to her mistress, and Vicky and James followed her into the shop.

Chapter Five

Vicky had found time to write to Lady Taversham during that week telling her of their change of name and of James's having been accepted as a boarding pupil at Westborough Grammar School, but she said no more except to thank her again for her kindness and affection and to sign herself V. Macalister.

To the Sellinges she did not write, and on the evening of the day when Mrs. Sellinge had been told that Lady Taversham was not at home, Emily came downstairs to find her brother in the morning room writing a letter, before accompanying her and his mother to a dinner party.

Emily, whose conscience had not been very happy since she had ignored Vicky on Sunday, immediately told her brother that Vicky Lingford had left Lady Taversham's. "Mama went to call on Lady Taversham today and she was told she was not at home," she went on. "I expect she did not want Mama to know that she had asked Vicky to leave, knowing that she is a friend of ours."

"Ought you not to put that in the past tense?" asked Sebastian drily. "And knowing Lady Taversham even as slightly as I do I cannot imagine her turning her back on a friend when she was in trouble. I would rather think that it was Miss Lingford who suggested the move, not wishing to embarrass her ladyship with her continued presence in her house."

"In which case she showed very good sense," said Emily petulantly. "Uncle said this morning that Paul Lingford's children must be fully aware by this time that they have lost all their friends. He said he doubted if even their relatives would be charitable enough to take them in."

Sebastian's lips tightened a little, and he asked his sister if she knew of any relatives that the Lingfords might have.

"I think Mama said once there was a Mr. Harold Lingford

47

who lives in Westborough. Aunt Kitty knows him slightly. Otherwise I suppose Vicky will have to go and live with that dreadful aunt or cousin or whatever she was, Miss Crampton, who used to go and look after them before their father took up with those horrible Grammidges. She was so prim that Vicky and James and I did all we could to shock her. I cannot imagine her offering to have them in her house. She is much too full of good works."

"Which would not extend, naturally, to her own family," agreed Sebastian, and then his mother came into the room to tell them that the carriage was waiting and it was time they set off.

But although his partner at dinner that evening was Miss Adela Berney, somehow he did not find her so entertaining as usual, and he was afraid that she found him dull. She teased him once or twice on having his mind taken up with some "stuffy old law case," to which he gave a grave smile and did his best to behave with more courtesy. But all the time his thoughts were on the young Lingfords, and he was remembering that his Aunt Kitty in Westborough had written to him several times lately about the lease of her house.

Adelaide Villa in the Close belonged to the Dean and Chapter of the cathedral, and the Proctor had been suggesting to his aunt that at the end of her lease, which ran out in the following March, she should move to the Laurels.

When they returned home that evening, to find the Judge indulging in a nightcap before going to bed, Sebastian asked his mother why his aunt did not wish to move to the Laurels. "It appears to be a much larger house than her present one, and they are suggesting that she should pay the same rent," he pointed out.

"My dear, the Laurels is a horrid, damp dark house," his mother explained. "Half hidden by dank laurels and a large cypress tree and much too large for her. She could not possibly keep up such a house on her income. I feel very sorry for Kitty. She is very comfortable in Adelaide Villa, which is just right for her, but there appears to be some difficulty about extending her lease. I do not understand these things, but I wrote and told her that I thought her lawyer either did not understand the matter properly or was trying to curry favor with the Dean, who may want her house for somebody else."

The Judge said that he had had trouble in the past with

leases attached to cathedral bodies. The proctors usually had too many masters.

"Perhaps I had better go down and see Aunt Kitty tomorrow, then," Sebastian said. "It is a Saturday, and I have nothing pressing to keep me here in London. I will look at her lease and see if I can find a clause giving her the right to extend her lease if she so wishes. There usually are such clauses, I believe."

The Judge approved of this and so in consequence did his mother, and the following morning Sebastian set off on the eleven-o'clock from Paddington, having sent a telegram from the station to his aunt to expect him. As the telegram arrived in time for more mutton chops to be fetched by the boy from the butcher's, he had an excellent luncheon in Miss Sellinge's charming little house in the Close.

"The truth is, Sebastian," she told him as they ate their way leisurely through their luncheon, "Mrs. Burke, the Dean's wife, has had her eyes on my little house for some time." His aunt's large blue eyes were as round as an outraged kitten's. In fact, she was very like a kitten altogether. "The last time she came here to tea she looked about her as she left and remarked how comfortable it all looked. 'It is just the sort of house for which my poor widowed sister is searching,' she told me and then went into a long story of how poor dear Maria had been left with a mere pittance, and could scarcely pay her way at all. Such a large house that needed at least eight or nine servants, quite impossible for a widow with her slender means."

"And what did you say to that?" Sebastian smiled indulgently across the dining table at his charming little aunt. White-haired, with her wide blue eyes, she still had the laughter of a girl, and she laughed now at the thought of how she had worsted the Dean's wife.

"I said I *quite* understood, and it was indeed dreadful for her poor sister to feel that she must give up her home and live in a much smaller one, and she must feel it acutely. And I said I hoped she would soon find herself suited with a house like mine, because all I needed here was my cook, house parlormaid, Fenwick, who acted as my personal maid as well, a scullery maid and the boot boy, Albert, which was all that *my* means could afford. I did not go into details, of course. The discussion of money matters is so vulgar, dear."

"There must be a great many rooms to spare at the Deanery," commented Sebastian. "It did not occur to Mrs. Burke to offer her poor widowed sister rooms there, I suppose?"

"Oh no, dear. Maria does not get on with the Dean."

"That settles that, then. I will have a look through your papers after luncheon and we will see what they have to say about the lease of Adelaide Villa."

The meal being finished with a glass or two of excellent port, he followed his aunt into her little drawing room, and with her papers spread out at her desk he went through them carefully until he came upon what he had hoped to find, a small unimportant clause in her lease stating that if at the expiration of her seven years' tenancy of Adelaide Villa, Miss Sellinge wished to extend it to a further seven years, she would be at liberty to do so.

"There you are, Aunt Kitty!" he said, pointing it out to her. "I shall have infinite pleasure in writing to the Proctor, Mr. Hayes, on your behalf, and drawing it to his attention. Have you discussed it with him, by the way?"

"When I tried to discuss it all he would do was to advise me to go and look at the Laurels, offering to accompany me there himself. I told him there was no *need* for me to look at the Laurels. I have seen them and the ugly house they try to hide for years. I would not *dream* of living there, I said, and he knew I meant it." She paused and then she laughed. "It's because of the Dean, you know. Poor Mr. Hayes is terrified of him. If he catches sight of his gaiters he will run like a hare."

"I see that his letter to you is a very polite one, however, merely suggesting that you might like to exchange Adelaide Villa for the Laurels and stressing the fact that it is a much larger house and the rent would be no more than you are paying now. You are not attracted by that, I gather?"

"Certainly not. What would be the use of a larger house to me, my dear boy? I am not thinking of setting up a boardinghouse!"

"Then I shall write an equally polite letter to the gentleman on your behalf, saying that I have studied the terms of your present lease in detail, and that I find you are entitled to extend that lease to another seven years, and as this is in fact your wish I shall be grateful if he will have a new lease drawn up for you to sign as soon as possible."

"You do not think he will dispute it?"

"I do not. The Proctor knows very well that my knowledge

of the law is as good as his, if not better, and I shall be surprised if you do not receive the new lease for signature in the near future. If you do not, write to me and I will come down in person to interview the Proctor—or even the Dean, gaiters and all."

His aunt drew a sigh of relief. "As long as Mr. Hayes cannot compel me to leave this dear little house, that is all that matters."

"Nobody can do that, my dearest aunt, unless you have committed sundry offenses which I will not offend your ears by mentioning, as none is likely to apply to you."

The letter was written and left for Albert to leave at the Proctor's office on the following day, and then Sebastian stayed to have tea with Miss Sellinge before leaving to catch his train back to London.

It was over tea that he asked her if she knew a gentleman by the name of Lingford living in or near Westborough.

"Do you mean Mr. Harold Lingford of Westborough Hall?" She made a small grimace. "He is a very grand gentleman indeed. He is on most of the charitable committees in the town—I think he is now governor of the St. Francis's Alms-houses and not liked very much, as he has been cutting down the old people's fuel. He says they have been given an extra blanket apiece and that should be enough. And then there is the hospital. He has given extensively to the hospital, and he likes everyone to be aware of it."

Sebastian thought that under those circumstances the young Lingfords might have found a haven with their uncle for a time, at all events. His aunt's next words, however, made this more doubtful.

"I do not know him very well, because I must admit I dislike the man. He has such a very good opinion of himself, and his wife is an extremely overbearing sort of woman. They do their best to keep in with the county set, but I do not think they succeed very well. What is your interest in them, my dear?"

"There was a certain Paul Lingford who left the country rather suddenly about a fortnight or so ago to escape being arrested for fraud. I wondered if Mr. Harold Lingford could be related to him."

"Oh yes, my dear, he was his brother. But Mr. Harold Lingford has completely disowned him. He says he is not going to acknowledge relationship with a swindler and a thief."

In that case it did not seem as if the gentleman would have felt inclined to help his brother's children.

"You have not heard what happened to Paul Lingford's children, I suppose?" Sebastian waited with some anxiety for his aunt's reply.

"I did not know there were any," she said.

"There were two. A boy and a girl. The girl was a school friend of Emily's, and the boy is I believe at St. Chad's."

"Then I am very sorry for the poor young creatures. I cannot see Mr. or Mrs. Harold Lingford extending any sort of helping hand to either of them."

Privately Sebastian agreed with her, and his anxiety for the two young Lingfords grew. He supposed they must be at the Sackville Street lodgings or at Costerley, and he thought that when he got back to London he would visit Paul Lingford's old lodgings and find out where they were.

After eating all he could of the muffins and bread and butter and homemade raspberry jam and cake dusted with sugar, he removed his long legs from the comfort of his aunt's fire and said he must go. Fenwick came in to light the gas lamps on either side of the fireplace, and the evening dusk outside was suddenly turned into night. He got up and kissed his aunt goodbye and went out into the hall, where Fenwick had his overcoat, hat and gloves ready for him.

"I wish you would allow me to send Albert for a cab," said Miss Sellinge. "It would not take a minute. There is a cab rank next to the almshouses."

"My dear Aunt Kitty, it is a lovely evening and the stars are out. I shall enjoy the walk to the station, and the exercise will do me good."

He went off lightly down the path from Adelaide Villa to its little gate, turning left along the south side of the Close into St. Francis's Row and then on down a winding old street, St. Francis's Lane, into the High Street, where the shops were all lit up and the lamplighter had finished with his ladder, and the gaslamps were like glass beads strung along the streets.

He was just about to cross the road to Railway Street and was standing by the milliner's shop where his aunt bought her bonnets when a boy came dashing out of the doorway and cannoned into him, sending his silk hat flying.

"I beg your pardon, sir." The boy picked up the hat and brushed it off with his glove. "I hope I did not hurt you, but I have been sent to find a doctor and I am afraid I did not look where I was going." Then as he raised his eyes to the gentleman's astonished face, "Why," he exclaimed, "it's Mr. Sellinge."

"You appear to be in a hurry, James." Sebastian took his hat from him and replaced it on his head. "Why are you needing a doctor so urgently?" Then his expression changed to one of concern. "Is your sister with you, and has she been taken ill?"

"Oh no, sir. It's the poor woman in this shop. Her maid came running out and said she was dead, and Vicky followed her in, and I must say she looked pretty rum, lying there with her face a sort of gray color. But when Vicky asked for one of the hand mirrors in the shop—it's a milliner's, you see, sir—and held it against the woman's mouth, she said she was still breathing, but she thought she ought to have a doctor quickly. The maid says her doctor is Dr. Warren in Bridge Street. Do you know where that is? Vicky is staying with her while I fetch him."

"Yes, of course. I will take you there." It would mean that he might miss his train, but there were others, and Sebastian wanted to know what Paul Lingford's children were doing in Westborough. He hoped it meant that their uncle had decided to help them after all, in which case he was more charitable than his aunt had thought. They started off toward Bridge Street, and as he kept up with his long strides James told him that he had come to join the grammar school that afternoon as one of its pupils. "Vicky came with me to see my dormitory and look over the school before going back to London. I was walking back with her to the station when this happened."

"But why Westborough Grammar School?" asked Sebastian.

"Well, you see, sir, I have to leave St. Chad's."

"Why was that?"

James was embarrassed and said that Dr. Dacres had been afraid that the other boys' fathers would not like him to continue there.

"In case the son of a black sheep should contaminate the snow-white fleeces of their pet lambs, I suppose," said Sebastian, and James laughed.

"Something of that sort. I believe old Dacres was really sorry about it, and he has sent a rattling good report of me to Dr. Eccrington. I hope I shall be able to live up to it."

"You have an uncle here, have you not? I expect your sister will make her home with him?"

"I only wish she could, but he showed us the door very quickly, and because of that Vicky and I have changed our name to Macalister—our mother's name. You will not forget that, will you, sir? Vicky does not want to be associated with the Lingfords any more, and neither do I. Not only because of what my father did, but because of what my uncle said, if you understand what I mean."

Finding that his aunt's opinion of Mr. Harold Lingford was in fact a correct one, Sebastian felt he understood perfectly.

"Did you tell Dr. Eccrington all this?" he asked.

"Oh yes. And he did not mind a bit. He said we were wise to change our names, and he assured us that I would be known simply as James Macalister in the school. He's an awfully decent sort of man, sir, and Mrs. Eccrington is a stunner."

They had by this time reached Bridge Street, and it did not take long to find the doctor's brightly polished brass plate winking under the lantern that hung above his door. Fortunately he was at home, and when he heard what had happened he did not seem surprised.

"It is Mrs. Snow, the milliner," he said, as he fetched his bag from a bench in the hall and shrugged himself into an overcoat before coming out on the steps to join them. "The woman is not strong, and the last time she had one of these fainting fits I warned her not to lift down any of those heavy bales of silk and velvet by herself. She was to leave that sort of thing to her assistants, or her maid, Polly. Wasn't Miss Fosbery there tonight, boy?" he demanded, turning rather fiercely on James.

"There did not seem to be anybody there, sir, except the poor woman on the floor and the maid who came running out to ask my sister's help," said James. "I think there was a bale of some colored material on top of her, though, because the first thing my sister did was to throw it off and find out if she was still breathing."

"Mrs. Snow is a very stupid woman," said the doctor, an energetic man with an air of authority. "The next time she lifts down one of those bales by herself she may not be breathing by the time she is found."

They arrived at the shop, and though he knew he must miss his early train to London, Sebastian told James to cut along back to school.

"I will see your sister back to the station later," he said. James ran off greatly relieved, and Sebastian followed the doctor into the shop, fascinated by the little scene in front of him.

Vicky, with the cape she had been wearing folded to make a pillow for Mrs. Snow, was kneeling beside her, her gloves and hat thrown on top of a bale of purple silk nearby. She was wearing her gray silk dress, and under the gaslight in the shop her hair was ash-fair.

During her brother's absence she had told Polly to close the shutters outside the shop windows, as they did not want a curious crowd gathering there. The gas lamp above the window had also been extinguished and the shop door closed, and at Vicky's request Polly had fetched a lighted candle from the kitchen. The little maid was horrified when the strange young lady calmly removed a scarlet feather from one of Mrs. Snow's best bonnets to hold it in the candle flame for a minute before holding it smoking under the milliner's nose. It had little effect, however, and the destruction of the feather only caused the lady on the floor to sigh and turn her head slightly away.

Encouraged by these signs of returning life, Vicky took her hands in hers and began to rub them briskly, sending Polly to fetch a blanket to wrap around her mistress.

She was still on her knees rubbing her patient's hands when the doctor arrived. She looked up with relief at his arrival, not at first seeing Sebastian behind him, and she waited until Dr. Warren had taken her place beside the unconscious woman. He noticed with approval the makeshift pillow under her head and that the tight collar of her dress had been loosened.

After a cursory examination he said that she must be taken upstairs to her bed, and Sebastian stepped forward to offer his help. Vicky stared at him, taken aback as seeing him there, and he went on hurriedly, "I told your brother to go back to school, and that I would see you to the station later on, Miss—"

"Macalister," she said quickly as he paused. "That was

kind of you, sir. I would not have liked my brother to be late on his first night at the grammar school."

Sebastian bowed and joined the doctor. "If I take her head and shoulders and you take her feet, Dr. Warren," he said, "I think we can manage her between us. She does not look very heavy."

"Polly, go in front of us and show us the way with that candle of yours, my dear," said the doctor. "I know these stairs. They are awkward and narrow."

They got her up the stairs between them, Polly lighting the way to her mistress's bedroom, a surprisingly large apartment next to an even larger apartment overlooking the street. They laid her down on her bed, and Vicky joined them there, while the doctor pulled the coverlet over the still-unconscious woman.

"I do not quite know what to do," he said, speaking to Vicky almost as if she were in charge of the situation. "She should have somebody reliable to sit up with her tonight." He turned to Polly. "Isn't there a cook here?" he asked.

"Oh yes, sir, but she's in the kitchen trembling like a leaf. I dursn't ask 'er to sit up wiv the missus. She'd have one of her turns."

"Heaven forbid." The doctor was evidently acquainted with the extent of Cook's turns. "What about Miss Fosbery, then? She lives on the premises, doesn't she?"

"Oh yes, sir, but she's been away to Clapham since Wednesday to be at 'er uncle's funeral, and she's not coming back till Monday."

"She will come back to another funeral if we are not careful." The doctor mulled over the problem aloud. "The work girls have all gone, of course."

"They go early, five o'clock of a Saturday," agreed Polly. "And Miss Silcocks and Mrs. Bellon don't live in like. Couldn't I sit up wiv 'er, sir? Anything I kin do fur the missus, only tell me and I'll do it. Wunnerful kind she's allus been to me, ever since I come to 'er when I were ten year old."

Vicky glanced at the maid with an expression of wonder. Ten years old seemed a tender age to be sent out as a servant.

"I am afraid it is too much of a responsibility for you, Polly, my dear," said the doctor kindly. "There are drops to be measured out carefully and given her directly she recovers consciousness, and so on." He paused, and it was then that Vicky made the offer that was to settle her future.

"Would you like me to sit up with her, Dr. Warren?" she said. "There is nothing important to require my immediate return to London now that my brother is at school. My time is my own, and if necessary I need not return until Monday."

"It is very good of you to offer your help in this way, and in fact it is what I could wish for most," said the doctor, showing considerable surprise, however. "But will not your relatives or friends be anxious about you?"

"I have neither relatives nor friends there," she said with a slight smile. She glanced at Sebastian. "If this gentleman is returning to London tonight, perhaps he would be so good as to call at my lodgings in Sackville Street and tell my landlady that I shall not be back for a day or two. That is, if it would not take him too much out of his way?" she added.

"I will do it with pleasure if you will give me the number of the house in Sackville Street," Sebastian said gravely.

She gave it to him with composure, as she would have done to a stranger, and as he left her in the milliner's shop and made his way to the station to catch the next train, he could not help comparing this very self-possessed young woman with the girl who had asked his advice at her coming-out ball at Costerley, and who, only last Sunday, had looked after his mother and sister, puzzled by their coolness. Then she had still been a young girl, happy to enjoy life with her mother's old friend, rather charming with her pretty clothes and her puzzled dark eyes.

There was no puzzlement now in those eyes, nor in her face. She knew what she intended to do and she would do it, and it occurred to him as he traveled back to London that in the short space of a week Vicky Lingford had grown into an extremely attractive woman.

Chapter Six

"Your name is Macalister?" Dr. Warren said after he had left drops and directions with Vicky and packed his bag ready to go.

"Yes. Victoria Macalister."

"Your brother is at the grammar school here?"

"Yes. He has been at a school in London, but he was not happy there, and our lawyer thought it would be better for his health if he could be accepted down here in Westborough. Our lawyer, who is responsible for my brother's education, has a very high opinion of the school."

"It is an excellent school. But have you no parents, then?"

"They are both dead." There was a note of hardness in her voice, and he did not pursue the subject. He returned to the grammar school, saying that he had two sons there himself and he would tell them to show young Macalister round.

"That will be very kind of you."

After he had gone, with Polly's help Vicky got Mrs. Snow undressed and into her nightdress, moving her gently and with great care. The milliner seemed to be breathing rather more easily when they had finished, and Polly went down to the kitchen to fetch a shovel of hot ashes with which to start a fire in the bedroom, accompanied by Cook, a large stout lady who said that when she had seen Mrs. Snow drop down like that she had come over all of a shake.

"It's me nerves, Miss," she said. "Never could bear the sight of illness, dear, ever since me dad was brought 'ome dead after being kicked by an 'orse in the 'igh Street."

Having satisfied her curiosity about Vicky and being assured that she was not the sort of young lady to give much trouble, she went away downstairs, and later on a plate of bread and butter and a pot of tea was brought up by Polly for Vicky's supper before Cook went off to bed.

"If the missus wakes in the night and you wants anything

fur 'er, Miss, put your 'ead out of the door and 'oller," she said. "I'm just above you in the attics, and you needn't be afraid of waking Cook. She sleeps like the dead, she do."

Vicky promised. "But I do not suppose I shall need help, and I shall not call you unless I do," she added, smiling. "We have got to face Miss Fosbery on Monday."

"Lor' bless you, Miss, you needn't be frit of her. Most like she'll 'ave the high-strikes, but not much worse'n that."

After Polly had gone to her attic the place seemed very quiet. Even the few horses and carriages passing outside did not seem to make the clatter of the London ones. She kept herself awake by getting up and walking up and down the room every now and then, and it was when she was doing this at about three o'clock in the morning that a surprised if weak voice spoke from the bed.

"Who are you, if you please?" it said. "And what are you doing in my room? And who had that fire lighted?"

Vicky turned quickly and came to the bed, smiling her pleasure.

"You are better!" she exclaimed. "I am so glad. You fainted, and my brother fetched Dr. Warren, and he and another gentleman carried you up here, where Polly and I put you to bed."

"But why are you here? Where did you come from? Were you wanting to buy a bonnet?"

"No. I am a stranger in the town. My brother, who is at the grammar school, was seeing me back to the railway station and I had crossed the road to look at the bonnets in your window, when Polly ran out and begged me to come in and help her. As it was not urgent that I should return to London tonight and the doctor thought you should not be left, we arranged that I should sit up with you and stay here until Miss Fosbery returns on Monday. The doctor said you were not to move from your bed until he comes to see you again."

Mrs. Snow did not seem to think much of that. "I suppose he will scold me," she said resignedly.

"I daresay he will," said Vicky cheerfully. "He said he had forbidden you to lift anything heavy from the shelves, and there you were, with a great bale of silk on top of you, in a dead faint." She turned in a businesslike way to the small table by the bed. "Do you feel able to take this medicine that the doctor left? I will put my arm under your pillow and raise you a little. We will try the drops first."

She measured them with care and raised her patient so skillfully that Mrs. Snow seemed less concerned as she laid her back gently on the pillows again.

"You did that as if you were accustomed to doing it," she remarked in a softer tone.

"I used to be allowed to help my mother when I was a little girl," Vicky told her.

"Was she ill then?"

"Very ill. She died when I was twelve, seven years ago."

"So you are nineteen now? You look older." She turned her head on the pillow. "Will you stay with me for the rest of tonight?"

"I have every intention of doing so." Vicky took the hand that was held out to her and held it in hers, glad to feel the warmth returning to it, until Mrs. Snow slept. She was a nice-looking woman, gray-haired, her face marked with the kindness that Vicky learned later was extended to all who worked for her.

When she was asleep Vicky freed her hand and sat by the window, until the dawn rose over the castle. She pulled the shutters open a crack and watched it, wondering what the future would hold for herself and if Mr. Larkin would be able to find her employment not too far away from Westborough, so that she could see James sometimes. She supposed she would have to go out as a companion, and not all old ladies were so charming and thoughtful as Lady Taversham, and even she gave Miss Sedge an active life of it. Not that Miss Sedge complained. She was always ready to run upstairs for knitting wools and spectacles, and books that had been left upstairs when they should have been downstairs. She wondered if she would have the patience to be an old lady's companion.

It was a depressing thought, only softened by the beauty of the sun's rays behind the old gray castle on top of the hill. They were turning it and everything else to rose color, and beneath the castle a group of beech trees that had not yet shed their golden leaves were turned to copper.

Plumes of smoke began to rise from the chimneys in the town as fires were lighted in kitchens and breakfast rooms, and she heard Polly moving about in her room above as if she too were on her way to light the kitchen fire and get a kettle boiling.

As the light grew over the castle and the city and reached

the cathedral spire in the midst of it, Vicky suddenly wished that she did not have to go back to London on Monday, and that she could make a home for James and herself in Westborough. Her thoughts too went to Sebastian Sellinge. How careful he had been—no doubt warned by James—not to show that he had met her before! There was cold comfort in the thought, however: no doubt he had no wish to be acknowledged as a friend of Paul Lingford's children.

The day passed quietly, Mrs. Snow sleeping a great deal and Polly coming in and out with trays of custards and port wine for the invalid, and at midday a generous helping of the Sunday roast beef for her nurse.

At eight o'clock on Monday morning there came the sound of running feet in the street below and a side door being opened and girls' voices raised in laughter and chatter until they were hushed by Cook.

After that heavy boots crept up an uncarpeted staircase to a corridor that seemed to be situated at the back of the house, but quiet as they were Mrs. Snow awoke and heard them.

"Those are my work girls," she told Vicky as she drew back the curtains and opened the shutters on a rather gray morning. "They always arrive at eight punctual. I won't have them late, and they know if they are they will not be able to leave at seven at night." She added with some concern that Vicky looked tired. "You have not taken your clothes off or lain down for one moment, have you?"

Vicky told her she had had a little sleep, sitting in the armchair by the fire, and apologized for her untidy appearance, as she had no brush or comb with her to do her hair. She felt, however, that she could wait until Miss Fosbery arrived to take her place.

Miss Fosbery arrived with the junior assistant, Miss Silcocks, soon after the work girls, and she came upstairs at once to hear all about the happenings of Saturday night, reproaching herself for not having come back sooner, but showing no signs of the hysterics that Polly had foretold.

Mrs. Bellon, the corsetière, then joined them around Mrs. Snow's bed, and remarked how fortunate it had been that Miss Macalister was passing at the time. "My dear Mrs. Snow," she said, "you might have laid there and died."

"I ought never to have stayed so long," put in Miss Fosbery. "I had a feeling that something might go wrong." She appealed to Vicky. "You know how you have such feelings, dear?"

"Me mam had a feeling like that," said Miss Silcocks. "It was the night me dad dropped down dead outside the Castle Arms."

"You go downstairs and start getting the shop ready, Miss Silcocks," said Miss Fosbery severely. "We don't want to waste time gossiping, do we?"

Miss Silcocks disappeared with an injured air, and Mrs. Snow remarked that as Miss Macalister had been sitting up with her for two nights she would appreciate a wash in Miss Fosbery's room while Mrs. Bellon sat with her while she had her breakfast.

Vicky was shown at once into the room on the other side of the upstairs parlor. Miss Fosbery's bedroom was very neat and tidy, with a muslin-draped dressing table and a honeycomb white cotton quilt on the brass bedstead. Polly quickly brought her a can of hot water, standing it in the flowered china basin on the washstand and covering it with a clean towel. She also provided her with a clean brush. "It's one of the missus's, Miss," she told her. "She allus has her brushes washed every day, does the missus."

Vicky thanked her, and left to herself she got out of her clothes to wash, shook the creases out of her gray silk dress, and having dressed again twisted her hair in its knot at the back of her head and felt very much better. She felt better still when she returned to Mrs. Snow's room to relieve Mrs. Bellon and found that Cook had sent up a breakfast of freshly boiled eggs and toast and tea for her breakfast.

Mrs. Snow was sitting up in bed consuming a similar breakfast and looked a great deal more ready to face the doctor when he arrived.

"As soon as he has gone you will be free to return to London, dear," she told Vicky. "But before you go you are to go into the shop downstairs and choose the best bonnet you fancy there. It will be a present from me for all you have done."

Vicky thanked her but assured her that she needed no more bonnets. "We will see what the doctor has to say," she added.

Dr. Warren examined Mrs. Snow, scolded her gently and told her that he did not want her to sleep alone for another night or two.

"I know you have a little brass bell beside your bed that you can ring if you want Polly or Miss Fosbery," he said. "But they may not hear it, and you might not be able to find it in the dark." He glanced at Vicky. "I suppose this young lady could not spare another couple of nights and sleep in your room?" he suggested. "There is a nice long settee in your parlor next door, and if it were to be moved in here I think she could stretch herself out on it, tall as she is, and snatch a few hours' sleep."

Mrs. Snow looked questioningly at Vicky. "I do not like to trespass on your kindness any more," she said. "But of course I cannot expect Miss Fosbery to work in the shop all day and sit up with me all night. And the boy and Polly will make nothing of moving the settee in here. But you want to go back to London today, do you not, dear?"

Vicky said she was in no hurry, as long as she might write to her landlady and her lawyer, and added that she thought the settee would make an excellent bed for her. When approached, Miss Fosbery was delighted to lend her a nightgown, wrapper and slippers for the night, and Vicky wrote her letters telling Mrs. Norris and Mr. Larkin not to expect her until the following Thursday.

Mrs. Snow was happy to have her with her in the daytime, although she did not talk a great deal. As for Miss Fosbery, she was filled with gratitude.

"I do not know how I should have managed had you not been here," she told Vicky. "Miss Silcock—our junior assistant—is leaving at Christmas, and we have a great many orders to be finished before she goes. And Mrs. Bellon is in such request with her corsets that I do not like to ask her to sleep in at night."

Mrs. Bellon was a somewhat imposing lady, portly of figure and round of face, with a lace cap hiding the widening center parting of her graying hair, and a worn pincushion attached to the waist of her black alpaca apron.

The back staircase led to the work girls' quarters, in which were four workrooms, two of which had sewing machines devoted to the making of Mrs. Bellon's corsets, and when Vicky glanced at them she did not wonder, as the seams in them were almost too many to count, what with the boning and the gussets and the opening at the back for lacing.

"You have no idea the lengths young ladies will go to make out they have only eighteen-inch waists," she told Vicky.

"They never mention the gap at the back where the laces let them out to twenty or twenty-two. But there we are. We must satisfy and humor our young ladies, must we not?"

During the day Mrs. Snow still slept a great deal, but at night Vicky, clad in one of Miss Fosbery's voluminous flannel nightgowns and a red wrapper, with blankets and a pillow to turn the settee into a bed, slept most of the night as well. In the dawn, however, thoughts came back to worry her, as she woke and lay wondering what she should do to earn a living.

The more she thought of it the more she felt she hated her father, who had deserted her in such a callous fashion. He must have known that his brother would never acknowledge her and her brother as any relations of his: he had thought by leaving him no option he would force him to give them a home. And what a home it would have been, she told herself bitterly, taking charity from a man like Harold Lingford.

By Wednesday, Mrs. Snow was very much better and insisted on getting up in the afternoon to sit in her dressing gown by the fire, and as they sat there together she asked Vicky why she was in lodgings in London and if it was because she had no home.

Vicky admitted that their home was gone, and on a sudden impulse decided to tell the milliner the truth about her parents. "My mother did indeed die when I was twelve," she said, "but my father is still alive, although to my brother and to me he *is* dead. A few weeks ago he left England suddenly, without leaving me a penny."

"He was in trouble?" asked Mrs. Snow quietly. She did not seem to be at all shocked.

"I am afraid he was."

"I have had such trouble myself," said Mrs. Snow sadly. "My son—my only child—robbed our oldest friend of one hundred pounds. Instead of prosecuting him, however, our friend gave him his passage money to America, and a few years later he died out there."

"I am sorry." Vicky felt her own troubles fade a little beside such a tragedy. "What happened?"

"I could not find out, but our friend went out to America himself, and he could not tell me much when he returned, except that Charlie had got into bad company." Polly had brought them a tray of tea, and as Vicky poured her out another cup she asked who was paying for her brother to go to the grammar school if their father had left them without money.

Vicky explained the conditions under which their grandfather had promised to educate James, and Mrs. Snow agreed that it made it difficult for Miss Macalister to claim any interest for herself from the old gentleman.

"That is why I am going to see my lawyer when I return to London," explained Vicky. "To ask him to find me employment of some sort. I am afraid it is not possible to discover any in Westborough, though this is where I should like to be most. I can only hope it will not be too far away."

Mrs. Snow thought it over, sipping her tea by the fire in the gathering dusk. The girl was a lady, and few chances of employment were open to ladies. Companion or governess— it would have to be one or the other.

Then suddenly she thought of Miss Silcocks, leaving to be married at Christmas. A superior young lady serving in her place in the shop would be the very thing. Miss Silcocks was never so refined as Miss Fosbery—in fact, Mrs. Bellon had once called her common to her face.

She said hesitatingly, "What sort of employment are you seeking?"

"I do not know." Vicky tried to smile. "I feel I would take anything—I would be a scullery maid even—rather than take a situation as an old lady's companion, but I suppose that is the only thing open to me."

Mrs. Snow's eyes went to the girl's slender figure, to the expensive dress, to the knot of fair hair at the nape of her neck, and she almost dismissed what she was going to say. Then she thought: Why not? She might take it for a time. She said aloud, "You said you would be a scullery maid. Well, I have a situation not quite as low as that to offer you, but it is yours if you would like to take it, shall we say, on a month's trial. Miss Silcocks is leaving at Christmas, and if you would like to take a situation as an assistant in the shop you could start there next Monday. Naturally I will have to discuss it with Mrs. Bellon and Miss Fosbery, and if they agree there would be time for you to learn what would be required of you in the millinery department. You will then be able to make up your mind if you would care to take Miss Silcocks's place permanently after Christmas."

For a moment Vicky was too astonished to speak, then she

took a deep breath, and suddenly her eyes began to shine and she gave a little laugh of pure pleasure.

"Do you really mean that, Mrs. Snow?" she asked.

"I would not suggest it to you, my dear, if I did not mean it."

"Then, if Mrs. Bellon and Miss Fosbery consent, I will accept with pleasure." Her own world had turned its back on her, and here was a new one willing to take her in. She had wished for obscurity, and where could she obtain it more easily than here, serving as an assistant in a milliner's shop in a country town? When she had visited the big London stores had she ever given a glance at the young women who had served her? She would be simply one of the assistants in Mrs. Snow's shop, and Vicky Lingford would have ceased to exist.

Before Mrs. Bellon left that evening she was asked to step upstairs with Miss Fosbery to Mrs. Snow's bedroom, where the three ladies discussed Vicky's future.

While they talked in low tones behind the closed door, Vicky went into the large parlor next door to admire the ready-made corsets, the work of Mrs. Bellon's hands, that stood about the room on stands. They were named respectively the Duchess, the Countess, and Her Ladyship, and were boned and gusseted to a remarkable degree, the seams and gussets reaching from below the hips to under the armpits. They confined the bust, the waist and the hips, they expanded the figure here and contracted it there, and Vicky did not wonder that the machines in the workrooms were kept so busy all day until ordered garments were finished, when they still had to be trimmed by hand with Valenciennes or torchon lace.

Mrs. Bellon had served an apprenticeship of seven years in a London corseterie, and Vicky could appreciate the skill with which the corsets in the parlor had been made, while she also appreciated that Mrs. Bellon's apprenticeship had given her an authority that Mrs. Snow and Miss Fosbery appreciated.

It was at Mrs. Bellon that she looked most therefore when she was asked to return to the bedroom.

"Mrs. Snow has told us that you are willing to take a temporary situation in the salesroom downstairs, and if you are efficient and you like the situation enough you will be prepared to stay on permanently when Miss Silcocks leaves," she said. She then went on to say that while they all felt it would be an advantage to have a refined young lady like herself in Miss Silcocks's place—who was, she felt bound to say, sometimes downright vulgar—they were not quite sure if Miss Macalister realized what would be expected of her.

"I am very willing to learn," said Vicky.

"I daresay you are, Miss Macalister. Indeed, if you had put on any airs I would have advised Mrs. Snow not to consider you for one moment," said Mrs. Bellon severely. "But there is the question of your dress, for one thing."

"My dress?" Vicky glanced down at the gray silk dress, more than a little creased from her having spent two nights in it.

"Yes, your dress, Miss Macalister. Mrs. Snow could not allow you to serve downstairs in a dress like that. I have suggested that something plainer would be more suitable, and Miss Fosbery tells us that Mr. Cumberledge has some ready-made dresses in his window—quite a new venture—and that there is a black silk one there for seventeen shillings. She thinks it would do very nicely for you to wear in the shop, and if you will purchase it she will be pleased to alter it for you to wear when you start work on Monday."

Vicky thought of her dwindling sovereigns and said she would certainly purchase the dress if it was thought to be more proper wear in the shop.

In the end it was Miss Fosbery who bought the dress for her, and when she returned with the black bodice and skirt and Vicky tried them on, she knew at once what Mrs. Bellon meant. The country-made dress was a poor imitation of the London fashion. It had a high neck and long tight-fitting sleeves, but the bodice and skirt were plain and badly cut. Miss Fosbery pinned it to fit, however, and when it was done it was certainly much more like the dress of a young woman who served in a shop. And the black alpaca overall that covered it was exactly right.

Vicky was delighted with it. Even if Emily were to walk into the milliner's now she doubted if she would recognize her.

As she looked at her reflection in the cheval glass in the parlor upstairs she told herself: Now, Miss Lingford, you are dead indeed, and thank heaven for it. I wonder what lies ahead for Miss Macalister? At least nothing could be quite as bad as what occurred to Miss Lingford.

Chapter Seven

The milliner's shop was old-fashioned. The windows were small and bow-fronted, and Mrs. Snow had resisted the advice offered from time to time by Mr. Cumberledge, the owner of what was locally termed the Westborough Whiteley's three doors away, to replace them with a large one of plate glass, such as those that enclosed his shop windows from top to bottom.

Inside the shop too she had kept the downstairs showroom, with mirrors where ladies could see the bonnets and hats they fancied tried on Miss Silcocks and decide if they would suit them or whether they should be trimmed in different fashions, before copies were made and sent for their approval.

A door on the landing at the top of the stairs that led to the corseterie showroom shut it off from the back corridor and the workrooms, and beyond the four workrooms at the very end of the corridor was a fifth room that was used for holding spare dummies for displaying corsets and stands for hats and bonnets, and this little room was to be cleared of its contents for Vicky's use.

It was a bare little room, but there was just enough space for a bed, one chair, a corner washstand with an enamel bowl and jug, and a tiny painted chest of drawers holding a swing mirror with a great deal of mercury gone from the back.

It was enough, however, to show her if she had put her hat on straight when she went out, and that her hair was tidy when she went downstairs to have her meals with Miss Fosbery and Miss Silcocks in the room that served as a dining parlor after the work girls had finished theirs.

On Thursday morning Mrs. Snow was so much better that Vicky felt no qualms in leaving her, and she set off for London to repack her trunk with the plainest of garments, to settle up with Mrs. Norris, and then to see Mr. Larkin before leaving for Westborough for good on Friday morning.

It was only natural that after she had gone Mrs. Snow, acting on advice from Mrs. Bellon and Miss Fosbery, sent a note down to Mr. Cumberledge, asking him to be good enough to step around that evening to give her the benefit of his advice.

When he was fourteen William Cumberledge had been apprenticed for seven years to a London warehouse near St. Paul's. At that time his father, Josiah, owned a small draper's shop in Westborough High Street, and before launching out on anything more ambitious sent his son to be trained in the ways and methods of London drapers. Fortunately William was sharp-witted as well as sharp-eyed, and he used his ears and eyes to some purpose. He soon learned the trades that paid best, and one of the most flourishing was that of the supply of family mourning.

For the first year after a husband's death his widow had to wear best dresses entirely covered with crape, bonnets of crape with long veils, parasols covered with crape, and parametta mantles lined with silk and trimmed with crape. For the second year they were expected to wear black dresses with crape in tucks, and during the two whole years they wore caps with streamers, and collars and cuffs of muslin and lawn, while their families remained for seven months in black crape, six in black, and three in slight mourning. Then for a relative outside the family there were black-edged handkerchiefs, and black ribbons were threaded through little girls' underclothes.

Indeed upon a death in a family the whole household went into mourning, including the servants, and every kind of relation was mourned in some way, which made the business of supplying mourning a very profitable one.

It so happened that Westborough was badly supplied with mourning facilities, and when he came home from London in the beginning of 1861 the first thing young William did was to persuade his father to buy a derelict leather-goods shop next door and convert it into a general mourning and mantle warehouse.

"It was so fortunate for William that the Prince Consort died just after his father had constructed his mourning warehouse," William's mama was apt to say to her friends, almost as if it had received the seal of royal patronage.

There had been no doubt in the town that William Cumberledge was a very go-ahead young man, and when his father died, leaving him in possession of his shop, gradually the premises of William Cumberledge, General Outfitters and Drapers, extended to several more businesses, including those of carpets and furniture and hardware.

At forty, Mr. Cumberledge had developed into a rather tubby little man with sleek dark hair, a flowing dark mustache, and a pleasing way with his customers. He had early fixed upon Miss Fosbery as a suitable partner for his future domestic life, but in the meantime, allowing for Mrs. Snow's delicacy, he was content that an understanding should exist between them. He took her once a month to the Haberdashers' Meeting, and on Sundays for a walk before going home to the rooms above the shop where his mother had tea ready for them. She was a good-natured old lady with an affection for William's intended.

On Thursday evening he listened to what Mrs. Snow and Miss Fosbery had to tell him about Vicky and considered the matter deeply before replying.

"There's two things as strikes me as being queer about Miss Macalister," he said then gravely. "You say she is a lady, and that her clothes is fashionable, and her brother has left a good school in London 'because he was unhappy there' to join our grammar school in Westborough. Why did he leave his London school so sudden? Boys don't go to school to be happy, Mrs. Snow. Most of 'em 'ate school, but their parents don't take 'em away from a fust-class London school and put 'em to our grammar without some other reason."

"She told me what I believe to be the truth about herself in strict confidence," said Mrs. Snow gently. "I know I can trust you and Miss Fosbery to let it go no further. Her mother died when she was twelve, seven years ago, and although her father is alive she and her brother regard him as being dead."

"Indeed? Why, what has he done?"

"She told me he left the country a few weeks ago without leaving her a penny piece."

"Ah, now I begin to understand." Mr. Cumberledge pulled at the ends of his mustache. "You say she is well dressed?"

"Very fashionably dressed, Mr. Cumberledge," said Miss Fosbery. "Quite the lady."

"So that it looks as if her dresses have been supplied by London dressmakers and shops where no doubt her father had accounts." Mr. Cumberledge smiled and shook his head. "You see them sometimes, gentlemen what you think are of substance and wealth. You let 'em run up bills, counting on their position to reimburse you, even if they're late in settling accounts when you send 'em in. And then sudden-like they're up and off abroad and you find they're wanted for debt, and if they had stayed in the country they'd hev been put in prison most like for owing thousands of pounds."

"Oh no!" Mrs. Snow was shocked. And then she remembered that Miss Macalister had admitted that her father had been in trouble.

The next thing Mr. Cumberledge wanted to know was who was paying for her brother if she had no money, and while Miss Fosbery gazed at him admiringly for his sharpness Mrs. Snow told him about the grandfather in Edinburgh and how his granddaughter dare not apply to him for help in case he refused to pay out any more for James.

"She shows more consideration for her relations than they do for her," was Mr. Cumberledge's remark when he heard this.

"But as Dr. Eccrington has taken the boy at the grammar school without question, do you not feel that is recommendation enough for his sister?" asked Mrs. Snow timidly.

Mr. Cumberledge was not entirely satisfied about that.

"Could not Mrs. Snow write to Miss Macalister's lawyer?" asked Miss Fosbery brightly. "Miss Macalister wrote to him on Monday last and asked me if one of the work girls would post the letter for her, but I said I would post it myself with some of mine. And I took the liberty of copying down the name and address before I went to the post office. It was addressed to a Mr. Larkin in a firm of lawyers in Lincoln's Inn Fields."

"That is the gentleman to write to, then," said Mr. Cumberledge, relieved. "He will tell Mrs. Snow if there is anything against her, and coming as a stranger, nice as she may appear to be, you cannot be too careful, ma'am."

Mrs. Snow, after protesting that Miss Macalister was a sweet kind girl and she could not imagine her ever doing anything wrong, was at last persuaded to write to Mr. Larkin for a reference. Mr. Cumberledge posted her letter in time to catch the last post, and on Sunday morning a reply was received that set all their minds at rest. She read it to Miss Fosbery and Mr. Cumberledge on Sunday afternoon, while Vicky was out with her brother.

Circumstances over which his client had no control, Mr.

Larkin wrote, had forced Miss Macalister to face the necessity of earning her living. She came from a good family and he had no hesitation in recommending her for any situation that Mrs. Snow might care to offer her.

Vicky was rather apprehensive at first as to what James would think of his sister's taking a situation as a shop assistant, but she need not have worried. After an astonished and incredulous look at her he burst out laughing. "I say," he said, "what a lark! Where is the shop, Sis?"

She told him it was the milliner's and that he would not have to be ashamed of her because it was not likely that any of the grammar school boys would want to buy anything from a ladies' hat and bonnet shop.

"But most of their fathers are tradesmen anyway," he said. "And very good sort of fellows they are, too. Now if I'd still been at St. Chad's—" He paused with a comical look at her.

"You would have been sent to Coventry forever!" she said, and they laughed together over the thought. He asked how much she was to be paid, and when she told him fifteen shillings a week he declared it to be riches.

"I am to have my board and keep free," she went on. "So that it is not at all bad. I shall save up and when you have a half-holiday we'll have a nice dinner again at the Mitre."

When she said goodbye to him at the school gates it was with the promise that she would see him again the following week.

"Miss Fosbery says I am allowed Sunday afternoons off," she said, smiling. "So they will be kept most jealously for you. In the winter we will go for walks as we have done today, and when summer comes we will venture farther afield."

On Monday morning Miss Fosbery submitted her to a critical examination, tying the alpaca overall over the ready-made dress herself, and approving of her hair.

Miss Fosbery, a thin lady with a carefully refined way of speaking and a pair of pale-blue eyes, had hair of bright chestnut, with a false fringe in front so that she would not have to cut her own hair. Vicky's naturally wavy fringe she considered attractive, although she thought a false one of a slightly darker color might be better. "It would not be easy to match, however," she said. "It is so fair that it is almost white, isn't it?"

Vicky said she would prefer not to wear a false fringe. She

had heard of a lady whose maid had not pinned hers in place securely and it had fallen into her soup at a dinner party.

Miss Silcocks, who had been listening entranced, here burst out in a loud laugh, and Miss Fosbery turned on her indignantly and told her to fetch some of the new bonnets and place them on stands in the window instead of listening to other people's conversations.

"She will laugh so loud," she said in a whisper behind Miss Silcocks's back. "When improvers was fashionable a year or two back, some of our ladies would come into the shop with them fixed inside the backs of their dresses. They was real 'ideous and when they come in I had to send Miss Silcocks off for something from upstairs while I attended to them myself. I was afraid she'd offend them by bursting out laughing as she did just now."

"But even improvers were better than crinolines, don't you think?" ventured Vicky.

"Oh, I agree, dear. Nasty dangerous things, them crinnies. Vulgar, too. Why, I've seen a lady get into her kerridge in the High Street and when she lifted her crinny you could see her drawers!"

She praised Vicky's dress once more, saying that Mr. Cumberledge told her ready-made dresses were sold quite frequently to ladies in London. "From the perfessional classes, you know, dear, what has not got the means to employ London dressmakers. Why, a Court dressmaker, Mr. Cumberledge says, will charge as much as twelve shillings and sixpence for making a lady's dress."

Vicky was unable to comment on this, as her upbringing had not brought her into contact with the charges of Court dressmakers.

That first week behind the counter at the milliner's was one fraught with ignorance and the desire to please, and she was encouraged at the end of it to be told by Miss Fosbery that she had done quite well.

She found time to write a few lines to Lady Taversham, keeping what she had to say to a minimum. She had found employment in Westborough and would be able to see James frequently at the grammar school, to which he had moved from St. Chad's. She wanted to add that she hoped they would meet again soon and could not. She wanted to put her address at the top of her letter and left it blank. She had made up her mind to disappear from sight and sound of her friends, and she must hold to that decision, even if it included dear Lady Taversham. So having given as little information as possible, she just signed herself "Your always loving Vicky."

"There," she said, as she folded the letter and put it in its envelope and addressed it. "That is done. I must forget her now and hope that in time she will forget me."

The little window of her room looked over the intervening roofs up toward the castle ruins, and somehow the strength of those old walls, ruined as they were, gave her too a feeling of strength. With her father had gone the dreadful Grammidges and their still more awful friends. There was no Costerley now. Those days had gone and gone for good.

When Lady Taversham received her letter, however, its reticence and air of finality touched her conscience. If the child was not living with her uncle, why did she not say so? And if he had found her a situation, as seemed likely from her letter, why not say what it was and give her address?

She thought of all the people who had known Vicky. Mrs. Sellinge she dismissed at once, and others who would be as eager to forget that they had ever been acquainted with Paul Lingford's daughter.

There was, of course, Sebastian Sellinge, who had been exceptionally courteous on the Sunday when his mother and sister had been so rude; he was level-headed and not likely to say as her son had done that she was wise not to encourage the girl.

She remembered Vicky's dark eyes, so like her mother's, expressive and beautiful, and her heart smote her afresh. She sent a slightly imperious summons to Mr. Sellinge at his rooms in Gray's Inn asking him to dine with her that evening at eight o'clock, and when he presented himself in Brook Street he found himself to be the only guest.

The dinner was excellent, however, and the wines of the best—her ladyship understood the entertainment of gentlemen—and afterward she took him into the small drawing room, Miss Sedge excusing herself tactfully and leaving them alone.

"I asked you to dine with me tonight, Mr. Sellinge," Lady Taversham said, "because I am hoping you have news of the young Lingfords. Has your mother or Emily heard from Vicky lately?"

Sebastian said he was sure they had not, although he did

not see as much of his family as when he'd lived in Brook Street.

She then handed him Vicky's letter, which he read with slightly lifted eyebrows.

"I suppose that uncle of hers down there has found her a situation?" said Lady Taversham questioningly.

"Oh no, he would not have done that." After a moment's hesitation Sebastian described his last meeting with Vicky and her brother and how James had told him that they had been utterly rejected by Harold Lingford. He added that when he left Vicky she had been offering to act as night nurse to a milliner in Westborough.

"A night nurse? What can you mean?" Lady Taversham was shocked, and he explained the situation and how the poor woman had been found unconscious on the floor of the shop.

"But somebody could have been found to sit up with her. Vicky need not have offered to do it in such an impetuous way. But of course that is her all over. She is much too impulsive."

"Quixotic," Sebastian suggested and smiled. "Do you not think, Lady Taversham, that she may have felt she needed time in which to think out what she was to do next? Her uncle had refused to take her in, she had very little money, and only Mr. Larkin to appeal to for help."

"She had me," said Lady Taversham indignantly. After a moment she went on in a quieter tone, "The day after she read that paragraph in the newspaper about her father she seemed to grow up. Until then she had been a pliable, charming girl, but overnight she changed into a young woman with a mind of her own. Did you not notice it when you saw her in Westborough?"

"Oh, certainly." His thoughts went back to the composed young woman he had left in the milliner's shop.

"I would dearly like to know what she is doing down there in Westborough all the same," complained her ladyship. "That stilted little letter tells me nothing. I am worried about her, Mr. Sellinge. Have you not an aunt in Westborough whom you visit occasionally?"

"I had been to see her when I last saw the Lingfords—or rather Macalisters, as they wish now to be called." He paused again and then continued more slowly, "I do not think Aunt Kitty would be able to help, and I would not ask her, because in my view I think these two young people *want* to disappear—as Lingfords, that is to say. And if two more young people have appeared in Westborough in the name of Macalister, and we raise a hue and cry after them, we might only succeed in revealing that which they most want to conceal—that they are the children of Paul Lingford. It might cause them to take flight again to some quite unknown destination, which would be even less satisfactory to friends who wish to help them."

"You appear to have thought it out more carefully than I have," said Lady Taversham. "And with more wisdom. Forgive me, Mr. Sellinge. I did not think of that side of it. Of course they must wish to hide from a world that holds their father in contempt. I can see now that we must move carefully in order to preserve their secret. But I wish all the same the next time you are in Westborough you will do your best to discover where Vicky is and what she is doing and if she needs help. My purse is at your disposal where she is concerned. I know I can trust you to be discreet."

"I will do my best." He told her that he had a trying case that promised to drag on for a few more weeks, but that at the end of that time he would go down to Westborough to see his aunt.

"I might inquire how the milliner progresses," he added, smiling. "Possibly she can tell me where Vicky—Miss Macalister—is now."

Lady Taversham noticed his use of the Christian name, and although she was glad she had sent for this usually reserved young man, she had seen the compassion in his face when he had stopped to speak to Vicky that Sunday morning, and she hoped his interest in the girl would not deepen into anything else later on.

A rising young barrister like Sebastian Sellinge could not permit himself the folly of falling in love with Paul Lingford's daughter.

The taint of the girl's father would not fail to touch him, and it would certainly ruin his career at the bar.

Paul Lingford had a great deal to answer for, and not the least the way in which his criminal behavior would always lie like a shadow over his children's lives.

But Vicky's short letter to herself had told her that she too was aware of it and that there was no way in which they could escape.

76

Chapter Eight

The first three weeks of Vicky's employment went by like a flash. She found herself beginning to enjoy the work, because it was all so different from anything to which she was accustomed.

Her acquaintances now were among entirely different people. The work girls had a bright "Good morning, Miss Macalister" for her when she came out of her room to go downstairs in the mornings, and she liked to hear their laughter and chatter and gossip as they gathered in the workrooms. It reminded her a little of the days at the select academy in Chiswick that she had attended with Emily.

James seemed to be settling down well at the grammar school, too. He had made friends with Dr. Warren's sons and had been asked out to tea at their house one Sunday afternoon.

It was now well into November and a lovely crisp afternoon, though cold. Vicky put on her gray silk dress and furlined cape and a little black bonnet and took herself for a walk alone in the Palace Gardens.

Every Sunday afternoon from two o'clock until dusk, winter and summer alike, the Bishop's Palace Gardens were open to the people of the town.

Naturally the Bishop's private gardens were enclosed with a high brick wall, and entrance there was gained only by invitation. Outside that wall in the days when bishops were princes of the church, there had been a spreading park, which was now laid out in spacious lawns and wide gravel paths, with fountains and flower beds and a large lake to the north of the palace. There were park benches placed at intervals along the paths, interspersed with notices asking the public to keep off the grass, informing them that no children's games were to be played there, and that it was not necessary to feed the ducks on the lake, the latter order always flagrantly disobeyed. They were also warned to keep away from the swans, which could be dangerous.

Nevertheless, in spite of these warnings that could have had a sobering effect upon those who wished to stroll there on a Sunday afternoon, the gardens remained popular with the townspeople of Westborough. They would conduct their families sedately along the gravel paths and around the lake, and in the summer they would make their way to one path higher than the rest from which it was possible to obtain a view of the Bishop's wife holding her garden parties on the lawns inside the high brick walls.

On this bright November day the leaves of the beech trees in the park had gone, leaving a carpet of coppery gold beneath them. The last of the dahlias were doing their best to survive the frosts that had touched their petals with brown, while the Michaelmas daisies were a bedraggled, sorry sight, waiting to be cut down by the gardeners the following week.

Vicky walked slowly, her cape held close against her, drawing in deep breaths of cold country air to her lungs.

When she came to the lake she found it to be more sheltered than the open park and chose a bench that was unoccupied and sat there for a few moments, watching the swans and ducks. She had been there only a little while when a gentleman came by, glanced at her, and then came back, lifting his hat.

"How do you do, Miss Macalister?" he said.

She looked up, startled. "Mr. Sellinge!" she exclaimed. "How did you find me?"

"Quite simply." He sat down beside her. "You wrote a little while ago to Lady Taversham, and your letter worried her. She asked me to dinner in order to find out if I could discover where you were, as you had given her no address. She knows that I do sometimes visit my aunt in the Close here. She also asked me to find out if I could discover the kind of employment you had undertaken in Westborough, and if all this appears to you to be unbearably interfering on my part I can only assure you that your old friend is extremely concerned about you."

"I suppose you made inquiries at the school?" Vicky said resentfully.

"I did not. I went to the milliner's in the High Street, and the maid told me you were living there, and that you were out walking. She thought you had gone to the Palace Gardens,

78

because you had asked her where they were situated." He frowned at her downcast face. "I suppose you are in lodgings at the milliner's?"

"No," she said, a note of defiance in her voice. "I am employed there as an assistant in the shop."

"What?" He could not hide his astonishment. "You cannot mean that!"

"But I do mean it." She got to her feet. "Come, let us walk to the gates. It is cold and they will soon be closing the gardens."

"But you cannot possibly be a shop assistant," he protested as he accompanied her. "You are a lady, and ladies do not take such situations."

"It is very kind of you to take so much trouble on Lady Taversham's behalf," she said crisply. "But I think you forget that I am Paul Lingford's daughter. The daughter, as anyone will tell you, of a man who is a common swindler. I know James and I have changed our name to Macalister, but the stain is there. I shall always feel smirched by it, and that is why I have not told even my dear old friend where I am."

As he remained silent she went on after a moment, "There is really no more to be said, Mr. Sellinge. I wrote to Lady Taversham to bid her goodbye, and I am sure she knew it. I am sorry she gave you the task of finding out where I am."

"And I am very glad she did. You cannot possibly continue in your present employment. No friend of yours would allow it."

"A friend of mine?" She laughed. "Mr. Sellinge, do you not understand that I wish to forget the friends I knew when I was Vicky Lingford as much as, I am sure in their hearts, they wish to forget me?"

"Lady Taversham has no intention of forgetting you."

She drew a sharp breath. "She will in time."

"And in the meantime you must find different employment."

"So you said before, but can you suggest anything from your store of wisdom?" Vicky's voice was heavy with sarcasm. "To be an old lady's companion, perhaps? Lady Taversham is a darling, but poor Miss Sedge showed me what I might expect from such a situation. 'Miss Sedge, will you please run upstairs and fetch my embroidery wools?' And when she came down again, 'Miss Sedge, I am sorry to trouble you again, but I think I must have left my spectacles up there somewhere.

Will you see if you can find them?' And then Pug had to be taken out, and the mud washed from his paws when he came in, and so it went on. I made up my mind then that if ever I had to earn my bread it would not be by being a lady's companion! And what else is there for me to do? I cannot go out as a governess. I am far too ignorant. At school I always sat at the bottom of the class. The only thing I enjoyed doing was writing essays, and who is going to pay me for writing essays?"

There seemed to be no answer to that, and as he remained silent she went on in a quieter tone:

"Mrs. Snow is kind and considerate. She accepts the fact that I must earn my living, and she is happy to employ me as an assistant. I am beginning to be quite clever at making bonnets, and I assure you that I am not likely to be recognized in a milliner's shop. In my plain black dress and overall I lose my identity completely. Nobody would look at me a second time, and I doubt if even you would know me if you entered the shop."

"Do not be too sure of that." They were nearing the gates, and he was frowning and unhappy. "Will you let me speak to my aunt about it? Will you come back with me now to meet her and confide in her? She may have friends who would be prepared to engage you."

"No." Vicky was quite decided. "Thank you very much, but I do not wish to meet your aunt, and I would not at all like to be employed by one of her friends. Do you not see what would happen? For a time all would be well, and then one day I would meet somebody I had known before—an old school acquaintance perhaps—and she would say, 'Are you not Vicky Lingford?' And immediately all the shame and horror and disgrace would come back."

She put her hand on his arm, and he was reminded of her coming-out ball and how they had stood on the terrace in the dawn of a summer day, while she asked his help. It was plain that this very determined young woman needed no help today.

"Please," she said, "do as I say, Mr. Sellinge. Do not tell your aunt anything about me, and do not tell Lady Taversham where I am living. You may, if you like, tell her how I am employed if you think it will not shock her too much. But please do not give her my address. Will you promise me that, Mr. Sellinge?"

The hand on his arm was small but firm, and the eyes that met his were resolute. He guessed at the torture she must have endured since her father left England, but he also knew that he and Lady Taversham must leave her to fight a lonely battle to regain her self-respect. To interfere, or to let Lady Taversham do so, would not only hurt her the more but might, as he had said to her old friend, drive her away from the haven she had found for herself and James.

"I will promise," he said. "And my name is Sebastian."

She shook her head. "I think it must remain Mr. Sellinge, don't you?" she said. And taking her hand from his arm she gave him a bright little smile that touched him deeply with its courage, said goodbye, and hurried away.

He was very silent over tea with his aunt, and she begged him not to take his work so seriously, thinking that it was a tiresome client that was worrying him. He caught an early train back to London, and in the morning he called on Lady Taversham to give her Vicky's message, steadfastly refusing to reveal her address.

"At least you can tell me what she is doing," she said at last.

"She said I might tell you that, although she was afraid it would shock you. She has taken a situation as an assistant in a milliner's shop."

"A milliner's shop? Vicky?" Her ladyship was horrified. "But my dear Mr. Sellinge, she cannot possibly do that."

"That was what I felt at first, but since then my feelings have changed. You see, she wants not only to forget but to be forgotten—at least for a time. And what is a better hiding place than a shop? Do you ever look at a shop assistant when you are ordering a bonnet or a gown?"

"Never." Lady Taversham's frown lifted, and she smiled suddenly, a smile that was full of charm and understanding. "It is the best hiding place in the world, as long as that odious uncle of hers does not find her out."

"I do not see what he can do if he does. He cannot make life uncomfortable for her without making it more so for himself. If he should ask Mrs. Snow to dismiss her she will want to know why, and what is to stop Vicky from telling her? No, I think his hands are tied."

However much Vicky wished to be forgotten, in the days that followed Sebastian found that he could not forget her easily. Her face, with its small determined chin, her dark eyes, now scornful, now laughing and defiant, haunted him. Her voice too and her slender figure, with her head held high, defying a critical, condemning world.

On her side the meeting with him on that Sunday had shaken her more than she had allowed him to see. She longed to go back to her little room and write a long letter to Lady Taversham, pouring out her heart to her, begging not to be forgotten.

She thought of the way she had dismissed Sebastian's suggestions for her future, and her mind went back to that other Sunday when Lady Taversham had spoken of him as chivalrous because he had walked home with them. She had taken that "chivalry" as being caused by pity for herself, and she had been angry with him for it, but now she saw that his action had also been intended to protect her old friend, and a new understanding replaced the resentment that she had continued to show him that afternoon.

In the first week in December a carriage stopped outside the milliner's shop and two young ladies alighted and came into the shop, and directly she saw them Mrs. Snow came hurrying from her office in the back parlor to greet them.

"Lady Eleanor, Miss Lingford, this is a great pleasure," she said. "What can I do for your ladyship? And for you, Miss Lingford?"

"Mrs. Snow," said the prettier of the two, Lady Eleanor Graham, "I must have a fur bonnet to match this jacket by next week at the latest. I know if I leave it until I go to London my London milliner will take at least a week before she matches the fur, and another to make it, and by that time I shall have set off for my grandfather's place for Christmas. We shall be going to Savering as usual, and I must have it before then."

"I hope his Grace is well, m'lady?"

"Except for the gout my grandfather is never ill."

Mrs. Snow examined the smart little fur jacket that her exalted young customer was wearing, and remarked that it was made of golden sealskin and of a most unusual color. "Very beautiful, but not very common, m'lady, and difficult to obtain. I know I have none in stock."

"But can you not get some for me? It is really important."

Mrs. Snow considered for a moment. Usually in such cases of emergency she would go herself to London to buy the fur, but she had been forbidden by Dr. Warren to risk train journeys in the winter. She wondered what she could do, because the young lady and her mother, the Marchioness of Evensbury, were her most valued customers. And then she caught sight of Vicky placing a black astrakhan hat in the window.

"Miss Macalister," she said, "come here, please."

Vicky came and was shown the fur and agreed that it was an unusual color.

"You know London well, do you not?" said her employer anxiously. "Have you ever been to Mr. Bradley's Arctic Fur Store in Chepstow Place?"

"Yes," Vicky answered without hesitation. "It is off the Bayswater Road." She had visited it only recently with Lady Taversham to match a favorite mantle where some of the fur had faded a little.

"You would be able to find the shop tomorrow, if I sent you there with a pattern to match this jacket? I think we may have some scraps in the iron box in my office. Go and see if you can find some."

Vicky went into the office and lifted the lid off the iron box containing lengths of furs and a strong smell of camphor, and after a few minutes' search came upon a scrap of golden sealskin. She returned with it, and Mrs. Snow held it against the jacket, and it was pronounced to be a perfect match.

Miss Silcocks was then called forward to try on some of the fur bonnets from the window so that her ladyship could select the one she liked best, and with promises from the milliner that the sealskin bonnet would be ready for a servant to fetch on the following Monday the two young ladies left the shop.

"So that is Mrs. Snow's new assistant," Miss Lingford remarked as the carriage moved down the High Street toward the Bishop's Palace, where they were both to take tea that afternoon. "Miss Burke was talking about her the other day and said how ladylike she is."

"I did not pay much attention to her, I am afraid," said Lady Eleanor. "It is fortunate that she knows London, and I hope she will be able to match the fur."

She began to talk of the party they were going to at the palace and said how much such affairs bored her. "I am quite sure the Dean's daughters will be there," she added. "And although I know they are friends of yours, I find them intensely boring."

Miss Lingford asked why she had accepted the invitation and was answered with a slightly wicked laugh.

"I find the Dean's daughters boring," Lady Eleanor said, her pretty eyes demure. "But I find his son Charles extremely amusing. He is in the Life Guards, and I saw quite a lot of him during the summer."

"And is he going to be there today?"

"Do you suppose I would be going if he were not?" Her ladyship glanced at Miss Lingford provokingly. "Oh, I am not serious about him, I promise you. Charles adores me, and I like to be adored. It relieves the boredom of the country in the winter." And she laughed again.

Miss Lingford felt sorry for the Dean's son.

The thought of Mrs. Snow's new assistant remained in her mind, however, and that evening she went to her mother's boudoir to tell her of her visit to the milliner's shop with Lady Eleanor and how she had seen for herself the new London assistant that the eldest Miss Burke had been praising so much.

Mrs. Lingford put down the novel she was reading to stare at her daughter. "I'm afraid I do not understand you, my dear," she said, smiling indulgently all the same, because Susan was always full of some new enthusiasm or exciting piece of news that usually turned out to be of no consequence whatever. "Since when have the Dean's daughters been interested in shop assistants?"

"Oh, but Miss Burke always buys her hats ready-made," said Susan. "And you know how full of good works she is, and Mrs. Snow always keeps her best bonnets and hats for her in any case. And this Miss Macalister, Mrs. Snow's new assistant, *is* very ladylike, because I saw her myself today. She made nothing of going to London tomorrow to match Lady Eleanor's fur jacket. Perhaps she could not obtain anything better than a situation as a shop assistant, and she wanted to be near her brother. Deering told me he is at the grammar school in Westborough. She has quite the fairest hair I have ever seen, and very nice dark eyes and a quiet, refined voice. You would almost take her for a lady."

The dressing bell sounded, and her mama said that instead of talking about shop assistants she should go and get dressed for dinner or she would not be ready by the time their guests arrived. The Harold Lingfords were entertaining a few friends to dinner that night. "And you know how your father dislikes it if you are late down," she added.

"I know. I will tell Deering to hurry. But I was *so* interested in this Miss Macalister at Mrs. Snow's. Elsa Burke is so full of her praises."

She ran off, and left to herself, her mother put aside her novel and dismissed the milliner and her assistants from her mind. Really, she thought, she could not imagine where Susan got this absurd fascination for the lower orders.

After their guests had gone that night and she sat for a few minutes in the library with her husband, joining him in a weak brandy and soda before going to bed, she remarked that she was glad to see that their daughter still appeared to enjoy the company of her own class.

"Why should she not, my dear?" Mr. Harold Lingford helped himself to a stiffer brandy than he had given his wife and stood with it in his hand with his back to the fire, warming his posterior.

She told him of her remarks about Mrs. Snow's new assistant. "It is all because of Elsa Burke," she added. "She seems to think that this Miss Macalister in Mrs. Snow's shop is a very superior young woman, but you know what Elsa is. Full of enthusiasm for the lower orders and wanting to start night classes to teach them to read and write and become equal to their betters."

"Which is nonsense," said Mr. Lingford. He put his glass on the chimney piece for a moment, however, frowning down into the fire. "What did you say the girl's name is?" he asked.

"Macalister, I think Susan said, but I cannot be sure. She saw her this afternoon when she went into the shop with Lady Eleanor to order a new bonnet."

"Did she describe the girl at all?"

"I did not pay all that much attention, I am afraid. I think she said her hair was extremely fair and she had dark eyes and was very ladylike." Mrs. Lingford laughed. "A ladylike assistant is nothing new. One expects them to be ladylike. I hope Susan will not pick up any unfortunate ideas from Miss Burke."

"I hope so too." Mr. Lingford continued to stare down at the fire, and his frown almost deepened to a scowl. He was remembering a girl with very fair hair who had put up her head and said that she wanted no kinship with the Lingfords and that in future she and her brother would use the name Macalister.

He said that perhaps in a few days' time he might indulge his wife too in a new fur bonnet. "Her ladyship must not be the only one in the fashion," he remarked with the playfulness of an elephant.

Two days later the carriage was ordered and took Mr. Lingford and his wife to the milliner's shop, and the moment he saw Vicky there he knew that his fears were realized.

But if the girl had been impertinent in his study it was nothing to her impertinence now. She came forward when Mrs. Snow called her, smiling, her eyes meeting Mr. Harold Lingford's without the slightest recognition.

"As Miss Silcocks is fitting a lady in the country this afternoon, we will try some shapes on Miss Macalister," said Mrs. Snow, perfectly unaware of the fury that was bubbling up in the husband of one of her prized customers. "Miss Macalister, fetch the latest bonnets for Madam and try them on for her."

"Yes, Mrs. Snow." Vicky fetched bonnets and hats from the window and put them on, under Mrs. Lingford's critical stare. Mrs. Lingford could not imagine what Elsa Burke had been making such a fuss about. The new assistant was merely a tall, plain girl whose fair hair showed off the fur bonnets and hats very well, but otherwise she appeared to be no different from any other assistant.

She ordered two of the bonnets to be made up for her and sent out as soon as possible. "I would like Miss Silcocks to bring them," she added. "She knows my tastes, does she not, Mrs. Snow?"

"Certainly, Madam." Mrs. Lingford bowed them out of the shop, and as Mr. Lingford followed his wife into the carriage he ordered the coachman to drive home at once. Directly the carriage door was closed he gave vent to his wrath.

"That girl," he said, "that Miss Macalister as she calls herself, is none other than Paul's daughter."

"What?" It took some minutes for his wife to digest this unwelcome piece of news. "You cannot mean," she said at last, "that she is the girl who came to see you at the end of October? The girl you said was so insolent?"

"The same." He folded his arms, his face like thunder. "She has, of course, taken this situation with the milliner with one purpose only, to make me the laughing stock of the town. I knew there was no good in her the moment I set eyes on her the day that she came to the Hall. She is the sort who will stop at nothing to get her own way. I daresay she thought I would hear of her situation in that shop and feel bound to do something for her."

"But as she calls herself Macalister, and her brother, one presumes, is at the grammar school under the same name, I see no reason why we should come into contact with either of them. That young woman at the milliner's knows very well that you will not brook her claiming any relationship with us. Why, if she did you would have her out of Westborough in five minutes."

There was sense in what she said, but it did not prevent him from feeling uneasy about the girl who had defied him last October, and as they drove home he wondered if he had been wise to dismiss Vicky and her brother so summarily. He could perhaps have obtained a post for her as a governess somewhere on the other side of the county, while the boy could have been sent to school in Edinburgh, near his grandfather. Both of them would then have been as far away from Westborough as possible.

Mr. Lingford found it vexing as well as alarming to discover that as a result of his bad temper that October morning they had both settled down almost on his doorstep.

Chapter Nine

On the morning following Lady Eleanor's visit to the milliner's, Vicky received many instructions from Mrs. Snow before starting out for London and Mr. Bradley's Arctic Fur Store in Chepstow Place. The small piece of golden sealskin was wrapped as carefully as if it had been a string of pearls and placed in a small cloth bag together with her purse.

"You will, of course, look for a Ladies Only compartment on the train, dear," Mrs. Snow warned her. "And when you arrive in London, take an omnibus to the Bayswater Road. When you find the Arctic Fur Company, ask for Mr. Sedgewick. He always supplies me with furs and will know exactly what I want directly you show him the piece you have with you. Tell him I want enough for one bonnet only, her ladyship's jacket being the only one of that color in the neighborhood. I think I should like some more black sealskin, however—enough to make four or five bonnets. Ladies still seem to wish to buy them, and sealskin jackets are popular at this time of year for carriage ladies."

"Am I to pay for the furs?" asked Vicky.

"Oh dear me no, my dear. I have an account with the wholesale department there, and Mr. Sedgewick would not dream of taking a cash payment for anything I ordered." Mrs. Snow smiled. "He will probably summon one of his lady superintendents to take you to the staff dining room for a good dinner before you go. He is so thoughtful over such matters. And she will let you use the staff washrooms, I have no doubt. It is impossible to visit these public lavatories that one sees sometimes in London. You might catch some fearful disease. And when you have finished at the Arctic Fur Store, be sure and catch another omnibus to Paddington Station. It is not very far, and because the fares are dear you do not find a lot of vulgar people using them. I shall expect you back on the train that arrives at five—or before, if you should take less time than I think."

Vicky carried out her employer's instructions scrupulously, and it was nearly two o'clock when she caught the omnibus to Paddington Station, and she was looking about her, thinking of happier times when she and Emily had been at school together, and of Lady Taversham, wishing she could see her just for a moment or two, when the omnibus stopped to take another passenger aboard and Sebastian Sellinge took the vacant place beside her.

"You do turn up in the most unexpected places, do you not?" he said. "I thought it was you, but I could not be sure. What are you doing, Vicky, in a London omnibus at this time of day?"

Her eyes met his mirthfully. "I have been on an errand to Mr. Bradley's Arctic Fur Store in Chepstow Place to match a pattern of fur for my employer," she said.

"But—have you had luncheon?"

"Yes, thank you. I had an excellent dinner with the work girls there—about forty of them, I should say. They were all very interested in me and my clothes, not being able at first to make out who I was or what I was doing there. At last I heard one of them say to her neighbor, 'You know what she is, don't you? *She's* a lady's maid, that's what she is. They allus gits their ladies' clothes given 'em. Them's the lucky ones, them's is, though they are so 'igh and mighty.' So mind your manners, in future, Mr. Sellinge. I am 'igh and mighty and as such I am to be treated with respect."

He laughed in spite of himself. "Where did you learn cockney?" he asked and added, "I believe you will always treat everything as a joke."

"What would you have me do? Sit down and cry?" She was looking ahead of her out of the omnibus window, and her head was held as high as it had been on the night of her coming-out ball.

"I cannot see you doing that," he replied and changed the subject abruptly. "I am glad I met you, because I wanted to ask you where you and James will be for Christmas."

She turned a radiant smile on him. "Oh, it is such luck. James had one great friend at St. Chad's, Tom Timberloft. His father was in command of an Indian regiment, and Timbers used to spend his summer holidays with us at Costerley. It now appears that Colonel Timberloft's father died during the summer, and the Colonel has retired from the army and is home in the family place—now his own—in Norfolk. Timbers will, of course, go there for Christmas, and his father has said he may bring a school friend with him if he likes. So of course dear Timbers thought of James. They are starting out together on the twentieth of December, and I am so glad. Mrs. Eccrington is the kindest soul on earth, but having Christmas at school is scarcely the same as having it in a proper home."

"And you? Are you going with them?"

"Great heavens no. I have not been asked, and if I had I could not go. I do not believe the milliner's shop closes until midday on Christmas Day."

The omnibus arrived at Paddington, and after he had helped her down and accompanied her to the ticket office and bought her ticket for her, he went with her to the train and said that if she would let him know the arrival of James's train on the twentieth he would be there to meet him and see him across London.

"Young Timberloft will know the time the Norfolk train starts," he added. "And I will see that he is there to meet him in good time."

"You are very kind." He found a first-class carriage with Ladies Only on the window and two ladies inside, and as she held out her hand to him he kept it for a moment in his.

"I shall think of you on Christmas Day," he said, 'Especially when Mama proposes the toast of 'absent friends'. I hope you will think of me too."

"I shall think of you on Christmas Day," he said, "Especially when Mama proposes the toast of 'absent friends.' I hope you will think of me too."

He said that he would and seemed about to say something more, and then changed his mind. He dropped her hand, and as she got into the carriage he closed the door on her and with rather an abrupt goodbye stood back from the train. The guard waved his flag, and the engine began to pull out with a shriek from its whistle and great puffs of smoke rising into the station roof.

As she sat back in the carriage the thought of spending Christmas alone at Mrs. Snow's became a trifle more bleak, not entirely because it was the first time in their lives that she had been parted from James at that season of the year.

She began to understand why Sebastian had wanted her

to find an occupation more in keeping with the life to which she was accustomed. If she were a governess or an old lady's companion there would have been a celebration of Christmas in some big house that would have given her at least a feeling of having been included in it. And then she pulled herself up with the stern reminder that in such houses there would always be the chance that some friend, asked for Christmas or for Christmas dinner, would recognize her as Paul Lingford's daughter. Her father had spoiled Christmas for her as he had spoiled everything else.

Looking out at the wintry countryside, she clenched her hands inside her muff, and her eyes suddenly misted with tears. She felt that she hated her father as she had never hated anyone before in her life. There was nothing that his behavior had not ruined, no enjoyment that it had not spoiled.

After the milliner's shop closed at midday on Christmas Day, Mrs. Snow was accustomed to take dinner at Mrs. Cumberledge's, accompanied by Miss Fosbery, with Polly to help with the serving. Cumberledge's too closed at noon, and Mr. Cumberledge always carved the Christmas goose and poured out the wine on that occasion, and this year his hospitable old mama insisted that Miss Macalister should be with them as well.

"The poor thing cannot be left alone with nowhere to go," she told Miss Fosbery. "You must bring her with you."

So Vicky opened her trunk and unpacked a green velvet dress for the occasion and enjoyed it all very much. Mr. Cumberledge became quite mellow under the influence of the wine and held Miss Fosbery's hand under the tablecloth, while Mrs. Cumberledge reminisced with Mrs. Snow on what Westborough had been like in the old days before the railways came to take everyone to London to do their shopping.

"I remember when the Mitre yard was full of post horses in them days," said Mrs. Snow sadly. "And the fine gentlemen's carriages came down the High Street with their post boys all in livery. It was a grand sight."

"Not but what William's store and your millinery and corsets isn't as good as any to be found in London, my dear," Mrs. Cumberledge said, following her own train of thought. "As William says, we 'ave to move with the times, and if you don't give people what they want they'll natural-like go elsewhere. But we do get a deal of carriage trade now, in spite of them nasty railways. It's selling fust-class goods what brings in fust-class customers, William says."

James came back from his holiday in Norfolk full of the house and the family and the fun he and Timbers had had with his older brothers and sisters. He did not tell his sister that he had not told Timbers or his family that she was employed in a milliner's shop. In fact, when he was told that he should have brought her with him he had replied that he did not think she would have been able to come, as the lady she was with could not spare her.

"I know old ladies are very strict with their companions," said Mrs. Timberloft, smiling. "I wish she could have come all the same."

Privately James was relieved that she could not. Vicky had a way of speaking out and would have thought nothing of telling his friends about her occupation in Westborough, and somehow he found that he did not want them to know. When he took out the little gift she had given him at parting to be opened on Christmas Day, however, he felt more than a little ashamed of himself, because it was a purse in Russian leather with one of her precious gold sovereigns inside.

When he saw her and thanked her on the Sunday after he arrived back at school he told her that the Timberlofts wanted him to go back with Tom for the long summer vacation, and he had said that he would very much like to go.

"What did you tell them about Papa?" asked Vicky, and James flushed up under her eyes.

"I just said that my parents were dead and my father had left us very badly off," he said quickly, but she thought he was not telling the truth.

He went on to tell her that Dr. Eccrington had decided to enter him for a bursary that was to be competed for in April. It seemed that there had been several benevolent old gentlemen in the past who had left sums of money for such purposes.

"I do not think I have a chance of winning it," James said. "But if I should it would mean that I'd almost certainly be able to go to Oxford and take a degree there in engineering." He dived his hand into his pocket. "Oh, and I almost forgot. You know that Mr. Sellinge met us when we got back to London, and having put Timbers into a cab for St. Chad's saw me across to Paddington. Just before the train left he asked me to give you this. I expect it is something from Lady Taversham."

It was a small flat package, and as it was beginning to rain Vicky left him at the school gates and took it back with her to her room.

There she opened it and found a little watercolor drawing of Costerley and a short letter from Sebastian.

"As I expect you know," he wrote, "Costerley came under the hammer at the beginning of December. I went to the sale and obtained this little drawing, which I thought you might like to keep. I drank to you in champagne at our Christmas dinner, and I hope Mr. Cumberledge supplied you with some in which to drink to me."

He signed himself Sebastian.

Vicky laughed over the letter, dropped a kiss on the picture of Costerley and suddenly found that tears were not far away. She scolded herself roundly, packed away the little picture and the letter into her trunk, washed her face and went into the best parlor upstairs to have Sunday tea with Mrs. Snow among the stands of corsets that stood about them like bulbous waiting maids.

Miss Silcocks had left before Christmas, and Mrs. Snow had asked her to stay on permanently in her place, to which she gladly consented. She was getting to know the customers and the work girls, and although she missed Miss Silcocks's bright chatter in the shop when there was nobody there to be served, she was kept busy most of the day and the time passed quickly.

January was cold, with snow making roads and pavements dangerous and dirty, and then February came in with pouring rain to fill the River Westerley that ran through the town until it almost burst its banks and some cottages near the water meadows were flooded out.

In the Close, however, snowdrops were pushing up in the gardens and spearheads of daffodils were showing among their spiky leaves, and one bright morning Miss Kitty Sellinge left Adelaide Villa with Fenwick carrying her last year's spring hat in a bandbox, intent on visiting Mrs. Snow's in the High Street.

She had heard a great deal about the new assistant in the milliner's shop, and those who had seen her were loud in their praises. She was, they said, evidently a lady, or alternately, that she was a very ladylike young woman, or again—even from Mrs. Burke—that she was a nice young woman with refined manners.

So Miss Sellinge determined to see for herself and satisfy her curiosity, as well as asking Mrs. Snow's advice on the renovation of her last year's hat, which she felt was far too good to dispose of to Fenwick or to one of the parlormaid's pert nieces.

Mrs. Snow was in the small parlor that she referred to as her office at the back of the shop and hurried out to greet her with the pleasure she always showed for her best-liked customers.

"Why, Miss Sellinge, ma'am," she said, "it is nice to see you in my shop again. What can I have the pleasure of doing for you?"

Miss Fosbery was busy with a lady who could not make up her mind whether to have trimmings on her new bonnet to match a new dress or to have a complete contrast, while beyond her at the counter the new assistant was getting out ribbons in various colors to help the lady in her choice. Miss Sellinge's blue eyes rested on her thoughtfully. The plain black dress and overall the young woman wore could not be said to be exactly refined, but her pale, straw-colored hair and large dark eyes gave her face a character of its own.

She explained to Mrs. Snow about the retrimming of her last year's hat, and it was removed from the bandbox and layers of tissue paper for her advice.

"I know it is a spring hat," said Miss Sellinge, "and it is cold outside, but one feels that spring must be on the way."

She took off her bonnet and Fenwick placed the hat on her head, bringing to the fore those pieces of trimming that had faded in order to show it, Miss Sellinge thought vexedly, at its worst.

Mrs. Snow merely remarked, however, that it was a good straw and if she remembered right, had been an expensive one, so that it was well worth retrimming. As Miss Fosbery was still occupied with her customer she summoned Vicky to fetch a box of lace trimmings and artificial flowers that might freshen it up.

The hat was a small one and sat rather uncomfortably on the top of Miss Sellinge's head. The milliner held first one ribbon and then another against it without any promise of improvement, until Vicky produced a soft length of lace ruching, suggesting that it might soften the hardness of the straw inside the front of the hat.

It was tried and judged by Mrs. Snow and Miss Sellinge

to be just the thing. A spray of blue gentians was then discovered at the bottom of the box of flowers, and on adding it to the brim so that the blue only just peeped through the white lace, it was found to be the exact color of Miss Sellinge's eyes.

It was a simple matter then to select blue ribbons to match, and the hat was left in Mrs. Snow's care, with the promise that it would be returned, restored to a new glory, on the following morning.

"I shall send Miss Macalister with it," the milliner said, with a smile for Vicky. "She is my new assistant and very careful. I will not trust it to that boy of mine, who is quite capable of dropping a bandbox in the river."

After Miss Sellinge had gone, Mrs. Snow asked Vicky if she thought she could get the hat trimmed in time.

Vicky said she would do most of it before she went to bed that night, putting in the lining and ruching and pinning the flowers and ribbons in place. "Then you and Miss Fosbery can see it first thing tomorrow," she added, "and if I have done anything wrong I can easily alter it. It will only take a few minutes to stitch the flowers and ribbons in place."

Her willingness pleased Miss Fosbery as well as Mrs. Snow, because it happened to be the day when Mr. Cumberledge took his intended to the Haberdashers' Friendly Meeting after the shop was closed and any extra work had to be done before she left.

By the following morning the hat was finished, and pronounced by both ladies to be excellent, and Vicky was allowed to pack it up in its bandbox and take it to Adelaide Villa herself.

"Thursdays are not very busy days," Mrs. Snow told her. "And Miss Fosbery and I can manage the shop until you come back. It will do you good, my dear, to get out into the fresh air, and you need a reward for all the hard work you have put into it."

Vicky set out with pleasure, the bandbox on her arm, enjoying the walk through the winding St. Francis's Lane and on past the St. Francis's Almshouses to the Close. She guessed that Miss Sellinge was the aunt that Sebastian visited from time to time, but she did not think he would have told her anything about her, and in the meantime it was nice to be free from the shop.

Miss Sellinge was pleased to see her arrive so promptly,

and Vicky was conducted to her dressing room, where she helped to place the hat to the best advantage on the lady's head.

"It is very pretty," said Miss Sellinge. "How clever of you to find those gentians."

"Miss Fosbery had found them the day before," Vicky said quickly.

"Shall we say how clever it was of Miss Fosbery then?" The smile in the blue eyes was reflected in the dark ones behind her. One had to be tactful with Miss Fosbery: that was understood. "But I have a feeling that had the choice been left to dear Mrs. Snow or to Miss Fosbery a spray of lilac or a bunch of purple violets might have been suggested as more suitable to a lady of my age."

"I do not see that age matters, Madam, and you have such very blue eyes." Vicky began to pack the tissue paper back into the bandbox, and Miss Sellinge said that she had been told Miss Macalister had a brother at the grammar school.

Vicky agreed that she had, shut the lid on the paper and added that he was very happy there.

"Dr. Eccrington and his wife are friends of mine," said Miss Sellinge. "A dear couple. I expect that is why you obtained employment here—to be near your brother?"

"Yes, Madam. I was very fortunate." Vicky was not forthcoming, remembering Miss Fosbery's warning that she must never gossip with customers. "I hope you will be satisfied with the hat, Madam. If it should need any further alteration, Mrs. Snow will be pleased to do it for you."

And off she went, carrying herself as straight as a dart, with more dignity than many a lady of Miss Sellinge's acquaintance.

Sebastian's aunt thought about her for some time, wondering why she was here working in a milliner's shop. She was quite sure she had been brought up to a very different life, and she wondered, with compassion for the girl, what had brought her down to this.

She was not the only lady in Westborough who heard Miss Macalister's praises sung by her friends. Mrs. Lingford came into her husband's study one afternoon after paying some calls and was fortunate to find him there alone.

"Harold," she said angrily, "that wretched girl is still serving in the milliner's shop."

"What girl?" Then, as he saw his wife's face, "Oh, you mean Miss Macalister, as she now calls herself."

"I would like to know what she hopes to gain by this piece of play-acting," said his wife. "One would have thought she would have returned to London long ago, now she knows there is nothing to be gained from us. Sooner or later somebody is going to recognize her as Paul's daughter, and it is going to make things very unpleasant for us. You must get her out of Westborough, Harold."

"That is all very well, my dear, but it is not as easy as it sounds." Mr. Lingford had had a word with Dr. Eccrington at a meeting a few days back and had asked him if he had had any new pupils at the grammar school that autumn. And the doctor had told him that he had had one of quite outstanding merit, a boy by the name of James Macalister, and that he intended to put him in for a bursary examination that April and had every hope of his winning it. Not only had the information been unwelcome, as such a scholarship would ensure James's being at the school for several years, but there had been a certain look in the good doctor's eyes that made Mr. Lingford think he knew the boy's real name and history.

"You are right, my dear," he said. "Both those young people must be got out of Westborough, but one does not quite know how to set about it."

The following day, however, he had to see his lawyer, Mr. North, about a notice he wished served on a tenant on his land. The man, Downer, was a small farmer and a very bad one, and invariably behind with his rent. While agreeing that it was bad for the landlord if a farm was allowed to deteriorate as Downer had allowed his to go down, Mr. North added that it was a pity his son had not the same liking for farming as he had for the drapery business.

He then told a suddenly interested Mr. Lingford that he had had the young man in that morning wanting to raise a loan so that he could rent the two empty shops opposite Mrs. Snow's, the milliner's, in the High Street.

"He has great ideas of converting them into one larger store, and his enthusiasm was so great that I was sorry to have to tell him that the little money he had saved during his apprenticeship in Birmingham would not stock one of those shops with goods, let alone two."

"Opposite Mrs. Snow's, you said?" Mr. Lingford became thoughtful. Those two dingy-looking shops had been empty for the past six months and would need a certain amount of repairs before they could be used for anything, but all the same there was a possibility there that appealed to him. "I wonder if I could help him?" he said. "I have money to invest, and if he is an honest, hard-working young fellow, perhaps I might delay that notice to his father for a little while. I should be obliged if you would find out for me who owns those empty shops and what sum would purchase them. Once that is discovered we can proceed to the next step. You will arrange for me to meet the Downer lad, and I will find out for myself of what his knowledge consists and what sort of store he has in mind."

"I think he has dreams of being a second Cumberledge," said Mr. North, smiling.

"You mean selling furniture and carpets as well as being a ladies' outfitter? Perhaps he could be persuaded to sell millinery as well?"

"That would scarcely be fair on Mrs. Snow, sir." Mr. North shook his head. "She is an elderly lady and has had a first-class millinery business in the town for a number of years."

"There is no harm in competition," said Mr. Lingford brusquely. "I have heard it said that trade flourishes on it. In any case, I would like those inquiries made as soon as possible. My name is not to come into the transaction, of course. You will act for a client who will be nameless."

And Mr. Harold Lingford went on his way with a feeling of satisfaction. A shop like the one he had in mind might not touch Cumberledge's trade, but it could easily, if handled right, put the milliner out of business altogether.

He could not have known that in starting this scheme he had taken the first step toward giving his niece Vicky Lingford not only a lucrative future but an independence that he would come in time to regret.

Chapter Ten

When work started on the two empty shops opposite the milliner's, for a time speculation in the town was rife. It was said that the new shop was to be a grocer's with a wine department, which drew forth a great deal of ridicule. Whoever had heard of the gentry buying their wines from a grocer? Then it was said to be a furnisher's, selling everything from carpets and mahogany wardrobes to brass fenders. This was abandoned in favor of a large dress shop, with materials and silks from France and the best tartan satins as worn at Balmoral.

Walls between the shops were knocked down and replaced with wooden pillars, and the little bow windows gave way to long ones of plate glass, quite as large as Cumberledge's, but even so, Mrs. Snow and Miss Fosbery watched the progress of the new emporium with only a passing interest. Mr. Cumberledge's position in the town was unassailable, and they only hoped that their work girls would not be tempted to desert them with offers of higher wages.

James was now working hard for his bursary, and there were several Sunday afternoons when he could not come out with his sister, staying in school at his books, which was really against the rules but forgiven by Dr. Eccrington because of the short time he had been at the school and the nearness of the April examination.

Vicky took to going out by herself on such afternoons when the weather was fine, preferring the fresh air of the Palace Gardens to her little room at the shop. It was on one such afternoon in the middle of March that she heard her name called and turned to see Rose Dalling, one of their work girls and a very pretty one, on the arm of a nice-looking young man who, from his appearance, was the farmhand to whom she had been engaged for the last two years.

"Oh, Miss Macalister," she said, "you must listen to what my Joe 'as to say about that thur new shop. You tell 'er, Joe."

Thus prodded, Joe Webber touched his hat and told her what he had heard.

"It's owned, they do say, by 'arry Downer, son of old Downer what's got the name fur being the worst farmer fur miles. 'Is farm is on Mr. 'arold Lingford's estate, and why that 'arry of 'is wants to go in fur retailing is beyond us all. 'Adn't the brains to git a pig to market, 'adn't 'arry, when he was a boy, but now 'e's bin away to Birmingham, 'prenticed to a wholesaler before old Downer broke the contrack after three year, 'e thinks 'e's big a chap as Mr. Cumberledge, shouldn't wonder."

"But what is he going to sell?" asked Vicky.

"They've put blinds in the winders," said Rose. "But there's a gap in one of 'em where it hasn't been drawed right, and I peeped in, an' what do you think, Miss Macalister? You know them pillars they put in where they took down them walls? They've painted 'em all white, and there's rods between 'em wiv drapery 'ung on 'em, and the walls is all papered in French wallpapers, and Joe hears as there's to be three departments like, one fur china and glass, another fur furniture, and the last one fur materials and all kinds of ladies fashions, including millinery."

"But that would be trying to outdo Mr. Cumberledge and Mrs. Snow," said Vicky, dismissing it as another rumor. "And I cannot see anybody doing that."

She went on into the Palace Gardens to write a letter to James, asking him not to work too hard and relating the latest in rumors about the new emporium. She sat wrapped in her gray cape, because the March wind was keen, and she had just finished the second page when a young man came and sat down at the other end of the bench.

He watched her pencil flying over the paper, and after a moment remarked enviously that he wished he could write as freely. "When you're working on a newspaper and your editor wants a weekly article on popular subjects it ain't so easy to find a flow of words," he said.

"I am writing to my brother," she told him, smiling. "And there always seems so much to tell him." She glanced at the young man with interest. He was the sort she supposed that Mr. Sellinge and his friends might refer to as a cad, but he had a nice open face under his brown bowler hat, and if his checked suit and the yellow uppers to his boots were a little on the loud side it did not make him any the worse. She asked him which paper he was writing for, and he said the *Westborough Echo*.

"It comes out weekly, as I expect you know, Miss, but it is read by many of the gentry as well as Westborough folk."

"I am sure it is. I work for Mrs. Snow, the milliner, and she always looks forward to her copy."

"Of course," he went on, "all news editors like scandal. Murder and burglary and sudden deaths and things like that. That's meat and drink to a reporter on a newspaper. Good news isn't wanted by anyone."

"If what I heard this afternoon about the new shop is true," said Vicky gravely, "it may be needed badly enough by Mrs. Snow. It is directly opposite us in the High Street, and they have just finished painting the name Pounce and Dart over it, and I have heard today that not only do they intend to set up as a second Cumberledge's, but as a milliner as well."

"They won't hurt Cumberledge," said the young man confidently. "But I wouldn't like to see them harm Mrs. Snow. She's a nice old lady and well liked in the town."

"But is it true, then?"

"I am afraid it is. We had an advertisement in yesterday— it's opening in a fornight's time—and the ad is going into the *Echo* this week. There's to be drapery, china, ironmongery, kitchenware, ready-made boots, ready-made dresses, a haberdasher's department, a fust-class millinery and ready-made corsets, if you will pardon me mentioning them, Miss."

"I cannot believe it." Vicky spoke with a sinking heart. As her companion said, Cumberledge's was not likely to suffer, but a new milliner's opposite her might ruin Mrs. Snow. Her bonnets and hats were copied by hand from Paris fashions, and although they might cost as much as two guineas, they could compete with any London milliner. But could they compete with this newcomer down here in Westborough? While as for Mrs. Bellon, ready-made corsets might be more appealing than the carefully fitted ones she created for each customer.

The young man said that he had been invited to go around the new store the following day so that he could write an article about it the following Friday in time for the grand opening.

"I don't know what to say about it, and that's a fact," he

added ruefully. "If I praise it as an excellent emporium, Mr. Cumberledge is going to have something to say, and if I say it is a shop nobody in their senses would patronize, Messrs. Pounce and Dart are going to sue the *Echo* for damages."

"It is possible to damn by faint praise all the same," said Vicky with a faintly wicked smile. She thought it over for a moment. "I suppose you could not arrange for me to accompany you tomorrow? I come from London, and my name is Miss Macalister, by the way. I could wear one of my London dresses and a bonnet with a fine veil over my face. You could say I was a lady superintendent from one of the big London stores looking for new ideas. I am sure if I tell Mrs. Snow what is in the wind she will let me go."

He admitted that it was an excellent idea. "Coming from London as you say you do, Miss Macalister," he said, "you will be able to speak with authority and advise me what line I should take. I should be very much obliged to you if you will do that."

"I will do it with pleasure." Anything, she felt, to save Mrs. Snow from annihilation by the odious Pounce and Dart.

He told her that his name was Smithson and he would be waiting for her at the *Echo* offices the following morning at eleven o'clock.

She hurried back to the milliner's and told Mrs. Snow and Miss Fosbery what she had heard that afternoon, and while Mrs. Snow was indignant, Miss Fosbery was more concerned about Mr. Cumberledge.

"It's enough to give him a seizure," she said. "After all he's done to build up the best business in Westborough. And I'd like to know where that Pounce and Dart have got their money from to start up such a thing."

Vicky said she would too.

The following day, veiled and in a hat and dress she had not worn in Westborough, she left by the work girls' entrance in St. Francis's Lane and made her way by back streets to the *Echo* offices.

Mr. Smithson was waiting for her, notebook in hand, and he took her at once to the new emporium, where he was met by a young man whom she took to be the Harry Downer of whom Joe Webber had spoken.

It was obvious that Mr. Smithson was astonished to find him there in charge.

"Why, Harry," he said, "never thought this would be your

line of business. Suppose you are here to show people around in Mr. Pounce's and Mr. Dart's absence? Or are they in the manager's office?" He looked about him curiously, and Mr. Downer laughed.

"Tell you the truth, Smithson," he said, tucking his thumbs into the armholes of his waistcoat and swaggering a little, "the business belongs to me. The names of Pounce and Dart is a sort of accommodation address, as you might say, fur me and me partner—the gentleman what is interested in it."

"You mean the gentleman what is putting up the money?" said Mr. Smithson. "Thought there must be something like that in it. Well, now I'm here, let me and this London lady see what you've got to offer."

Mr. Downer took them through the various departments with pride, while Vicky took a few notes in her own small notebook. It was when they arrived in the millinery department that Smithson gave vent to his indignation.

"Why, you've enough here to put Mrs. Snow out of business! I hope you'll never do that, Harry."

"I don't want to spoil her trade," said Harry Downer complacently. "But she will have to smarten her shop up if she don't want to close down. Not but what my partner wouldn't be pleased to see that 'appen," he added in a low voice. "He don't like Mrs. Snow, fur some reasons of his own, and I've thought lately he's only opened this business with the intention of ruining her. But don't put that in the *Echo*, for Gawd's sake!"

"Wouldn't dream of it," said Mr. Smithson. "Why, if a hint of anything like that got around, your winders would be smashed long before your shop was open, that I can promise you. Anyone what touches Mrs. Snow will get their fingers burned."

Vicky left the new emporium with Mr. Smithson and walked back to the newspaper offices with him, and as they went Mr. Smithson repeated that he could not think why anybody should wish to harm Mrs. Snow. He was evidently as surprised and upset as Vicky was herself. "I wouldn't have said she had an enemy in the world."

Vicky agreed that she could not imagine such a thing and added that she wondered who was financing the new emporium.

"Oh, I should say that's Mr. Harold Lingford," said Mr. Smithson easily. "It wouldn't be the first time he's had a finger in a local pie, and usually he sees that he comes out of it with a profit. Very astute gentleman is Mr. Harold Lingford."

Vicky found that she was unable to reply. A thought as absurd as it was stupefying entered her mind. Surely Harold Lingford would not try to close down Mrs. Snow's shop in order that his niece would be forced to leave the town? She could not imagine that he could stoop to such a thing, but the whole business of the new emporium struck her as being very odd, and on her way back to the milliner's she purchased some sheets of writing paper and pen and ink from a stationer's, and a pound of candles from the chandler's next door.

That evening she went up her room directly after supper on the pretense of having to finish her letter to James, and she took the writing materials to the tiny table in the window that she used as a dressing table, work table and everything else, cleared its top, lighted one of her candles and began to write.

As she wrote about the new shop, ideas began to form in her mind, making her smile as she wrote, because from a quick survey of its contents she was quite sure Mr. Harry Downer knew very little about the art of retailing, and by the time she was ready for bed the first draft of an amusing and provocative article was finished.

The next night she spent in improving what she had written, deleting anything that could be construed as a personal attack upon anyone, and with the excuse that she needed some stamps she went out during the dinner hour and hurried to the *Echo* offices, leaving her work in a sealed envelope addressed to Mr. Smithson. Inside she had put a short covering note saying that she hoped the sketch would be of help to him when composing his article on Messrs. Pounce and Dart.

The following day a letter came from him acknowledging the receipt of the sketch and asking her to meet him on Sunday afternoon in the Palace Gardens.

James was occupied once more with work, as it was now only a fortnight before the bursary examination in April, and as the afternoon was fine and dry she went to the Palace Gardens and found Mr. Smithson waiting for her there, with a nice-looking girl whom he introduced as his wife, and young Master Smithson, walking along beside his baby sister, who was sitting up and looking very alert in a basket-sided perambulator.

Mrs. Smithson went ahead with the children, and her husband followed more slowly with Vicky.

"First of all, Miss Macalister," he said, "I must congratulate you on your sketch. I showed it to my editor, Mr. Driffle, and he was chuckling over it before he'd finished the first few lines. When he came to the end of it he said to me, 'By gum, she's got the trick of writing, has that young lady. This is finer stuff than you'll ever write, Smithson.' I said I was well aware of it and asked if he would print it. He said with your permission he most certainly would, and what is more he will pay you for it."

"But of course he can print it." Vicky was flushed with gratitude and delight. "But it must not come out under my name."

"Then let us think of a name for you," said Mr. Smithson. "What name do you fancy?"

Her eyes followed Master Smithson ahead of them, throwing some crumbs to some very greedy duck, and as she watched, a lame duck waddled out of the bushes and came for his share before going into the water.

"I think perhaps 'A Lame Duck' might be suitable," she said, and they both laughed.

As they caught up with the little boy's mother, Mrs. Smithson asked her if she had many friends in Westborough, and when she replied that she had none apart from Dr. Eccrington and his wife and Mrs. Snow at the milliner's shop, the young woman asked her rather shyly if she would like to come to tea with them on the following Sunday. She accepted the invitation with pleasure, and Mr. Smithson gave her their address, in an unfashionable quarter of the town.

"I might have some more news for you from Mr. Driffle," he added.

As she parted from them their warmth and friendship went with her, so that she arrived back at the milliner's in a happier frame of mind than she had known for some time. She was, however, quite unprepared for the following Friday morning, when the *Echo* came out in time to catch the country people thronging into town for market day.

Mr. Cumberledge sent a copy of the paper around to Miss Fosbery, marking a page in black pencil. "Mrs. Snow has one defender in Westborough," he wrote in the margin. "And how pleased her friends are going to be when they read this!"

Miss Fosbery ran with the paper to Mrs. Snow and read out the article on the marked page, the words audible to Vicky, who was serving a customer with bonnet ribbon in the shop.

"'The opening of Messrs. Pounce and Dart's new emporium in the High Street has, we feel, fulfilled a long-felt want experienced by the wives and daughters of farmers visiting our city on Market Day. Its furniture department exhibits massive sideboards in mahogany that would not disgrace any farm parlor and large enough to take the most generous harvest supper dishes. The china department too deserves comment. The ornaments, tastefully shaped like urns for the most part and decorated with Italian views in colors so vivid as to startle even the most insensitive of observers, will grace any of the overmantels which the furniture department has in such profusion. And then there are materials for curtains and for domestic use. Such thick flannel and such hard-wearing calico at prices that compete with those in the market. Patterned cottons and silks too, some in gay tartans of no known clan, and velveteen, much patronized these days by those whose means are not sufficient to include silk velvet in their purchases. But what words could describe the millinery department, with its choice of hats and bonnets for country wear? Mrs. Snow's Paris creations, known and admired by all, are naturally not suitable for farmers' wives and daughters, but they need not be ashamed of going to church on Sunday morning with Messrs. Pounce and Dart's erections on their heads. The shapes and sizes of these elegant creations are sufficient alone to captivate and—dare we say astonish?—all beholders.'"

The article then touched on the more delicate matter of ready-made corsets, which though not being fashionable in shape, had the advantage of not being likely to confine ample forms uncomfortably. It ended with an account of the kitchen utensils in the store, which might not last as long as the superior ones at Cumberledge's, but one could not have everything, and to those who liked to save a penny on an inferior article this new emporium would be just what was needed. The article was signed "The Lame Duck."

Friday was a busy day, numbers of people visiting the new emporium on their way to do their usual market-day shopping, some of them only walking through the millinery department before crossing the road to the established milliner's shop opposite.

Messrs. Pounce and Dart could never say that the *Echo*'s account of their new shop had spoiled their sales, which remained brisk all day, but by the time evening came Mrs. Snow found that she would be obliged to send to her London warehouses for more materials to be dispatched as soon as possible. The Paris bonnets and hats mentioned in the Lame Duck's account had greatly interested many country farmers' daughters who had never thought of purchasing them before.

On Sunday afternoon Vicky set out for Mr. Smithson's house, a small, semidetached villa on the outskirts of the town, with a low brick wall in front and a neatly cut privet hedge sheltering some early primroses that bordered a patch of grass no bigger than a kitchen tablecloth.

Mr. Smithson had been watching for her, and the maid opened the door almost as soon as Vicky touched the brass knocker, and she was shown into the front parlor, a small room with a bay window looking out on the privet hedge.

The room was made even smaller by a horsehair-covered sofa, a fern stand with a palm in it in the window, three or four rather stiff-looking chairs and an upright piano with a branch of candles on either side. Above the fireplace there was a large steel engraving of "The Monarch of the Glen."

Mr. Smithson was not alone. A tall thin man of fifty or so, with grizzled hair and beard and a rather mournful face, was sitting with him, and was introduced proudly to Vicky as "my editor, Mr. Driffle."

He shook her hand warmly and congratulated her on her article. "And before I forget," he added, "will make payment for it at once." He dived into his pocket and produced a battered purse from which he took fifteen shillings. "I hope this will be acceptable, Miss—er—Lame Duck?"

Vicky laughed at the droll look he gave her as she accepted the money. "Until Miss Fosbery read it out from the paper on Friday morning I'd no idea that you really intended to print it," she said.

"I wanted to meet you," said Mr. Driffle, as they sat down again. "I feel that a young lady like yourself might find a place on the paper, and I had a long talk with Smithson about it yesterday evening. We came to the conclusion that if you felt yourself able to contribute one article to the paper every week, on any country subject you fancied, such as market days, or harvest homes, or anything else that might come into your mind, we would be glad to print them and reward you with fifteen shillings each. Would you like to consider this, Miss Lame Duck? It is a serious offer, seriously made."

Vicky, whose recent experiences in her nineteen years had made her cautious, suggested that he might like to see the next article she wrote before making further offers.

He appreciated her wisdom at not jumping at it. "It is only a beginning," he told her. "I think you have the talent to write things that people will want to read, but we shall see. I shall await your next contribution with interest."

And then Mrs. Smithson appeared, with Master Smithson beside her, her finger clasped in his fist like a sheet anchor, and the baby on her arm, and they went into a dining room that was even smaller than the front parlor, to sit around the table for tea.

As she walked back to the milliner's shop that evening, Vicky remembered a conversation she had had with Sebastian when he had been trying to persuade her to take employment more suited to her class. She had told him that she had no talents and in fact that at school the only thing in which she had been successful had been essay writing. "And who will pay me for writing essays?" she had asked.

It now seemed as if somebody would, and from that evening the dullness of her life disappeared overnight. No matter how trying customers might have been during the day, no matter how the hours had dragged, how irritating the alterations to be made, and what tempers had to be placated with words of praise for a bonnet and its purchaser, it ended at last, and after a frugal supper with Mrs. Snow and Miss Fosbery she was free to escape to her candle, her paper and her pen.

Chapter Eleven

The first article to follow Vicky's "Our New Emporium" was entitled "Market Day" and described in detail and with amusement the different stalls, the cheap crockery, the sunbonnets, the rabbits in hutches, the chickens in coops, the piles of fruit on the barrows and the raucous voices of the cheap-jacks, holding up such items as gold watches for sale at half a crown. "And when the buyer gets it home," Vicky concluded, "not only does he find that it is not gold, but the salesman has omitted to tell him that it has no works."

This sketch was accepted for the same fee, and another was demanded, and this time Vicky had as her title "From a Park Bench," describing with delicacy and charm the families who enjoyed taking their Sunday-afternoon stroll in the Palace Gardens.

One sketch was entitled "Shadows" and described how a little girl dancing ahead of her family in the park did her best to tread on her shadow, cast before her by the sunlight of the April afternoon, but try as she would she could never catch up with it. In her description of this little scene Vicky ended, "So we all, when we are young, pursue our shadows, dancing after them, laughing in anticipation of the joy that will be ours when we catch them up. And then suddenly the sun goes in and the shadows are gone and our laughter and dancing steps with them. We wait for the cloud to pass, indeed sometimes we think it will never pass, but when the sun comes out again our steps are perhaps slower, our dancing is finished, and we build castles of more substance, remembering the shadows that have gone."

Miss Sellinge soon became one of the Lame Duck's most devoted admirers. She discussed the articles in the *Echo* with the Dean's wife, in an effort to make her peace with her over her refusal to leave Adelaide Villa, after which a certain coolness had existed between the two ladies.

Mrs. Burke replied with some acidity that she never read the *Echo*. "My husband is forced to glance through it, of course, in case anybody has been unwise enough to criticize the cathedral or the Chapter. But I am not attracted by the gossip of local tradesmen."

"The articles I mentioned are not gossip, nor are they written by an ill-bred person. There is a freshness and a gentleness in them that I find most consoling these days when you cannot pick up a newspaper without seeing dreadful things written by people calling themselves Freethinkers. You really should read the Lame Duck articles, Mrs. Burke. They are so well written that I almost thought they might have as an author one of your clever daughters."

Mrs. Burke said that neither of her daughters would dream of writing anything for a vulgar little local paper, but nevertheless when the next week's copy of the *Echo* was delivered at the Deanery it was the Dean's wife who carried it off with her before her husband could see it to read the Lame Duck article for that week with far more interest than she had thought possible.

So the Lame Duck was launched, and Vicky found not only the writing of the articles rewarding, but the payment for them. She was bound by contract to a dozen at fifteen shillings apiece, riches beyond her dreams.

Supposing, she thought, she wrote a novel? Supposing she became a successful authoress, like Miss Yonge or Mrs. Henry Wood? She would be free from the milliner's shop and her own mistress, and what was better still, that small house of which she and James dreamed might be theirs far sooner than they had anticipated.

Easter came, with the bursary examination over, and on Easter Monday the school had organized a paper chase. James, because of his long legs, was selected as one of the hares, and old lesson books were torn up to lay the trail.

Mrs. Snow had closed her shop, as usual on a bank holiday, and early in the morning Mrs. Smithson sent a note to Vicky asking her to spend the day with them. They planned to take a picnic lunch with them to the castle ruins, and Vicky was delighted to accept.

The sun was shining, blossom was breaking out everywhere on fruit trees and May trees in the city dwellers' gardens, and the Palace Gardens were full of daffodils. Vicky put on a short walking dress and a pair of stoutly made boots that she had purchased at Cumberledge's and on arriving at the Smithsons' little house found Mrs. Smithson in the act of putting the baby into the perambulator while Master Smithson was vociferously refusing to ride at the other end.

Vicky had never explored the castle and was delighted to be conducted around the remains of the old fortress by Mr. Smithson, making notes as she went for a future article. They planned to return home for tea, the baby having become slightly fractious and Master Smithson not objecting by this time to a ride in the perambulator with his sister.

"We will take the short cut through the Close," said Mr. Smithson as they approached the cathedral. "There will not be anybody about today."

They went down a narrow lane between a row of small houses reserved for certain minor canons and circumnavigated the cathedral, where an asphalt path made a smooth way for the perambulator.

It was just as they drew level with the Deanery that Miss Sellinge and her nephew came out of the gate, having had luncheon with the Dean, his wife and their two daughters. They were evidently on their way back to Adelaide Villa, and Sebastian was carrying a flower pot in which was growing a straggling but sweet-scented oak-leaved geranium for his aunt's conservatory, graciously given her by the Dean.

The Judge had taken his sister and his niece to spend Easter with him in a hotel in Brighton, remarking that he would not invite Sebastian to accompany them as he was sure he had not time for such frivolities. Sebastian, who could not conceive for one moment that a visit anywhere accompanied by his uncle could be termed a frivolity, was thankful that he did not have to get deeper into the old gentleman's black books by a refusal. Instead he invited himself to his Aunt Kitty, drawn to Westborough by the thought that he might see Vicky again in the Palace Gardens.

He did see Vicky, but not under any such circumstances. It had occurred to the Dean's wife that Miss Sellinge's nephew, although he had made himself tiresome over her lease of Adelaide Villa, was nevertheless spoken of everywhere as one of the coming men in his profession, and she remembered that she had two unmarried daughters. Therefore a gracious invitation was extended to Miss Sellinge and Sebastian for luncheon on the bank holiday, and Sebastian was wearing his most formal clothes while Miss Sellinge was wearing her retrimmed last year's hat with her garden-party dress under a long black coat.

As she caught sight of the Smithsons and the tall girl with them she exclaimed, "Wait for me a minute, Sebastian. I must go and have a little chat with my dear Christine."

Sebastian's eyes lingered for a second on the group with no sign of recognition, for which Vicky was thankful, and he waited politely some yards away, while Miss Sellinge greeted the Smithsons and Vicky with the kindly air of interest that she reserved for old servants who had moved away from Westborough.

"Miss Macalister," she said, "how nice to see you free from your duties at the shop for once, and with my dear Christine." She beamed at Mrs. Smithson, who smiled timidly back. "Mrs. Smithson was nursery governess to the Archdeacon's children until they were old enough for a proper governess," she explained. "So I used to see a great deal of her at one time when she was taking her charges for a walk in the Close or the Palace Gardens. And when she married Mr. Smithson, the Archdeacon married them, did he not, Christine? In the Bishop's private chapel, too! Such an honor. But Mrs. Spender, the Archdeacon's wife, was so fond of Christine, and she insisted on giving a small wedding breakfast for her at their house. And now you have two children of your own to take for walks, my dear. Where have you been today?"

They told her they had been to the castle ruins and were taking Miss Macalister home with them to tea, whereupon Miss Sellinge smiled again, said it was so nice to see Christine and her family looking so well, and with a gracious goodbye that included Vicky rejoined her nephew and walked on with him to Adelaide Villa.

"I am glad Miss Macalister has made such nice friends," she told Sebastian. "Smithson is a reporter on the *Echo*—a most polite, unassuming young man—and his wife is one of my favorites. Miss Macalister is quite a mystery in the town."

"Indeed?" Sebastian did not sound interested.

"One can see at a glance that she is a lady," went on Miss Sellinge. "That is to say, unless you saw her in the shop in her black badly fitting dress and that horrid overall. But she speaks in a very refined way, and when she is out she wears clothes that have been expensive and well cut. People say that her parents are dead, and indeed it is more than probable, because I cannot imagine any lady allowing her daughter to become a shop assistant. And her brother is paid for at the grammar school by a Macalister relative, so I am told. Somebody said it was Sir Hector Macalister, but that is sheer nonsense, of course. Macalister is a fairly common name. But one wonders what Miss Macalister was doing before she came to Westborough."

Sebastian hunted in his mind for a plausible explanation and suddenly remembered Vicky's visit to the Arctic Fur Store. "Could she not have been a lady's maid?" he suggested. "Do not ladies give their old dresses to their personal maids? But you will know more about that sort of thing than I do, Aunt Kitty."

"Of course!" Miss Sellinge stopped short at her little iron gate, looking at her nephew with admiration. "How clever of you to think of that. It solves everything—not only her clothes but her refined accent, which no doubt she picked up from her mistress. A lady's maid. Yes, I should say that is exactly what she was, and that, of course, is why Mrs. Snow took her as an assistant. Lady's maids are usually very good with their needles."

So Vicky's past was solved to Miss Sellinge's and her friends' satisfaction.

The new assistant at the milliner's had been a lady's maid in possibly a titled lady's establishment—it soon grew to be a duchess's establishment, and there was even a hint of her having attended a lady-in-waiting at one time—and she had left in order to be near her brother at the grammar school.

The mystery was solved. Indeed, there was no mystery about it. The thing was as plain as the nose on your face.

Sebastian lay awake for some time on the night of that bank holiday, his thoughts with Vicky and her new friends. What had she not come down to that she was glad to make friends of a reporter on a country newspaper and his wife, who, moreover, had been the Archdeacon's nursery governess? Had she deliberately chosen these people, turning her back resolutely on those like himself who would have done all they could to help her?

His anger with her soon faded, giving way to compassion. Who were to be her friends if she turned her back too on people like the Smithsons? There was the milliner and her head assistant, who, according to his aunt, was to marry the draper, Cumberledge; there were the work girls in the shop, and though he might curl his lip at them they would help her to hide from her world far more easily than he could.

Determinedly he put Vicky out of his thoughts. Her chin was much too determined, he thought, just before he dropped off to sleep. A chin like that on a woman could be her downfall. Or on the other hand, of course, it could be her salvation. And in any case he was thinking far too much about Miss Macalister.

As for Vicky, she too had been sleepless that night. She could not forget for some time that much as Sebastian seemed to want to regard himself as her friend when there was nobody near to observe them, he would not acknowledge that friendship in public or in front of his aunt. Remembering how he had asked at one time if he could not take her to his aunt and ask for help, she was thankful now that she had refused to consider it. The charming patronage with which Miss Sellinge had greeted her and her new friends had made her feel half sad and half indignant. The Smithsons had been so kind, were being so kind. Sebastian, who had so many friends, could not understand what it meant to have none in a town where, if only her uncle had shown some Christian charity, she should have had some of her own class, if not many.

You could change your name, she thought, but you could not change the past. The stigma of her father's behavior remained, and would remain forever among those who had once been her friends.

If ever the day comes when I am rich, she told herself, I hope my father will hear of it and come back to England, thinking to find me waiting for him. Because I shall never wait for him or welcome him in my house, however rich I may be.

The hurt he had inflicted was too deep and too lasting to be forgotten or forgiven. And if ever an opportunity should come when she could teach him the lesson of heartlessness as he had taught it to her, she would grasp it with both hands.

A few days later, however, a letter arrived for her, directed in a handwriting that she knew. She thrust it into the pocket of her overall to be read at the end of the day in the privacy of her little room.

"My dear Vicky," Sebastian wrote, "I feel I cannot allow another day to pass without apologizing for my boorishness last Monday. I did not even have the courtesy to take off my hat to you. But I remembered that when I asked you once if

I might introduce you to my aunt and enlist her help on your behalf you refused so emphatically that I could only respect your wishes. I understand from my aunt that she always attends Speech Day at the grammar school at the end of June, and she tells me there will be many people there. I intend to make one of them in the hope that I may be able to exchange a few words with you. Crowds are sometimes as good hiding places as milliners' shops. Yours as ever, Sebastian."

The kindness, the thought for her in the letter, brought a warmth to her heart. She locked it away in her trunk with the picture of Costerley that he had given her at Christmas, and the following evening she took it out to read it again before replying to it.

"Dear Mr. Sellinge"—she refused to call him Sebastian—"It was very kind of you to write, but there is nothing for which you had to apologize, and I was glad that you respected my wish for privacy. I shall hope to see you at Speech Day, in the distance if not to speak to, because I understand the winner of the bursary is to be announced. James is refusing to talk of anything but cricket: he is in the second eleven and I am learning a considerable amount about the game. Yours sincerely, V. Macalister."

Speech Day was certainly the most eagerly awaited day of the whole school year. It took place on the last Saturday in June, the long summer vacation beginning in the following week.

As James's only relative, Vicky had been invited, and when she asked Mrs. Snow if she could be spared that day she was told that of course she must go. Mrs. Snow studied her carefully, head on one side. "If you will show me the dress you intend to wear I will give you a new hat for it, and I will trim it myself."

Vicky unpacked a simple white dress with a short train from her trunk. It was made of white silk with a large bow of white silk tied at the back of her slender waist. Its lace neck was boned up high under her chin, and after approving of it heartily Mrs. Snow produced a chip straw hat trimmed with white daisies, their yellow centers accentuating the dark eyes beneath them. With white kid gloves cleaned with Fuller's earth on her hands—Mrs. Snow would not allow cleaning with benzine, saying that it was much too dangerous—Vicky felt that she would not shame James that day.

She was met at the school gates by her brother, who had

been keeping an anxious watch for her. Relatives and friends of the boys were pouring into the big hall where the speeches and prize-giving were to take place, and he took her straight to the place he had kept for her beside the Warrens.

Mrs. Warren could not quite hide her surprise that a shop assistant or even a lady's maid could wear such a dress and hat with the air that was natural to Vicky. The girl was a lady born and bred, she thought, and there was a mystery about her that could not be explained away by stories in the minds of the town's gossips. But as a doctor's wife she had been trained not to probe into other people's business, and she greeted James's sister kindly, saying she was glad to meet her at last. As for the doctor, he had only time to ask after Mrs. Snow before the proceedings began, with the arrival on the platform of Dr. Eccrington and the Dean, who was to present a few prizes before making his speech.

The report on the school year was read out first by the headmaster, dwelling with pride on successes, and regret but encouraging words on certain failures, before handing over to the Dean, who spoke for such a long time on the dangers of the world outside that waited for the boys when they entered on manhood that Vicky found it hard to keep awake.

And then at the end of it all, after giving out a few prizes in the shape of Latin dictionaries and volumes of sermons selected by himself, the Dean stated that he had to announce the name of the boy who had won Bishop Bridie's Bursary, and she sat up again, very wide awake. It was, said the Dean, a boy who had been in the school less than a year, a boy by the name of James Macalister.

In the outburst of clapping that followed, James went scarlet, and Vicky put out her hand to grip his, ready to weep with delight. "I *knew* you would do it!" she whispered.

"Well then, I did not." He gave a small grimace. "There were a lot cleverer fellows than I am in for it."

The clapping died down, with whispered words of congratulations from the Warrens and their friends, and then the headmaster rose to his feet again and said that as everyone knew this bursary was awarded not only for the pupil's ability in taking the necessary examination, but in his ability to work, and this—perhaps owing to his Scots blood—was what had secured the coveted prize for young Macalister.

When it was all over the relatives and friends who had been invited to luncheon with the boys made their way to a couple of large marquees that had been erected on the school lawns.

Mrs. Warren asked Vicky and James to join them, and they were following the doctor and his wife and their sons toward a table large enough to accommodate them all when they were held up in the crowd, and a well-known voice said softly beside her, "I told you we might meet. Will you please congratulate James for me? You must be very proud of him."

She turned her head and smiled up at the man beside her. "Oh, I am indeed. Where are you sitting for luncheon?"

"At the head table with the Dean and his family."

"You will enjoy that." The eyes under the pretty hat laughed up at him.

"That is unkind." But a smile lurked around his grave mouth. "Have you a holiday today?"

"For the whole day. Am I not fortunate?" And then as James found an opening in the crowd through which he could lead his sister to join the Warrens, Sebastian was forced to seek his aunt and conduct her to the large table at the top of the tent.

Miss Sellinge was seated on the Dean's right, and her nephew was placed firmly between the two Miss Burkes, who asked him if he was staying for the cricket match in the afternoon. He said he thought his aunt intended to stay for it and that therefore he would too.

"Young Macalister is clever," said the Dean to Dr. Eccrington. "Is not that his sister with the Warrens?"

"It is."

"Hm." The Dean studied Vicky with interest. "What was their father?"

"A gentleman who was unfortunate in money matters, I think," said Dr. Eccrington suavely, and across the table Sebastian inwardly applauded him for his caution.

"I doubt if he was a gentleman," said the Dean. "I think he was more likely to be a head clerk in an office in the City. There is nothing like it for inflaming such a man's sense of importance. No doubt he attempted to bring his daughter up as a lady, seeing the daughters of his employer driving about with their mama in grand carriages. Not being able to afford such luxuries himself, he used his employer's influence to obtain the post of lady's maid in some grand household for his daughter. I have seen these things happen so often, where men ape their betters and come to grief in the end."

Sebastian regarded him with some wonder and not a little relief. He had worked the thing out to a nicety, and nobody would contradict him. Vicky's past and present were now firmly fixed in everyone's mind, sealed by the Dean himself.

He turned to the eldest Miss Burke and asked her if she played tennis, receiving an emphatic denial.

"Oh dear no, Mr. Sellinge. I would not attempt to play it. In my opinion it is a game that should be left to the gentlemen."

"It makes one unpleasantly warm," said her sister, Louisa, on his other side. She was more frivolous than Elsa and fancied it attractive not to sound her r's. "So vewy, vewy warm, Mr. Sellinge. Mama says a lady playing at tennis is the most undignified sight in the world."

He glanced at the girls' dresses, the skin-tight fashion that had succeeded the crinoline, with short trains that swept the grass, and could not think they would find it comfortable to play an energetic game in such garments. He became aware that Miss Sellinge was addressing a question to him from her place beside the Dean.

"Yes, Aunt Kitty?" he said.

"We were talking about those articles in the *Echo* written by somebody calling themselves 'A Lame Duck,'" she said. "I sent some of them to you to read, Sebastian. Did you not think them good?"

"Those I have had time to read remind me a little of Elia," he admitted. "Who is the gentleman? Does anybody know?"

They all exclaimed, and his aunt cried out, 'My dearest Sebastian, they are not written by a Lame *Drake*—they are by a Lame *Duck*. It must be a lady who writes them."

"Now, how can you be so sure of that, Aunt Kitty?" Sebastian was not alone in waiting for her answer.

"Well, you know, my dear, I have a slight acquaintance with Mr. Smithson, that nice reporter on the *Echo*. I saw him only the other day outside the newspaper's offices, and I said, "Mr. Smithson, we are all dying to know the identity of the Lame Duck." He replied that he was very sorry to disoblige a lady but his lips were sealed. So I said that at least he could tell me if she was a local lady, and he admitted that she is."

The Dean congratulated her on having discovered as much about their mysterious authoress. "The articles she writes remind me a little of Miss Mitford's," he conceded graciously.

"They have the same country flavor. You have read this week's 'Country Epitaphs,' I suppose?"

"I have indeed. Though my favorite is still 'Shadows.' It is charmingly done."

Sebastian sat silent among all this discussion, deciding that he would read the bundle of cuttings from the *Echo* when he returned home. In the meantime he found his eyes straying every now and then to Dr. Warren's table, far away to the right of the headmaster's, where there was a great deal of hilarity. Vicky seemed to be thoroughly enjoying herself: she was laughing as he had seen her laugh in the old days before her father had deserted her, and he wished he were at her table instead of with the two Miss Burkes.

He decided that he must see her and speak to her again before he left. Somehow he must find an opportunity to discover what had changed her since he last saw her. She looked happy as well as completely self-possessed—in fact, there was a secret radiance about her that he failed to understand. He hoped with all his heart that she had not fallen in love with one of Mr. Smithson's vulgar friends.

Chapter Twelve

After luncheon there was the annual cricket match between the first and second elevens, and as the Dean's party made their way toward the seats that had been placed under the trees that surrounded the pitch, Sebastian found himself for a moment beside James, on his way to the pavilion and carrying his bat.

He asked him where he was going to be for the long summer vacation, and the boy told him that Colonel Timberloft had invited him there again with Timbers.

"You will enjoy that," Sebastian said. He put his hand in his pocket. "Perhaps this will help with pocket money."

"Oh, thank you, sir. You are very good." James pocketed the sovereign gratefully. "Although Vicky has given me quite a lot of tin lately. I do not know where she gets it from because Mrs. Snow does not pay her a fortune."

"I expect she saves it up for you," Sebastian said, smiling. He wished him luck in the match and looked for Vicky but could not see her anywhere. He was forced to return to his aunt and endure the vapid conversation of the Misses Burke for the rest of the afternoon.

Vicky was not at the match because she had gone indoors to consult with Mrs. Hall over James's clothes, both those that he wanted for his holiday with Timbers and the repairing and renewing of any that could be made to do for the coming term. He was growing so fast, however, that they both agreed some new suits and a new overcoat would be essential.

She made a note of everything that he would require, to be sent to Mr. Larkin for his approval before they were purchased, and it all took a little while. The match had finished, not ingloriously for the second eleven, who had held their own remarkably well against the first, and tea was over too when she came out of the school gates.

Most of the guests had departed to catch local trains, and

the day boys were going home with their parents. Vicky had promised James that she would come for him as usual the next afternoon, when the boys had been allowed longer leave than usual as it was the last Sunday of the term, and as she left and turned up into College Street she paused for a moment beside a small bookshop on the corner that catered to the school.

A tray of fourpenny books, marked down from one shilling and sixpence, was standing there, and she took from it a copy of *Cranford,* one of her favorites.

It was as she was turning the pages that Sebastian said beside her, "Do you mind if I walk a little way with you? My aunt has been offered a lift in the Dean's carriage."

"If you do not mind waiting while I buy this book," she said, smiling.

"What is it?" And then she gave it to him, *"Cranford!* But what a dirty, tattered copy. I think we might find something better than that inside."

"But it is only fourpence. You cannot expect a great deal for fourpence!" she protested, but he had already disappeared into the shop. In a few minutes he was out again with a finely bound copy of the book she wanted in his hand.

"But that is more than fourpence!" she said, shaking her head.

He glanced inside the cover. "One shilling and sixpence," he said. "Allow me to give it to you as a small celebration of James's success." And then as she took it from him with a smile of thanks he went on: "Which way shall we go? Is there no place less public than the Bishop's Palace Gardens?"

"There is the path down by the water meadows," she said. "It is one that I often take, because there are so few people there. Indeed, except for a few small fishermen with broomsticks for rods and dough for bait on bent pins, sometimes I have met nobody at all."

"Then let us go there."

She turned to the left as they reached Bridge Street, into a lane that led past a few cottages. The lane then petered out into a path where the river descended into the meadows, old willow trees on either side casting reflections in the water.

"In the spring," she told him as they entered this path, "there are kingcups growing on the banks. They are quite lovely and I have picked them from time to time to bring sunshine into my little room." She glanced at his absorbed face. "You are very silent," she said.

"I beg your pardon." The fact was that as she mentioned the small fishermen with their bent pins he had suddenly remembered one of the few Lame Duck articles that he had read. It had described just such a river as this, with kingcups out and a small boy fishing there, and was entitled, "Philosophy of a Fisherman," with a delightful report of the lady's conversation with the lad. He was also remembering the conversation about the Lame Duck's identity at luncheon, and James's casual reference to his sister's increase of "tin," and above all he recollected Vicky's recent friendship with Mr. Smithson of the *Echo*. Putting all these things together, he found that they might add up to an astonishing but quite credible whole.

They had come to a part of the river where a narrow wooden bridge spanned it to the other bank, and she led him onto it, pausing in the middle to lean on the rail and point out to him the fish that darted like shadows in and out of the weeds that were being swayed and flattened by the current of the stream. "I love watching the fish," she said. "They are almost transparent, are they not? I believe they are mostly dace." And then, as he still remained silent, "May I ask what you are thinking about so deeply?"

"I was thinking about the Lame Duck," he said and saw her quick look at him and the accompanying flush.

"What do you mean?" she asked.

"We were talking about her at luncheon," he said quietly. "Her work is very generally admired in Westborough—the Dean compared her to Elia, and others compared her to Miss Mitford. Everyone was making guesses as to who she could be, and only agreed on one point, that she must be a Westborough lady."

"I do not see why they should think that." It was obvious, however, that she was embarrassed. "The articles have not been very unkind, I think—not even the first one about the new emporium."

"Nobody mentioned unkindness in that connection," he assured her. He rested his elbows on the rail and looked down into the clear water with her. "Everyone said how charming they were. My aunt is giving me a bundle of them to take home with me to read." He paused and then added deliberately, "I think you told me once that you were good at essay writing?"

She turned to him protestingly. "It is only guesswork on your part!" she said.

"But correct, I think. You gave yourself away when you spoke of your small fisherman just now. 'Philosophy of a Fisherman' is one of the few I have read." He raised himself, and for a moment his gloved hand covered hers on the rail of the little bridge. "I can promise you one thing. Your secret is as safe with me as it is with Mr. Smithson and his editor."

She looked relieved and pleased. "They are giving me fifteen shillings for each one," she told him in a low voice as if even the fishes must not hear. "That, with Mrs. Snow's fifteen shillings, makes me a rich woman. Do you not think so?"

"It is a good start," he agreed. "But now you have started you must go on. I have a friend who is a publisher, and when I have read the articles my aunt has cut out of the *Echo* for me I will with your permission show them to him and discover if he thinks them good enough for publication in book form. Will you allow me to do that?"

"With all my heart." She was radiant, and he thought with relief that he had found the secret of her happy looks at luncheon. It was not a friend of Mr. Smithson's who was the cause of it, but Mr. Smithson himself. "Oh, would it not be fun," she went on, "if I became a famous authoress—like Ouida, you know. I could rent that little cottage that James and I have often talked about, and he would be able to come there for his holidays. He would have a home of his own once more, and even if he goes abroad to build bridges and railways and harbors when he is a man it would be there for him to come back to in the end."

He wondered, not for the first time, if she ever thought of herself.

"I don't think you need have any fear for James," he said. "He is well able to look after himself."

"Yes." She smiled at her thoughts. "I sometimes think he has forgotten that his name has ever been any other than Macalister."

"Whereas you," he said, watching her, "will no doubt change it again."

"What do you mean?" She saw him smile and colored a little. "Oh, you mean that I shall marry?"

"Exactly. If you were to marry me, for instance, you would then automatically become Vicky Sellinge."

He saw her eyes dance, and her laughter rang out, happy and sweet. "If I were to do that," she said, "can you *imagine* what your uncle the Judge would say?"

"I can imagine very well," he replied composedly. "But I cannot say that I allow myself to be guided very much by my uncle these days."

Her eyes returned to the darting fishes in the weeds, and the smile died from her face. "I shall never marry," she said quietly. "That I have quite decided."

"Are you not rather young to make such a decision?"

"My father decided it for me," she said. "I am now twenty, and if I were to choose a man of my own class to fall in love with and to marry, can you imagine him choosing *me*—the daughter of a swindler and a thief? And I could not marry anybody like my dear Mr. Smithson, nice as he is. Oh, he amuses me enormously and I am very fond of him and his wife, but we do not speak the same language. If I were to marry a man like that the day would surely come when I would quarrel with him and he would round on me, asking what right I had to dictate to one who had never known anything but honesty all his life."

Her eyes had lost their laughter as they left watching the river and studied his face instead. "You must agree with me there?"

"I do not agree with a word of it," he replied. "Of course you cannot marry a chap like Smithson—that goes without saying—but you will marry all the same." He changed the subject abruptly. "Have you no assets on which Mr. Larkin could advance you some money?"

"I have some jewelry that was left me by my godmother— a Scotswoman—and it may be valuable or it may not. But in any case it cannot be mine until June of next year, when I shall be twenty-one."

"And I suppose if it is valuable you will sell it in order to buy a large house for James?"

She shot him a queer little glance, almost as if she pitied him for his ignorance. "Oh no," she said. "I know exactly what I am going to do with it."

She walked on across the bridge to the other side, and he followed her, finding a wider path this time that led back to a deserted Market Street and from thence into Mitre Lane.

As they walked she changed the subject by referring again to the Lame Duck articles. "I have dreams about those," she said. "You have started a whole host of them in my mind."

"Can you confide in me what they are?"

"Why yes. If I made a fortune as an authoress the news of it might reach my father. He might even manage to slip back into the country and come to my house and ask if Miss Lingford was at home. And do you know what I should do?" Her eyes were somber and she gave a hard little laugh. "I'd send my servant to tell him that nobody of the name of Lingford lived there or ever had. And then he would go away, as he left me, penniless and without a friend in the world. Is not that a lovely dream?"

He did not answer for a moment, and then he said, "But it is not a dream with which I could possibly credit you, Vicky. *I* would do it, if the chance were mine, but for all that determined chin of yours, you would not."

She pulled down her mouth. "You speak as if you know me better than I know myself."

"I am beginning to think that I do." After a moment he added, "Have you always hated your father?"

"Oh no. When I was a child I adored him. He was such fun to be with, always laughing and joking. He used to insist that when there were no guests present James and I have our luncheon with him and Mama in the big dining room. Once when James was about five years old we had been having a lot of rabbit for our schoolroom dinners, stewed rabbit, roast rabbit and so on, and that day there was rabbit again with onion sauce. James pulled a long face and sighed and said he was rather tired of rabbit. Papa looked at him with concern and apologized and said, "Well, James, what shall we give you as a change the next time you come down to the dining room? Shall we perhaps try a piece of the sideboard?" You should have seen Jamie's face as he stared round-eyed at the massive piece of mahogany, wondering how on earth he was going to get his teeth into it. And then Mama asked Papa if he would like it roasted or boiled and we all laughed, and nobody laughed louder than James, who suddenly saw that it had been one of Papa's jokes." She frowned. "That is one of the things that makes me so angry with my father. He has destroyed all our happy memories of our old home. He spoils everything, even the little things."

They stopped by the empty marketplace, and she was silent for a moment before going on.

"You do not know how much I would like to have your little picture of Costerley hanging over my bed. But it would lead to questions that I cannot answer. Those are the things for which I hate him most, almost more than the loss of my friends."

"But you have some friends still," he said quietly. "Do not forget that, Vicky."

"And they are worth all the others who have left me," she agreed. They walked up Mitre Lane toward the High Street, and just before they came to the High Street she stopped and held out her hand.

"You have been a good friend to me, Mr. Sellinge," she said. "And I would not have you think me ungrateful for your friendship."

He took her hand in his and held it for a moment before saying a rather abrupt goodbye and leaving her to walk on to the milliner's shop alone.

But as he left the High Street for St. Francis's Lane and climbed its winding way to the almshouses and the Close beyond, he knew that he had never been so attracted by any woman in his life before, and he wondered if the time would ever come when he would be able to make his proposal to Vicky in earnest and she would not laugh.

The beginning of July meant that for a time at least no more of the Lame Duck's articles were needed by the *Echo*. There were garden parties to be reported upon by Mr. Smithson, especially the Bishop's. There were Sunday-school outings and treats, there were outings to the seaside arranged by local factories and shops. Mr. Cumberledge had one such excursion for his people, closing his shop for the whole of one Wednesday and giving each member a half-sovereign to spend on souvenirs and going on the pier. A midday dinner was provided for them, and before they came home a high tea in the largest restaurant.

All this was Mr. Smithson's territory and his alone, just as were cricket matches organized by local squires of the villages around Westborough, and when August came in the harvesting to report on and cattle shows and plowing matches.

Not until September could Vicky hope to send in any more of her sketches, and so she started work on a book. In the same way as she had written her Lame Duck articles she would take a notebook with her out into the country on a Sunday afternoon, jotting down descriptions of villages and great houses, watching the wildlife in the hedgerows, and writing it down when she got back to her room.

In the evenings she worked on her novel, the plot forming slowly in her mind; it was not until one Saturday when she had been sent out by Mrs. Snow to post a parcel just before the last parcel post left that it took a definite shape.

As she was coming back from the post office she caught sight of a rather fine young gentleman standing nonchalantly at the corner of St. Francis's Lane, as if he were waiting for somebody.

A few seconds later the work girls poured out of the back entrance of the milliner's shop in the lane and she saw one stay behind, making a pretense of fastening a boot button.

The gentleman walked on, taking a narrow turning to the left in the lane, where it led behind cottage gardens to a more deserted part of the town, and after the girl had finished with her boot she looked quickly around her to see if any of the other girls remained before running across to take the same turning. And before she disappeared Vicky saw that she was Rose Dalling.

The young gentleman had obviously made an assignation with the girl, and it troubled her not a little as she went back into the shop and up to her room.

Rose was not only extremely pretty but she was also vain and empty-headed. If some young spark came after her he would not find her a difficult conquest, in spite of the devotion of Joe Webber.

As she thought it over her sympathies were more with Joe than with Rose, touched with a certain amount of apprehension. She recalled the young man's fine physique; if he discovered that this young gentleman was attempting to seduce his Rose he would be quite likely to take the law into his own hands, risking transportation or even hanging.

She did not wish to speak to Mrs. Snow or even to Miss Fosbery about what she had seen, because after all there might be nothing in it. The following Monday, however, something happened that made her not quite so ready to dismiss it from her mind.

Rose was early for work that morning, having been given a lift into the town in her father's cart. He had a small holding out at Duxbury, a village five miles outside Westborough, where he grew fresh vegetables for a small shop belonging to his brother.

Rose was sitting alone in her workroom as Vicky passed the open door, admiring a gold bracelet on her wrist. She hastily pushed it up her sleeve, but not before Vicky had seen it too.

"Why, Rose!" she said, smiling. "What a lovely bracelet. Did Joe give it to you?"

"No then he didn't." Rose's pretty face clouded over, and she looked up angrily at Mrs. Snow's assistant. "And it ain't nothing to do with you, any road, Miss Macalister."

Vicky flushed at her rudeness but told her quietly that she had seen her follow a young gentleman into Pyke's Passage off St. Francis's Lane on Saturday evening and she wondered if he had given it to her.

Rose shot a quick glance at her and went red. "Don't know what you mean, I'm sure," she said. "What young gentleman? I never met no young gentleman in Pyke's Passage."

"I was worried," Vicky said, "because of Joe."

"Oh, *him!*" Rose tossed her head and laughed. "A fine life I'd 'ave if I married a chap like 'im. I'd be wasted on 'im, I would. All a man like Joe wants of a wife is somebody to scrub at the washing, cook 'is meals, look arter 'ens and 'ave children under 'er feet till in a matter of a few years 'er looks is gone and 'er figure too. It ain't fair to expect a girl like me to 'ave a life like that with Joe."

Vicky was silent, seeing the force of the argument. Certainly pretty girls did lose their looks quickly when they married farm laborers, even if such laborers were, like Joe, employed on Lord Evensbury's estate.

"It's all very well for you," went on Rose, more aggrieved than ever by her silence. "*You* wouldn't marry a chap like Joe, and you know it. You're a lady, you are, though you 'ave come down 'ere to 'ide from something what you've done. Mebbe a young gentleman took advantage of you, Miss Macalister, and that's why you're ready to cast doubts on Mr. Victor Lingford!" She clapped her hand over her mouth. "There. I didn't ought to 'ave said that."

"I will forget it," said Vicky coldly. "But if you continue with his acquaintance you will regret it." No Lingford would ever be a Prince for a Cinderella, she thought, as she went on down to the shop.

The following Sunday was a beautiful day, and Mrs. Snow

asked her if she intended to take a walk in the country, as she often did while James was away.

Vicky said she thought of walking out toward Duxbury, and the milliner asked her if she would be so good as to take a little bonnet to a cousin of hers who lived on the Duxbury road.

"I always give her one of my old bonnets on her birthday," she said. "She looks forward to that, though they may be two or three years old. Her husband was head gamekeeper on the Evensbury estate, and when he died his lordship's agent, Mr. Richardson, told her she could live on in the same cottage rent-free for the rest of her life. Ever so good he's been to her, has Mr. Richardson, because his lordship was so fond of her husband. Rabbits she gets, and ducks, and corn to feed her hens—she keeps half a dozen and they lay real well. And always a leg of pork come Christmas. It isn't more than three miles or so to walk, if you take the path across the fields. You can't miss the cottage. It's whitewashed outside with a thatched roof, and it stands by itself almost opposite the bridle track through Duxbury woods."

Vicky accepted the errand with pleasure and started out with the bonnet parceled up in her hand and her notebook and pencil in the pocket of her dress.

The fields were now turning into deep gold, and as she took the footpath to Duxbury she delighted to see the scarlet poppies on either side with the corn cockles, and the scarlet pimpernel, the poor man's weather glass, opening its tiny faces to the sun.

When she reached the end of the path and had climbed the stile she saw the cottage opposite the woods about half a mile up the road. She walked toward it slowly, taking her time and noticing all the birds and the different kinds of flowers and the small animals in the hedgerows as she went.

The cottage door was opened by a splendidly clean old lady with a white lace cap on her head and a spotless apron tied over her Sunday dress of purple cloth.

"I thought my cousin would not forget my birthday," she said as she welcomed Vicky inside the cottage. "She never does. A new bonnet, too. She always sends me one, and my neighbors in the village is right down jealous of them when I wears 'em to church of a Sunday." She dusted a chair for Vicky to sit on and took a cup with roses on it from a cupboard by the fireplace, poured out a cup of tea from the pot on the hob, and produced a slice of cake from her larder.

"You set you down and rest," she said. "I daresay you come over the fields, which is two mile short of the road, but it's hot outside today and you must be tired." She gave Vicky a penetrating look. "You're the Miss Macalister what everyone is saying used to be a lady's maid," she said.

Vicky admitted that she was Miss Macalister but said nothing about being a lady's maid, and the old lady continued.

"Being as you are new to working in a shop I expect you found it strange at first, but I daresay you find my cousin's place nice to work in."

Vicky said she was very happy there, and the old lady went on: "I wouldn't say a word of this to my cousin, dear, but one of her girls is heading for trouble if ever a girl did. It's that Rose Dalling—a very pretty girl, but with no more sense in her head than I have in my little finger. I am told that she meets Mr. Victor Lingford, Mr. Harold Lingford's son, in them woods opposite every Sunday afternoon. I daresay they are there now, because I saw him ride by only a little while ago, and he turned up into the bridle road, what my husband used to take every day of his life. When I saw him today I thought to meself, I know where you are heading for, my fine young spark—it's that silly Rose waiting for you at the other end of the track. My husband would never allow anyone into them woods when he was head gamekeeper up at the castle. Said he had more respect for his pheasants than he had for lovers." She chuckled knowingly, and then became grave again. "But if Mr. Victor Lingford seduces Rose and Joe Webber finds out he's going to wait fur him one dark night and half kill him. Joe's deeply in love with Rose, worthless little piece as she is, and he'd risk hanging if he thought she had a lover besides himself."

Certainly it seemed that Victor Lingford was playing with fire, and it also seemed that the whole of Duxbury knew about it. Vicky wished she could warn him, not for his own sake but for Joe's. He was too good a young man to be hanged for what was only a game to young Mr. Lingford.

Having drunk a cup of bitter tea and eaten the slice of dry cake, Vicky took her leave, being entrusted with many messages of thanks to Mrs. Snow for the bonnet, which was tried on in her presence before she left.

It was still early, and with much to employ her mind that

could not be written down in her notebook, she mounted the stile that led to the path across the fields back to Westborough and wondered if she should impart any of the warning about Rose to Mrs. Snow. She had no wish to get the girl into trouble with her employer, however, and it was as she sat there with her notebook in her hand that she heard a horse's hooves approaching from the direction of the Duxbury woods.

It took only a glance to see that the rider was Mr. Victor Lingford, and on an impulse she slipped down off the stile and stood in his path.

"Wait a minute, if you please, sir," she said. "I wish to speak to you."

He drew on the bridle and stopped his horse, and she saw the surprise in his face before he took off his hat to her.

"I beg your pardon," he said. "Have I the honor of your acquaintance?"

"My name is Macalister," she said. "But that is of no consequence. I think you may have been meeting a work girl from the milliner's shop, a very pretty girl by the name of Rose Dalling, in those woods. If you have, I must ask you, sir, to discontinue such meetings. You may not know that she is promised to a laborer on Lord Evenbury's estate, and that his lordship's agent, Mr. Richardson, has promised them a cottage next summer. Rose's future husband is deeply in love with her, and your meetings with Rose are already widely known in Duxbury village. If they should come to his knowledge he is quite likely to wait for you one dark night and have it out with you with his fists. He is a very large and powerful young man, and I would not put it past him to have the best of the encounter."

"If he attacked a gentleman of my standing he could face transportation." Victor Lingford's face was dark with anger. "And in any case I am not quite sure I know what you are talking about."

"I think you do." The dark eyes met his with contempt. "Young laborers of Joe Webber's standing do not give gold bracelets to their promised brides."

"Oh, so that was it. You saw the bracelet I gave her—" He broke off, knowing he had given himself away. "I would like to know what right you have to interfere."

"Perhaps I have more right than you know," she said and walked back to the stile, leaving him to whip up his horse and canter furiously up the lane.

She made her way back to the shop slowly, hoping that she had persuaded him to leave off pestering silly pretty Rose. Nobody, even Victor Lingford, wanted a scandal to blow up in Westborough over an affair with a little work girl in the town.

Chapter Thirteen

The only boy in a family of girls, Victor had always been more than a little spoiled, and he had also been run after by a considerable number of fond mamas who wished to win a rich marriage for their daughters.

Very seldom, if ever, had a young lady spoken to him as Miss Macalister had spoken that afternoon, and as he rode back to Westborough his temper gradually cooled and he wondered where he had met her before. He was quite sure that he had at least seen her somewhere in or near Westborough, and not so very long ago.

As he neared the Hall, memory came back to him in a flash. Of course, she was the young lady he had seen leaving his father's house one morning last October. He had been out riding and had come around the corner of the house to see her and a boy of about fourteen or so walking away together. They had not seen him, and the boy's voice had come back to him, half laughing, half angry. "He might have given us luncheon," he had said.

"He" was apparently Mr. Harold Lingford, but why should he have given them luncheon? At the time Victor had dismissed the boy's words without another thought, concluding that the two had come from some charity to beg assistance from his father.

But now his memory went back still further as he recollected that it had been at the beginning of that October that his Uncle Paul had left the country, taking with him a great deal of money that rightfully belonged to other people. A fraudulent railway company or some such thing. Could those two young people that October day have been his cousins, then? The parting remark of the young lady that afternoon that she might have more right to protest over Rose Dalling than he thought suddenly took on a new meaning. If she was Vicky, then most certainly she would have the right as a cousin, if not as her father's daughter. He wondered if his father knew that she was employed in the milliner's shop. If he did it would be amusing to enlighten him, and perhaps turn the situation to his own advantage. He smiled a little and let his horse sample the grass verge in the lane for a few minutes while he thought it out.

There was always a cold supper at the Hall on Sunday evening, and they waited on themselves, the servants being expected to attend church in the town. There were only four of the family there that evening, his youngest sister, Sue, their parents and himself, and when the meal was ended and the two ladies went to the drawing room, where Sue amused herself by playing the piano and singing a few old ballads, Victor asked his father if he might speak to him.

Harold grunted and said he supposed Victor had more debts to be settled and led the way into his study, where his son sat himself down in a large armchair and said that his father might be relieved to hear that he had not come to discuss any debts this time.

"I only wanted to tell you," he went on, watching his father's face carefully, "that I met my cousin Vicky Macalister—as she now calls herself—when I was out riding this afternoon."

If he had any doubt that his father knew of whom he was speaking it was dispelled at once by the purple flush that invaded that gentleman's face.

"You *what?*" he spluttered.

Victor repeated what he had said, adding that he believed his cousin was now an assistant in a milliner's shop in Westborough.

"*That* young woman!" Harold had time to recover himself. "I know all about her, thank you. Whatever she may have told you it is common knowledge in Westborough that before she came here she was a lady's maid, and she is the daughter of a common city clerk."

"She told me nothing about herself except her name, and I only concluded that she was employed at the milliner's because—" He stopped abruptly. "But she is no more the daughter of a common city clerk than Sue is. She is a lady, and I think you know it, sir."

"She is Paul's daughter," growled Mr. Lingford. "And her damned brother is a pupil at the grammar school here. I suppose Paul left them with no money—I know the boy has always been supported by his grandfather, old Sir Hector—but the girl took this situation to be near him and to hold a threat over my head. That was the whole purpose of their visit to me last October, I am quite sure. I should have received them, calling them Smith or Robinson and saying they were the orphaned children of an old friend, and I could then have used my influence to get the boy placed in some school in Scotland and the girl could have been found a situation as a companion or governess as far away from Westborough as possible. I know what I should have done now that it is too late, and in the meantime the girl works in that shop where many of your aunt's friends go for their bonnets and holds an eternal threat over my head."

"I do not think she intends to claim any relationship with our family, all the same," said his son. "I would not do so if I were a child of Paul Lingford. If the truth got out it would harm her and the boy. But it might harm you more, sir."

"What do you mean?" Harold looked sharply at his son and saw the complacent smile on that young man's face with some misgiving. "How could it harm me?"

"Oh come, sir, you do not need me to explain, surely? If somebody in the town were to learn the truth of the story about Miss Macalister and that in fact she had been turned away by her uncle, who is always too anxious to have his name heading every charity committee in Westborough, without a penny piece—" He stopped and watched his father's face, his smile deepening.

"Who is going to spread the story? And who will believe it anyway?" But Harold was blustering, and Victor knew he was winning.

"I have an unfortunate habit of telling stories against my family when I am among certain of my friends in London," said Victor. "I do not mean any offense, I promise you, only a joke. And you must admit there is some humor in the situation—my cousin Vicky serving my aunt's friends with their bonnets while her uncle sits here wondering when everyone is going to find out who she really is."

"I see no humor in it at all," said his father. "And if you are wise, sir, you will hold your tongue."

"I have every intention of doing so," said Victor complacently. "As long as I get what I want."

"So!" Mr. Lingford was so angry that for a moment he could not speak. Then he said in a stuttering way that seemed as if he might be going to have a seizure, "My own son—blackmailing me. My own son. I did not think it possible."

"Blackmail nothing," said Victor contemptuously. "But I do find it extremely hard to manage on the thousand a year that you give me, sir, and I would like it increased to five—as I am now of age, and you are extremely rich."

"Five thousand a year!" This was too much. "I will never do such a thing."

"You must please yourself, of course." Victor got out of his chair. "I am afraid my sisters—all so well married, and one with a husband who is a member of Parliament—will be a trifle embarrassed when the truth about their cousin comes out. People have such a horrid habit of believing the worst of their friends. While of course Westborough is a hotbed of gossip, and such a piece of news would be handed about for months. I am afraid you and Mama and perhaps Sue might find it very unpleasant for a time." He sauntered toward the door and had almost reached it when his father called him back.

"You shall have the money," he said bitterly. "I have no choice, have I?"

"Very little," agreed his son cheerfully.

"But don't expect me to pay any more of your debts in future." And then as Victor did not answer, Harold Lingford inquired what Miss Macalister had been doing in the Duxbury lane.

"She was sitting on a stile writing something down in a notebook," said Victor. "But I did not ask what she was writing and she did not tell me." And this time he was allowed to go.

For a long time Harold Lingford sat there bitterly regretting his conduct toward Vicky and her brother, and he made up his mind that somehow at all events he must get the girl out of the town. If she had stopped Victor in the lane to speak to him she would stop others. And why was she writing things down in a notebook?

It bothered him so that when he went to bed he could not sleep, and when he eventually dropped off he was prey to nightmares. Then quite suddenly in the early hours of the morning he woke up, remembering the last occasion when his brother had visited them, in order to try to persuade him to put money into his fraudulent railway. He had asked him if Vicky was good at the piano and if she had a good voice, and Paul had laughed and said the only thing Vicky was good at was writing essays at school and stories for her brother in the holidays, and he hoped she would not grow up into a bluestocking.

A bluestocking. Writing essays and stories. And she had had a notebook with her that afternoon. Supposing she were the Lame Duck of the *Echo*, writing articles about people and places, and damning the opening of the new shop in the High Street so that it had never properly recovered?

Supposing she went further and wrote articles about relatives who refused to help nephews and nieces?

"I will go and see Driffle in the morning," he said aloud. "Those articles must be stopped. I'll make him tell me the name of the writer."

He flung himself back on his pillows with such force that he woke his wife.

"You've been kicking about all night," she told him reproachfully. "You ate too much of that cucumber. I told you it would give you indigestion, and it has."

But Mr. Lingford had turned over and was already asleep.

For a time Rose openly sulked, and Vicky heard that Mr. Victor Lingford had gone to Scotland for some shooting. After a time, however, Vicky saw Rose out with Joe one Sunday afternoon with her sulks all gone, and the next Sunday he came to Duxbury in a trap borrowed from the Evensbury Home Farm to fetch her out. The object of the expedition was to show his future bride the cottage that Mr. Richardson was going to have ready for them by Michaelmas, when Joe was being promoted to head herdsman on the farm.

Vicky heard Rose telling the other work girls all about it. It was to have a proper cooking range fitted into the kitchen, one from Cumberledge's down the street. There was to be an oven on one side of the fire in the range and a boiler for hot water with a tap to it on the other. And there was to be a pump in the back kitchen so that she would not have to carry a bucket into the yard to get water.

In the meantime Vicky wrote to James every Sunday and received scrappy letters from him in return. They were near enough to the sea to go swimming every day, they went out fishing, and they played cricket with the families of neighbors, the boys of those families like themselves home for the long summer vacation. There were accounts of picnics and excursions and rock climbing, and he was so full of what he and his new friends were doing that Vicky was sure he had not the time to miss her, and she was glad of it.

He was back at the end of September, and the school term commenced, so that she was no longer left to her own devices on Sunday afternoons. Her brother had grown at least two inches, she told him, and she had never seen him look so well or be in such good spirits.

She let him into the secret of the Lame Duck articles, which delighted him very much. Then one Sunday soon after the term had started and she was walking with him in the Palace Gardens she saw Mr. Smithson there, evidently looking for her, because directly he caught sight of her he hurried toward her.

She introduced James to him and told him that James knew all about the Lame Duck articles and they could speak freely in front of him, but she saw that he looked worried and his usual cheerful smile of welcome had left him. She said: "Have you come to see me about those Lame Duck articles, Mr. Smithson? Does Mr. Driffle not want any more?"

"He wants them enough," said Mr. Smithson, looking very cast down. "And I can only guess at why he is not continuing with them. Miss Macalister, have you offended some grand lady in Mrs. Snow's shop?" He broke off. "Oh, but it is impossible. Of course you have not."

"Please explain," she said. "What is it that concerns you so much, Mr. Smithson? You are a friend, and I would like you to be frank."

He hesitated and then he said, choosing his words carefully:

"A certain gentleman who lives in a large place outside Westborough came into the *Echo* offices a few days ago to see Mr. Driffle about some small advertisement to do with farming implements, and just before he left he spoke about 'Those little articles by the lady who calls herself a Lame Duck.' He asked who she was, and Mr. Driffle said he had to respect your wish for anonymity. The gentleman said he was aware of that, but he had had a hint that the authoress was in a humble position in a milliner's shop in the town. Mr. Driffle admitted that it was true, but said he trusted the gentleman to keep it to himself. 'Oh, of course,' said the gentleman with one of those wolfish grins of his, 'it is nothing to do with me, but I believe it would pay you, Mr. Driffle, to use the column you have been devoting to this little shopgirl's efforts to something more worthwhile.' And then he stalked out." Mr. Smithson paused, looking more unhappy than ever. "The thing is the Town Clerk is a great friend of this gentleman—a horrid toady of a man detested by everyone—but he is the owner of the *Echo* and if he agrees with Mr. Lingford that those articles must not be published then they will not be."

"I see. So it was Mr. Lingford who came into the *Echo* office that day?" Vicky spoke thoughtfully.

"Why, yes. And I know that Mrs. Lingford patronizes Mrs. Snow's establishment, which is why I wondered if you had offended the lady—quite unwittingly—at some time."

"I may have done. Some of these fine ladies are hard to please." Vicky forced herself to speak unconcernedly and squeezed James's arm, guessing at the outburst that hovered on his lips. "Think no more of it, Mr. Smithson. I can only thank you and your editor for printing so many of my little stories, and in any case I do not think I would have had time to continue with them this autumn. Every one of our customers appears to be needing new bonnets all at once, and Mrs. Snow scarcely knows where to turn to make them all."

She smiled at the worried little man, sent her love to his wife and children and walked on with James.

"Well," the latter exclaimed when they were out of earshot. "Could you believe it possible? For our uncle—having treated us in the first place like beggars—to try and stop you from earning another few shillings a week by printing those little Lame Duck articles! I read one of them last week, Vicky, and I thought it was damned good. It is the meanest thing I ever heard. Why is he doing it?"

"I daresay because he has guessed the Lame Duck's identity correctly and he is frightened."

"Frightened? Of you?" James was scornful.

"Not of me. Of his own conscience."

"You will never convince me that he has such a thing."

"I daresay he has not. In which case it is just another point that I have to score against Papa. At every turn he comes to the surface to remind me that I am his daughter. I hate him, James. I cannot tell you how much I hate him—far more than I hate Uncle Harold. For him I've only contempt. But Papa I hate with all my heart, and I am sure you must hate him too."

"No," said James thoughtfully. "I do not think I do, because I have never believed that the things people said about him were true. Papa was not the sort of person to defraud people deliberately. I am sure that man Grammidge had him in his clutches and he could not escape. And what is more, Colonel Timberloft thinks so too."

"Colonel Timberloft? You did not tell him, James?" She was horrified.

"Of course I told him who I was, last Christmas when I first went to stay there. Timbers is my friend, Sis. I could not take his parents' hospitality on false pretenses." And then as she remained silent he went on, "I talked it over with Timbers on the way down and we decided that I would see his father that evening. So after dinner I asked him if I could speak to him privately, and he took me into the gun room and asked me what it was."

"And you told him you were Paul Lingford's son?"

"Yes. I can't tell you how nice he was about it, Sis. He put his hand on my shoulder and thanked me for telling him, and said that lots of people changed their names—some just to inherit a fortune. He said he had known Papa years ago and he was quite sure the day would come when everything would be cleared up and I would be able to be proud of him again, and that he was not the sort of man to defraud people, and he was certain there was some mistake. And he told me that I was welcome in his house as often as I wanted to come."

Vicky was silent for a long moment, and then she said with a little sigh that she wished she could believe it but she could not.

She was remembering a day in the week before when she had been arranging some hats in the shop window and Miss Fosbery caught her arm, pointing out an old clergyman who was walking on the far pavement. He had a stick on which he appeared to lean heavily, he looked tired, and his clothes were very shabby.

"You see that poor old gentleman?" Miss Fosbery said. "Well, it was Mr. Harold Lingford's brother that ruined him. He has a living in a village just over five miles on the other side of Westborough Hall, and the stipend is no more than fifty pounds a year. He had a small private income that enabled him to keep a pony and trap, though, and to buy a few extras for his invalid wife. And then he saw this paper advertising railway shares and Mr. Paul Lingford's name on the paper, promising a larger income than what he was getting on his money. So the poor old gentleman put all he had into that dreadful railway, and of course he lost it all. Now he has to walk to the palace when the Bishop's chaplain wants to see him, and his poor wife is so ill I'm told she can't last much longer. And all because of that brother of Mr. Harold Lingford. I sometimes wonder that Mrs. Lingford has the impudence to walk into this shop and order bonnets and hats as she does, knowing that the old gentleman isn't the only one as has suffered in that way."

Vicky had felt then that every word Miss Fosbery uttered found an echo in her own heart, and as she listened she was sickened afresh by what her father had done. And here was James, saying that he had not known what he was doing, encouraged by Colonel Timberloft. And what did that gentleman know about it in any case, as he had been out of the country for years?

She could not speak of it any more and walked to the school gates to kiss her brother goodbye.

"What will you do, Sis?" he said anxiously then. "Without the extra money from the *Echo?*"

"Oh, I shall manage very well, as I did before." She smiled at him reassuringly. "While you were away I started to write a book, and I shall go on with it now. But instead of turning it into a novel as I had intended, I shall write another series of articles, all about the grand ladies who come into the shop, and the way they behave—both to Mrs. Snow and to her assistants—and the hats that looked so pretty on Miss Silcocks and will look so ridiculous on some of our customers."

"But you will not be able to use real names," he said, horrified.

"Oh no. Do not look so alarmed, James. It will not have Westborough as its city, and neither will any of the characters be easy to identify."

"And what will you call your book?"

"Oh," she said lightly, "there is only one title for it, and that is *The Milliner's Shop.*" She laughed, kissed him again, and left him, walking back up College Street with her determined chin in the air, as if she were meeting a new challenge and finding it worthwhile.

She had been looking forward to the addition to her income that the Lame Duck articles would give her that autumn, but she put it behind her with resignation, thinking that perhaps they had not been as good as everyone said they were. And as she had no word from Sebastian she concluded that his publisher friend had thought the same.

She continued to write her book at night, however, and she enjoyed it because she was able to lose herself in the writing. Imaginary characters took shape interwoven with real-life stories, gathered from the gossip of Miss Fosbery and Mrs. Bellon, and the work girls, and Polly and even Cook. She had managed to put by nine pounds from the money she had earned from the *Echo,* and she added to it as many shillings every week as she could spare from her salary from the milliner's shop.

So the autumn passed, and then just before Christmas the weather turned bitingly cold, snow in the Palace Gardens with a bitter northeast wind making it too unpleasant to contemplate a walk. So she spent a little while with James at the school and returned to the milliner's shop to find it in chaos.

Miss Fosbery was at the Cumberledge's as usual, Cook was having one of her turns in the kitchen, and upstairs in the best parlor Mrs. Snow was stretched out on the settee unconscious, with Dr. Warren beside her and Polly standing as still as one of the stands of corsets around them, too frightened to speak.

The doctor was glad to see Vicky as she came into the room. "Thank heaven for the bad weather that sent you home so early," he said.

"Is she very ill?" asked Vicky anxiously, looking down at the gray face of her employer.

"It's an aneurysm," he told her quietly. "I am afraid it is only a matter of days—maybe of hours."

"You mean—she is dying?"

"I am afraid so. Perhaps Polly could run down the street to fetch Miss Fosbery."

Polly snatched her shawl from a peg on the kitchen door and ran, leaving Cook to recover from her turn as best she might, but fast as she ran and quickly as Miss Fosbery and Mr. Cumberledge hurried back with her, by the time they arrived in the upstairs parlor Mrs. Snow was dead.

Chapter Fourteen

The shop was closed for a week, and most of the shops in the town closed for the day of the funeral, their owners crowding into St. Francis's Church near West Gate, which Mrs. Snow had attended for so many years. Having paid their respects, they then left Mrs. Cumberledge and her son and Miss Fosbery, Vicky and Mrs. Bellon and Polly to see her buried in the churchyard under the yew trees there.

The lawyer, Mr. Mellis, came back with Miss Fosbery, Vicky and Mrs. Bellon to the parlor behind the shop, where wine and biscuits had been set out for his refreshment, and as they sat in the little room that the milliner had used as her office he told them the terms of her will.

She had only one sister, living in Wales, with whom she had quarreled many years ago, her only son was dead, and as she had no other living relative Mrs. Snow had left the shop and its contents, including goodwill and what money she possessed, to her devoted friend Miss Eliza Fosbery. There was only one bequest, that of one hundred pounds to Mrs. Bellon.

The news of her inheritance nearly sent Miss Fosbery into a fit of hysterics, fortunately forestalled by Vicky with a glass of sherry wine. The lawyer congratulated the lady, told her that when she had time to think about what she was going to do—she might for instance, contemplate selling the business—she was to let him know and he would come and see her with all the legal parts of the contract to be signed and witnessed.

"And although you will miss your friend," he added, as he shook hands with her before he took his departure, "you will also be comforted to know how much she appreciated you by leaving you a business and a competence which many would envy."

He went away into the dark December afternoon, and for

a time Miss Fosbery was too overcome to speak. Then she asked Vicky if she did not think she should send for Mr. Cumberledge.

"He was at the graveside with his mother, you know, dear," she said tearfully. "But he was very discreet and tactful and left me to come back here alone with Mr. Mellis. He was never one for pushing his way into other folks' business, wasn't Mr. Cumberledge, though we have been walking out together for ten years. 'I shall wait for you,' he said, when I told him I could not leave Mrs. Snow, 'and when she goes, my dear Eliza, the banns will go up the following week.'" She sighed. "But with dear Mrs. Snow scarcely cold in her grave as you might say, I feel it might look a little indelicate to send for him today."

Vicky disagreed stoutly. "Nobody could have shown more devotion to Mrs. Snow," she said. "And Mr. Cumberledge has been equally devoted to you, as well as being helpful to her with his advice and help whenever she needed it. I think it would be only kind and appreciative if you sent Polly down with a note asking him to step up at once."

The result was that directly they had finished an elaborate tea provided by Cook, who knew what was due to mourners after a funeral, Mr. Cumberledge appeared, full of sympathy for Miss Fosbery and equally anxious to know if she had been left anything by her late employer.

When he heard of the extent of the legacy he was reduced to silence for a few minutes while he digested it. "She left you the business and her money as well?" he said then incredulously. "Did Mr. Mellis say how much you could expect to inherit?"

"He said that apart from the business it might be as much as five thousand pounds," said Miss Fosbery faintly. "I cannot believe it, William. It seems like a dream."

"But not a bad dream, my dear, sorry though we all are for the loss of Mrs. Snow. You are a rich woman, Eliza." He put his hand on hers. "And nobody deserves it more, if I may say so. I am sure Miss Macalister and Mrs. Bellon will agree with me there."

"We do indeed." Mrs. Bellon, however, was a trifle put out that she had not been left more than a hundred and soon took her leave, while Vicky took the tea tray out to Polly, and as Cook had retired to her room, saying that funerals always brought on one of her turns, helped Polly to wash up the crockery in a bowl of hot water on the kitchen table.

She then went up to her cold little room and sat there with her fur-lined cape around her shoulders and a rug around her knees, wondering what would happen to the milliner's shop, and if the go-ahead Mr. Cumberledge would advise Miss Fosbery to sell it. Or would he marry her and include the business with his own, putting in a saleslady to take charge of the millinery and corsetry department? One could not forget that he had served his full apprenticeship in London and had a very good head for business.

She wondered uneasily what the future held for her and if her work here in the milliner's shop must end.

The following morning, over breakfast in the little parlor downstairs, the shop not being due to be opened until after the following Sunday, Miss Fosbery told her that she and Mr. Cumberledge planned to be married in February.

"In the meantime, William intends to advertise for a head saleslady for this shop," she went on. "He does not wish me to have anything to do with it after we are married. We shall live with his mother for the time being, but he intends to have a house built for us on the outskirts of the town on the Duxbury road—it is so nice and open out that way. He says we shall be able to afford a house that will need at least two or three servants and he will have a garden large enough to employ at least one full-time gardener, if not two. And he intends to set up his own carriage."

As Vicky sat silent, struck dumb with the ambitions of the go-ahead Mr. Cumberledge, Miss Fosbery went on to impart more of his ideas for the milliner's shop.

"The staircase, he thinks, can be widened and made to lead directly into the large parlor downstairs. He wants that room to be turned into a larger showroom for millinery, while the room that is at present my bedroom will be turned into a fitting room for corsets. Although a number of ladies now buy their corsets ready-made, there are still some, as we know, who like Mrs. Bellon to make theirs for them."

The alterations to the shop would take place while Mr. Cumberledge and his bride were on their wedding trip in the Isle of Wight, and it would be followed by the installation of a leading saleslady who would take charge.

Mr. Cumberledge was already drafting an advertisement

to be put in some of the trade journals and hoped they would be suited before long.

"I did suggest you for the post, dear," added Miss Fosbery. "But William thinks you are too young."

Vicky was relieved to hear it. She wanted to stay in the milliner's shop until James had left the grammar school, but after that she had no wish to be tied down to Westborough. At the back of her mind there was still the dream of the little house she and her brother would share one day, although since he had been a visitor at the Timberlofts he seemed to have grown away from her in a way that she tried to understand while it hurt.

Once more Christmas had taken him away from her to Norfolk, and although she was invited to take her Christmas dinner with old Mrs. Cumberledge as the year before, it was not a festive occasion.

The meal was accompanied by tearful recollections of Mrs. Snow from Miss Fosbery and her future mother-in-law, and Vicky was glad when she could leave with the excuse of leaving Miss Fosbery to discuss future arrangements with her William and find her way back to the shop with Polly.

Her room was too cold to sit in, and so she sat downstairs with Polly by the cheerful kitchen fire and listened to the girl's stories of the orphanage where she had been before being rescued by Mrs. Snow.

It was cozy sitting there roasting the chestnuts she had bought and sharing them with Polly, Cook having stayed behind to gossip with Mrs. Cumberledge's cook and be regaled with port wine, poured out with a generous hand by Mr. Cumberledge.

There was a heavy snowfall that Christmas, and when it melted the water meadows were flooded and then froze hard, providing grand skating for the youths of the town and the boys from the grammar school.

The first Sunday in January, Vicky made her way down to the frozen expanse of water, watching James in the distance as he performed figure-eights in competition with the less accomplished Warren boys.

She was smiling as she watched them, her hands tucked into a small fur muff, when a deep voice said behind her, "And is not Miss Macalister skating this afternoon?"

She turned quickly and greeted Mr. Sellinge with a quiet delight that quickened his pulses.

"Why are you in Westborough?" she asked, and then, "No, do not tell me. You are visiting your aunt."

"As I had neglected her throughout the Michaelmas term and the Hilary term is not burdening me with quite so many briefs, I felt I should come down here to see how she is."

"I hope she is well?"

"Very well. She does not like venturing out in this cold weather, however." He paused, his eyes taking in the pale-gold hair that curled under her little fur hat, the sparkle in her dark eyes, the warm generosity of her mouth and her deplorably determined chin. "I hoped I would find you here with James. Did you spend Christmas with him at the school?"

"Oh no. He went to the Timberlofts in Norfolk. He has struck up a great friendship with the family." In spite of herself she could not help bitterness creeping into her voice. "The Colonel knew my father many years ago and has convinced himself—and my brother—that he was merely the victim of the villain Grammidge, and as innocent of any intent to defraud as a babe unborn." She frowned at the skaters. "It is a point of view that I cannot—that I will *never* share."

"I am glad I have found you," he said, changing the subject abruptly. "Because I have wanted to apologize for being so neglectful in writing to you about your Lame Duck articles. They are quite charming, and are now in the hands of my publisher friend, Philip Brent. He has had them for some time and I am seeing him next week in the hope of getting a decision from him to publish them in a book."

She shook her head sadly. "I am afraid there is no future in that sort of thing for me," she said, and told him of Mr. Harold Lingford's successful wrecking of her contributions to the *Echo*.

Mr. Sellinge appeared to be quite unmoved. "That is the sort of thing that every writer encounters, I believe," he said equably. "I hope you have not let it put you off writing any more articles?"

"Oh no. If anything it has made me more determined to continue writing," she told him, her chin well up.

"So there will be another book to follow the first," he said with satisfaction. "When I have seen Philip next week I will have that amount of ammunition against him. If anything comes of that interview—and it will not be my fault if it does not—might I suggest that you take a day off from your mil-

147

liner's shop and come to London to see him? I will meet your train and take you to his office, and afterward perhaps you will lunch with me in my rooms in Gray's Inn. You need have no fear of not being properly chaperoned," he added hastily. "Although Herbert is sufficient in himself."

"So Herbert is with you?" She remembered the staid gentleman's servant with pleasure.

"He is my valet, messenger and general factotum." He saw her shiver in the cold air. "You are cold, and as James shows no signs of joining you, may I walk with you back to your shop? You had better take my arm. The paths and the streets are like glass."

She took his arm, careless of what any townsfolk who saw them might say, and felt its strength warm and comforting under her hand. When they reached Mitre Lane he took something from his pocket and slipped it into her muff.

"Look at it when you get back to your milliner's shop," he said. "It is a small Christmas gift—rather late, I am afraid."

He saw her as far as the shop door, and there he left her, and when she reached her room she sat down on her bed and untied the string of the little parcel, breaking the Sellinge seal.

Inside the packet there was a jewelers' box, and in the box, on a bed of velvet, a small oval locket. The locket was of gold with V in pearls on it, and when she opened it she saw the tiny figure of a duck in diamonds, with sapphires for eyes, and one scarlet-enameled foot lifted a little as if it were lame.

It was far too expensive a present for her to accept from any man, but she knew at that first sight of it that she would never part from it. She held it against her cheek, remembering the look in Sebastian's eyes when they had met that afternoon, and the warm strength of his arm under her hand, and she knew that he was the one man in the world with whom she could fall in love. If falling in love were possible for the daughter of Paul Lingford.

Sadly she opened her trunk and packed the little locket and the gold chain that had accompanied it away with the little watercolor drawing of Costerley. Such things as eligible young men and pictures of Costerley and lame ducks in diamonds belonged to the life she had left, the world that her father's behavior had closed to her for ever.

* * *

Mr. Cumberledge selected a lady who signed herself Madame Rene from the many answers to his advertisement. She said she had been head saleslady in a large store in Regent Street and furnished him with glowing references as to her ability and character, and as February was fast approaching and there was no time to be lost she came down to Westborough to be interviewed.

She was a large lady with a massive bust, black hair frizzed into a fringe under an extremely smart hat, and eyes that were black and sharp. Her expression too had a sharpness about it, as if she were daring anyone to try to deceive her. Her smart tailored costume was of navy-blue serge, and her hands were thrust into tightly fitting black kid gloves, embroidered on the back in jet.

She wore high-heeled boots, with yellow kid uppers, and her skirt rustled as she walked as if there was a silk petticoat beneath it. Vicky took a dislike to the woman on sight: she was so hard, so sure of what she would or would not have in the shop, and so very different from gentle Mrs. Snow. She was sure too that her dislike for Madame Rene was reciprocated.

When, for instance, she inspected the workrooms and Vicky's tiny bedroom at the end of the passage she turned to Mr. Cumberledge and said with her hard bright smile that she had no doubt Miss Macalister would not object to finding herself a lodging in the town.

"There must be plenty of rooms to be had in a cathedral city of this size, and I shall need her room for another workroom. You say you have six work girls here—I have never worked with less than fifty, and even in a little business like this I would require at least ten and another sewing machine or two. There is so much machining to be done in corsetry, as I know Mrs. Bellon will agree."

She agreed to start work on the day after Mr. Cumberledge returned from his wedding trip, in return for a salary of two hundred a year all found, and after she had gone back to London Miss Fosbery asked Vicky with some anxiety if she would mind looking for a room while they were away.

"Of one thing you may be quite sure, my dear," she added. "We shall never turn you out. It would be quite unthinkable after all you did for dear Mrs. Snow."

Vicky assured her that it would be no trouble for her to find a room and she would arrange to move before the wedding day so that the workmen who came in to do the conversions to the stairs and the parlor would not be hindered by her.

That night after she had undressed she took the little key to her trunk from the gold chain around her neck and counted out what she had managed to save from her salary and the Lame Duck articles. It amounted to thirty-five pounds, which would be a temporary help toward a furnished room, which with attendance and a fire but without food must be all of ten shillings a week.

She went to see Mrs. Eccrington, who was as kind and helpful as ever and gave her the names of several houses where there were rooms to be let. "The relatives of several of our boarding pupils have been very comfortable with Mrs. Giles in Bishop's Court Road," she told her. "I should try her first if I were you, my dear."

Certainly Mrs. Giles was the sort of landlady for whom Vicky was looking. She had been a housekeeper in a gentleman's family, and she showed Vicky a nicely furnished room that was vacant. It was large and quiet and looked out on the trees surrounding the Palace Gardens, but unfortunately Mrs. Giles knew a lady when she saw one and charged accordingly. Her terms, she told Vicky, were a pound a week, and that would include attendance, a fire in her room, and all meals, including a hot midday dinner on Sundays.

She seemed shocked when Vicky told her that she would be working at the milliner's in the day and would only require breakfast and a light supper at night.

"Well," she said in an altered tone, "of course I have a smaller room you could have, but it has no outlook and there is always a great demand for my rooms, being so near the palace and the school. I could not charge less than fifteen shillings a week for it."

Vicky thanked her and said she had a few more rooms to look at and if she found nothing to suit her she would come back, which gave some offense, Mrs. Giles saying that she did not think she would find better rooms in the town.

In her heart Vicky agreed with her, and as she explored the other addresses her opinion was confirmed. They were all situated in noisy streets, near public houses, or too near the river, and their prices did not vary very much from Mrs. Giles's. At last, however, she settled for a small house in Railway Street, situated in a row of similar red-brick villas.

Although it smelled of oilcloth and cabbage, the charge for a small back room looking out on the neighbor's washing was only ten shillings a week "and all found."

The landlady, Mrs. Jorrocks, was of a very different class from Mrs. Giles and was interested to hear that Vicky worked at the milliner's.

"Mrs. Snow was a lovely lady, dear," she said. "Nothing unfriendly about her, was there? I remember one of me daughters going in there once to look at a wedding bonnet, and the one she saw in the window was all of three pounds. She was almost in tears. 'Oh,' she says, 'I can't afford to pay all that, Mrs. Snow. And it is such a pretty bonnet.' 'It suits you too, my dear,' says Mrs. Snow. 'I'll give it to you for a wedding present,' she says, 'and I'll put a piece of orange blossom around the brim.' I've never forgotten that, and neither has my Lucy. Fancy you working for her, Miss. And now Miss Fosbery's been left the shop and 'tis said she'll marry Mr. Cumberledge next month."

Vicky said the wedding was to take place in the first week of February, and before they parted she agreed to take the room on the day following. The furniture in it was of the simplest description, but everything was spotlessly clean, and what attracted her to it the most was the sturdy table placed under the window, just right for holding paper and ink and a tray of pens as well as a candle.

Vicky explained that Mr. Cumberledge wished to have alterations made to the shop while he was away on his wedding trip and that as the new saleslady intended to use her bedroom there as another workroom she wished to leave as soon as possible.

"Much better to be independent, dear," agreed Mrs. Jorrocks. "If you're on the spot you'll be at everyone's beck and call. But I daresay you'll have your dinner there?"

Vicky said she would, and Mrs. Jorrocks said in that case she would reduce the charge by one shilling a week. "Mr. Cumberledge will make a big thing of that shop, you mark my words," she said. "He'll go a long way, will Mr. Cumberledge. Everybody says so. I'd never be surprised to see him Mayor of Westborough one day."

They parted on very good terms, and Vicky thought she would be happier there than at Mrs. Giles's, where the fact that a lodger was working in a local shop was bound to be regarded with suspicion and disapproval.

Mr. Cumberledge was in the shop when she got back discussing the alterations with the head of a building business in which he had an interest. A tall thin man with a drooping mustache was introduced to her as Mr. Crowhurst, the head sales gentleman of Mr. Cumberledge's furniture department. "He will be looking in every day while I am away," he told Vicky, "just to see that everything is being done as I want, and he will measure for the new carpeting and see there are new Nottingham lace curtains at the winders before the shop opens the Monday after I get back." It had all been planned to the last detail in Mr. Cumberledge's orderly mind, just as the wedding was planned to take place in St. Francis's Church, followed by a small wedding breakfast in the restaurant at Cumberledge's. The main shop had been closed for the day in honor of the occasion, and after the bride and bridegroom had left for the Isle of Wight Vicky returned to the milliner's shop. There she finished packing up her belongings and sent Polly for a cab to take her and her trunk to Mrs. Jorrocks's. Just as she was leaving Polly came running after her with a letter in her hand.

"This came for you this morning, Miss," she said. "I forgot to give it to you wiv the weddin' an' everything. I shall miss you something dreadful, Miss. I don't fink I'm going to like that new Madame Rene very much. She looks a real bossy sort to me."

"But we do not know her yet, do we, Polly? She may be very nice." Vicky put half a crown into her hand and stooped to kiss her. "And thank you for all you have done for me while I've been living here. I shall not forget it."

And she got into the cab and drove away to Railway Street. It was not until after the cabby had got her trunk upstairs to her room that she remembered the letter.

It was from Sebastian.

Chapter Fifteen

She left the trunk in the middle of the floor where the cabby had dumped it and sat down on her bed to read the letter. It was written with a lack of gravity; indeed, there was about it an air of exuberance and congratulation.

He had seen his friend, Philip Brent, and he had agreed to publish the Lame Duck articles in book form in the summer. He was to pay forty pounds for the first edition, but Sebastian thought it might go into several more. In any case Mr. Brent would like to meet the authoress to discuss it with her and also any further projects. She had mentioned that she was writing another book when he saw her last. If she had finished it perhaps she would bring it with her. He suggested that she should come to London next Thursday, when he would be happy to meet her train and take her to Paternoster Row himself to introduce her to Mr. Brent. He signed himself "Yours as ever, Sebastian." And he added a postscript: "Wear your little fur hat."

She had to read the letter twice before she was able to take it in. Forty pounds! Why, with her savings of thirty-five pounds added to it she would be the possessor of seventy-five. It was riches indeed. And then she read the postscript and smiled and shook her head.

"Oh, Sebastian, Sebastian!" she said aloud. "Have you not learned anything yet?" But she thought she would wear her fur hat all the same.

She unpacked the few dresses that the one small cupboard in her little room would hold before going downstairs to an appetizing midday dinner of stewed rabbit and dumplings, with Mrs. Jorrocks's three other lodgers to keep her company.

They were a queer unmatched trio, she thought, looking at them with an eye to future books. There was old Mr. Sumpton, a retired newsagent, with a habit of clearing his throat every other moment as if he had a bone stuck in it. There was a Miss Gaunt, a spinster lady who was dressmaker at Mrs. Carey's establishment in Castle Street, one that the Dean's wife and daughters patronized. And there was a schoolteacher, Miss Loder, about forty years old, who had brought her school manners with her in a very ladylike fashion.

When the meal was over Vicky went back to her room to write to Sebastian, giving her new address and telling him that as the shop was closed for a fortnight she would be free to meet his friend Mr. Brent on Thursday and that she would arrive by the train that arrived at Paddington at eleven.

As the train pulled into Paddington that Thursday she saw him waiting for her, and she wished that her dress were more fashionable. She was conscious that the gray silk dress under the fur-lined cape was at least two years old, and that the cape itself was becoming slightly worn. But it was not at her dress or cape that Sebastian looked as he lifted his hat to her and took the hand she extended to him in greeting. His eyes were on her face, glowing with happiness, on her sparkling eyes and the ash-fair hair curling up so charmingly under the little fur hat.

He took the brown paper parcel she was carrying, asking if it contained the next book, and when she admitted that it did he added that Mr. Brent would be delighted to see it. "I am hoping for a great deal from this meeting with Brent," he said.

As they drove off toward Paternoster Row he enlarged on the subject. "Brent is a good fellow and a friend," he told her. "But publishers are not in the trade for the good of their health, and one has to remember that. I presume you hold the copyright for the articles?"

"Oh yes. The last time I saw Mr. Smithson I told him there was a chance of their appearing as a book, and he was delighted, and said that I was to send him a copy when the book came out and he would give it a 'thumping good review' in the *Echo*. Wasn't it kind of him? He has been such a good friend to me."

Mr. Sellinge did not know whether he liked or disliked Mr. Smithson more, and remained rather silent until the cab reached Paternoster Row. Here Vicky was conducted through a low doorway into a dark passage to a flight of stairs. At the first half-landing there was a door with "Mr. Philip Brent, Publisher" on it, and she was ushered through an outer office into a smaller one, lined with shelves bulging with manuscripts and tin boxes.

A cheerful fire was burning in the grate, and a gentleman rose to greet her from his writing table in the window. He was about Sebastian's age, with upstanding fair hair and a long fair mustache, and he put her at ease at once by saying that she looked far too young to be the authoress of the charming Lame Duck articles. "From their simplicity of style and gentle country air I expected a lady of more mature age."

They then got down to business, Sebastian referring to the terms that Mr. Brent was offering for the book and suggesting that as each new edition was issued the price should be raised.

"You are offering forty pounds for the first edition of two thousand copies," he said. "I suggest sixty for the second edition, eighty for the third, one hundred for the fourth and so on."

Mr. Brent raised his fair eyebrows. "While I like the book immensely," he pointed out, "I cannot guarantee that it will exceed the first edition."

"Then you will only be required to pay Miss Macalister the sum of forty pounds," pointed out Sebastian urbanely. Vicky sat silent while the fate of her little book was decided, and after Mr. Brent had agreed to Sebastian's terms the question of the authoress's name was discussed. While "A Lame Duck" was a good one for newspaper articles it would not serve for that of the authoress of a book. After a few minutes' thought Vicky suggested her mother's name, Mary Macalister.

Sebastian glanced questioningly at Mr. Brent and saw him smile. "An excellent name," he told her, adding, "And now we come to another proposition my firm would like you to consider. We publish monthly magazines and journals—*The Mayfair Gentlewoman* is one with which you are no doubt familiar. We are always in search of articles and stories with a feminine interest, and do you think you could write some for us? I suggest that I give you a copy of the journal to read so that you may study it at your leisure. We usually pay thirty shillings to two pounds for each article or story, according to its length."

Vicky said she would do her best, and after thanking him and tucking the copy he gave her into her muff, she left, leaving her new book with him. He said he would have her contract ready for signature in a few days, and perhaps Mr.

Sellinge would bring her to his office to sign it. Sebastian said he would be delighted, and added that once signed, he presumed the payment of forty pounds would be paid in advance.

Mr. Brent shook his head at him. "You're a damned tough customer, Sellinge," he said. "I would not like to fight you in court." And then with some cheerfulness he agreed and let them go.

"And now for luncheon," Sebastian said as they came out again into Paternoster Row and made their way to Ludgate Hill. "I am taking you to my rooms, and as I promised there is an excellent chaperon waiting to meet you."

His rooms were on the second floor of a beautiful Queen Anne house in Gray's Inn, and as they arrived at his front door, where his name appeared on a small brass plate, it was opened by Herbert. He greeted Vicky with a grave smile of pleasure and conducted her to a spare room where a can of hot water stood with a clean towel over it in the washbasin. On the bed there was a long sealskin coat and a lady's slightly moth-eaten fur tie, and as she added her cape to them she thought both looked familiar.

She washed her hands, however, and tidied her hair under the fur hat and emerged to be shown into the drawing room looking out over lawns.

Two ladies were sitting in this room waiting for her, and Vicky gave a cry of delight.

"Lady Taversham!" she said. "And dear Miss Sedge. How lovely it is to see you again."

Her ladyship embraced her tenderly, while Miss Sedge took her hand with tears in her eyes and retired to the edge of her chair looking more like a fox terrier than ever.

"You are thinner," Lady Taversham then pronounced, holding her at arm's length and looking her up and down. "But as usual you are well turned out and have that air of dignity that you will never lose. The wretched shop does not appear to have done you a great deal of harm. And I hear from Mr. Sellinge that it has turned you into an authoress. That is the best news he has given me about you all the time you have been there." She drew up a chair for Vicky beside her. "And now tell me all about the book. When is it coming out? Of course it will mean that you will leave Westborough. No authoress of any standing could work in a milliner's shop. You will have to find some nice rooms in London. Perhaps that nice woman in Sackville Street would accommodate you."

Here Sebastian added his persuasion to her ladyship's. "I'm glad you said that, Lady Taversham. If Vicky becomes a well-known authoress she must live in London."

"This is a conspiracy!" cried Vicky, her dark eyes full of mischief and her mouth smiling in a way that he found extremely provocative. "You have forgotten, I think, Mr. Sellinge, that I wrote those articles that your friend Mr. Brent likes so much while I *was* working in the shop, and that in fact the little collection of stories that I left with him this morning have as their title *The Milliner's Shop*. I feel it would be most ungrateful of me to hand in my notice there now."

"So wonderfully clever," sighed Miss Sedge. "What are the stories about, Miss Macalister? Or must we not ask?"

"Certainly you may ask, and I will tell you. They are about some of the people in the town, and some of the customers who come into the shop. They are about the rustic romances of work girls and the grandeur of town clerks and lord mayors. Very simple little stories because they are mostly true."

Lady Taversham, who had been noticing the expression on her host's face as he listened to Vicky and the way his eyes did not seem able to remove themselves from her glowing face for long, was relieved when luncheon was served and there was the view of the courtyard to be admired and the few family portraits that Sebastian had brought with him from Brook Street. It was impossible, thought her ladyship, that a young man with such a brilliant career in front of him as was foretold for Sebastian Sellinge should mar that career forever by an unfortunate marriage.

She was forced to admit that Vicky was very attractive and that Sebastian was fully aware of it. But Vicky had grown up indeed since they had last met: she was now a young woman with a mind of her own, and her ladyship felt she must utter a word of warning.

She waited until they were all settled at luncheon and then she remarked lightly that she thought Sebastian's aunt, Miss Sellinge, must have sometimes wondered at her nephew's frequent visits.

"The truth is, my dear," she told Vicky, "that I sent him down to Westborough to see if he could find out where you were living, what you were doing, and how you looked. Every time he visited the place he would write me a note on his return or come and see me, to reassure me that you were not as wretched as I felt you might be and that you were facing your impossible situation with your usual courage." She smiled at Vicky across the table. "I have been more than grateful to him for the trouble he has taken on my behalf."

Vicky's eyes met hers with a twinkle as if she fully understood what her ladyship was trying to say, but Sebastian looked annoyed and changed the subject to James, asking how he was getting on and if there was any chance of his being selected as captain of the second eleven that summer.

After Lady Taversham had gone, with Miss Sedge in her wake, and Vicky said she must visit Mr. Larkin, Sebastian said he would walk with her to Lincoln's Inn Fields.

They set out in silence, and it was quite a while before Sebastian broke it by saying briefly that he was afraid Lady Taversham prevaricated.

"In what way?" Vicky glanced at him with amusement.

"She indicated that my visits to Westborough had been at her bidding alone, and that is not true. When she knew you had taken a situation in a milliner's shop she was naturally as horrified as I was myself, but I managed to persuade her that you had probably chosen the best possible hiding place from your world and hers. She agreed to pry no more into your whereabouts until you wished it, and when I asked her to be your chaperon today and also revealed the secret of your little book I never dreamed that she would imply that my visits to Westborough had been taken entirely on her account. They were also on mine, Vicky."

"Do not say any more, Mr. Sellinge." Vicky turned her head to smile at him gravely. "Even if I stayed only a fortnight with Lady Taversham it was long enough to teach me all her little fancies and prejudices, and I know exactly what she was trying to tell me today. She was warning me not to let the feelings of friendship I might have for you go any deeper." Her eyes left his face and stared steadily ahead. "She need not have done it, although I am sure it was kindly meant. I am never likely to forget that I am my father's daughter."

"But if my feelings for you should be deeper—" he was beginning when she stopped him with her hand on his arm.

"Do not spoil it!" she pleaded. "Please, Mr. Sellinge, let me keep your friendship. It is—the most valuable one I know. One day you will meet a lady who will be exactly what you need and you will marry her and I trust live happily ever after. But until that time comes let our friendship remain as it is. Please!"

Her voice shook a little and he could refuse her nothing. He put his gloved hand over the one on his arm. "Very well," he said equally unsteadily. "If that is your wish, let it be that way between us."

But it did not stop him from wishing he had not asked her ladyship to be her chaperon.

As he left Vicky at the lawyer's he knew that if he wished to retain even such a fragile thing as her friendship he must try to conquer at least for a time the love he now knew he felt for her.

If he did not marry Vicky he would marry nobody, of that he was quite certain. Her visit to his rooms that day had shown him how much she meant to him, and unfortunately Lady Taversham had seen it and taken immediate action.

He thought his safest course was not to see Vicky again until he could control his feelings better than he had managed to do that day, and he wrote to Mr. Brent asking him to post the contract to her with the request that she sign it and return it to him.

Mr. Larkin received Vicky courteously, asked how she was progressing in Westborough and congratulated her gravely when she told him about the acceptance of her book.

"It will mean that when I have that forty pounds, together with the thirty-five that I have put by, I shall have seventy-five," she told him. "If I were to leave the milliner's shop, would it be possible for you to find me a small cottage not too far from London where I could work in peace?"

The lawyer considered the matter with his usual calm and then agreed that sometimes he had clients who had small properties—lodges and cottages and the like—that they were ready to let for a few shillings a week. "But I must warn you to think carefully before you make any change in your present plans, Miss Macalister," he added. "Seventy-five pounds may sound like a lot of money, but it will not last very long, especially if you intend to have your brother to stay with you during his holidays."

She agreed with him that it might be too slender a sum to start out on her own. "Although Mr. Brent has asked for some stories for his magazines and I have left another little book with him, which he seemed pleased to have. If he wishes to publish that as well as *From a Park Bench* I shall be able to look forward to another sum in the autumn perhaps."

Mr. Larkin agreed that the prospects looked good but still advised caution. "For an author to starve in an attic while pursuing his trade is one thing," he told her. "But for a young authoress like yourself it is impossible. And in June you will have your godmother's bequest, which may make you independent for the rest of your life."

She shook her head. "Oh no," she said. "I have other plans for that, and there I need your help—help for which I am very willing to pay." She told him what she wanted and saw his kind face exhibit a shocked disapproval.

"But my dear Miss Macalister, it is nothing to do with you," he protested. "I could not possibly advise you to do such a thing."

"I am not asking for your advice, Mr. Larkin," said Vicky, her determined chin much to the fore. "I am asking you to *do* this thing for me—and before June."

Most reluctantly he agreed, and then she took her leave, making her way to Paddington with a mixture of feelings. She had not let Sebastian see how much Lady Taversham had hurt her by her warning. Did she not know, she wondered, that with her father at the back of her, she could never marry anybody? As she traveled back to Westborough she felt more cut off than ever from the friends she had known.

A few days later she had a short letter from Sebastian pleading an important brief that would prevent him from meeting her in the following week, and telling her to expect the contract from Brent to be signed and possibly witnessed before she returned it to him. The letter was cool and restrained and saddened her a little, but she knew that he was only carrying out her wishes. That he was attracted by her she knew, but that he was really in love with her she would not believe. Because if she did believe it, it would break her heart.

The contract arrived by almost the same post, and on Monday morning she took it to Mr. Driffle to ask him if he would be kind enough to witness her signature, which he did willingly, congratulating her on the successful outcome of the little book. He was pleased to hear that Mr. Brent was studying another collection of stories, and as she returned the contract in its envelope said with a twinkle in his eye, "And now I suppose the next thing will be a novel?"

"A novel?" She smiled and shook her head. "That would be beyond me, I am afraid."

"Nonsense, my dear. You are a born writer, and with such a gift it will be easy. There are only three plots that appeal to ladies, and after all ladies are the people who read the most novels."

"And what are those plots, Mr. Driffle?"

"One might call them fairy tales," he said. "First we have Cinderella, or in other words the governess who marries her employer."

"Like Jane Eyre and Mr. Rochester?" she asked, her eyes dancing. "And the next?"

"Dick Whittington, or the poor boy who has such success that he comes home to marry his first love. You must remember always to have a first love, Miss Macalister, to whom the hero, after many vicissitudes, returns."

She waited. "You said three, I believe?"

"Ah yes. The third is of course the princess and the swineherd."

"You mean somebody like a shop assistant marries an aristocrat's daughter?"

"Oh no. Not as severe as that. Ladies who read novels would not appreciate a shop assistant as a hero."

Her thoughts went to Mr. Cumberledge, tubby and brisk, and to Mr. Crowhurst, tall and thin with a drooping mustache, and she was inclined to agree.

"Could he not be a young gentleman without a penny who is forced into such a situation to support an aged mother?" she asked. "He might even be a blacksmith and a rich young lady would come to the forge to have a loose shoe mended."

"I see you have the notion of it." He nodded approvingly. "Go back to your lodgings and write it all down. And when you are a famous authoress, don't forget your friends on the *Echo.*"

"As if I ever could!"

Having posted the contract back to Mr. Brent with a covering letter of thanks, Vicky returned to her lodgings in Railway Street and started on her novel.

Once the story was in her mind her pen traveled fast over the paper, her heart uplifted by her interview with the kindly Mr. Driffle, and her happiness spilling over with every word she wrote.

She spent the rest of the week in a happy dream, sharing

the news of the success of *From a Park Bench* with James that Sunday, and her hopes for their cottage that might now become a reality.

Even the information that she had sent the check for forty pounds to Mr. Larkin to put into a London bank for her did not impress her brother a great deal. He described it as a nice little nest egg for his sister, but he dismissed the idea of a cottage as slightly absurd. It was evident that Colonel Timberloft had shown him how a gentleman should live.

"Colonel Timberloft thinks we should wait until you inherit your godmother's jewels in June," went on James. "They may be worth a great deal of money that could set us up forever."

"I see." Vicky was thoughtful. "He did not think any of that money should be paid back to the shareholders in the fraudulent railway of which our father was a director?"

"Certainly not. What an extraordinary idea, Vicky!" James stared at his sister in consternation. "I hope Mr. Larkin will not encourage you in any ideas of that sort. It is not our fault that people put money into it, after all."

"No," she agreed. "It is not our fault." But her memory went back to an old clergyman tramping wearily along the High Street to the Bishop's Palace because he had had to give up his pony and trap. She said goodbye to her brother as usual at the school gates and went back to Railway Street to continue with her novel. But somehow words would not come that night. She could only think of James and how Colonel Timberloft had taken him away from her. She held no resentment against him for it. It was once more at Paul Lingford's door that the blame must be laid.

And then she took out her black dress and overall ready for Monday morning and her return to the milliner's shop.

Chapter Sixteen

Vicky had disliked Madame Rene when she first saw her, and it seemed then that the dislike was mutual. The new lady superintendent of the milliner's shop had arrived the previous Saturday, bringing with her a great deal of luggage, some of it very heavy.

It did not help Vicky's future relations with Madame Rene that she was five minutes late on Monday morning, but good Mrs. Jorrocks had no idea of time. When Vicky had come down at half past seven that morning it was to find her landlady on her knees in front of a sulky dining-room fire, trying to put life into it with a pair of punctured bellows. The kettle on the hob was stone cold, but on the table there was a loaf of bread and some butter and a jug of milk. Vicky hastily disposed of a slice of bread and butter and half a cup of milk before starting off for the shop.

Madame Rene was there, with Miss Folkestone, a young saleslady from Cumberledge's who had been sent to replace Miss Macalister as she was moved up to what had been Miss Fosbery's place. Madame was very grand in a black silk dress with many flounces, a high lace neck to it, several gold bracelets and a large jet brooch pinned to her bosom. When Vicky arrived she greeted her with extreme coldness, staring at the fur-lined cape.

"You are late, Miss Macalister," she said in her most refined accents. "Kaindly do not let it occur again. The work girls 'ave been 'ere at least half an hour."

Vicky apologized and promised to be more punctual in future, and went on into the passage behind the shop to hang the cape beside the work girls' hats and jackets.

Her first morning under Madame Rene was not an auspicious one. The new saleslady found endless fault with the way the stands were arranged in the windows downstairs, and she did not like the hats and bonnets that were displayed in the large showroom upstairs, but fortunately she could not find anything to say against Mrs. Snow's chairs and settees that had been newly and elegantly upholstered in pale-blue striped rep, and made excellent resting places for ladies who climbed the stairs to examine hats and bonnets and corsets.

Ready-to-wear corsets were displayed in what had been Miss Fosbery's room, with Mrs. Bellon there to advise.

After that first morning Madame could not complain of Vicky's unpunctuality. Often she would have a slice of bread for her breakfast and hurry away, hoping to make up for it at dinner in the middle of the day with the work girls in the dining parlor at the back.

Madame would allow her no more than a quarter of an hour for her meal, however, and then peremptorily recalled her to take charge while she had her dinner brought up to her room by Polly. The dinner that was taken to her was infinitely superior to that of the work girls, consisting of chicken, or mutton chops, or a steak, followed by pastries from the pastry cook down the street, and cheese and a glass of beer or porter.

She would come down from her meal looking flushed and well satisfied and sucking a violet cachou, which Vicky regarded with suspicion, remembering a housekeeper at Costerley who had been addicted to violet cachous and was finally dismissed for drunkenness.

One day after she had been there a week she told Vicky, Miss Folkestone and Mrs. Bellon that it would not be long before she had the milliner's shop on its feet. It occurred to Vicky that Mrs. Snow's shop had never been anything else but on its feet, and perhaps unwisely she said that Mrs. Snow always had had most of the country trade, a remark that was instantly resented.

"I'll thank you not to back-answer me, Miss Macalister," snapped Madame.

Vicky held her tongue with difficulty, conscious of the startled glances of the others, but after that unlucky occasion she became the target of Madame's temper. She would invariably select a moment when a customer was in the shop to criticize or scold her.

"I said at once, Miss Macalister," she would rail at her. "Do not dawdle like that. We have not got the whole day in front of us. Bring the bonnet over 'ere, as I told you."

Vicky would bring the bonnet, often to find the work she

had put into it destroyed, with ribbons and flowers ripped off. "That's not the way to put ribbon on," Madame would say. "Reely, Miss Macalister, you should know better by this time."

The days were a misery, subject as she became to Madame's bullying, but every night when she returned to her little room Vicky happily forgot it in working on her book, and on stories for *The Mayfair Gentlewoman*. Mr. Brent took two of these without question, forwarding to her a check for four pounds, which she sent to Mr. Larkin on Saturday morning.

When she started out for work in the mornings she would arm herself against Madame's insults by telling herself that she knew no better, that maybe she was jealous, knowing how much the Cumberledges liked and trusted her. Her determination was strengthened by a letter she received one morning from Mr. Brent saying how much he liked *The Milliner's Shop*, that he would like to publish it before Christmas, but the contract and the terms on which he could buy it must wait until he was assured of the first book in June. This struck Vicky as being very sensible, but it seemed that he wished in any case to buy the second book and she would be quite content if it was to be on the same terms as the first.

The letter made her happy all day, and she was quite unprepared for the scene that awaited her that evening.

At about eight o'clock, after she had been kept busy on trifling alterations that could have been done in the morning, she found Madame waiting for her, a gleam in her eyes.

"One moment, Miss Macalister," she said, "and there's no need to look at me like that as if I was dirt. You've no right to put on airs, if anyone did. I 'ad a young man in here today, name of Slide, what is traveler for the firm of Makins and Shrub, what makes velvets."

"I know the firm." Vicky stopped in the empty shop to face her enemy and waited.

"He happened to tell me your true story, Miss Macalister," said Madame Rene triumphantly. "Not the true story as you told Mrs. Snow, though I've no doubt Mrs. Snow knew it but was too good-natured to refuse to take you into her shop."

Vicky frowned. "I have not the slightest idea what you are talking about," she said.

"Haven't you reely?" said Madame. "Then I'll tell you. Mr. Slide was in the commercials bar at the Red Lion and he sees there a man that was footman to Mr. 'arold Lingford at Westborough Hall." She saw Vicky's expression change and suddenly become more intense. "I see you know what I've heard this afternoon."

"Perhaps you will be kind enough to tell me." Vicky's voice was cool.

"That footman, what has just been dismissed from Mr. Lingford's service because of some trifling offense what didn't please 'is lordship, said as how you and your brother came to call on Mr. Lingford a year ago last October, and Mr. Lingford sent you both off in a fury. The footman said it was his opinion as you was Mr. Lingford's children by some woman in London and she had sent you down 'ere to make him pay up, and that all he could do to keep her quiet was to find you employment with Mrs. Snow and pay for your brother's schooling and board at the grammar school."

She paused, and seeing the expression on Vicky's face, became suddenly uneasy. "Well?" she blustered. "What 'ave you to say to that, Miss Macalister?"

"That there is not a word of truth in it." Vicky's voice was like ice. "My brother, if it is of any interest to you, is paid for by my grandfather, Sir Hector Macalister of Edinburgh. We were sent to Mr. Lingford, as he is a well-known gentleman around here, to ask if he could help me obtain a situation. This he was unable to do, and as I was anxious to be near my brother, when Mrs. Snow offered me a situation here in this shop I was glad to take it. If you dare to spread such a story as the one you have just told me abroad, Madame Rene, you will hear from my London lawyer, who will explain to you the penalty you might have to pay for defamation of character. I should think it over very carefully before you believe any more tales from a dismissed footman."

She fetched her cape from its peg and left the shop, but not before she caught a glimpse of the frightened look on the woman's face. It was evident that she did not like the thought of facing London lawyers, or being taken into any courts of law.

When Vicky got back to her lodgings, however, she found herself unable to dismiss the odious Madame Rene with a shrug before continuing writing her book.

She sat for a long time staring at the empty page in front of her and not once did she dip her pen into the inkwell that had been James's gift to her last Christmas.

She could not help wondering who else had heard the foot-

166

man's story. It sounded plausible enough. Many gentlemen like Mr. Harold Lingford, grand as they might be with their attendance at the cathedral every Sunday, did keep illegitimate families elsewhere.

In the morning she was surprised to find her tormentor all smiles and honeyed words, which she found almost more unpleasant to endure than the bullying had been. Everything she did was right, and she wondered if the threat of legal action had had a salutary effect. But the man's story could not be lightly dismissed, and she found herself looking for any small groups of women standing talking on the pavement to see if they would favor her with a hard stare as she passed. Sometimes she found herself too looking back to see if they had begun a renewed and more animated conversation, as if they were discussing her behind her back.

Madame Rene certainly continued to treat her with more civility, however, and for some weeks the shop appeared to flourish under her management. And then, not long before Easter, her behavior became so strange that Vicky suspected the heavy trunks that had been carried up to her room had contained a good number of bottles, and if so that they were being emptied at a fairly smart pace.

These suspicions were confirmed when one evening she came down from a workroom where she had been putting the finishing touches to a bonnet that had been ordered for the next day, with nothing more to be done than to fetch some Honiton lace to gather up under the brim, and some yellow roses to tuck into it. The work girls and Mrs. Bellon and Miss Folkestone had gone, and as she entered the shop, expecting to find it empty, she discovered Madame seated on the bottom stair of the staircase to the large showroom, an empty gin bottle beside her and another full one in her hand.

She had already had far too much, so much was evident from her flushed face and bloodshot eyes, but when she saw Vicky she got to her feet, strode up to her, snatched the bonnet out of her hands and tore it to pieces, before flinging the bits on the floor and stamping on them.

"That's what I think of your work, Miss Macalister," she shouted. "You and your 'aughty ways. You came to Westborough because you was in trouble. I dessay you'd been caught by the perlice for stealing or worse and you came 'ere to 'ide. Ladies don't work as shop assistants, and that fur cape of yours was given you by some rich genleman in Lunnon."

Her speech became blurred and she took a draft of the full bottle to steady her nerves but became so unsteady on her feet that she had to sit down again on the stairs.

Vicky looked down at her with contempt. "I do not know how you are going to get another bonnet made for Lady Perriton by the morning," she said crisply. "Because I shall not do it. I rather think your references should have mentioned that you were dismissed from your last situation because of drink. I shall not be here in the morning in any case. I shall give in my notice to Mr. Cumberledge on my way home."

She saw the glazed eyes of Madame follow her to the door and she heard her mutter "Good riddance to bad rubbidge" before lifting the bottle once more to her lips, the ruined bonnet scattered about her feet.

Mr. and Mrs. Cumberledge were sitting by their snug little fire upstairs when Vicky arrived.

"Why, Miss Macalister!" Mr. Cumberledge got to his feet. "What has happened? Is the shop on fire or have you had thieves?"

"Neither," said Vicky, standing in front of him white-faced but extremely determined. "I have come to give in my notice, Mr. Cumberledge. I am very sorry to have to do it, but I cannot work with Madame Rene another day." She explained how she had been working late on a bonnet for Lady Perriton so that it would be ready for her servant to fetch the next morning, and how Madame had torn it to pieces. "I cannot possibly remake it in time," she finished.

"But—is the woman insane?" asked Mr. Cumberledge.

He was answered by Polly, who had followed fast on Vicky's heels.

"Oh, Mr. Cumberledge, sir," she cried. "Can you come at once? Madame Rene is lying on the floor of the shop and Cook says as she's drunk as a lord. I 'eard a thud and Cook told me to go and see what it was and there she was, wiv two empty gin bottles beside 'er and the shop smelling something 'orrible."

The shock to Mr. Cumberledge, a teetotaler and leader of the city's Band of Hope, was terrible. At first his wife was afraid he was going to have an apoplectic fit, and then he pulled himself together, told her to stay where she was with Miss Macalister and went back to the milliner's shop accompanied by Polly.

His head saleslady there was still insensible and snoring,

and he left a note for her, giving her notice on the spot and a request that she should leave for London by the first train in the morning. He told Cook that he would send Mr. Crowhurst to see that she did so.

After he had gone his wife burst into tears, but his mother said it was no more than she expected.

"That's what comes of putting in some London saleslady what he didn't know," she said. "Much better to have one that he does know, like Miss Macalister or Miss Folkestone."

"I shall go back to the shop tomorrow," said her daughter-in-law tearfully. "I have nothing to do here over Cumberledge's, and I've been twiddling my thumbs and longing to get back to the millinery ever since we got back from the Isle of Wight. After that dreadful woman has gone I shall take my old place there until we can find somebody really reliable." She sighed. "I am afraid we shall lose Lady Perriton's custom."

Vicky relented a little, and said she would see if she could find a shape similar to the one that had been spoiled and the same trimming and ribbons. "If I work at it in my rooms tonight it might be ready by the morning," she added.

"You are a good girl, Miss Macalister. I don't know what we shall do without you, I'm sure." Mrs. William Cumberledge looked at her pleadingly. "I do hope now that Madame Rene is going you will withdraw your notice."

Vicky said she would consider it, but after she had fetched the new shape and worked on it in her room in Railway Street, stitching at it by candlelight until the cathedral clock struck twelve, she felt that Madame Rene had succeeded where her uncle and Lady Taversham and even Sebastian had failed.

She had had enough of the milliner's shop.

At the end of the week she packed her trunk, paid Mrs. Jorrocks what she owed her, received her week's wages from a tearful Mrs. William Cumberledge, and set off for Sackville Street and the warm welcome of Mrs. Norris.

Her old landlady was very apologetic because she could not offer her anything more than two small rooms on the second floor, but after Railway Street they seemed spacious and even luxurious, while Mrs. Norris's cooking was a dream.

Fortunately James was spending Sunday with the Warrens, and she wrote to him to tell him of her change of plans.

Until he heard from her again, she told him, she would be at their old rooms in Sackville Street.

She felt that he might know a sense of relief that she had left Westborough. Although he had always been pleased to see her on Sunday afternoons the intervals between them when he went to visit the Warrens were becoming ever longer.

On Monday she went to see Mr. Larkin, who received her with his usual courtesy and read the letters she had received from Mr. Brent with pleasure and congratulation.

"I feel," Vicky told him, "that the time has come for me to try to launch out on my own. I am staying in Sackville Street for the time being, but I should dearly like to have a house, however tiny, of my own."

Mr. Larkin thought for a few moments, pressing the tips of his fingers together and regarding her over the steel rims of his spectacles as if he were summing up several alternatives. Then he hunted through his desk until he found a letter and, placing it in front of him, tapped it with his finger.

"A client of my firm, an old lady by the name of Miss Ellis, has recently died," he said. "She lived in a small house in a country lane leading onto Hampstead Heath, and the relatives to whom her property was left do not quite know what to do with it. They have taken the family things, like pictures and china and so forth, but it is left amply if plainly furnished. The problem is that although none of them wishes to live at the house they do not like the thought of depriving Miss Ellis's old housekeeper of a place that has been her home for forty years. Neither do they wish to discharge the gardener, who has cherished the garden for almost as long. They have asked me to help them out of this quandary by finding a lady, preferably single, who would be prepared to move into the house regarding it as a temporary abode, keeping on both housekeeper and gardener, until she decides if it would suit her as a permanent residence. Does this offer appeal to you at all, Miss Macalister?"

"It appeals to me very much indeed," Vicky said. "But I could not afford to pay a housekeeper and a gardener. And what rent is being asked for the house?"

"None," said Mr. Larkin, smiling. "And Mr. Ellis is willing to pay the wages of the two old servants. All you would be required to pay are your own and your housekeeper's food bills."

"But—why?" Vicky could not understand such generosity.

"They do not wish to make any formal arrangement until they can find somebody ready and willing to take the house permanently, and even then the tenant would have to be willing to take the old servants on. But naturally it is very difficult for them to find the right sort of lady, although when I mentioned yourself and that you were an authoress they seemed to think you might suit admirably. I did not know, of course, that you were in London and was about to write to you this morning. Mr. and Mrs. Ellis are at the house this week, and I could take you out there in a cab this afternoon to meet them and to look at it if you wish."

Vicky said she would be ready at any time he liked to call for her, and two o'clock was arranged, and punctual to the minute the gentleman arrived to assist her into the cab and start out with her for Hampstead, telling her as they went that he had referred to her only as Miss Macalister to Mr. Ellis, but had also said he had known her family for years and could vouch for her in every way.

"I mentioned that you were related to Sir Hector," he added. "But I did not specify the relationship."

His caution pleased her. Sir Hector was a well-known man of letters and had written several abstruse books on ancient manuscripts that had won him a certain amount of attention in the world that had once been her world too.

Directly she set eyes on the little house at the end of its countrified lane she knew it was just what she was seeking.

It stood back from the lane, surrounded by a high garden wall, broken in front by a wooden gate with the name "The Witchery" painted on it in white letters.

The gate opened onto a flagged path, bordered with bright spring flowers, and the house was square, like a house that a child might draw, built of red brick with a blue slate roof with two dormer windows. A sturdy front door had an iron knocker and a fanlight above.

"You have to knock hard," Mr. Larkin said, suiting his action to his words. "Old Martha—the housekeeper—is rather deaf."

Martha heard his knock, however, and in a suprisingly short time she was there to let them in, an old apple-cheeked woman with white hair under a snowy cap and a white apron over a print dress. A gray shawl was over her shoulders, its ends tucked into her waistband. But as Vicky looked at her she saw in her face the same kindness that had been in Mrs. Snow's and Mrs. Norris's.

The lawyer sent in his card to Mr. and Mrs. Ellis with a scribbled request that he might bring Miss Macalister in to meet them.

He was at once invited into a little drawing room to the left of the front door, where Mr. and Mrs. Ellis were engaged in going through some old letters in a small desk.

They left their task at once to greet Vicky and the lawyer, and they were happy to show her over the house and the garden, where the old gardener, Barlow, was planting out young cabbages. She liked the Ellises as much as they liked her. Mr. Ellis was a middle-aged man with grizzled hair and beard, and Mrs. Ellis was a pleasant-faced woman with a quiet gentle voice and serene manner that won Vicky at once.

They both told her that she looked far too young to be an authoress, and she explained rather shyly about the two books she had written and the novel she was engaged upon, which startled Mr. Ellis considerably.

"A novel, eh?" he exclaimed. "That sounds ambitious."

She laughed and assured him it was not a learned book, nor indeed a very exciting one.

They gave her tea in the little drawing room, and both tea and interview ended satisfactorily. They agreed to let her have the Witchery on the terms Mr. Larkin had explained to her for the space of three months, and she would be free to move in at the end of April.

When she arrived back in Sackville Street she wrote at once to Mr. Brent telling him of her change of address, and then she wrote once more to James, describing the Witchery with delight and quoting its many advantages. There was, for instance, the omnibus that had to have trace horses harnessed to it to help pull it up Haverstock Hill. It was a very useful omnibus, and it did not take a great while to reach London. And then from the Heath she could see the corn that was now showing green between Parliament Hill Fields and London. In August it would be golden, just as if they were living in the country.

Her brother's letter was short but approving, although he said he thought the Witchery sounded rather small. Still, anything was better than those dreadful rooms of hers in Railway Street, and he was extremely glad that she had finished with the milliner's shop. He would come for a week at the end of June if he could, but he thought he would probably go straight to Norfolk with Timbers.

It seemed that he had forgotten the cottage that they had talked of sharing only two years ago. He was too grown up now, she thought sadly, to be tied to his sister's apron strings. And his relief that she had left Westborough and the shop was evident in his letter.

Resolutely she made excuses for him. Those rooms in Railway Street had been the final humiliation, and she was glad she had been able to free him from that at least. It was not his fault if he enjoyed his holidays in Norfolk. There would be little for him to do at the Witchery, after all.

On the first of May she settled in there happily enough, however, selecting as her study the little morning room behind the dining room. The little house was very like a doll's house after Costerley and the big London houses, but every day the charm of it grew on her, and her work on her book went on apace. She found she could add mischief and good humor to situations in which she had found little humor at the time.

May went by so fast that she was surprised when June came in. The lilacs at the gate were over, but the roses were coming out around the windows of the little house and over the wall that enclosed the small kitchen yard at the back.

And then one morning the front door knocker sounded and Martha came to ask if she would see a gentleman, a Mr. Sellinge.

Chapter Seventeen

Vicky had not allowed her thoughts to dwell on Sebastian too often ever since that luncheon party in his rooms in February. She had reminded herself of Lady Taversham's warning, and tried her best only to remember that Sebastian Sellinge was not in the world to which her father had abandoned her.

But still on quiet evenings sitting alone in the Witchery after old Martha had closed the shutters and gone to bed she had found her thoughts going to him, wondering if he thought of her, missing his quiet common sense and the friendship that had meant so much to her.

"So I have found you at last," Sebastian said as she came forward to greet him with a smile of welcome and an outstretched hand. "It seems that our authoress has found herself a dwelling."

"And she also has a housekeeper and a gardener," she told him. "So that she is really living like a lady, and you need not be ashamed to call on her."

"But had I not called on Brent yesterday to ask when your book was coming out," he said reproachfully, "I would not have known where to find you. It seems you gave your publisher your address and neglected your friends."

"I am sorry." She tried to find an excuse. "There was so much to do."

"And you did not forget that unlucky luncheon party of mine, I have no doubt." His gravity left him, and he smiled. "I will forgive you if you will show me around your small domain."

She did so happily, and introduced him to old Barlow, whom they discovered up-ended in the vegetable garden weeding the strawberry bed.

"It is mine until the end of July," she said, as they returned to the house. "And then I shall have to discover how much

174

money I shall be likely to earn during the next year, and if I can take it on a proper tenancy."

She told him of the terms of the tenancy, which interested him, and he said he did not think she would find much difficulty in finding a rent for the place and even in paying the two servants.

"I have brought a parcel for you from Brent," he said, taking it from the table in the little hall. "And I am happy to tell you that half the first edition was sold before publication, and he is preparing a second to appear at the end of July."

She took the parcel from him and ran into the drawing room to find her embroidery scissors, much too excited to untie any knots in the string. "It's *From a Park Bench?*" she said.

"From a Park Bench it is," he assured her, "and I hope when you see it you will forgive me for my surliness when I arrived."

"But you were not surly," she said. She cut the string and looked into his nice kind face. "I did not forget you, Mr. Sellinge. Indeed I did not."

"I know. I was angry because old Larkin had found this refuge for you and I had not." He watched her undo the paper and take up the first of the six complimentary copies of her little book with an exclamation of delight.

It was a beautifully produced little volume, with the title and the name Mary Macalister in gold on a soft blue leather cover. The pages were nicely spaced, the print clear, the edges of the pages brushed with gold. There were picture headings to the essays—ladies and gentlemen strolling in the park, children bowling hoops, a little girl trying to dance on her shadow, and at the end of each essay a twisted ribbon into which was tucked a flower according to its season.

"I did not think it would ever be like this." Her cheeks were flushed with pleasure and her dark eyes shone. "How beautifully Mr. Brent has produced it."

He watched her face with a feeling of tenderness that he dared not show. "Brent intends to publish *The Milliner's Shop* in October," he told her then. "And he has agreed to pay you the sum of one hundred pounds for a first edition of two thousand copies, but if he should decide because of the success of this little book that the first edition should be four thousand copies he will pay you two hundred. You are going to be a very successful young woman, Vicky."

"And it is all because of you," she said penitently. "Which you must think I have often not appreciated as I should. But I do thank you, Mr. Sellinge, for all you have done, and I would like to give you one of these little volumes, if I may, to show it."

He accepted the volume with pleasure and made her write her name on the flyleaf, and then Martha knocked at the door to ask if the gentleman was staying to luncheon.

"He is certainly," Vicky said, not giving him time to answer, and as the old woman went back to the kitchen she told him that he would have to open a bottle of wine that Mr. Ellis had left with her to drink to the success of the book when it came out.

Over luncheon and a glass of the wine he asked her if she was happy at the Witchery, and she told him she was completely and utterly happy.

"The Ellises have been so kind," she told him. "They sent their married daughter, Miriam Southern, to call on me. She lives in a rather larger house than this, in St. John's Wood, and I have been to her house to dine and met there all sorts of interesting people. The Ellises have a nice place in the country, and their eldest son is managing the estate for his father. Their second son is a commander in the Royal Navy. Miriam says that directly he comes home on leave, which he hopes to do very soon, she is going to have him to stay with her, and I shall be one of the first to meet him there. She calls him a charmer." She laughed, the happy laugh of a girl who was enjoying life again, and although he was glad to hear it he was not quite so pleased with the cause of it. Being entertained by young ladies with brothers who were charmers might be dangerous for anyone like Vicky.

He asked after James and was told that he was planning to spend his holidays in Norfolk. So once more the little bread-winner was to be left on her own while Master James enjoyed himself. He was too angry with James to continue, and Vicky said gently that she was so glad he was going away to Norfolk. "He loves the country life and country sports," she pointed out. "He never has had a chance to enjoy them ever since we left Costerley. And Colonel Timberloft almost looks on him as another son."

"And the novel?" he asked abruptly, putting down his

empty glass. "What is its title, if one may ask? Or have you not chosen one for it?"

"Not yet. What do you suggest?" She gave a wicked little smile. "Does *The Burglar's Daughter* appeal to you? Or *Child of a Thief,* perhaps?"

He looked across the table frowning, and then suddenly he laughed. She would always be herself, unpredictable, infuriating, and yet holding his heart as no other woman could. "So you have not forgotten your hatred for your father?" he said.

"I think I hate him more than ever," she replied, the laughter dying in her face. He changed the subject to her grandfather. Had she never heard from him? Had he not offered her any help? Did he still know nothing of her own situation?

"Nothing," she said, getting up from the table and leading the way back to her little drawing room. "And he must know nothing, in case it should hurt James."

"In case it should hurt James?" He was angry again. "Do you never think of how *you* have been hurt?"

"But I do not think I have been hurt." She thought it over. "I have had difficulties, but they are never so bad when you are prepared to face them, are they? I detest people who pull long faces and go around wringing their hands."

He walked to the window and stood there looking out at the front garden with its trim lawns and the well-kept borders of flowers, and the little wooden gate beyond which could be seen glimpses of the Heath. "Have you no relative who would come and live with you here?" he asked abruptly. "You should not live here alone, Vicky."

"You mean I should have a duenna?" she said, smiling. "But how could I keep her on the little money I have—even if I do receive more in the near future? And in any case I do not think I have any relatives who would oblige me in such a way." She thought of Miss Crampton and dismissed her at once. "I have been alone so long, Mr. Sellinge, that I do not mind it at all. There is, as you see, a good supply of books on that shelf that old Miss Ellis left, and I am enjoying them very much." She glanced at his grave face. "I hope you are not angry with me for it?"

"I am not likely to be angry with you ever, Vicky. Angry with others on your behalf, perhaps. I am glad you have found friends in the Ellises' daughter and her friends, but I do not like to think of you being alone here, on the edge of the Heath, with only a rather deaf old housekeeper to look after you."

She assured him that she was quite able to look after herself, but he did not seem convinced, and then he said goodbye and made his way back to Haverstock Hill and the omnibus that would take him back to London.

She watched him go with her hand on the little wooden gate, feeling happier and reassured by his visit.

Across the Heath and the green of the cornfields that soon would be turning she saw the gray outline of London, dominated by the dome of St. Paul's, against a pale-blue sky where mackerel clouds were threatening a change in the summer weather. She went back slowly into the house feeling the warm grasp of Sebastian's hand, and for the first time since she had come to the Witchery the sense of being entirely on her own in the small house was not as welcome as usual.

In the meantime, having arrived back in London, Sebastian made his way to Mr. Larkin's offices, ostensibly to discuss a brief with which the lawyer had supplied him, and having disposed of that, he mentioned that he had been to visit Miss Macalister that morning in Hampstead.

"I was glad to see her so nicely settled for the moment, if not for longer," he commented. "And I understand that it has been entirely by your efforts. But I would like you to elucidate a mystery for me, Mr. Larkin, if you are able to do so. I always understood that she was to receive her godmother's bequest of jewelry when she became twenty-one. From her conversation today it did not seem as if she expected to receive much from it. At all events she did not mention it. Was it worth nothing?"

"On the contrary, Miss Macalister's inheritance is expected to fetch at least sixty-five thousand pounds."

"Sixty-five thousand!" Sebastian stared. "But in that case she will be a very wealthy young lady."

"Unfortunately not." Mr. Larkin shook his head. "She came to my office one afternoon last February—I believe she had been lunching with you and Lady Taversham—"

"She had." Sebastian's voice was grim.

"She asked me to obtain for her a complete list of the shareholders in the fraudulent railway company that had been sponsored by her father. I managed to get the list from a man who had been clerk to the company and had lost five hundred pounds of his own in it. He had kept the list in case the time should come when he would be able to give evidence in court against what he termed 'those two scoundrels.' Naturally I did not tell Miss Macalister this."

"Naturally." Sebastian did not ask why Vicky had wanted the list. He had a very good idea of her reasons, and it dismayed him utterly.

"When at the beginning of this month I put the jewel case into her hands, it being now her twenty-first birthday and hers to do with as she liked, she opened it with the key that had been left in my possession, and I could see at once that some items were extremely valuable. There was a diamond necklace that was especially beautiful." Mr. Larkin appeared to be depressed at the thought of the necklace. "I told her that in my opinion that necklace alone was worth at least twenty thousand. 'Then sell it,' she cried, her delight almost that of a child with a new toy. 'Sell the lot, Mr. Larkin.' I asked her if she wished the proceeds from the sale to be invested for her, and she said no, she wished me to hold it and from it to repay as many as I could of the shareholders in the railway company. She ignored my protests and said only that I was to repay the smaller ones first. The clerk to the company was to receive his five hundred back at once, and she was especially concerned about an old clergyman living near Westborough who had lost two thousand pounds. 'And in all these cases,' she said, 'I want them to be paid two years' interest on their money.' I said that all that could be arranged, but I begged her to keep at least a few thousand for herself. This she utterly refused to do and would only agree to keep one thousand in case her brother should need it in the future."

James, thought Sebastian bitterly. Never herself. Only James. And those damned shareholders.

"Miss Macalister impressed on me that it was the shareholders who could not afford to lose their money that were to be repaid first. The rich she cared nothing about. They could bear their losses, she said, and it might teach them to be content with what they had. I assure you, Mr. Sellinge, I did my best to dissuade her from giving it all away, but you know what she is like when she sets that chin of hers."

Sebastian knew all too well.

"She was persistent that her father had robbed these people and as his daughter it was her duty to repay as many of them as she could." Mr. Larkin sighed and smiled. "She is, in my opinion, Mr. Sellinge, a very remarkable young lady."

Sebastian could only agree with him. Nine out of ten of the girls he knew would have taken the jewels and sold what they did not require for pin money and been happy to do it. But not Vicky. Her conscience would never have let her rest.

"No woman should be born with a conscience," he muttered angrily as he strode back to his chambers. "They ought to run true to form—looking to men to provide incomes for them."

He wondered if the time would ever come when she would allow him to help her in her difficulties, or if she would go through life with her mind made up as to the direction she was to take and the way in which she would take it by herself. He found it a depressing thought.

He went on to his chambers and found in the afternoon post a letter from a troublesome client in Edinburgh. The gentleman was disputing his London cousin's claim to some property in Islington, nothing of any value but rousing all his Scottish obduracy, a quality unhappily shared by his cousin.

The Edinburgh gentleman owned the original deeds to the property, in which, he stated, it was set down clearly that it was his, while his cousin owned a copy of the deeds setting down equally clearly that it belonged to him and him alone. Sebastian had been briefed by Mr. Larkin to act for the Edinburgh gentleman, but a great difficulty arose because neither gentleman would part with deeds or copy until they came to court. If Mr. Sellinge wished to see the deeds in Edinburgh before the case came off in the Michaelmas term he would have to travel to Edinburgh.

"Do neither of these blockheads comprehend that the value of the property is so small they will spend far more in litigation than it is worth?" groaned Sebastian. And then suddenly a thought came to him. Awkward as it might be to leave London in the middle of Trinity term at least some good might come of it. He sent for his clerk and told him to step around to the nearest bookseller and buy if he could a copy of *From a Park Bench* by Miss Mary Macalister.

The clerk came back to say that he had been fortunate in discovering a bookseller that had one copy left. "He says he has sold nearly a hundred copies in the last few days, sir," he told Sebastian. "He thinks it is because there was an advertisement in one of the newspapers referring to the authoress as a second Miss Mitford."

It was sufficient for Sebastian. That night Herbert packed for himself and his master and the next day they caught an early train to Edinburgh.

Having met his client and studied the deeds and made a few notes, Sebastian spent the second morning in Edinburgh in renewing his acquaintance with the city, still uncertain if what he was about to do was right, before finding his way in the afternoon to the New Town and the beautiful Georgian house where Sir Hector lived.

The door was opened by an austere-looking housekeeper, an elderly lady in a black alpaca dress and a plain alpaca apron, and with a small lace cap on her iron-gray hair.

When he asked if he might see Sir Hector and gave her his card, she viewed it and him with the deepest suspicion before observing that her master did not usually see persons without an appointment. She agreed to see if he was disengaged, however, and led him through the stone-floored hall to a small paneled room to wait. The room overlooked the square in which the house stood, it was extremely cold, his reception had been equally cold, and he began to wish he had not come. He hoped that his visit would not make things worse for Vicky.

After a few minutes the woman returned and asked him to follow her and showed him into Sir Hector's library, where the gentleman was sitting at a writing table poring over a volume with the aid of a magnifying glass.

It was undoubtedly the room of a bibliophile; so much was evident from its condition. Books were piled on the shelves that surrounded the room, on the floor, on every chair, even on the library steps.

Sir Hector withdrew himself from his study of the ancient volume he was inspecting and turned to greet his visitor with some impatience, glancing at the card in his hand.

"I hope you will forgive my intrusion, sir," said Sebastian pleasantly. "But as I had to visit Edinburgh to visit a client, and knew you to be interested in books, I have taken the liberty of presenting you with a copy of your granddaughter's book, *From a Park Bench,* which I hope you will do me the honor of accepting. You will see that she writes under the name of her mother, Mary Macalister."

The old gentleman looked at him sharply and then glanced

at the book in his hand. "You say my granddaughter has written that book," he said. "Are you referring to Miss Victoria Lingford?"

"I am, sir."

"But how did you come by it? Is she not in France with her father?"

"No. He left her in England with instructions to go to her uncle in Westborough."

"That fellow! Never did like him. Well, and so she has written a book while she has been living in his house."

"On the contrary, Sir Hector. Her uncle refused to take her in."

"Refused? But in that case where has she been living all this time? At Costerley?"

"No, sir. That had to be sold after Mr. Paul Lingford fled the country. The bank had a mortgage on it."

"But I suppose he made other arrangements for his daughter? He must have left her a competence?"

"He left her without a ha'penny, and until this spring she has been working in a milliner's shop in Westborough, where her brother, James, is now a boarder at the grammar school. Lately, however, she found a publisher who agreed to publish in book form some essays that she had written for a local paper."

"And that is the book?"

"It is." Sebastian put it down on the writing table beside the rare volume and the magnifying glass, and Sir Hector took it up with the sensitive touch of one who loves books and glanced through it while Sebastian considered him in silence.

He had had the chestnut hair that James had inherited, though now it was very gray, and his eyes were a clear blue under thick reddish brows, giving him an air of fierceness. As he examined his granddaughter's book one fact stayed in his mind with some force.

"You say that Vicky has been a *shop assistant* in Westborough?" he said, a rumble of anger in his deep voice. "May I ask who persuaded her to do this?"

"She took it on herself to do it, I'm afraid," Sebastian said. "She is an exceptionally determined young lady."

"But why did she not come to me? Why the devil did not that damned lawyer tell me what had happened?" Sir Hector was now very angry indeed. "By God, sir, I'll write to that Larkin fellow and tell him exactly what I think of him."

"I think that was what Miss Vicky was afraid of, sir." Sebastian spoke coolly and firmly. "She found a letter you had written to her father years ago in which you stated that you would educate your grandson on condition that his father took charge of his sister. She was afraid that if you knew that Mr. Paul Lingford had broken his side of the bargain you might refuse to have anything more to do with James."

"Those were my conditions, certainly," agreed Sir Hector and thought it over, evidently at a loss. "But all I meant to do in laying them down was to instill in my son-in-law the sense of responsibility in which he was sadly lacking. I'd no idea, and certainly no intention, of abandoning the girl or of harming young James if their father showed himself to be the weakling I took him to be. James, I hear from Mr. Larkin, has obtained a bursary—I suppose at this grammar school in Westborough. I was not told why he was moved there from St. Chad's."

Sebastian explained how when the news of his father's flight from England was known Dr. Dacres had asked Mr. Larkin to remove James from his school.

"But why Westborough?"

"I think Mr. Larkin hoped that Mr. Harold Lingford would take the two young people in. And although he turned out to be as anxious as Dr. Dacres had been over James to rid himself of them, the lawyer had already made an appointment for Miss Lingford and her brother to see Dr. Eccrington at the grammar school, and there was no reason why James should not be moved there. I would add, Sir Hector, that it is an old school with an excellent reputation for learning as well as for discipline, and Dr. Eccrington had no hesitation in accepting him as a boarder. He appears to be happy there and plans to go on to Oxford now that he has obtained this bursary."

Sir Hector, who had listened to this account of James with interest, took up the little book again. "And his sister, little Vicky, has turned authoress," he commented. "This has been well produced. Is it going to sell?"

Sebastian repeated what the London bookseller had said, and told him the terms of Vicky's contract with Mr. Brent. "He is honest enough," he added. "I had to bully him a little, but with good result."

"So you think she should receive a hundred pounds or more for this little book and the next?"

"It certainly seems probable."

"Where is she now?"

He was told of Mr. and Mrs. Ellis and their kindness to his granddaughter and emphasized that both James and his sister had abandoned the name of Lingford and taken that of Macalister.

The old man thought it over, walking to the fireplace and back. "What is she like?" he asked then abruptly.

For the first time during their interview Sebastian found himself at a loss. How could he describe Vicky, with her hair the color of ripe oats, her great dark eyes, her sensitive mouth and the way she laughed?

"Is she pretty?" asked Sir Hector impatiently.

"I do not think most people would call her that," said Sebastian slowly. "No, I would not call her pretty. She has a very determined face and the spirit of a lion. Resents advice or interference. I have been in her black books more than once for trying to persuade her to leave that damned shop and earn her bread in some way more suited to her class." He added that she was working hard in the cottage in Hampstead, with the Ellises' deaf old housekeeper to keep her company. "And that brings me to the object of my call upon you this afternoon, sir. Is there not some relative of independent means on her mother's side who could be persuaded to go and live with her there and act as her chaperon for a time? She would not consider a Lingford, even if there was one to be found."

Sir Hector considered the matter, and then a gleam appeared in his eye. He stalked to the bell rope and pulled it violently, and when the housekeeper appeared asked that Miss Jeanie be requested to come immediately. In a short while, no longer than was necessary for Miss Jeanie to exchange her everyday cap for a better one, the door opened and a short brisk little woman entered the room, her face lined and her red hair turned sandy with years of fierce Indian suns.

She was introduced to Sebastian as Mrs. Jean Clonmell, the widow of the late Colonel Clonmell, who had been killed in a skirmish on the northwest frontier five years earlier. Under the hastily donned cap with its purple ribbon her face showed the same determination as Vicky's, and her plaid dress had evidently been purchased out of deference for Her Majesty's love of the Highlands. A gold brooch pinned a gold watch to her bosom, and at her throat was a Cairngorm ornament.

"You wanted me, Father?" Her sharp dark eyes, so like his, looked from Sir Hector to his visitor.

"Yes, my dear. This gentleman, Mr. Sebastian Sellinge, has come to me with news of my granddaughter, your sister Mary's child, Victoria." He told her Vicky's story in outline, details supplied from time to time by Sebastian.

"Paul Lingford was always a fool," said Mrs. Clonmell when he had done. "Unfortunately a good-looking one, and nothing would make poor Mary give him up, not even the threat of disinheritance."

"I did not disinherit her!" exploded Sir Hector. "I settled five thousand pounds on her when she married, as I had done with you."

"Knowing full well that her husband would use the last penny of it in buying Costerley Park, much too large and far too ruinous for his means." Mrs. Clonmell tossed her head. "Why, when Meg went to stay there once when Mary was alive she was quite horrified at the state of the place. She wrote and told me that only half the rooms were furnished, and when there was a storm what few servants there were had to run about with buckets and baths to catch the water that dripped through the ceilings."

She paused and then went on more quietly, "All the same, Mr. Sellinge, although Paul was weak and easily led, with no sense of responsibility where money was concerned, he was a gentleman, and neither I nor my father can believe that he would deliberately defraud anyone. We have no doubt that his partner kept him ignorant of the true state of affairs, using him as a cat's-paw. But for his daughter to be allowed to serve in a milliner's shop is quite incomprehensible, and unforgivable in her lawyer. Is there any explanation for his conduct?"

Sebastian repeated the explanation he had given to her father, and once again the sandy head was tossed, rather more ferociously than before.

"I never heard of such nonsense! Well, Father, what steps are we going to take about this? Mr. Sellinge says that Victoria is living alone in a cottage lent her by these Ellises, but we cannot permit her to continue there without some sort of chaperon."

"Exactly my thought, my dear." Sebastian caught a hint

of cunning in Sir Hector's eyes. "That is why I sent for you. I was certain that you, as a married woman, would know better how to deal with the situation than your sister."

"Certainly I know what should be done, and I am willing to see that it is done." Mrs. Clonmell had made up her mind before the words were out of her father's mouth. "As Meg managed your household perfectly well while I was in India, and will no doubt be very well pleased to manage it once more without my help, I suggest that I should be the one to act as Victoria's chaperon. I am the eldest of the family and a widow with no family of my own, and therefore perfectly free to go to Hampstead at once. No question of means need stand in my way. My husband left me with a good income, and I shall naturally pay for my own board and that of my maid, Saunders, who will accompany me."

"If it will not be too great a sacrifice on your part, Jeanie, my dear, to leave your friends in Edinburgh," said her father mildly, "I really do think it would be the best solution to the problem. When could you be ready to start?"

"Early next week," said Mrs. Clonmell briskly. "I will write to Victoria and acquaint her with the time of my arrival."

"She does not use the name of Lingford," Sebastian reminded Vicky's aunt. "Both she and her brother are now known under their grandfather's name, Macalister. They say they will have no further intercourse with the family of Lingford."

"Sensible," commented Mrs. Clonmell. "But it would have been unnecessary if their father had not lacked the courage to stay and face his accusers." She asked Sebastian to stay to dinner, and on being told that he had to start his journey back to London that night bade him goodbye with the hope that she might see him again when she was established in Hampstead.

As the door closed behind her, Sir Hector chuckled and rubbed his hands with satisfaction.

"Your visit this afternoon," he told Sebastian, "has lifted a weight from my shoulders. My two remaining daughters, the eldest and the youngest, have never got on well together. Mary was the one who held them together, and when Jeanie came back from India as a colonel's widow naturally she returned here to her old home. My youngest daughter, Meg, is unmarried and had for years been mistress of this house, and she much resented having that position usurped by her eldest sister. As two women cannot act as mistress of the same house, there has been some friction between them over the years. If Jeanie goes to Hampstead, however, Meg can resume what she sees to be her rightful place and harmony will be restored. Books, you see, Mr. Sellinge, are my hobby and my delight, and I dislike that interest being broken into every now and then to demand if I would prefer beef or mutton for my dinner. Food is the least of my interests, and I do not care what I eat as long as I have my bowl of oatmeal for my breakfast. You have therefore come in the welcome guise of a peacemaker, and I am grateful to you on that account. But little Vicky shall not suffer—that I promise you. She has claimed her right to my protection as a Macalister, and that protection she shall have."

And after Sebastian had left him he sat down to write a strong letter of rebuke to poor Mr. Larkin, ending by telling him that he might draw on his bank to the amount of two thousand pounds, the money to be invested in Consols at five percent in the name of Miss Victoria Lingford, now known as Macalister.

Chapter Eighteen

Vicky received her aunt's letter with dismay.

This is all Sebastian's doing, she told herself ungratefully. He has gone to Scotland and he has called on my grandfather and this is the result. Why cannot he leave me alone?

Even a letter from Mr. Larkin containing the news of the money that Sir Hector had settled on her did little to console her, and her irritation was increased when she was forced to rearrange the bedrooms that she had settled with so much satisfaction.

The two best of the three front bedrooms she had reserved for herself and for James, and rather than give his to her aunt she decided to move her own belongings to one of the three small back bedrooms, which left her only a dressing room for Tom Timberloft if he should elect to visit them, as the small room in front would have to be reserved for her aunt's maid. When she visited Miriam on the afternoon before Mrs. Clonmell's arrival she was further annoyed by that young matron's delight at the news of Mrs. Clonmell's impending descent on the Witchery.

"It is just what you need," she said. "My dearest Vicky, did you never think how strange it seemed for you to be living there on your own? If as you suggest Mr. Sellinge interfered in the matter, I am only glad that he did."

"He is inclined to interfere too much in my affairs," said Vicky.

"Perhaps he is in love with you?"

Vicky dismissed this idea with a somewhat heightened color. "I do not think it shows a sense of devotion to send me an aunt whom I have never met," she remarked.

"But I know you will welcome her when she arrives all the same. Vicky, my love, you cannot say that you enjoy lonely evenings at the Witchery with only deaf old Martha to keep you company."

"I like reading," said Vicky, stubbornly defending her independence.

"But you cannot entertain your friends there alone," pointed out Miriam. "It would not be at all the thing. And next week my brother Aubrey will be on furlough, and he is such fun. Naturally he will spend a little while with our parents first, but he will come to me as soon as he can, and the very next day I shall drive him over to introduce him to you and your duenna. And I am ready to promise that he will charm her as much as he will charm you."

Vicky laughed and went back to the Witchery, where Martha too, instead of resenting the extra work that would be put upon her, expressed great pleasure at the thought of the company it would make not only for Vicky but for herself.

"It ain't right for a young lady, Miss, to live 'ere alone," she said when Vicky first broke the news to her. "And it will be company for me in the kitchen, and Miss Saunders will 'elp me plan the meals. So long as she don't make 'aggis," she added, "which I've 'eard tell is a terrible 'orrible dish."

When Mrs. Clonmell arrived, she was as charmed with the house as she was with her niece, and on the following morning directly they had finished breakfast, she insisted on being taken over it from top to bottom.

When she had done she said she saw no reason why one of the best bedrooms should be reserved for James.

"As he does not propose visting you for more than a week, if that," she pointed out, "he can very well do with that nice large attic with the dormer windows. One can see that it had been used as a nursery—possibly for Miss Ellis's great-nephews and nieces and their nurses—and it will make an ideal bedroom for a boy. Or for two boys for that matter, if young Timberloft should accompany him. One of the Norfolk Timberlofts, I believe. I met the Colonel and his wife in India some years ago. We can easily hire a couple of beds from the furniture warehouse in the village while they are here."

Not only was her aunt prepared to take over the arrangement of her rooms, Vicky discovered, but from the start she had very rigid ideas of how they should plan their days.

In the mornings directly after breakfast, Vicky must go to her little study and write her books, while Mrs. Clonmell saw Martha in the dining room to arrange the day's meals. She would then see the gardener and order from him whatever was required in the way of vegetables and fruit from the kitchen garden.

"You have quite a well-stocked garden here," she told Vicky after she had inspected it with Barlow. "There is nothing like fresh vegetables and fruit to improve a young lady's complexion."

The end of term came, and James and his friend descended upon the Witchery, and from the first moment they met Mrs. Clonmell showed him that it was his sister and not himself who had to be considered first.

It did the young man no harm, and the two boys were sent out on excursions together, leaving Vicky to write and Mrs. Clonmell to plan gargantuan meals for their return. James won his aunt's heart by informing her that Colonel Timberloft agreed with her and Sir Hector about his father's lack of culpability over the spurious railway.

Vicky listened in silence, not satisfied and with her opinion unchanged.

Her father had been no fool, she told herself. He must have known what Grammidge had been about. And what about Grammidge's talk with his wife about pigeons for the plucking? Did he never discuss such things with her father?

Her hatred for him increased if anything with her brother's and her aunt's defense of him. They had not been left without a penny and nobody to turn to for a roof over their heads. Bitterness built up in her, and she was glad when the time came for the two boys to depart for Norfolk, full of expressions of gratitude to Mrs. Clonmell and promises to come again.

The following afternoon, while Vicky was out visiting Miriam in St. John's Wood, an open carriage drew up in front of the Witchery with two ladies in it. One of them was helped out by a footman, the other settled herself under a shabby parasol to wait for her companion's return.

When Saunders announced Lady Taversham, Mrs. Clonmell got up to greet her visitor in some surprise.

"It is most kind of you to call," she said. "I am afraid Victoria is out this afternoon. She will be sorry to have missed you. Will you not sit down?"

Her ladyship sat down, the smile fading from her face. She was not accustomed to being greeted in such a manner, and she almost thought she could read animosity in the small Scotswoman's eyes.

"The last time we met was, I believe, at Mary's wedding,"

continued Mrs. Clonmell, not in the least overawed by her distinguished visitor. "That must be more than twenty-two years ago."

"I was very fond of Mary," said Lady Taversham warmly. "And I am also very fond of her daughter."

"Yes, Victoria told me how kind you were to her before her father left England," agreed Mrs. Clonmell crisply. "It is a pity that so many of their friends deserted the poor child at that time. I am afraid my father and I assumed that she had gone with Paul. It was most reprehensible in Mr. Larkin not to inform us that she had been left behind."

"But—" Her ladyship was shocked. "Surely you could not have wished Vicky to go with her father?"

"I do not see why not, Lady Taversham."

"But he had defrauded hundreds of people!"

"Is it not more correct to say that he was *said* to have defrauded them?" corrected Mrs. Clonmell firmly. "My father and I will never believe that Paul had anything to do with promoting that railway knowing it to be bogus. He had been persuaded, no doubt, by the man Grammidge that there was a railway there and that it was a good investment. I am afraid my brother-in-law had no idea of business matters and was very easily taken in. But at least he was a gentleman, Lady Taversham, and gentlemen are not thieves."

"That was not generally believed," said her ladyship, reddening a little.

"Oh, I daresay his friends may not have wished to believe it," agreed Mrs. Clonmell. "It is quite likely that they preferred to think of him as a swindler. Have you not noticed how people are far more ready to believe the worst than the best in their friends? I saw so much of it in India, where society was more limited and tightly knit. However," she went on cheerfully before her visitor could get her breath, "Victoria has at least had one good kind friend, and if it had not been for his visit to a client in Edinburgh we would still be in ignorance of the state of her affairs."

"You are referring to Mr. Sebastian Sellinge?" Lady Taversham set her mouth disapprovingly.

"Yes." Mrs. Clonmell smiled, reading her thoughts. "You need not be alarmed on his account, Lady Taversham. If he were so unwise as to fall in love with Victoria and wish to marry her, she would not have him. Most unhappily she believes that her father was fully aware of what Grammidge was doing, and she has made up her mind that because of that she will never marry. So Mr. Sellinge is safe from her and always has been."

It is possible that at that moment her ladyship remembered a day when she had acted as Vicky's chaperon in Sebastian's rooms in Gray's Inn, and it made her feel slightly uncomfortable, but she did not mention it. She remarked acidly that she did not see how anyone could blame Vicky's friends for her behavior over the last two years. "It was entirely her own choice that she took this absurd position in a milliner's shop, Mrs. Clonmell."

"In order to hide from her friends?" hazarded Vicky's aunt. Really, thought her ladyship, she had an unfortunate way of putting things.

"Or to hide from what her father had done," she said sharply.

Mrs. Clonmell ignored this. "The person who was most to blame was, as I said before, Mr. Larkin," she observed. "Directly Paul left without Victoria, he should have traveled to Edinburgh and told my father what had happened. I should then have gone to Westborough or Sackville Street, wherever she happened to be, and removed her at once to Edinburgh. I can assure you that there she would have been accepted by all our friends as Mary's daughter, and my father would have taken care that James was placed at a good Scots school. Sir Hector Macalister is not without influence, Lady Taversham."

Her ladyship said she was extremely glad that dear Vicky had at last found relatives ready to take care of her, and having shot this last bolt, refused the little Scotswoman's offer of tea, sent her love to Vicky, and got up to go.

Mrs. Clonmell watched her departure with some satisfaction. She was glad that Vicky had not been there when her ladyship had called and decided to say nothing to her of the visit. She had been hurt enough, she felt, by the neglect of her friends.

Lady Taversham lost no time in expressing her opinion of Mrs. Clonmell to Miss Sedge as they drove back to Brook Street.

"A self-opinionated little Scotswoman," she said wrathfully. "I did what I could for Vicky, but after her father left England I could not prolong her stay in my house for her own sake as well as for my own. How was I to know that the stupid child would take a situation in a shop, of all things? And as for saying that Paul Lingford was innocent of that railway swindle, everyone knows that he was as guilty as his partner. Why did he run away if he was not? I shall not call at the Witchery again."

"Did Mrs. Clonmell say how Miss Vicky was?" asked Miss Sedge timidly She had been very fond of Vicky, and her heart had often ached for her.

"I did not ask," snapped her ladyship. Girls who behaved like that and produced such obstinate and wrongheaded aunts did not deserve to be asked after.

And yet the thought of Vicky and the indomitable Mrs. Clonmell remained with her ladyship uncomfortably for some time to come.

The following week, Miriam Southern came over to the Witchery, ostensibly to bring her brother, Lieutenant Ellis, to call on Mrs. Clonmell, but it was obvious that the Lieutenant was chiefly interested in Vicky. Miriam had not exaggerated when she had called him a charmer: he was extremely handsome, very light-hearted and always ready to laugh.

When Miriam said she had come to invite them to a small dance during the next week, however, Vicky screwed up her face and said that she had not danced for more than two years.

"But you must come all the same," said Miriam. "I shall not forgive you if you do not, and neither will Aubrey."

Lieutenant Ellis added his persuasions to his sister's. "You cannot write stories all day long," he protested. "Only a bluestocking would do that, and you are far too charming to be a bluestocking."

So the invitation was accepted, although after the brother and sister had gone Vicky said she did not think she had a dress suitable for a ball.

"Probably not for a ball," agreed her aunt. "But as this is only going to be a small dance I am sure we can find something suitable in those trunks of yours from Sackville Street."

A pale-yellow silk was selected by Mrs. Clonmell as being not too much out of fashion, and what alterations should be done were soon put in hand by Saunders. It was a simple dress with a low-cut neck and tiny sleeves gathered into straps over the shoulders. The skirt was plain and fitted snugly to her slender figure, with flounces at the bottom that ended in a small train.

Looking at her reflection in the long cheval glass in her room before they started out for Miriam's house, Vicky could scarcely believe that the young woman she saw there was the same as the assistant in the Westborough milliner's shop. And when old Barlow produced a small bouquet of Gloire de Dijon roses for her to carry and a spray for the shoulder of her dress, even her aunt admitted that it looked charming. "The fashion of having bare arms to the shoulder is not one that I approve," she remarked. "But you have pretty arms, Victoria. I am extremely thankful that those abominable bustles have gone out."

"Miriam says Paris dressmakers are trying to bring them in again even larger than before!"

"Then I hope you will never wear one, my dear."

"I can safely promise you that. How could I sit at my writing desk with a great platform built out at the back of my skirt?"

Miriam's drawing room was full when they arrived. It was a large room at the front of the house, with dividing doors shutting it off from a smaller room at the back used as a morning room. The doors had been removed for the evening and both carpets taken away, and the result was a nice little ballroom. Flowers had been banked in both fireplaces, and there were fairy lights strung up in the little conservatory that led from the morning room to the garden below.

Their hostess lost no time introducing them to her friends, all strangers to Vicky until she said, "Oh, and I have a surprise for you here, Vicky. Here is somebody who says she thinks she was at school with you." And she found herself looking into the eyes of Emily Sellinge.

"Emily!" she exclaimed. "I did not think to see you here."

"It is quite a time since we met, is it not?" Emily spoke coolly, her eyes taking in the yellow silk dress, the beautiful roses and her only ornament, a gold locket with V on it in pearls, suspended around her neck on a fine gold chain. Then she said deliberately, "The last time I heard of you I believe you were a shop assistant."

"A shop assistant!" Miriam repeated the words rather louder than she had intended, and the circle of her guests around them suddenly fell silent. And then from behind his sister Sebastian spoke, smiling, treating the thing with a lightness that saved the situation.

"Mrs. Southern is looking shocked," he said. "But now that my sister has given her away I am sure Miss Macalister will forgive me if I explain the circumstances. Miss Macalister is, as you know, Mrs. Southern, becoming a well-known authoress, and she wanted some stories of a simple nature for a book that my friend Mr. Philip Brent is publishing this autumn." He paused, and seeing that he had gained not only his hostess's interest but that of her friends, went on imperturbably, "Mr. Dickens, we have been told, prowled the streets at night to find his stories, but a young lady is more limited in her approach. So, with considerable courage, Miss Macalister decided to take a situation for a time as a shop assistant, and I believe she had an amusing experience, did you not, Miss Macalister?"

His eyes met hers, and saw in them relief and at the same time a sparkle that might have been anger.

"Yes," she said with a slightly strained smile. "It was at times, as Mr. Sellinge said, quite amusing."

Like the time when Madame Rene had got drunk, but one did not mention that.

Emily, unsmiling and with an edge to her voice, said she did not see how anyone could find working in a shop amusing, but her voice was lost by Aubrey Ellis demanding the title of the book. "I suppose it will be called *The Shop*," he said, his eyes dancing as they rested with admiration on Vicky's face and the beautiful lines of her neck and shoulders.

"The Milliner's Shop," she corrected him, smiling.

"And what is this novel about that you are working on now?" asked Miriam. "Let me guess, as Aubrey did. It will be about Hampstead and all the queer characters that inhabit it. I had no idea, Vicky, that you were such a dangerous person to know!"

Laughter finally defeated the tension that Emily's words had caused and her brother had done his best to dispel, and the orchestra struck up for the first dance. Aubrey Ellis claimed Vicky at once, and as he put his arm around her waist and took her onto the floor for a waltz she said she hoped he was a good dancer, because her own dancing had become rusty with lack of use.

"Did you never indulge in dances in the milliner's shop?" he asked wickedly.

"Never."

His eyes sought hers admiringly. "I agree with Sellinge that you needed great courage to do that," he said. "Not many girls would."

"They might if circumstances forced them to it." She was relieved to see that Miriam's drawing room, with the exception of Emily and her brother, was full of people she had never known, but as she looked she saw a tall gray-haired man enter and shake hands with Miriam and her husband. His face was vaguely familiar. She knew she had seen him before, and that their meeting might have been at Costerley, but she could not put a name to him and trusted that he would not remember her.

The Lieutenant monopolized her most of the evening, and only once or twice did she catch Sebastian's eyes on her, gravely watching them. It was not until the last dance of the evening that she felt his hand on her arm and heard his voice.

"Will you have this one with me, Vicky? I think Lieutenant Ellis will not grudge me one dance with you."

She turned quickly.

"He has made me dance too much," she said, smiling. "I am quite exhausted."

"And this room is appallingly hot. Would you like to find a little coolness in the garden as others are doing?"

They made their way through the conservatory, heavy with the scent of ferns, and down the twisting iron stairs that led from it, Sebastian giving her his hand to steady her. But when they reached the lawn he dropped it and strolled with her toward a garden seat under a large old apple tree.

"I want to apologize to you," he said, sitting down beside her, "for Emily's abominable behavior. I told her that you were to be here and I also told her she was to behave herself."

Vicky played with her fan for a few moments, opening and shutting the ivory sticks. Then she said quietly, "But her behavior is only what I have grown to expect from my former friends, Mr. Sellinge. It did not surprise or shock me in the least."

"It was designed to do both." He was silent, as if considering something of considerable importance, and then he said quietly, "Vicky, do you remember that afternoon after you had lunched in my rooms, when we were walking back together to Larkin's office?"

"I remember," she said, but the light had gone from her eyes and she sat very still.

"You asked me then if we could not always be friends, and put any deeper feelings behind us," he said. "I promised you that I would, but I must break that promise. You see, I have been in love with you ever since that evening when I saw you on your knees beside that poor woman in the milliner's shop. I want you to marry me, so that I can stand between you and such attacks as my sister made on you tonight. Do you think you could bring yourself to it, Vicky?"

She sat silent for a long moment, gripping the ivory sticks in her hands until it seemed that they must break. Then she shook her head.

"You know I cannot marry you," she said in a low voice. "I told you some time ago that I could not marry anybody, because of my father."

"But if you could care sufficiently for me to marry me, he would be forgotten—" He broke off as she put her hand gently on his arm.

"Do you not see," she said, "it is because I care so much for you, Sebastian, that I could not do it? I would drag you down into the same depths that he has dragged me, and it would be impossible. All the time, when we went out together, I should know what people were saying about us—about *you*—behind our backs. 'He could have gone a long way, poor fellow, if he had not married that wretched girl, Paul Lingford's daughter.' My father's shadow has always been over everything I've ever done since he left England, and it always will be. He stands between every happiness I have found, and he will continue to do so, even when he is dead." She paused and then in a voice that broke a little she said, "You referred just now to that afternoon when I told you I valued your friendship. I still do. But if you feel after this that you cannot continue with it I shall understand."

He covered her hand with his, and presently he took it to his lips. "Vicky, my darling love," he said, "if you want me at any time, you have only to send and I shall come."

The last of the guests had left the garden and were mounting the staircase back to the ballroom, where the last dance was still going on. He accompanied her to the foot of the stairs, and there he left her to go back alone.

As she reached the conservatory she found that she had to wait for a moment until her legs had stopped shaking, and she stood in the doorway watching the dancers. The smell of the ferns would always remind her of that evening, and as she stood there, scarcely able to stand, a voice said beside her, "I was sure we had met before. My name is Bassett, and I believe, Miss—Macalister—you were once the means of saving me from losing a great deal of money."

She turned her head and suddenly recognized the gray-haired man who had puzzled her all the evening. The library at Costerley came back to her, and she heard her own voice there begging him not to offer himself to Grammidge and her father as a pigeon for the plucking.

As she stood there, not knowing what to say, he continued: "I was very grateful to you, as I still am. Do you ever hear from your father?"

"Never. And I do not wish to hear from him. To me he is dead."

"I can quite understand your feeling there." He was quietly sympathetic. "But I can see that you have the same courage that you showed me at Costerley."

And then her aunt was at her side, concerned for her.

"Vicky, my dear, you look very white. Do you want to go home now?"

"If you please, Aunt Jeanie. I am very tired."

"Then come and let us fetch our wraps and say goodbye to Mr. and Mrs. Southern."

She bustled her niece off with some energy, said goodbye to their host and hostess, complimenting them on a delightful evening, and carried Vicky off with her to the waiting cab.

As it moved off toward Hampstead she asked if anything had happened to upset her. "I saw you go out with Mr. Sellinge and come back without him," she added. "I hope he did not upset you, my dear?"

"He asked me to marry him, and I refused him," Vicky said, her hands clasped tightly in her lap and her eyes fixed on the dark streets outside.

"Do you not care for him, then?"

"I love him with my whole heart, too much to ruin his life." She passed the back of her gloved hand over her eyes like a child trying to wipe away tears. "Aunt Jeanie, how could I subject a wonderful person like Sebastian to the sort of things that I have to endure? He thinks he would be able to protect me, but he could not protect himself. It would bring nothing but misery on us both."

Mrs. Clonmell comforted her as best she could, but there was little she could say, and when they reached the Witchery although they went straight to bed neither of them slept much that night.

In the meantime in St. John's Wood, Sam Southern, always hospitable, and knowing Mr. Bassett to be living at his club, asked the gentleman to stay for a nightcap in the library before he left.

The rest of the guests had gone, and Mr. Bassett joined Sam and his brother-in-law and Miriam in the library, where glasses and brandy and soda water had been set out on a silver tray.

As Sam poured out a brandy and soda for Mr. Bassett he remarked on Miss Macalister's striking looks. "I saw you speaking to her just before she left," he said. "Had you met her before?"

"Miss Macalister?" Mr. Bassett sipped his drink slowly. "No, I had never met Miss Macalister before."

"Aubrey has lost his heart to her," said Miriam, laughing.

"Aubrey is always losing his heart to somebody when he is on shore leave," commented her husband. "But in Miss Macalister's case I would advise him to pursue it no further."

"What do you mean?" asked Aubrey lazily, while Miriam perched herself on the arm of her husband's chair with a glass of soda water in her hand, waiting too for his explanation.

"It was something I heard from a friend of mine in the City," Sam Southern told them, speaking with some authority because he was a partner in his father's private bank in Lombard Street. "And also something I have been working out for myself."

"What can you mean?" His wife shook his arm impatiently. "Tell me at once, you irritating man."

"As long as you do not spill my brandy I will." He smiled at her genially. "Your friend says her name is Victoria Macalister, eh, Miriam?"

"Well, and so it is."

"In that case she must be the daughter of Sir Hector Macalister's son, as she claims him for her grandfather."

"I suppose so. I have never thought about it."

"But Sir Hector had no son." Sam watched the expressions on their faces with amusement. "He only had three daughters—Mrs. Clonmell, who was here tonight; the youngest one, Margaret, who is unmarried and living with him in Edinburgh; and the third, who was your Vicky's mother and died when she was twelve years old. So who, my dearest girl, was her father?"

There was a dismayed silence while Mr. Bassett continued to sip his brandy and soda with watchful eyes on them all. Then Miriam said breathlessly, "You cannot mean that she is—illegitimate?"

"From what I have heard it would have been better if she had been. No, my dear, I am afraid it is worse than that. Your new friend, Miss Victoria Macalister, is the daughter of Paul Lingford, one of the biggest scamps of the last decade."

"Paul Lingford!" Aubrey whistled. "Didn't he help to float a spurious railway company?"

"And he left England taking with him thousands of pounds that he had filched from trusting shareholders," said Sam grimly. He turned to Mr. Bassett. "I have no doubt you know all about it? Were you not going to put some money into it at one time?"

"I was, but fortunately I was saved from doing so by a warning I received from a friend," said Mr. Bassett pleasantly.

Sam patted his wife's hand consolingly. "Never mind, my dear. We will say nothing about it to your parents. It is very convenient for them to have her and especially her aunt living at the Witchery keeping old Martha company. Nobody could be more respectable than Mrs. Clonmell, after all."

"Poor Vicky." Miriam got up off the arm of his chair and stood by the fireplace, looking down at the cones that were heaped in its hearth with troubled eyes. "What am I to do, Sam?"

"Go and see her from time to time and invite her here—to tea, perhaps, with her aunt, when you do not expect any other callers. And be very careful about introducing her to your friends."

"But that would be quite dreadful." Miriam's eyes were wet. "I am much too fond of her to cast her off like that. I will not do it, Sam. She had nothing to do with her father's dishonesty."

"But you must have seen Emily Sellinge's attitude toward her when you presented her to her tonight? I know Sellinge was quick to cover it all up, but I think the poor fellow is in love with her. He couldn't take his eyes off her all the evening. But that is as far as it goes, of course. He would never marry

her. A barrister with his reputation cannot very well entertain the thought of having a rascal like Lingford for his
father-in-law."

"And who could blame him?" Aubrey laughed and held
out his glass for a refill. "Do not look so miserable, Miriam.
I am leaving the day after tomorrow to rejoin the parents.
Why don't you come with me? I shall be there until I go back
to sea."

Sam said it was an excellent idea, and rather dejectedly
Miriam agreed.

"But I still say it was not Vicky's fault if her father swin-
dled all those people," she said.

"Nobody ever said it was her fault," replied her husband
sensibly. "But the fact remains, my dearest, that she *is* Paul
Lingford's daughter, and from what my friend told me he is
still on the Continent somewhere, no doubt spending his ill-
gotten gains."

"He will probably turn up again in England one day," said
Aubrey carelessly. "Bad pennies usually do—when they are
least wanted."

Mr. Bassett took his leave thoughtfully. He felt very sorry
for Paul Lingford's daughter, and he could not forget that she
had once saved him thousands of pounds by begging him not
to be one of the pigeons for Grammidge's plucking.

But she had courage and her novels to employ her and the
Macalisters to stand by her, and many girls, he thought, had
less with which to face a hard and unfeeling world.

Chapter Nineteen

Having sent his sister home in the carriage, Sebastian took a solitary walk back from St. John's Wood to Gray's Inn. The moon was swinging low over the housetops and Orion was up there somewhere stamping on the smaller stars, but Sebastian was blind to everything except Vicky.

The worst thing he had to face was that she had been right. He could protect her to a certain extent with his name, but there would be critical looks and sweetly acid smiles against which there was no defense. Drawing rooms, for instance, in which Vicky would be introduced as his wife. "Oh, Mrs. Sebastian Sellenge. Of course." A look up and down and a smile that had no warmth in it. "I think I've heard about you." And more wounding still, "Mrs. Sebastian Sellinge? Are you not an authoress or something of the kind?" And a turned shoulder and conversation continued with somebody else.

Her father in the background refusing to set her free. It was no good to damn the man or to wish him dead. He would reach out from the very grave to torment them and to spoil their lives. There was no way to free themselves from him and what he had done.

He came to the gates of the square and rang the bell, and the porter roused himself from his bunk to open up and let him in. But once up there in his chambers after he had sent Herbert to bed and left his evening clothes in the dressing room for the valet to put away in the morning, he sat for a long time in his dressing gown at the windows, looking down at the quiet square and thinking of nothing but Vicky.

It was because she cared too much, she had told him, that she could not marry him. But he knew, staring down at the silent square, vast and deserted at that time of night, that if he could not have her he would have nobody else.

The next morning Vicky received a hurried note from

Miriam telling her that she would call for her in her little carriage at eleven o'clock. It was a warm morning and promised to be a hot day, and when she arrived Vicky was waiting for her with a shady hat and a parasol.

Miriam refused her invitation to come in, and when she climbed in beside her, raising the parasol against the hot summer sun, Vicky told her that Mrs. Clonmell was going to call on her that afternoon.

"A courtesy call after the dance, you know," she added.

"Don't talk to me about the dance," Miriam said, her lips trembling. "I wish I had never thought of it."

"Why, what is the matter?"

"I am angry with Aubrey," Miriam burst out. "And angrier still with Sam for spoiling it all."

Vicky tried to remember any extraordinary behavior on the part of Mr. Southern and her brother-in-law and failed. "What did they do?" she asked.

"It was what Sam said, after everybody had left," said Miriam miserably. She lowered her voice so that the coachman could not hear. "Sam said he had been discussing you with one of his horrid friends in the City and he had said that—that your grandfather, Sir Hector, had no son."

Light dawned, taking the smile from Vicky's eyes. "I see," she said slowly. "Sam's friend told him the name of the man my mother married?"

"Yes," said Miriam more miserably still. "Oh, Vicky, is it true?"

"That I am Paul Lingford's daughter? Yes, Miriam, my dear. I am afraid it is."

"And that was why you changed your name?"

"Of course."

Miriam shot a timid glance at her friend's set profile and saw the tired lines around her dark eyes. "I am so dreadfully sorry," she said.

"I suppose your husband wishes you to end our friendship?"

"Oh no. And I would not if he did. I know I swore I'd obey him when I married him, but I shall not allow him to tell me how I am to treat my friends."

"You need not blame him or yourself, Miriam. Everybody else—or nearly everybody else," added Vicky, remembering Sebastian, "have turned their backs on me. It is a thing I have come to expect."

The sadness in her voice stabbed Miriam's soft heart. "I

shall not turn my back on you," she said. "Sam graciously says I may ask you and your aunt to tea at our house—when I have nobody else there that afternoon—and I may take tea at the Witchery with you when your aunt is kind enough to invite me."

"Come, that is better." Vicky put her hand on the little gloved one beside her. "You have told me, Miriam, and I am glad that you did. My father's conduct has ruined my future."

"Ruined your future? Why, Vicky, you are only just twenty-one. You have your whole life before you."

"No, my dear. My life ended nearly two years ago. I think I am strong enough now in my own right, however, to fight the world and its censure, and I am fighting it with all my strength. When you are permitted to come to tea with us, my dear, we shall welcome you as warmly as we have always done. And my aunt and I will come and see you sometimes and sit in that nice garden of yours." For a moment her voice faltered as she remembered how she had sat there with Sebastian only a few hours before. "So cheer up. All is not lost."

"And you are still my friend?"

"Of course I am. No City friends of your Sam's can break our friendship, and it was not his fault, after all." Vicky asked to be dropped before they arrived back at the Witchery, and after she had seen a somewhat comforted Miriam drive away the thought came back to her with some force how she continued to be indebted to her father for behavior such as Sam Southern's.

She strolled onto the Heath and sat down on a bench high enough to look toward the blue-gray line of London in the distance, but it failed to give her its usual pleasure. There lay the City, where Sam worked as a junior partner in Southern's Bank. She had to face this new challenge to her battle against the world. Her father thwarted her at every turn, and this was the latest in a series of skirmishes that he had won against her. He was her enemy and she must always be on her guard.

I shall never forget and I shall never forgive him, she told herself fiercely. Aunt Jeanie is wrong, and so is Colonel Timberloft. I hope Papa is destitute at this moment and longing to come back to his own country, knowing that it will never receive him. But he does not know yet that his own family will not receive him either. He has that to learn, and when he learns it I think I may have won.

And yet she could not win, because she could never defeat the censure of the world that included her as well as him.

She got up, bitter anger in her heart, and walked back slowly to the Witchery. She was surprised to see a cab drawn up outside its gate. When she reached the front door it was opened to her by Saunders with a very grave face.

"Oh, Miss Vicky," she said. "Your aunt wishes to see you at once in the drawing room. Mr. Larkin is here, and I am afraid he has brought some very bad news."

Vicky left her parasol in the little hall and hurried into the drawing room, where Mr. Larkin was sitting with her aunt.

"Is it news about James?" she cried, as the lawyer came forward to take her hand, a look of compassion on his face. "Has he had an accident? Is he ill?"

"No, it is nothing to do with James, my dear," said her aunt. "I will leave Mr. Larkin to tell you. I shall be in the dining room if you want me." And the door closed behind her.

"It concerns your father, Mr. Paul Lingford, Miss Macalister," said Mr. Larkin gravely. "I am afraid that he is seriously ill."

"Is that all?" Vicky almost laughed. Did her aunt or this lawyer of hers believe that her father's being ill could be bad news? She could see that he was slightly shocked at her lightness, and he continued in rather a sterner tone:

"As the matter seemed urgent, I thought I had better come and see you myself. I had a letter this morning from a gentleman by the name of Mr. Alan Hayward, an Englishman living in Nice. He tells me that Mr. Lingford is lying dangerously ill at his house and has asked for his daughter. He did not know where she was, but he thought I would know her address."

"I see." Vicky's eyes were as hard as stones. "I am afraid I do not believe in this Mr. Hayward or his letter. I am sorry if I shock you, Mr. Larkin, but you are very well aware of how my father left me when he escaped from England and the consequences of his fraudulent activities. It has not occurred to him to write to you since he left to ask what I was doing or where I was living, or if any of my relatives had given me a home. But one thing I think he has remembered very clearly—that when I was twenty-one last June I inherited my godmother's bequest of jewelry, and he also knows no doubt that some of it was of considerable value. He concludes that as he left me no money I must have sold it, and he wishes to share the profits of the undertaking. I am afraid he is mistaken. I have kept only one thousand pounds for James, and he is not going to touch a penny of it."

"Then what would you like me to do, Miss Macalister? Shall I write to Mr. Hayward and say you are unable to go?"

"Not at all. I shall certainly go, and as soon as possible." Vicky's cheeks were flushed, her eyes bright with anger. "I shall leave as soon as you can obtain a ticket for me, and when I see my father in Nice I shall delight in telling him what I have done with the money from the sale of my jewelry. I shall tell him how he has lost me all my friends and drawn upon me the contempt of those who do not even know me, and how his own brother refused to take me in. I shall tell him how I hate him and that he may die in a French prison before I will lift a finger to help him."

She stopped, breathless, thinking of that first Sunday when she had read the paragraph that Lady Taversham had kept for her to see, of Lady Taversham's pity, of the slighting of old friends like Emily and her mother. She thought of her life in the milliner's shop, and the constant fear that she might see there somebody who knew her. Of Sebastian she would not think; the wound was still too raw for healing.

"Oh yes, Mr. Larkin," she said in a low voice. "I shall certainly go to Nice to see him, because there are a great many things I have to tell that cruel and wicked man."

"Very well." That he did not approve of her attitude was plain, but he did not discuss it further. "Then I will make arrangements for your aunt and yourself to leave London as soon as possible for Nice."

"My aunt? Is she coming with me?"

"She will not hear of you traveling alone, Miss Macalister." The lawyer permitted himself a dry little smile. "And she is taking her maid with her. If she had not been anxious to accompany you I would have gone myself. How soon can you be ready?"

"I do not know. I shall have to speak to my aunt."

"I have asked her already, and she thinks she could be ready in three days' time—say by next Monday."

"Why, yes. I can pack all I need in a few hours."

"You will not need passports for France, but there are tickets to be purchased and hotels to be arranged in Paris and at Marseilles. Mr. and Mrs. Hayward have kindly offered their hospitality for the time that you will stay in Nice. I will go at once to the offices of Thomas Cook in Ludgate Circus and buy your tickets there. They will take you through to Nice from London, and the clerks there will advise me on the best hotels for ladies traveling alone."

After he had gone, Mrs. Clonmell tried to offer some words of sympathy to her niece, and came up against a hardness in Vicky's face that checked the words almost before they were uttered.

"I have no love at all for my father, Aunt Jeanie," she said abruptly. "It is of no matter to me if he lives or dies. But I am quite sure that he is not ill at all and there is only one reason why he wishes to see me." She told her aunt what she had already told Mr. Larkin about Paul's wishing to share in her godmother's legacy, and although Mrs. Clonmell was shocked she could also understand her feelings.

"He has behaved abominably to you, my dear," she said. "But he may be ill, and there is the question of one's duty to one's parents to be considered."

Vicky said she did not think she had any duty to her father as he had shown none for her, and Mrs. Clonmell said no more except to discuss the clothes they must take with them.

"Thin dresses will be essential in the South of France at this time of year," she said. "And in traveling abroad I have always found a small hamper with my own cutlery, table napkins, glasses and plates very useful. One can generally find a hotel ready to supply one with a bottle or so of wine and croissants and cheese, which will sustain one on a long journey, so that one does not have to look for restaurants when the train stops at a station for a short while."

"But are there not restaurants as there are here?"

"There may be some, but the food and the service they offer will not be very nice. The retiring rooms, from what I remember of them, are quite terrible. Cattle could not be treated worse."

Vicky laughed and went upstairs to pack for the journey.

"Put in nothing that you do not wish to see spoiled." Mrs. Clonmell followed her to utter a final warning. "The Customs officials are quite dreadful over ladies' luggage. They ask for your keys and they turn the contents over with their dirty hands, expecting to find cigars or tobacco hidden away among your underclothing. They are not so bad at Calais, but exceptionally so in Paris."

"I will take nothing that dirty hands can destroy," promised Vicky. Really, her aunt thought, from the lightness with which she treated the matter she might be going off on a holiday trip.

The next morning a letter arrived from Mr. Larkin, telling them that he had arranged for them to stay at the Charing Cross Hotel on Sunday night so that they could be ready for the seven-forty train to Dover in the morning.

From Dover they would board the steamer for Calais, and at Calais they would take the train for Paris, arriving in time for dinner in the evening. They would stay the night in the Hotel Henri Quatre in the Rue. St. Honoré, a quiet but comfortable small hotel. The following morning they would take the nine-forty train from the Gare de Lyon to Marseilles. It was a very long journey, fourteen hours at least, and they would not arrive until nearly midnight.

At Marseilles, Cook's suggested that they should stay at the Terminus Hotel, and from there it was an easy journey to Nice, so that if they wished to have time in which to recover from the traveling from Paris they would not need to take any train until after they had had a substantial *déjeuner* at midday. But in Paris and in Marseilles they must be careful to look for the Cook's man. There would always be one there to advise them, and they would know him by his uniform and the name Cook's on his hatband.

He ended his letter by hoping that they would find Mr. Lingford not as seriously ill as his friend Mr. Hayward appeared to think he was.

So on Sunday evening a cab took Mrs. Clonmell and her niece and Saunders to the Charing Cross Hotel. The small hamper that was to help sustain them on their journey was clasped tightly in Saunders's capable hands, while two small portmanteaux held all that the ladies would require, and Saunders had packed hers in a basket hold-all secured with a leather strap.

It was bright and windy when they arrived at Dover the next morning, and the sea looked uncomfortably choppy. On stepping aboard the cross-channel steamer, Mrs. Clonmell and Saunders immediately went below, but Vicky, who was a good sailor, stayed on deck and made friends with an old gentleman, a Cambridge professor, who expressed deep concern over the submarine Channel tunnel and hoped it would never come to pass.

He expounded at length on the strip of sea that had protected England for many centuries and might do so for many more to come.

"Have you ever thought, my dear young lady," he argued, "what would happen if such a tunnel were not to be protected against the surprise of an invasion? Although it is said that the tunnel would in that case be destroyed I do not think such a thing could ever be done. Trains would be continually passing through it, and what general would give orders to blow it up under such circumstances? The loss of life would be too terrible to contemplate."

Vicky, who had never given a thought to a tunnel under the Channel, agreed gravely that there were many dangers attached to the scheme and let him run on, his sparse white hair blowing in the wind, his black-gloved hands grasping a Gladstone bag, reminding her of Tenniel's illustration of the White Knight in *Alice in Wonderland*.

Her enjoyment of the crossing filled her aunt and Saunders with wonder, and on the following day when they left Paris for the south her delight in the scenery as it unfolded about them was that of a child. To Mrs. Clonmell it seemed she never gave a thought to the father at Nice who might be dying.

The journey to Marseilles was a long and wearisome one, and Vicky would have liked to break it at Lyon, which looked from the train to be an interesting old city, if somewhat industrialized.

The vine-growing country about it fascinated her too, with the changes of scenery, and although they were all tired out by the time they reached Marseilles, there too she found time to exclaim with delight at the station's yards and garden with oleander trees and flowering myrtles.

The warmth of the south now began to welcome them, and she was up early the next morning, looking from the balcony outside her window across to sundry small islands to the east, wondering if one could be the Chateau d'If.

She would have liked to explore the older parts of the town, but Mrs. Clonmell was firm. They had had a long journey, and in order to be ready for what might lie ahead of them she must rest until it was time for *déjeuner*.

Reluctantly Vicky gave in, and they reached Nice in the late afternoon, surprised by the tourists and visitors of all sorts who thronged the station on their way to the casino at Monte Carlo.

A tall Englishman elbowed his way through the crowd to them and introduced himself as Alan Hayward. "From the description I had of you I feel you must be Mrs. Clonmell and Miss Lingford," he said. The little Scotswoman greeted him with relief.

"Is my brother-in-law very ill?" she asked anxiously.

"So ill that I began to be afraid you might be too late," he said. He took them to the waiting carriage outside the station and helped them inside with Saunders, while his groom helped their porter to lift their luggage to the roof.

"Too late?" Vicky repeated the words slowly as he got in beside them. "Do you mean, sir, that my father is *dangerously* ill?"

"Did not Mr. Larkin tell you?" Mr. Hayward spoke gently. "I am afraid that he cannot live." He spoke to Mrs. Clonmell, giving Vicky time to recover. "I discovered him in a collapsed state on the Promenade des Anglais about a fortnight ago and took him to my house, where he is now. I hope Mr. Larkin told you that my wife and I are hoping you and Miss Lingford will accept our hospitality while you are in Nice."

Mrs. Clonmell thanked him for his kindness and glanced at Vicky, who sat silent and stormy-eyed in her corner of the carriage. Could it be that she was more angry than sorry that her father was going to escape the tirade she had prepared for him? One could not abuse a dying man. "What is his illness?" she asked.

"He has consumption of the lungs, a very rapid kind. In England I believe it is known as galloping consumption. He came here to try to recover from it, but it increased with such rapidity that directly I set eyes on the poor fellow I knew there was no hope for him. The doctor my wife summoned gave him only a few weeks to live."

After a few minutes he continued, "I asked him where he was lodging, and on finding it to be in a poor quarter of the old town I took my man and fetched his clothes and a black deed box on which he seemed to set store. They are in his room now. It is the deed box that worries him most. He kept asking me to send for his daughter. 'It must go back to England by somebody I can trust,' he said. 'If her uncle will not let her go, write to Mr. Larkin and tell him to insist that she comes to me here.'"

"My uncle?" Vicky did not understand him.

"Are you not living with an uncle at a place called Westborough Hall?" asked Mr. Hayward.

"No." Vicky leaned back in the carriage looking so white that her aunt was afraid she was going to faint, but all she said was, "Please go on, Mr. Hayward. My father believed that I was there?"

"Yes. He was certain of it. He wrote to you frequently, and when you did not reply he concluded that your uncle had not allowed you to write to him."

"He must have destroyed those letters, because I never received them." The infamy of her uncle was suddenly far greater than anything his brother could have done. "Mr. Hayward, if I had ever had any of those letters, telling me where my father was, I would have reached him somehow, I would have been with him—"

"I am sure you would. Never mind, we have found you at last, and here we are at my house."

The carriage stopped outside a large white house in a pleasant square, and as they entered a cool hall with a marble floor to make it cooler, Mrs. Hayward, a kindly gray-haired woman, came forward to greet them. Vicky asked if she might see her father at once.

"I will send a servant to ask the nurse if he is awake," Mrs. Hayward said, and Vicky waited impatiently until the nurse appeared herself and asked her to follow her upstairs.

As the door was opened for her she found herself in a large room with a tiled floor and long windows that looked out over the sea. The slatted shutters that had been closed all day against the heat of the sun had been folded back, so that the man lying on the bed in front of them could get the cooler evening air.

Paul Lingford's eyes were closed, and for a moment she could not move, so shocked was she by what she saw. His face was so emaciated that the skin appeared to be tightly drawn over the bones, while his hair, which had been the color of hers, was now quite white. His beard had been shaved off for the sake of coolness, and it made him look very old.

The nurse drew out a chair for her to sit beside him. "Speak to him," she whispered. "Tell him you are here—he has wanted you so much."

Vicky sat down by the bed, looking down at what had been

her feckless handsome father, and she said softly, "Papa, dearest, I am here. Your Vicky is here."

He opened his eyes, and they were the same brilliant blue that she remembered, and as they rested on her he smiled. "So you came?" he said in a faint voice. "I did not think you would."

"But of course I came," she said. Came to thrash him with her tongue, to tell him how she hated him for what he had done to her. But now all she could think about was the father who had been such fun at dear shabby Costerley, the father she had adored when she was small, the father who had been full of jokes, inviting Jamie to start eating the sideboard. The hatred, the anger, the humiliation she had felt were there no longer. It was as if a great burden had slipped from her shoulders, lightening them, bringing an incredible relief to her spirit.

"The deed box," he said then. "Did Hayward tell you about it?"

"He told me, and I shall take it back with me to Mr. Larkin. There is no need to worry about it any more."

He gave a sigh of relief. "I told Hayward that if you came you would have the sense of a dozen. There is money in that box, Vicky—got to be paid back to the shareholders. Larkin will see to it."

"It will all be repaid, my dearest." She took a small bottle of eau-de-cologne from the pocket of her traveling dress, put a little on her handkerchief and held it to his forehead. He muttered a word of thanks, and his eyes closed again. She put her hand in his and felt his thin fingers close about it.

"Dear Vicky," he said, and then in a voice so low that it was like a breath, "Forgive—"

"There is nothing to forgive, my dearest," she said and stooped to kiss him. His fingers fell from her hand, he smiled, and his head dropped back on the pillows, the dying day turning his white hair once more to gold.

Sebastian had steadfastly kept away from the Witchery since the night of Miriam's dance. Fortunately the Michaelmas term was not far away, and briefs were beginning to build up and kept his mind occupied during the day. It was only at night when he saw the lamplight in some of the windows that surrounded the square and heard from the quarters occupied by married men the sound of a piano being played and a woman's voice singing some haunting air that the thought of Vicky would come back, fiercely agonizing in its hopelessness.

And then one morning he saw a small paragraph in the *Times* newspaper headed "Mr. Paul Lingford" in black type, stating that he had died ten days ago in Nice, and that his daughter, Miss Victoria Lingford, had been with him when he died.

Sebastian put aside all thought of work for the day and told Herbert to tell his clerk that he was out to all visitors. His carriage was still in Brook Street, but he did not waste time sending for it. He walked into Holborn and called a cab and told the driver to drive as fast as his old nag would let him to Heath Lane in Hampstead.

The driver was at first disgruntled and said 'averstock 'ill was enough to give his 'oss a stroke on sich an 'ot day, so Sebastian showed him a half-sovereign to encourage both horse and driver and they started off at a fairly brisk pace.

It seemed an unending drive, but at last he arrived at Heath Lane and the Witchery at the end of it, and the half-sovereign was pocketed by his cabbie, who said he would wait for him to give the 'oss a rest.

He pushed open the gate and went up the little path to the front door, and it was opened by Saunders. When he told her that he had just seen the news of Mr. Lingford's death in the paper and had come to see Miss Vicky, she said that she thought it would be better if he saw the mistress first.

"It was a sad business, sir," she said sorrowfully. "And I don't think the mistress wants Miss Vicky to see anybody yet."

In a few minutes he was with Mrs. Clonmell in the drawing room and listening with anxiety to what she had to tell him.

"I am so glad you have come," she said. "I suppose you saw the obituary in the newspaper this morning?"

He said it was that that had brought him to the Witchery. "When did Mr. Lingford die?" he asked.

"The evening we arrived, about an hour after we got to his friends' house. Mr. Hayward and his wife were so kind. They saw to the funeral for us—Paul was buried in the little English cemetery there, where the Haywards' two little girls are. They brought them to Nice some years ago, hoping that they would recover from the same dreadful disease that had attacked Paul, but in vain. Mrs. Hayward would not leave

Nice after they died, and both she and her husband do all they can to help English sufferers there. They are very good kind people."

"And Vicky? How did she take her father's death?"

"Very badly. She came out of his room dry-eyed and for a time had nothing to say. I realized that the shock had been greater than I had anticipated, and it upset her more than I ever dreamed it would. On the journey out, you see, she was as happy as a lark, quite certain that there was nothing the matter with Paul, and that he only wanted money from her. But after he died she seemed to be shocked into silence. I asked her if he had said anything, and she said that the last thing he said was something about forgiving, and she had told him there was nothing to forgive."

"Nothing to forgive!" Sebastian's voice showed his anger. "My God, if ever a man had anything to answer for—" He broke off. "You said Lingford's friends arranged the funeral?"

"Yes. No Scotswoman ever attends funerals, Mr. Sellinge. We leave it to the gentlemen. But Vicky insisted on going, and I felt I must be with her. She refused to wear a black dress—she said her father hated mourning and wearing of black. And when I would have ordered lilies to put on his coffin, she would not have them either. 'No lilies for Papa,' she said, and she went into a flower shop—there are so many flower shops in Nice—and she bought a great armful of gaily colored flowers, the most brilliant she could find. Roses, carnations, marigolds, everything you could think of, and she tied them up with a scarlet ribbon and left them there on his grave. I was quite horrified—or at least I would have been had I not known that the poor child was too distracted to know what she was doing."

"And you came home the next day?"

"Yes. There was a deed box of bank notes that Paul had asked Vicky to give to Mr. Larkin. I believe there was forty-five thousand pounds, money taken from the shareholders in that so-called railway started by the man Grammidge. Mr. Hayward wrote a letter to Mr. Larkin telling him what Paul had told him of his part in the swindle, and if was, of course, as my father and I and Colonel Timberloft believed. My brother-in-law was weak, but so trusting and honest himself that it never occurred to him that Grammidge could be untrustworthy and dishonest. He was paid a great deal to be secretary to the company, which as far as he was concerned simply meant allowing his name to be used on the company's prospectus. He had been in fact a sprat to catch a whale, and he never knew it until a prospective shareholder asked if he might send in an auditor to examine the company's books. It was only then that Grammidge told Paul there were no books and there was no company, and that he was leaving for France the next day and advised him to do the same. I think myself it was with an idea of compromising him that he gave Paul forty-five thousand pounds as his share of the swindle. Paul's first instinct was to go to the police and stop his former partner from leaving the country, and then he realized that with his own name on the prospectus he would not be believed. In fact, he would be regarded as guilty as Grammidge himself.

"He put the money in a deed box, intending to take it to Mr. Larkin in the morning, asking him to return it to the shareholders, and then he remembered that Mr. Larkin was a lawyer and would not be very likely to agree to handle stolen property without proper authority. So Paul too left the country, taking the deed box with him everywhere, living as cheaply as possible, and trying to find some old friends who could be trusted to take the money back to England and discover for him how it could be returned to some of the shareholders."

"And I suppose he never did find anyone?"

"No. Any old friend he met turned his back on him, and he was in despair and very ill indeed when at last, in Nice, he was taken into Mr. Hayward's house. He told him everything, just as I have told it to you, and Mr. Hayward wrote it down, made him sign it and had his signature witnessed.

"It is now with the deed box in Mr. Larkin's hands. He is preparing a statement for the newspapers that will completely exonerate Paul from any blame in the wretched swindle."

Hayward had been wise, Sebastian thought. Any English court of law would accept the signed and witnessed statement of a dying man. "The fact remains," he reminded Mrs. Clonmell, "he did not take sufficient care of his daughter." For that he could not forgive him.

Mrs. Clonmell then told him how Paul had written to Vicky and received no replies to his letters. "He was so sure that she was with his brother, Harold," she added.

"He might have written to Larkin to find out if she was

at Westborough Hall," pointed out Sebastian. "And he did not."

"I am afraid he was fearful of having anything to do with the law, until he knew that he could not live and it was imperative to find Vicky at all costs. My poor brother-in-law. Good looks and charming manners, added to a weak character, can lead a man into deep waters indeed."

"Where is Vicky now?"

"In her study. She has written to James to tell him of his father's death, and the letter has been posted, but I do not think she is working. I was in the garden a little while ago talking to old Barlow and I glanced at her window, and she was just sitting there at her desk, staring in front of her."

"Do you think I might see her?"

"I think you could do nothing but good."

She took him to the door of the little room that Vicky used as her study and left him there.

He opened the door and went in, shutting it behind him, and as Vicky got up from her work table to face him he found that he could not speak. He could only hold out his arms to her, and she ran into them and clung to him, knowing a comfort and love and protection that she had not known since she was a child at dear shabby Costerley.

A little while later two items of news in the *Times* newspaper were read with a rather painful interest by Mr. Harold Lingford and his wife.

The first stated that Mr. Paul Lingford, whose death in Nice had recently been reported, had left a statement that completely exonerated him from all blame in the spurious railway company of which Mr. Alfred Grammidge had persuaded him to be secretary more than three years ago. It was understood that Mr. Paul Lingford, together with his daughter, Miss Victoria Lingford, who used a bequest for the purpose, had already refunded the greater part of money owing to the shareholders in the fraudulent company, and that the interest on the money would also be gradually repaid.

The second item had a more human interest. It was simply the announcement of the forthcoming marriage between Miss Victoria Lingford, daughter of the late Mr. Paul Lingford, late of Costerley Park, and Mr. Sebastian Sellinge of Gray's Inn.

Both items filled Mrs. Harold Lingford with consternation.

"I told you not to destroy those letters from Paul," she told her husband. "They would have removed Vicky from Westborough far more quickly than anything we could do. And now she is going to be married to Sebastian Sellinge, and Miss Sellinge will be told all about it, and you know what a gossip she is. All our friends will cut us, and we shall be asked nowhere. You will have to sell the Hall and move to another part of the country. That is all you can do."

And in time Mr. Harold Lingford had to admit that she was right.

Both items of news were read by Sir Hector Macalister with some amusement, however.

"So Paul is exonerated," he said. "Must not speak ill of the dead, but he would not have got into such a mess if he had been a steadier fellow. No sense of responsibility. I am glad little Vicky is to marry Sellinge. Nice fellow. Thought he was in love with her when he came here with her first little book. No man who was not in love would have taken so much care to say that she was not pretty, and that he only called out of good manners. He appears to have taken a house in Hampstead, near Jeanie, who seems determined to keep on her tenancy of the Witchery. Her excuse is that James will have somewhere to bring his school friends, and later on those he makes at Oxford. An excellent idea, eh, Meg?"

His younger daughter smiled. "Will you go to Hampstead for the wedding?" she asked.

"Of course. I must give the bride away, and I have a desire to meet young James. I hope you will accompany me?"

Meg said that nothing would keep her away. She also wanted to meet her niece, and now that her sister had her own establishment she felt she would be delighted to visit her there from time to time, when she knew they would be the best of friends.

It was a quiet wedding, taking place in the middle of September to give the bridegroom time for a short honeymoon in Paris before the start of the Michaelmas term. The bride wore a simple white dress with a charming white bonnet, the ribbons embroidered by hand by the owner of a certain milliner's shop. With it she wore a beautiful diamond necklace, and carried a spray of orange blossom that had arrived that morning by express delivery from Nice.

After the ceremony at Hampstead Parish Church there was a small wedding breakfast in a small marquee erected on the lawn behind the Witchery. James had wanted to give his sister away, but gallantly relinquished that right to his grandfather, who thanked him for it afterward. James approved of his grandfather and his grandfather approved of his grandson, and a friendship was sealed that day that lasted the rest of the old gentleman's life.

On the whole the guests were a mixed bunch. Mrs. Sellinge and Emily were there, Emily annoyed because Vicky had chosen to have no bridesmaids. Lady Taversham was there, telling everyone who would listen to her how fond she had always been of dearest Vicky, and Miss Sedge, sitting on the edge of a chair sipping champagne and nibbling wedding cake and looking as if she did not know whether to laugh or to cry. The bridegroom's uncle the Judge was there, and after the toasts had been drunk and the wedding cake cut, entered into an argument with Sir Hector about Scottish law, in which Sir Hector proved to his own satisfaction, at least, that he knew considerably more about it than the Judge, who remarked to his sister later on that he had always found Scotsmen tiresome, opinionated fellows.

There were too Mr. and Mrs. Smithson and their children, and Mr. Driffle, and Mr. Brent with his charming wife, and of course the Timberlofts were there, to claim old acquaintance with Mrs. Clonmell.

Miss Sellinge was there, and Mr. and Mrs. Ellis, and Miriam and her repentant Sam, and Dr. and Mrs. Eccrington, and Mrs. Norris from Sackville Street in her best Sunday black.

Everybody admired Vicky's diamond necklace, which had been, she told them, left to her by the godmother she had never seen.

It was only when they were driving away to London en route for Paris that she explained the mystery of the necklace to Sebastian, who had remarked that he thought she had sold all her jewelry.

"So I did," she said. "But that diamond necklace has come back to me in a charming way. I kept the letter that came with it for you to see."

She took a letter from the little gold-mesh reticule that had been her aunt's present to her and gave it to him. It was written in a firm businesslike hand.

"Dear Miss Macalister," it ran. "When your future husband is a judge, or perhaps Lord Chief Justice, as I have every hope he will be one day, this may be a suitable ornament for his lady. I bought it at a sale of jewelry in the summer. I was told it was being sold by a young lady in order to pay some of her father's debts. I was reminded of another equally courageous young lady who, nearly three years ago, warned me against allowing myself to become a 'pigeon for the plucking.' May I offer this single plume as a token of my regard and wishes for a future that from now on may be given entirely to happiness?" It was signed, "Stephen Bassett."

Sebastian read it thoughtfully, and when he saw the signature he whistled. "Stephen Bassett," he said. "Why, he's one of the wealthiest men in London."

"Is he really?" She wondered if he had been the man who had asked to see Mr. Grammidge's books. "He seems a very nice man," she said demurely. "Do you not think it would be a good plan to ask him to be godfather to our first child, Sebastian dearest?" She caught his look of astonishment and said, "I believe I have shocked you!"

"Shocked me?" he said. "*Shocked* me? I'll show you what you have done to me—"

"Sebastian!" she protested, and then again, "*Sebastian!* Do not forget this is an open carriage—"

"What of it?" he said. "I do not think anybody is going to take legal proceedings against me for embracing my own wife. The only person likely to be shocked is Herbert, and he is behind us in a closed cab surrounded by our luggage."

The dark eyes under the pretty russet straw hat were sparkling now, and the lips, trying to be severe, were half parted in a smile. It was an invitation that he could not resist.

"Look, Mama," said a small girl passing the carriage as she walked sedately with her mother toward the Heath. "The gentleman in that carriage was kissing that lady."

"Then I do not think he could be a gentleman," said her mama severely. "No gentleman would kiss a lady in public."

But she had seen the white ribbon tied to the coachman's whip, and she sighed, her thoughts going back to the day of her own wedding when she had driven away with her bridegroom in a closed carriage. He was a man who preferred to keep his love for his bride to himself.

It seemed that the bridegroom in the open carriage, however, did not care if the whole world saw how much he loved his bride, and she sighed again, envying a little the radiant girl in the russet dress.

Let COVENTRY Give You
A Little Old-Fashioned Romance

NEW FROM POPULAR LIBRARY

☐ FALLING IN PLACE   04650 $2.95
   by Ann Beattie

☐ THURSDAY'S CHILD   04656 $2.95
   by Victoria Poole

☐ RIVIERA   04657 $2.75
   by Robert Sydney Hopkins

☐ THE ZERO TRAP   04660 $2.50
   by Paula Gosling

☐ FORCE PLAY   04658 $1.95
   by Anthony Stuart

☐ KEEPING TIME   04659 $2.25
   by David Bear

FAWCETT COLUMBINE
COOKBOOKS

Illustrated, specialty cookbooks in large format.

☐ THE CHICKEN COOKBOOK   90049 $6.95
By Sophie Kay and The Editors of Consumer Guide ®
Still one of the most economical and nutritious foods, chicken is also
one of the most versatile. This book contains over 200 recipes as
well as storage tips, cooking hints and nutritional information.

☐ CONVECTION OVEN COOKBOOK   90042 $6.95
By Beatrice Ojakangas and The Editors of Consumer Guide ®
Over 200 tasty, easy to follow recipes for broiling, roasting,
baking, slow-cooking and dehydrating. Also includes a section on
conversion of conventional oven recipes to convection oven.

☐ THE FOOD INFLATION FIGHTER'S
HANDBOOK   90030 $5.95
By Judith L. Klinger
A comprehensive guide on beating the high cost of food. This
book is filled with useful tips on saving money; from shopping to
entertaining. Also includes money-saving recipes.

☐ THE NEW YORK TIMES 60-MINUTE
GOURMET   90045 $6.95
By Pierre Franey
Gourmet recipes that can be prepared in an hour or less. Includes
nearly 300 recipes for main dishes as well as appropriate accom-
panying side dishes.

☐ THE WOMAN'S DAY GREAT AMERICAN
COOKIE BOOK   90032 $5.95
Edited by Julie Houston
An original collection of best-loved cookies from *Woman's Day*
magazine. Over 250 recipes which include useful tips on sub-
stitutions, storing and freezing.

Buy them at your local bookstore or use this handy coupon for ordering.

COLUMBIA BOOK SERVICE (a CBS Publications Co.)
32275 Mally Road, P.O. Box FB, Madison Heights, MI 48071

Please send me the books I have checked above. Orders for less than 5
books must include 75¢ for the first book and 25¢ for each additional
book to cover postage and handling. Orders for 5 books or more postage
is FREE. Send check or money order only.

    Cost $_____   Name _____

Sales tax*_____   Address _____

  Postage_____   City _____

   Total $_____   State _____ Zip _____

* *The government requires us to collect sales tax in all states except AK,
DE, MT, NH and OR.*

This offer expires 1 February 82   8169

Attention: Schools and Corporations

FAWCETT books are available at quantity discounts with bulk purchase for educational, business, or sales promotional use. For more information and a catalog write to:

EDUCATION AND SPECIAL SALES DEPT.
FAWCETT BOOKS GROUP
1515 BROADWAY
NEW YORK, NY 10036

Attention: Individual Readers

Are there FAWCETT books you want to read but cannot find in your local bookstore? You can order any FAWCETT title in print by completing the order form below, attaching it to your list of selections, and mailing both with your payment to the address indicated:

COLUMBIA BOOK SERVICE
P.O. BOX FB, 32275 MALLY RD.
MADISON HEIGHTS, MI 48071

Please send book(s) selected. Orders for less than 5 books must include 75¢ for first book and 25¢ for each additional book to cover postage and handling. Postage and handling are FREE on orders of 5 books or more. Send check or money order only.

Cost	$_____	Name_____
Sales tax*	_____	Address_____
Postage	_____	City_____
Total	_____	State_____Zip_____

☐ **8461** Check here if you wish Columbia Book Service catalog sent. Add 50¢ to help defray postage and handling costs.

*The government requires us to collect sales tax in all states except AK, DE, MT, NH and OR.